Praise for Rebecca Ore and *Gaia's Toys*

"A brilliant, macabre vision of America's not-too-distant future, Ore's new novel puts her squarely in the ranks of such leading-edge SF talent as William Gibson and Neal Stephenson. . . . Ore fuses slick and absorbing storytelling with sophisticated speculative science."

—*Booklist*

"Rebecca Ore is right up there with our best. Her work is madly inventive and full of insight into human foibles, and tremendously funny besides. And she writes with impressive skill, not a word too many or in the wrong place. What I feel, as I read her stuff, is a troublsome mixture of high admiration and downright envy for the deft way she does the things she does." —Robert Silverberg

"Dystopian, cyberpunkish, near-future paranoia . . . plausibly edgy and cynical and often absorbing." —*Kirkus Reviews*

"Ore writes of a disturbingly valid future, a world where, in the words of one of her characters, 'technology makes people into machine parts.' What Thea von Harbou accomplished with steel decades ago in *Metropolis*, Ore accomplishes today through the updated techniques of microbiology. But the beauty of the situation is that, despite being machine parts, Ore's characters still hold onto some small spark of what the reader recognizes as humanity.' —*Starlog*

Tor Books by Rebecca Ore

Alien Bootlegger and Other Stories
Becoming Alien
Being Alien
Gaia's Toys
Human to Human
The Illegal Rebirth of Billy the Kid
Slow Funeral

GAIA'S TOYS

REBECCA ORE

TOR®

A TOM DOHERTY ASSOCIATES BOOK
NEW YORK

This is a work of fiction. All the characters and events portrayed in this book are either products of the author's imagination or are used fictitiously.

GAIA'S TOYS

Cover art by Shelley Eshkar

A Tor Book
Published by Tom Doherty Associates, Inc.
175 Fifth Avenue
New York, NY 10010

Tor Books on the World Wide Web:
http://www.tor.com

Tor® is a registered trademark of Tom Doherty Associates, Inc.

ISBN: 0-812-55045-5
Library of Congress Card Catalog Number: 95-14724

First edition: August 1995
First mass market edition: May 1997

Printed in the United States of America

0 9 8 7 6 5 4 3 2 1

I'd like to thank Theresa Croft, Rebecca Wright, Jim Thomerson, and Bruce Turner for information that I used in putting this book together. Any mistakes of biology, psychology, or geography, however, are my own.

Rebecca Ore
April 5, 1994
Critz, VA

ONE

A MAN AND HIS MANTIS

Willie Hunsucker knew what the little nasty clerks whispered about him down at Social Services, "Hunsucker been on dole so long that the techs had to work the skull cutouts with abrasive grease last five times, scour them idea pits off the drodes."

Four of his buddies lay stretched out in interface, bodies dressed in gray welfare coveralls, bald heads, just like his, now surrounded by thick black halos, a machine puffing air down their windpipes through a hose that looked like something out of an automobile that brought air from the filter to the carburetor.

The apprentice clerk with his wispy chin beard pulled Willie's records up on the terminal, then showed the note he'd just scribbled to Jackson Sim's eyes. Jackson's eyes had just enough motor control to blink and scan. The note reappeared on the screen in yellow light dot alphanumerics. The clerk told Willie, "You got to go to Roanoke. Van'll take you to the vactube. Wait for the blue light. Next."

Jackson Sim wouldn't remember a thing the next time he and Willie met, say at the Tibetan War Vets' dance, full of old warriors' tales about how high, how cold, how Chinese bulleted down the high passes in jet snowmobiles guided by satellite.

Willie remembered how you blasted those fiberglass sleds and found no flesh smeared to paste and bone chips, just a hardened speaker giggling about how the Rimpoches fooled America into dropping all its iron and steel production down for Chinese scavengers.

Then it had become the perfect war—all automated, and Willie'd gone home with a useless knowledge of Tibetan, three trunksful of idolatrous art that some museum would steal from him if he was fool enough to let Welfare know he had it, and a house.

The land around the house was now part of a three-thousand-acre bio-engineered sheep and cow operation, mowers, fence-drivers, feeders, all as automated as the war. So no farming anymore, but he had the house and got on the dole.

You hand them your head. They fit you with drodes and lock 'um with key caps.

They feed you granola, only that wasn't what old granola had been, it was yeast mush.

The blue light over the back door went on, and Willie got up out of the Welfare's metal folding chair and climbed up in the van—*shaped a lot like a ChiCom bullet sled,* he thought the first time he saw it— and slumped down on a seat gritty with tobacco flakes and garden muck. Willie didn't make a garden himself—too many bugs.

Bugs made him scream—some hallucinogenic bugs got Willie in the Tibetan village where the soldiers had gone for R & R. Willie remembered the sting—like a curare shot, deep into his calf muscle—and the four days of fucking a dream Tibetan girl who was really wadded-up bedclothes. He came out of it with a cock half-regrown in a plastic sack glued to his belly and thighs.

No, he didn't like to garden, find ticks bored into his neck, legs, mosquitos tiptoeing over his eyelids; all those bugs drove him into screaming fits. He used the entertainment dole credits to zap all the house bugs except for an eight-inch-high mantis trained not to bite him. The Tibetan hallie bug that got him had looked just like a damn Japanese beetle, might have even been made from Jap beetle DNA. The mantis was big enough to trust.

A bug crawled out from under the floor mat, but Jubbie, the fat greasy white girl from up on the mountain, popped it with her red sneaker as she got in. "Hey, Willie, I saved you again. You know about Roanoke?"

"Just we're going."

Carter, the black guy who refused to do anything except play piano and dole his brain, climbed in, all bony and ashy looking, high nose like a TV Pharaoh's despite black grey skin. He said, "What say, Jubbie?"

The driver frowned at them. "No speculating."

*   *   *

Back at Willie's house, the mantis was considering its options. It bellowed slightly, thorax chitin hinged with leathery skin to allow lung movements, pumping air through its spiracles. If it'd had known how to really think, not just weigh the sight of mantis kibble against the tightness of its chitin shell, it might have realized that eight-inch-high mantises did well to trade off flight for better oxygenated tissues.

Since it didn't use language, perhaps it's better to say the mantis's neural programs were measuring growth variables. Triangular head with blue-black faceted eyes panning, it sidestepped around the mantis kibble Willie had left it before he went to fill his dole. *A mass of kibble a third its present volume.* Then it saw that Willie had left the lights on over its terrarium. The variables clicked, hormones cascaded through vibrating muscles. *Food, warmth, stuffed tight.*

It peeled off its skin. The wings came off last, and the mantis ate furiously. When the next wet wings popped out of their cases, it inflated its lungs to the fullest and cautiously climbed by the lights into the terrarium.

As growth torpor hit, it tried to play with rubbery feet the music that soothed its human. The lungs expanded. Oxygen filled its system.

To keep a check on the speculating, the van driver stood with the dole people at the tube train station. The train came, stopped by the station magnetic coils. The passenger insert moved in against the train. Paying passengers to Roanoke and beyond got in before the dole people. The insert slid out again, the gap sealed, the train accelerated out as fast as possible for human comfort. Had it been all dole people, the station would have sent the train out a little faster.

Five minutes later, Roanoke's coils caught them.

Willie and the other dole people went out to the coordinator who stood in her uniform waiting for them. Willie always felt like his joints weren't fastened solid around the coordinators. They moved like military people, no slop in the hips or knees. *Bam, bam, bam, follow the leader into the van and a two or three week blank.* Roanoke moved coal, microbio chips, dead trees, tobacco, quartz, red clay, bits and pieces of cultured steer.

And secret things.

"Why they blank us the whole time?" Carter asked. "Why not just in brain dole?"

"No speculating," the big fat girl said before the coordinator could say it.

Sometimes, but not in Roanoke, Willie remembered bits and patches of dole work—his brain and the computer flying a thousand alpha-whatsits, *letters and numbers, ah, alphanumerics,* a microsecond—bam, bam, bam, pattern and manipulation. But, nothing stayed with him in Roanoke—a whole two or three weeks blank, old electric fan noises his only memory ever.

They all climbed in the van. "I'd like to be up at night some," Jubbie the fat girl said wistfully. "They got good dancing on Center Street."

Carter spat out chewing tobacco before he got in the van, then looked at the fat girl. "Hell," Carter said, "you can't afford dancing those places on the dole."

Willie leaned back, staring at the old white wooden houses around the vactube station, wondering whether he'd remember seeing them. Sometimes, he knew he'd been to Roanoke, sometimes not. He felt a skull electrode itch—*tension,* they'd told him, *don't scratch and you won't get infected.*

He twisted around so his head was between the itchy terminal and the coordinator, then brought his hand up quick and rubbed around the terminal lock caps with his knuckles, not his nails. Willie knew better than to cut his skin around the terminals before a dole session. Cuts festered inside the halo.

Then he didn't remember anything from there—retro-wipe—and came out from under the halo dizzy, sirens in his ears, a med-tech bent over him, wiping the drode points with Betadine and recapping them, twisting the key into each cap, locking him down. Willie couldn't tell if the sirens were in his ears or outside, smart bombs hitting Roanoke, a psychic attack by radical Tibetan spirit masters? He never trusted them damn spirit masters, hoaxers or not.

"Willie, you with us?" the supervisor asked.

Willie blinked. Would he remember this? Yeah, there was that tension in his brain, like these seconds were logging on long time. But the siren? "Direh's?" His tongue tumbled numbly in his mouth. Tried again, "Sirens?"

"Ears ringing?"

"Sirens." Shit, he shouldn't sound so dumb.

The supervisor rolled him over and pulled two connectors out, wiped and capped the trode holes. The sirens faded. Faded, didn't go away completely. "What happened?"

"I don't know," the supervisor said like he really did and couldn't say. Willie suspected he'd been put to moving war materials. Bug images flashed by the corners of his eyes—not real. They faded when he looked at them, but he shuddered just the same.

"My time up?" Willie asked.

"No," the supervisor said. "But take a break."

Willie was going to be remembering Roanoke Central. The supervisor strapped a call watch around Willie's wrist and said, "You're not so dumb you'd get lost. Come right back when it beeps."

Willie asked, "How much time?"

"Couple of hours. Follow Alice out." The man slipped him a five chip. "Have a good time, but leave your brain clean."

Willie, wondering a lot, followed the coordinator who'd picked him up at the vactrain. *Alice, name's Alice. Bitch is human after all.* She hustled him out of Roanoke Central before he could have much of a look around, took him out to the street and said, "See the tower there, the holographic man on top of our building here."

The holographic man seemed suspended in a slab of plastic about three hundred feet high—he was marching, marching, constantly marching, all 250 feet of him. Willie wasn't sure whether the man was propaganda or what. "Ain't going no where, is he?"

Alice looked like she didn't know whether Willie was being extra dumb or joking. She decided not to decide, tapped his wrist, and said, "Be sure to come right back when the buzzer goes off."

Willie began walking toward the tower, looking at Roanoke, the jumble of old houses, pitted chrome, hearing the groan of vacuum engines sucking air out of the train tubes, smelling ozone and piss. *They didn't want me hanging around while they fixed something.* He hummed his mantis's saw leg sounds, but in a lower key. Still it comforted him as he walked away, free for a few hours, from the holographic man stuck marching embedded in plastic.

A woman, could he get a woman for five dollars? Willie ignored the hysteria hanging around the edge of the idea, suppressed memories of his hallucinations. He wanted to be normal. Fingering the chip the supervisor had given him, he knew he couldn't just spend it on liquor. If he got drunk, they run the kidney on him, for sure, rip up his veins for it with dull needles. Willie found a phone terminal and checked the Yellow Pad. *Nice they legalized it; too bad dole doesn't allot for cunt.*

Willie picked a brothel without a display ad, called. "At your pleasure," a woman said. She didn't sound sexy, more like a supervisor.

"What can I get for five dollars chip?"

The woman didn't answer for a second. Willie figured she was probably key-checking her computer, a straight one without a dole brain attached. "You can look, honey."

He hung up, thought about trying another brothel, didn't. *Just make*

dole man waste his time, he thought as he walked up the block. He
was also obscurely relieved.

Somewhere around here was the street with dancing and music, if
those bars opened during the day. Willie almost went back to check
the phone terminal, but decided to just walk. *Dole man, they can just
throw him out on the street, tell me don't get drunk.*

The mantis, now eleven inches tall, roused itself and drank water from
the tube sticking out of the bottle attached to the terrarium. It stared
through the glass at the remaining kibble, moved legs that were still
rubbery, drank more water and nibbled away an old chitin fragment
stuck to its right front leg. Blurred vision triggered a lens burnishing
reflex, bent legs moving over and over the bowed triangular head bent
at its swivel socket with the thorax. Flakes of very thin almost clear
scales came away from its eye facets. The mantis drank more water,
felt loose and small inside its new shell, so raised its legs to the rim
of the terrarium, awkwardly; the terrarium seemed to be smaller to the
mantis. Then it adjusted to its new size and raised the middle legs and
hoisted itself out, holding onto the rim with the rear legs as the front
legs reached down, took an astonishing weight. The mantis hung there
for a while, heavier, recalibrating muscle neurons, then dropped to the
table and climbed down its rope to the floor.

It nibbled more kibble, then saw a wasp hovering over the sink.
Calculations hardwired into the mantis's small brain ganglion kept it
stiff, attentive, but the wasp wasn't in jumping grasp.

Finally, the mantis, bored, crawled behind the toilet bowl and let the
cold from the water stiffen it.

Willie ignored the staring shoppers by the old Hotel Roanoke's arcade,
just kept plodding along in his dole clothes, drode caps glistening in
his bare skull, the black plastic call watch tight on his wrist. He felt
cut out forever, which bothered him one second and left him feeling
almost like a pure spectator the next. *Dole'd never let me starve. Dole's
got money under my skull.* Come the funeral, he knew Welfare would
get it all back before they rendered his fat and burned the rest down
to fine ash and spread him on a field mixed with composted sewage
gook. *Down again, can't think about that.* He felt the five chip in his
pocket and thought maybe he could go watch naked women, start talking to them, see if he could . . . Women, like vacations, were totally
beyond him now.

All around him, he saw women in silk, alpaca, silver, furs, and looked at them so hungrily that a couple became nervous, had him put on the street.

He went outside behind the officer without protesting. The call watch beeped and he looked for the tower, walked to it, then saw the marching man hologram and went inside. He stopped remembering beyond the door. . . .

. . . then awake again, trembling, his skin feeling lumpy as though bugs were under it. *No, a delusion.* He looked up at the supervisor as he and aides removed the halo. *Am I broken?* Willie never remembered this happening before and began to cry weakly.

"Damn, man, we don't want to have to drug you too far down," the supervisor said.

"Get someone else and let him . . ." the woman who'd picked him up at the station said.

"No, Jubbie's unstable and I don't trust Carter."

"I didn't spend your five-chip," Willie said, hoping they'd be nice to him.

"Oh, Willie." The supervisor patted his shoulder. It all disappeared again. . . .

. . . and Willie walked around a landscape like valley Tibet, rhododendrons and orchids, too gaudy to be real. His mantis, bigger now, eight-year-old child-sized, thorax bellowing air in and out of its body, came up to him and rubbed its rear legs together, making a deeper version of that soothing music his real-life mantis made. This wasn't real life, but Willie didn't worry as long as his mantis made its music.

He wondered if he could talk here. "Funny, all the pets they let me have is just a bug." *A Rimpoche must be behind this, spirit walking me away.* He thought vaguely about astral projection.

Then the bugs moved toward him, a wave of them. He and his mantis grabbed them, threw them various directions. Suddenly, Willie knew he was moving war material, lots of it. They trusted him, not the fat girl, not Carter, because he'd been a soldier.

With a security clearance, he remembered that now. He hadn't always been on the dole, wasn't born to the dole. The mantis turned to look at him. The bugs were gone.

Behind the peaks towering over the valley lightning flashed. Willie knew he'd targeted atomics, thrown hallie bugs in after. Hallie bugs that gas a man into brain-choking visions.

I couldn't help it. But having the war work from Roanoke was sweet, no battlefields.

The mantis said, "But you threaten the planet." Willie knew that the mantis meant humans, not him in particular.

"What you going to do about it?"

"We respond quickly," the mantis said. "You remake us and we respond even more quickly, genes unstable from the splicing."

I'm unstable from all the stuff they run through my head. I could remember all of it. Willie realized he'd remember this, in this form. Maybe he knew more.

The mantis looked to the left, as if hearing something. "You've started to stop forgetting. I don't know how, but you're learning to make your own data nests."

What will I remember? The mantis was still listening to something on the left when . . .

Willie was shivering, sitting in the van with the fat girl and Jubbie. He felt his face—depilated—and his head, still bald. They were back in Stuart leaving the vactube; he'd been walking on automatic up to just now.

"Three weeks?" he asked the driver.

"Yeah, man, three weeks."

Willie'd smuggled out memories of Roanoke this time, other memories his brain had hallucinated up—rhodedenrons, orchids, and a four-foot-tall talking mantis. Bugs, bombs over the peaks. "And any news we miss?"

The driver stiffened.

Willie felt the chip the supervisor had given him—five dollars. He'd sell some plasma once he tested the amnesia drugs out of his system. "Must be some news."

Jubbie said, "They did a neutron on Nakchuka. Not that there wasn't anybody home."

"Ain't nobody home but butterflies and Yetis," Willie said.

"And bugs," Jubbie said.

Willie went cold around the spine. "You a bitch," Carter said.

"What about the neutron, Willie?"

"Neutron? Wouldn't make sense."

"No speculating," the driver told them. The van pulled up by Bicycle Parking. Willie got out, found his bike, unlocked it with his fingerprint, and began riding home. *Maybe I bombed some bugs moving in on India?* His testicles drew up as high as they could, just thinking about bugs, round bugs.

Its human was back—the mantis felt Willie's warm hands and began wriggling its abdomen. Willie's breath vibrated the air and warmed the mantis's eyeballs. He put the mantis down on the kitchen table, on old newspaper, and it shat, then began stroking music out of its legs. The lungs, attached to the thorax and wing muscles, sucked air in, puffed air out. Willie sighed. The mantis walked off the paper and wrapped its legs around Willie's forearm, the warmth of it.

Willie looked down at the mantis and said, ''I bet you got the bugs out, too.''

The mantis felt the man vibrate the air, and it moved its head so the two focus areas of each eye, where the eye facets were smaller and thicker, caught Willie—the human's jelly eyes, the mobile flesh flaps, four of them. But still the mantis knew the man in a dim way, this pattern, these particular eyelids, lips, teeth, pores filled with red clay particles and black Roanoke dirt.

The mantis twisted slightly and rubbed human soothing sounds from its legs, then misted the air slightly with a pheromone that made them both happier.

Willie remembered the day the mantis came stepping through his door when he opened it, as though it had been invited. Just as he began to scream—bug even if not bug-shaped—the mantis made its music.

Wild or escaped recombinant-DNA insect tranquilizer military tool? Willie never found out for sure, but a couple of other dole people had them as pets already. *None of us talk much about them, but there's mantis kibble on the market, so I suspect they're made creatures.*

Male or female? Neither Willie nor the mantis knew.

The five-dollar credit chip made Willie itchy. He had it in his pocket when he called his caseworker. ''Hi, Eileen, it's me, Willie. I need to talk to you.''

''What about, Willie?''

''Well, about doing something, getting off the dole.''

''Willie.''

He remembered that she'd told him once that he had a good brain, but not enough determination to run it on his own. They'd been mad at each other that day, over something like him selling tap time to a private computer programmer who picked his electrode cap locks. Man wasn't caught with Willie's head in a vice, but when the wire patrollers caught him and another dole brain running a modem steal on the *Reader's Digest* database, he told them Willie'd laid for him, too. ''So, this time, I check with you, make sure I don't do anything illegal.''

''Willie, I'd love to see you get off the dole, okay. Now, can you come up with a plan?''

He was thirty-four years old—how the hell was he going to get someone to hire him, dole brain for seven years, military before that. ''Or at least do something besides sit around between plug-in times.''

"It's not a job, it's an adventure." That phrase floated through his mind. Like everyone said, he had plenty of free time between being blanked out into a computer. He fingered the five-dollar chip as Eileen said, "Willie, I can't come up with a plan for you. If you come up with a plan that's legal, I'll do my best to help you implement it, okay."

"Okay." He'd walk into town, take a train to a public tap and check out databases on jobs, IQ tests. Five dollars should buy something. Maybe he'd sell the mantis, if there was a market for mantises.

As he hung up, the mantis walked into the room and played its music. "No, baby, I can't sell you."

He got his wig out of the three-hundred-year-old walnut cupboard he'd painted with blue enamel when he realized Welfare wanted him to sell all his valuables. As he glued on the wig, he realized he wouldn't sell the cabinet nor the mantis—he'd be truly poor then. But he could sell the Tibetan art. He never looked at it anyway, not part of his cultural matrix as a man who owned his own brain might say. The wig covered his electrode caps. He checked himself in the mirror, tugged the wig to make sure the wig stayed put.

Town was a ways, but he walked, fast so the cold could get him through his Welfare cast-off coat. The plasma center was in an old storefront—chrome plate peeling off the trim, whitewash blanking the windows. They never said anything about Welfare. Stuart was a small town so they probably knew. The girl took his fingerprints and sat him down at a chair. He slipped his left arm under the cuff. The chair hummed, calculating his weight, setting up, then the needle and tube dropped out of the side of the chair arm. The girl inserted it into Willie's vein after the cuff inflated. From there on, it was automatic. The chair would spin the plasma off the blood cells, mix the cells with saline solution, and return the washed cells to Willie's arm. But it took a human to put the needle in. Or else, Willie decided, she was cheaper than a program and sensors capable of finding all veins. It was cheaper to use a human brain to scan handwriting than work up a computer to do that.

The blood drained down, red and warm, into the chair, then, about thirty minutes later, as Willie was dozing off, pushed back into Willie's veins his blood cells, some bent, mashed, suspended in chilly saline that tickled and chilled.

He took an alcohol patch from the container when the needle retracted and held it against the needle hole. The girl had him sign for his second five-dollar chip of the week.

He said, "Where would a man go if he needed to sell some Tibetan sculptures?"

"Know a man," she said. "In D.C. Yeah, but . . ." She shrugged thin shoulders. "I know another man closer, easier to deal with for a man with your connections."

"Can't hook up through these trodes. They put in screaming locks. Even Welfare can't cut out the message to Central. They just check to make sure I'm on time for dole duty."

"Sorry. I'll tell him it's impossible."

Willie shuddered, partly from the cold plasma dumped in his veins, partly from thinking about round, gas-squirting bugs. "What about the guy in D.C.?"

"He runs a shop in Old Town," the girl said. "I'll call him, give me a name or something."

"Mr. Jubbie Carter," Willie said.

The girl said, "You know I'm supposed to report a Welfare man's earnings if I know. From the plasma, anything else."

She'd get a cut of whatever deal he ran with the guy in Washington, a cut off of informing. Willie said, "Could you give me two fours for these fives?"

The plasma center bitch took the money and handed him back a five and three ones, not smiling at all. Willie smiled and said, "I don't have anything at my house, you know. I'll take up just one thing at a time." He'd always lie to the bitch about what he had and what he had left. Be just like her to let him sell everything, then inform on him so he'd lose his money. But money could be hid easier than sculptures.

Something in the big world was going on and he wanted to know why it bled into his work memories. He could get four dollars a week from plasma without fuss, buy keyboard time into a data base. Too bad he couldn't hook up through his dole 'trodes. But if he tried to steal brain time again, Eileen had told him, they'd give him bug hallucinations. Willie never asked if the hallucinations would be in reality from bug gas or data demons through computer chips. Only bug he wanted to see more of was his mantis.

I'm going to come up with a damn plan.

He put on his coat and walked home.

TWO

TO YOU PEOPLE WHO MUST LIVE IN THE FUTURE I AM MAKING

When I turned forty-three, I was Mattie Higgins, driving on fake ID and plate-grown fingerprints to New Orleans. The car trim, I'd been told, would explode when triggered by the right radio code. A 12-gauge shotgun, broke open and trigger up, rode like a person sitting beside me, Mr. Gun and his human girlfriend.

The barrel had been sawed off precisely as short as any state I went through allowed. Even though I'd fitted the gun with a shoulder pad, I hated to fire that big a load.

In Picayune, I pulled off the Interstate and parked the Xhoshiba at an old Winn Dixie and bought a six pack of maize beer and two cans of organic peanut and chile soup, then changed from the dress and heels to jeans and a tee shirt greasy with oil laced with something that broke cordite molecules—in case I had to shoot someone. My heels needed resoling badly. I heated up a can of soup in the car's microwave and put Yo Secuve on the stereo. The soup cost too much, but I preferred true agricultural product.

A truck full of swamp Cajuns pulled up, post-survivalist survivors bristling with old ASh-95s, needle barrels beside the slug barrels. The barrel ends looked like tortured metal faces with no noses—one steel eye bruised down to a tiny dot.

I smiled at them and memorized the plate number, in case they were in the way when I came back out of Louisiana. Drive, woman, I told myself, you've got bombs to plant. I donated can metal at the store crusher, then drove back onto the Interstate, seventeen hours out of Washington, just a lone middle-aged woman driving fast, shotgun on the seat beside her, too old, too short, and too slight to be a physical threat. Would have looked suspicious to be alone and unarmed.

Last night's nightmare replayed me trying to surrender to an orphanage. In the nightmare, I could never find the orphanage. In reality, I'd thought I was quite mature to look for an orphanage when my parents abandoned me in a river park. But I refused to tell the Cincinnati cops anything. Maybe prepping me for the drode world was the cops' and orphanage's payback for me not informing on my biologicals.

The orphanage numbered me, mapped my DNA and retinas, and sent me to play on educational machines. Orphanage educational machines produced students numerate and literate enough to be good scanners.

Machines fought formal wars. Humans fought little non-wars. I've battled to be more than a dole idiot scanning handwritten memos into computers. The long dream of the twenty-first century collapsed when the owners realized people bred at their own cost, but machines took capital. Making a computer to read brain output was cheaper than building pure artificial intelligence. Brains came preprogrammed with all sorts of equations we didn't have to be concious of to use.

I refused to be a computer's bio-component. I believed in tools people could build for themselves, a world rebuilt by people using those tools. Since my late teens, I'd been an eco-warrior. The Movement gave me my first kind lover and a real education.

Now, disguised by middle age and a lower mid-line car, I merged in the Interstate flow at 90 mph, the flat land around us cropped four times a year for fibers, oil, and feed meals, clear tubes running down out of the booster tanks as if the land were in intensive care.

Cruise by balloon-tired combines eating strips wider than half an Interstate.

Did the Picayune clerk have the flat affect of this overcropped land? The Pearl River lay walled in concrete—whoosh, behind me now. Now refineries—rock oil, vegetable oil, fish, bird and mammal fat, we burn it all. Crematories sold human fat as a side product. We had plenty of dead people. Welfare dole electrodes bring on brain infection to drode heads who don't keep clean. Sweat-vectored AIDS wasn't as lethal as the sexual varients, but it cropped weaker humans.

I switched lanes for the Canal Street exit, the fool sky raining on me. Minutes later, on Canal Street, I pulled over and put the shotgun in its case.

Illicher—what the Government called my kind. The high tech Survivalists call us Luddites, although we don't kick personal computers, okay. I pulled back out and drove into my hotel's garage building, punched the ticket clock for hanging storage. Clamps came down on my car's front end and hoisted it up like a bug in forceps, trunk down.

I had wondered if the new African cars were built to hang—obviously, yes. *Hang them all,* I thought as the hoist lifted the car up to the rails that whirled cars around like clothes at a personal dry cleaners.

The bombs stayed in the car. I wore the trigger—looking like a gold jewel dangling from an earring post.

The Movement always used my ambiguous look, not African-American, not completely white. Being small disarms people. I don't, though, remember my parents as being particularly small or dark. Actually, I don't remember my folks much better than I remember my nightmares. They dumped me after I began giving them grief like an eight-year-old might. I've figured since they lived in the cracks like Movement people, perhaps much more illegal—hustles and scams, scutwork that required more conscious judgement than a drode head and machine could give.

The State proved a lousy mother. I ran when I realized the nice surgery scheduled for my fifteenth birthday was for the computer interface module. If I'd screwed up at eight by surrendering to an orphanage, I'd be smarter at fourteen. I wasn't going to have wires in my head, no route for brain infections for this girl, not me.

From age fifteen, I've been a figment of other people's nightmares and fantasies. Renegade children live on theft and machine sex shows. Tolerated by the government, we provided a threat to more compliant urban masses. Buy more cops, we'll protect you from the kids.

But the police gun down kid gangs from time to time, as if shooting us made us more dangerous. I looked back once. A terrified adult shot at me as though I'd explode and take out his whole neighborhood.

Oh, well. Inside me, an eight-year-old girl walks forever through Cincinnati hunting for an orphanage. I wish she'd joined a kid gang early enough for that life to have seemed normal.

So, now, I was traveling in eco bombs. My own horrors locked in my skull bones, I made other people's nightmares come true.

Enough of me. Did I say that AIDS was to Africa what the Black Plague was to my European ancestors?

Did I say that to run a high-tech, ecologically sound world, a micromanaged environment, the controllers have to both believe their instruments and be looking for what else might be wrong, even if the corrections cost them? No humans are that egoless or honest or consistent.

So, we bomb tech back when we suspect the instruments show problems the controllers refuse to face. People die. So what? People were already dying. The individuality of people is as real and insignificant as the individuality of snowflakes.

I went into the hotel and gave them the fake fingerprints, then went up to shower in hot salt water, turning under the spray. Fresh for the hair—membrane distilled.

The bed I'd ordered was a cotton-stuffed mat covered with pure linen ticking. I stripped, turned off the air-conditioning, and lay down, finally tired.

Bombs away. Tech against tech. I paid the demons at night. Oil burned on the Mississippi. I died in the explosion. After I died, I wandered around trying to be dead, trying to find an afterlife that would take me.

I woke during the night, paralyzed by dreads I couldn't quite remember, sweating. Someone once told me dreams were the body trying to warn the intellect, but if my nightmares came from the body, then I wished I didn't have one. I lay listening to a midnight trumpet playing jazz until I slept again.

In the morning, rain slid through the ambient humidity, instantly recycled on the pavements. As I slid into my hose and shoes, I wondered if I'd live to get cancer from all the carcinogens dissolved in the city rain.

Probably not. I wiggled into a dress and went downstairs for breakfast. Today, I'd relax and be a tourist, wouldn't care if killers from all the factions followed me. The car would dangle, the bombs disguised as plastic seat trim. Returning to it was the hard part. Then, I'd worry, be careful.

I went through crowds of night people going back to their beds at sunrise. Beds or coffins—New Orleans pasty pale vampires feed on tourists who go home thrilled by their neck scars. Look, Henry, authentic fang marks.

As significantly individual as snowflakes—these pale ex-human beings, these dark antimated corpses. No, not really zombies and vampires. Too many people—that's what made me fantasize zombies and vampires out of tired strippers, musicians, bartenders, and dole heads.

Dole heads were true technological zombies. Too many people—planet, I have promised you relief. Turning the human surplus into the living dead isn't good enough.

I remembered the dream of being dead with no place to go, neither oblivion or heaven. Not even hell. My dead dream self asked *what should I do now?*

Push the dream away. Today I am a daytripper, too prim for the night shows, open bar doors displaying naked flesh swirling over the bar, teasing those gametes into more reproduction.

We can't live with the consequences of those gamete actions. Bomb the oil, pollute once, not forever. Break the dams that hold back the ocean. Tear down the levees and let the Mississippi run wild. Drag the solar reflectors out of orbit. Bring in the water that belongs here as the ice caps melt. Cut the human numbers.

I was Tech, once, but it requires too much honesty. Micromanaging the ecosphere requires perfect ego control.

But understand, I was a nervous kid renegade until I learned to shoot. Firing a .410 shotgun made me charitable to my neighbors. The 12-gauge made me realize that killing could be painful.

The clerk in the sex goods and liquor store was scowling at the television as a techno-punk and a Catholic argued. He saw me looking and went service-people bland, but I knew he hated one or the other of the debaters.

"So, who bothers you?" I said.

"All ideologues," he said, deciding not to give a damn about my opinions either.

I bought a vibrator, artificial jissom, and a bottle of Scotch from him. Just a tourist, out to have a good time, even if, in true Techie fashion, excessively private.

I went back to my room and used the vibrator to sex out the nightmare tensions. Going out for lunch, I felt post-coitally languid, soothed by fake prostate secretions. Too tired to walk far, I ate expensively on a credit card set to erase its records in three days.

Tomorrow, I'd contact the man who'd get me into the refinery. If he didn't show, I could always take out a sea levee and drown the city. That one was a suicide mission, but then I was just another human snowflake, wasn't I?

At night, I was a child bomb exploding on that terrified cop. The million flesh shreds didn't know if they were me or him. After I could move, I wondered if I could walk away from all these nightmares, leave the bomb hanging in the car, throw the trigger in the Mississippi, go.

I couldn't let my nightmares run me.

*   *   *

"The problem is that we humans breed like coyotes," the refinery man said as he gave me a pass card. "You kill us for the environment, we breed even faster." He was a small, slight guy with black hair and pale skin, blue eyes and plump lips, an indoor clerk, so I'd been told.

I said, "I'm killing oil, not people. If you don't like what we do, why'd you help us?" I didn't like to discuss politics when I was handling a situation.

He laughed, then patted my hand. "I'll be out of there."

"You don't know when I'm coming in," I said, holding the pass card set for my new fingertips and present face, that instant realizing he would know. "Not in advance."

"Not in advance," he said. "But won't you want to escape the blast yourself?"

"Perhaps not," I said. "But I've got more work to do." Not that I was special, but training a new operative could cost us operations.

The refinery clerk said, "I'm getting paid."

I didn't like hearing that. Should I abort the mission? But then, if he'd been bought out by a faction with more money, would he be saying this?

Perhaps. Perhaps I should get in touch with my cell leader. Perhaps I was supposed to get in touch with my cell leader. "Would you betray me for even more money?"

"You Luddites got a reputation for revenge," the clerk said.

"You don't care about the cause?"

"Some," he said.

Maybe I should make blowing the refinery a suicide mission to get this little fool. I said, "So I won't be seeing you again."

"No," he said. The plump lips glistened a bit.

I set up a remote disguised as a courier skitter to check to see if anyone followed me. The silver remote spun on its axis, danced from doorway to doorway, behind me, then ahead of me. Its whole surface was photon-reactive. Nothing of a constant size followed me or paralled me. If the little clerk had tipped them, then I might be getting relay spotted. I wondered if I should send the bombs in by remote, but I'd been told perimeter electromagnetic pulses would scramble everything.

The car swung around on its hooks and came to rest on its tires. I paid the garage in cash and drove the car off without checking for tamper marks.

How long has the human population been over the psychological carrying capacity? Since whenever we invented castes to break us up into pseudo-species. I drove the car by the docks filled with more African cars, various containers filled with rayon, and bales of oil-cake plankton. In the background, blue flames bouncing off towers, tended by humans who'd become their job categories so we, by thinking people into pressure gauge readers, pipe fitters, and remote operators, could reduce the population pressure. Technology makes people into machine parts. Don't think of them as people, they're not in the way.

The scanner sitting over the back seat said a constant volume followed us. I slowed down to see if the big Volvo truck would pass. It did. The side window opaqued and played a cock rising out of pubic hair and balls. I touched Mr. Gun sitting beside me. The window spelled out: BE THAT WAY, BITCH.

His gonads conned him into thinking he was special. The truck sped on. The scanner would have been happier exposed to all sides. I was going down Delta, on the west bank of the Mississippi, heading for shaky ground. I found the turn off to the refinery and drove the car up to the gate. The pass seemed good. Behind a long sheet-metal building I got out of the car and had to hold onto the hood for a second. My exhausted muscles seemed as though they'd trembled for hours without me noticing.

Next. I pulled off the plastic trim and slid it against a wall and an untrimmed edge of weeds. The car stayed here. Another cell member would pick me up. I'd been told to:

Walk back through the guard station, tell any humans around that you've had car trouble. Keep walking, we'll get you.

The plastic explosive will take out the whole refinery.

The place stank worse than crematory oil, this grease from pre-human times. I pulled off the clip holding the earring stud against my ear. It took two hands to do that, then I cupped my left hand under my ear and slid the stud out of the pierced hole with my right. I pressed the code holes to give me five hours, then pushed the trigger against the plastique.

I decided I ought to drive the car out. If something happened to the ride waiting outside the gate, I could get away faster.

The Xhoshiba wouldn't start. I wondered if I should change the timing and make this a suicide mission after all. But no, we needed to know if we'd been betrayed. I started running for the gate. If I had to be captured, then please let it be officials, I thought, not a techno-punk mob. I had to live to help analyze what went wrong.

As I turned back for the shotgun, an amplified voice called, "Don't move." Lights surrounded me. "Hands up, slowly."

I was a snowflake, melting in arc-light glare. The voice asked, "Do you want to use the suicide kit?"

"No," I said.

"You've been totally fucked, you know." The arc lights burned though my closed lids.

"I'll show you where the bombs are," I said. If I did, I might live. Or die, changing the explosion time to now. Nightmare, wasn't this? I could not move. The nightmares trained me for this horror.

The voice said, "Stay where you are."

A man walked out of the glare. The lights dimmed. He grabbed my arms and cuffed them behind me, then cut away my clothes. Being naked and light-blinded was bad, being exposed in dinged and wrinkled body was worse. "Step aside," he said.

Two other men scurried up to take my clothes away.

"I'll show you where the plastique is," I said.

"It's plastic, not plastique, and your trigger earring is electro-magnetically inert," he said. "So where is the bomb? And how were you going to get away?"

"Hitch out," I said. "The car wouldn't start." Who betrayed who?

"The car," the man said. "It's in the car, but put the clothes in the car just in case. Then we're out of here."

Shit, we'd been lured to a dummy refinery. I hoped the bomb blast would be significant.

From behind the lights, a voice said, "It's a baby nuke. Bomb team incoming. We're evacuating."

"I don't have any clothes," I said. The three men who'd stepped out from the lights grabbed me and hustled me off. Think of it as an operation, I told myself, being cut into, for the sake of the body politic. But another side of myself, the starving kid in the sex display, disease too common for men to do other than watch strange cunt, hated my nakedness.

Nightmares, what were you trying to tell me?

A freight helicopter landed. The men pushed me into it. We took off and flew at what must have been the machine's maximum speed. As the guards shoved me to the back compartment, I saw the little clerk dressed now in a suit with a private guard insignia in the button hole. "Hold her down," he said. "We've got to get her suicide kit."

I said, "Give me some clothes and I'll tell you where it is."

The men held me down. The suicide kit wasn't in my vagina where the fake clerk jammed his fingers. "Are the nipples real?" He twisted one of them, then reached further inside me, fingers stretching me. I wish he'd had a cut and I a disease.

At fifteen, I'd done sex shows for money. I could manage this.

"It's my lower right wisdom tooth," my body seemed to say for me. Two hands immediately went into my mouth and stretched my jaws. The fake clerk pulled out my tooth, then said, "X-ray her. I doubt she has a clue as to what she could be carrying."

I don't want to cry, but my wishes terrified my body. The eyes weeped. They spread eagled me in plastic restraints. Then the helicopter jerked and the whole sky lit up.

The fake clerk slapped me as the helicopter rocked in the bomb shock and the afterblasts of the real refineries up and down the river. He collected himself, drew himself up into being a pro, and stretched out a hand to block the other men.

"Bet the X-ray plates are fucked," one of the other men said. The fake clerk nodded.

Another man asked, "How big was it?" He envied the fake clerk my bruised eye.

I said, "I didn't know anything about it."

"Eighth Hiroshima-sized," the fake clerk said. "Bitch, your people wrote you off."

The naive-as-a-child bomb. I had another suicide kit under my left hand's little fingernail, but when I began flexing my fingers, the men taped them flat to the X-ray table.

"I'm just a dupe. You might as well kill me."

The fake clerk began pulling out my fingernails. I fainted, then came to. He held the second suicide kit in front of my eyes, curare needle bared.

"Cover her," he told the others. "You wouldn't want to die naked, would you?"

"Thank you," I said. Then I saw the men were carrying a black body bag, patched with blue tape in two places. Hell, a used body bag. They pulled the cold plastic over my skin. My dead body would go naked in the body bag.

"When we hit you with the curare, you'll smother," he said, moving the needle close to one eye. "We could just put you in the body bag now, without using the needle. You'd still smother."

I gathered my nerve. Please, do it quickly, I thought, afraid if I begged them out loud to be quick, they'd delay.

"Where are your politics now?" the fake clerk asked. He raised the needle.

"On the end of the needle," I said.

He pricked me. I continued breathing, my heart pounding. Please let me keep my courage until I'm paralyzed, I thought. Time passed. I kept breathing.

I began gasping. "Not a real refinery, not a real suicide needle," the fake clerk said. "Or perhaps I used the wrong needle. Your group sent you on a suicide mission without telling you. And you want to die for them?"

I turned my head to the side. The fake clerk came back with another needle, smaller. The real needle. He sat watching me, the needle embedded in a cork he held between his fingers. "We were fooled, too. We couldn't believe environmentals would steal a nuke."

"Good," I said. "At least the bomb crew died." I felt clammy under the body bag.

"I didn't mean to torture you by pulling out your fingernails. You're lucky I found the kit by the third nail."

"Use it," I said. Who had I offended? Who'd do this to me?

"We need you alive for a retina scan."

"If I tell you who I am, my birth ID number, will you kill me now?"

"How do I know you won't be lying? Your retinas will rot quick after you're dead."

"You can still do DNA typing."

"True." The fake clerk pulled his hand back. "So who were you?"

"Allison Dodge, ID #OHO27555121200. I wasn't registered at birth, but at age eight."

"An orphanage prefix. Lot of those kids disappear. If you're lying, how will we be able to punish you? You'll be dead." He asked someone else, "Can we tightbeam?"

"Sure. We're away now."

The tightbeam confirmed that there was an Allison Dodge and sent back retina and DNA prints, and my earlier arrest sheet, probation to a housekeeping service, spotted and IDed and wanted for various adolescent thefts and sexual misdemeanors. Shot at by cops while running. "Well, Allison," the fake clerk said, "I'm Mr. Kearney. You sure you'd prefer dying to an adjustment center?"

I said, "I know too much about reality. We're trying to save humanity from the planet's ultimate revenge, you know." I thought I sounded stupid as I heard myself speaking. From where I'd gotten in this maze, the only way out was death. If I lived, the nightmares would come back with yet more demons.

Kearney pulled out a stopwatch. "We'll put you in the body bag when you're good and dead."

Do you want to be doing this, a part of myself asked. Yes, I'm worthless now, I told myself. Kearney turned my head upright, leaned it back over a small pillow, and taped it in place.

"Don't want you flinching at the last moment," he said.

I couldn't see his hand, but I felt the prick against my neck. The stopwatch clicked when I stopped breathing.

I couldn't move. I wanted to move. Kearney pushed a stethoscope on my breast under the body bag. "Still with us," he said. Then he closed my eyes. I wasn't dead yet, then nothing.

I thought I died. I was in the body bag, my head numb. Was I still breathing? Kearney said, "Careful." The bag swayed. I was paralyzed, numb. I realized I was still alive, still paralyzed, numb around the neck. On a respirator.

I found myself very happy. Kearney was torturing me, but I was happy to be alive. The bomb that would have killed me did kill men and refineries that night.

They pulled back my eyelids and took retina prints. Kearney looked down at me. My eyes still wouldn't focus. I was still paralyzed, like the first moments awake from a nightmare. He said, "Allison, you played straight enough with us. Next we'll be asking who you've been. And who you've been with." He pushed my eyelids back down with hot fingers.

Hours or minutes passed. The respirator pumped my lungs. My body sweated. The helicopter landed.

Hands moved me to a gurney and covered me up with warmed blankets. Some time later, in a bed, other hands catherized my bladder. Kearney told me, "Technology is keeping you alive now." If I hadn't been paralyzed, I'd have told him we weren't opposed to technology, just its overuse.

Kearney's voice repeated, "Technology is keeping you alive now." Same exact inflections. Again, "Technology is keeping you alive now." A sound loop. For hours, forever.

I fell asleep against that noise, and dreamed I'd volunteered to be killed by a guy who was doing it slowly. People asked why I'd let him do this to me, he didn't really care for me. But before I realized I didn't want to die, I was too maimed to live.

The dream should have been a nightmare, but I was dead emotionally.

Then the real nightmare began, cars perched on precarious narrow bridges, a wordless terror, the whole dreamscape folding up around me. Kearney sat across the room reading printouts. "Hello, Allison," he said.

I was paralyzed, awake, trying to scream. Then I heard Kearney say, "Allison?"

"Damn you, Kearney. Why didn't you let me die?" I was in a windowless room with one door, three thick plastic viewing ports with cameras or people whirring behind them.

He came over with a needle set in cork. "I thought perhaps you'd changed your mind. We also needed to get you here so we could squid your brain." Catch my thought quanta. He went on, "Curare's so cruel. This, by the way, isn't a curare needle. It'll put you to sleep, just a pinprick. And it stops dreams."

"Could you not?" I didn't want to die, didn't want to be toyed with.

"Yes. Why shouldn't we kill you? You murdered thousands of people, destroyed millions of dollars worth of oil and equipment. We're fighting oil fires from the Mississippi to Galveston."

"A brain read-out goes better with my cooperation." I was telling him I wanted to live. I'd nearly died a couple of times in the past, I should have been more callous. "I really didn't know anything about the baby nuke." The Movement picked me off the street, educated and sacrificed me. Nobody had cared, except perhaps my first recruiter. "Does it really stop dreams?"

Technology kept me alive. Kearney smiled, to let me know that he knew I found a fear of death in that body bag, then said, "We could redo you, new retina prints, new, younger face. A prettier body. The orphanage said you were smart."

He'd seen me naked. The Movement doesn't pay for body work. "Witness protection?" I'd find a way to trick them. All of them, every faction.

Kearney said, "You have to be a witness first. Next we'd like to insert you as an operative."

I didn't speak. My body, riddled with DNA that wanted to extend itself, was relieved.

Kearney said, "If I'd been you, I would not have followed through on the operation after the man selling you access was so cynical. We were trying to get you to run backwards. Glad you were so blind to my cynicism. You'd have killed New Orleans, assuming the baby nuke would have gone off wherever it was. Your trigger was just jewelry."

"I didn't know anything about the baby nuke," I said, again, "but we Nortes do use more energy than the world can afford."

He said, "I'll order you clothes."

I asked, "Can you really stop nightmares?"

Kearney said, "If you cooperate. I'm taking you at your word, Allison. My superiors think you'll try to trick us." He left.

A woman brought me what I'd be wearing. No bra with its suicide straps, no panties with waistbands I could tear out with my teeth or stuff down my windpipe—I got what the jail crowd calls strong clothes, a heavy cloth dress with rolled up sleeves. If the prisoner gets rowdy, the sleeves unroll into a straight jacket.

Strong clothes can't be ripped with fingernails or teeth. Run it back and forth across brick for a few hours and it might fuzz up a little.

I pulled it on over my head. It fit like a sack, came down almost to my ankles. Bend my legs up, tie the dress at the bottom, tie the sleeves behind my back, I'd be very secure.

"Why?" I asked.

"You're a suicide risk," she said.

"I've blown up half the Gulf Coast. Don't you want me dead?"

"Mr. Kearney will be back this afternoon. Has the dietician been by to talk to you?"

"No," I said.

"We'll see to it," the woman said.

"Where am I?" I asked. The woman's face locked against saying anything. "What kind of institution? Jail? Hospital? Rehab center?"

"Does it matter?" the woman said. She went through the door. I heard the locks. Beyond that door, I heard another door. Excessive doors between me and the outside, but I was too shaken now to make any independent plans.

Lunch came with a plastic spoon and the same woman who'd brought my strong dress. The plastic spoon would shatter into rounded beads if I tried to bite it jagged. Whoever fixed the meal cut it into spoon-sized bits for me. Beef. They should know I don't eat red meat. I said, "I'm a lactovegetarian who eats fish."

"Pretty hypocritical. Calves die for milk. Fish wouldn't mind staying alive either."

"I'm not opposed to any meat-eating. It's just that the factory farm product requires too much energy waste."

"Imagine this is grass-fed," the woman said. "I can't imagine you're opposed to killing."

"As a prisoner, I have the right to a diet that doesn't offend my conscience."

"You weren't awake at processing," the woman said. "The dietician will see you some time between afternoon and day after tomorrow."

I was starved. *Eat the meat,* my body said. It was factory meat fed on chemical industrial by-products poor Asians had to eat straight. Whatever poisons, I gagged it down.

Another woman came in, wearing a uniform. She was skinny, late forties, with bright red fingernails, and eyeliner, like makeup would soften her. Otherwise, no nonsense, even her face was strung together with whipcord muscle. She said, "Allison, I'm Captain Gouge, in charge of the female detainees at this facility."

The strong dress wasn't made to bend to my shrug. The other woman nodded at Captain Gouge and left.

Captain Gouge said, "We will allow you one phone call. I think you know we'll tap it."

I thought it was unusual that the Captain would visit a new prisoner. Perhaps she was a sympathizer? I asked, "When will I be transferred out of the hospital unit?"

"You're not in a hospital unit. Do you want a court-appointed attorney? Or do you have an attorney you'd want us to call?"

"Court-appointed attorney would be fine." All anyone could do would be hold my hand while I got sentenced.

"You claim you didn't know about the baby nuke. We'd like you to cooperate with a brain scan. Otherwise, we'll have to execute you before the Amnesty representative makes his visit."

I should have wanted the death. "Okay." Some Luddie must have gone mad-dog, stealing a baby nuke. Maybe we could truce with the Feds and run down the mad dog together? "My group's officially opposed to nuclear bombs."

Captain Gouge sighed. "An Amnesty representative will see you before the first scanning session. Full implementation requires a tracheotomy."

Full implementation requires removing a few skull bones and laying read membranes on the brain, get close to those electrical potentials and chemical gradients. I'd be paralyzed again. My hands shook. The skull bones contained the nightmares. The terror dreams lay inside the brain jelly, too, could be read, could be recorded and played back, techno-looped.

"Your people claim you had full knowledge when you volunteered for the suicide mission," Captain Gouge said. "Your leaders are hypocrites, ranting against testing baby nukes for the battlefield, but perfectly willing to contaminate thousands of acres of Louisiana and Texas themselves. Tell us the truth and what you know, and we won't put you through the brain scan."

About twenty years earlier, my recruiter Jergen had told me, "You can't cooperate even just a little bit. They'll lie to you, make you think your leaders sold you out. Don't imagine that you can trick them. If you're captured, consider yourself dead."

Jergen disappeared about eight years ago. I said to Captain Gouge,

"Perhaps your people put the bomb in my car when it garaged. You've always wanted us to look like insane terrorists."

If the plastic had been plastique . . . if the car had started . . . if anyone had really planned to pick me up at the gate. . . .

Captain Gouge said, "They've been all the world you've known since you were seventeen, right."

"Between fourteen and then, I was with another group." That group stole and put on sex shows for men too afraid of disease to touch wild child flesh.

"A community. They'll never trust you again."

"I might as well die."

"You Deep Ecology people say individual human life is meaningless, but when we catch you, very few of you actually see your own lives as meaningless."

"I was ready to die, but Kearney kept me alive."

"Takes a lot out of a person to be ready to die."

Knowing that they'd deliberately exhausted my will to die didn't make me ready to die again. I was angry. I said, "You know the people you work for are capable of planting baby nukes to make us look bad."

Captain Gouge said, "You stupid bitch. You keep saying that, I'll turn you over to the boys before Amnesty knows you ever existed. Rape's rude and crude, but it does break people."

"What an awful thing to threaten another woman with."

"We had to see if you contained any surprises. You have a device in a vertebral spinous process. It wasn't broadcasting, so we'll take it out when we do the squid surgery."

I was surprised. The Movement medics must have put it in when I was in surgery for a bicycling accident three years ago. A spinal tap, indeed. "If it's a recorder, it will tell you I didn't know anything about the baby nuke."

"Recordings can be falsified. And you didn't even know you had the device in you."

"Would you really throw me to rapists if I wonder if your people set this up?"

Captain Gouge laughed. "When did you have back surgery?"

"I'd been in a bike accident. One of those car people turned right on top of me. The medics said they gave me a spinal. We don't need to know everything."

"When?"

"Three years ago."

"You could be more precise. The bomb was stolen three years ago."

"March, late March."

Captain Gouge said, "The bomb was stolen in September."

"No connection," I said.

"Perhaps," Captain Gouge said. "You know your people are ruthless enough to send in a dumb courier. Isn't the term a waster?"

"I'm too well trained to be wasted."

"Who did you threaten? Reject? One of your people must have it in for you."

"I've agreed to cooperate with the brain read. Leave me alone."

"Was lunch okay?"

"No. I don't eat red meat."

"You finished it off."

"I was starving. I . . ."

"You don't eat red meat. Your people are opposed to nukes. Yet."

"Unusual circumstances."

"I'm sure that's why your people used the nuke."

"The cow was dead already."

"They thought you would be."

"So you're going to force me to eat red meat."

"No, we'll fit the diet to your conscience."

"Yeah, you would have asked me at intake, but I was drugged out. And the dietician will show up not later than the end of the week."

"You won't get more red meat. You can discuss the further details of your diet with the dietician later."

Why did I feel like I'd been an unruly child being obnoxious about my school grades? I'd told them my training was special. "You're really good," I told Captain Gouge.

Captain Gouge said, "Everyone of you we've captured thinks your training was special. No surprise. You think you're so special your group wouldn't send you out on a really dangerous mission. Believing this makes you bolder."

"I said I'm going to cooperate."

"You think you'll beat the system. No surprise there either. You won't beat us. We understand you're subject to nightmares. We've got drugs that can tone down the dreams. We've also got drugs that will feed your demons."

I'd met the bad cop.

The ends justify the means. The means are the ends. The two big oppositions in the world today. We can't live in a degraded world. The life chains are fraying.

Mr. Kearney said, "The horrible predictions haven't come true, you know. We didn't have major fish kills in the 1980s. The Mohawk River and the Hudson were pollution-controlled by then. My grandfather swam in the Mohawk.''

I said, ''We've lost half the world's coral reefs, most of the virgin rainforests. The native peoples. . . .''

''Come on. Industrial societies are less damaging to the landscape than farming societies. We live in cities to save energy. We farm intensively. What you'd like is enough energy to live away from your manufacturing, entertainment, information. It's an archaic territoriality most of us don't believe in anymore. Having your own slice of woodlands, mountains, doesn't preserve ecosystems. Preserving ecosystems is a large scale endeavor.''

I said, ''First, I'm not a back-to-the-lander. Second, I did believe in something.''

He said, ''You believed you and your friends were superior to other people. When you were a street thief, you and your buddies felt martyred. In the Movement, you got to be both a social victim and very morally superior.''

''Better than being the scum you thought we were.''

''People willing to bomb with baby nukes are dangerous. We're going to open you, but I'd rather have you realize the stakes and agree with us of your own free will.''

''There was a past,'' I said, meaning once upon a time, America only had 120 million people living on her.

''I think the future is much more important.''

''Why are you doing this? You're going to change my mind electrochemically, aren't you?'' I suspected that if I held my core opinions, no brain work that left me still recognizable could eradicate them. I could always re-make up my mind. A hologram shatters into replicant holograms, still the same image in each fragment, only somewhat degraded. A bit of the authentic me could overwhelm the false ideals inserted by the Federal brain workers.

Kearney said, ''Don't turn this into a dominance struggle. It isn't *I win, you lose.*''

I said, ''The bayou country was already ruined. Most of the nukes these days are neutron bombs.''

''Not that one. Your people wanted the equipment dead, not just people.''

''Maybe we need to nuke ourselves away, give evolution another chance to make sense. Even if you stopped every Illicher, every Deep Eco group, you'd still have the survivalists, the techno-punks, city gangs, the mass murderers, the thousand and one factions that rise when humans need to thin their numbers.''

"First, it doesn't work that way. War breeds babies. Poverty breeds babies."

"You think we're on opposite sides, then? You want to pacify humanity so we don't breed like coyotes. My people bomb so we get strife-driven population increases?"

"What do you believe?"

I said, "We're not coyotes." Kearney sighed. I thought about Eastern Europe, Africa in the Twentieth Century, street girls who had AIDS and babies, and added, "I guess you're right, but you're a cruel bastard."

"You just killed friends of mine. The outlaws always hate us when we have to kill their people, but we're supposed to be professionals and not take it personally when you kill our colleagues. I'd have thrown you off the helicopter if you hadn't begged to die."

I could almost see my naked body spinning down, limbs spread to catch air and prolong life. This image fell into the nightmare vat. I said, "I thought outlaws were the ones whose mourning wasn't taken into consideration. You've killed my people, too, you know?"

"Scared you, didn't I, telling you I wanted to throw you off the helicopter. You are terrified of dying."

"That's just the body, the genes wanted to go on. Humans have to control their bodies. Just like I control my nightmares." I hadn't meant to say that. I couldn't really control my nightmares as well as I wanted to. I didn't want to have them at all.

Kearney said, "If you have nightmares, something's wrong with your daytime."

"Captain Gouge said she'd throw me to rapists if I suggested that perhaps your people planted the baby nuke in my car."

"I'd kill anyone who'd deliberately plant a baby nuke in my country. Do you want an attorney, or are you going to be fully cooperative?"

"Fair enough," I said. Whatever, I didn't knowingly plant the damn atomic bomb deliberately. "I want to cooperate."

"With that note, goodbye for now. I'll see you again under the squid."

That night, the sleeping injection chained the demons, but they moved through my night in their chains, reminding me of how fierce they'd be. The chemical bonds didn't exorcise them, but exercised them.

I couldn't even wake up to be paralyzed. *Look at us closely,* they told me. My mother and father said, *we just wanted to scare you, not abandon you forever. We'd have come back. But now we've given away all your things.*

The demons looked like Jergen, like me, like my mother and father. I remembered it all when I woke up.

The dietician came. As an IV dripped sedatives, beta-endorphins, and various neurotransmitters into my veins, I picked the modified Zen diet, vegan with fish, basically. Modified Zen was the easiest choice. My brain fuzzed, cleared, whirred. I was turning into a mechanical doll.

As a nurse with a razor shaved my head, a cute guy with a little blond beard held my hand, a nice warm fuzzy to soothe the patient. In a clear moment, I wonder if he'd known what I'd done, or if I was just another prisoner to be jollied out of panic. Whatever I thought, my body liked having its hand held.

"Will you be with me throughout?" I heard myself ask the cute guy who I thought was a hospital aide.

"I'll stay with you until they start reading. I'll come back to take you to recovery. It won't hurt. The brain's got no pain nerves."

I wanted to tell him I was scared, but he was on the enemy's team. He said, "I know you're scared. Everyone's scared the first time. But you're on our records now. Amnesty won't let you disappear."

My brain fuzzed, then began flipping through memories, then remembered what the aide said. "The first time? Amnesty?"

He squeezed my hand, then said, "Can you get on the gurney yourself or do you need help?" Another young man wheeled the gurney beside the bed. I'd have thought I could sit up and walk to it, but I could barely wiggle onto the gurney.

"It's the muscle relaxant," the fuzzy-bearded man said.

"I won't be paralyzed, will I?" I'd go insane if they paralyzed me and drew out my mind.

"No, just relaxed. You won't even worry as much as you're worrying now." He pulled a vial out of his pants pocket, stuck a needle into it, drew out a drug that must have been a worry-killer, and injected it through a valve in my IV drip. "Amnesty recommends this to make the interrogation more humane."

Nothing I could do to stop this. Might as well relax and not worry. The gurney moved me to the operating theatre. I smiled at the Amnesty boy who was still beside me, stroking my hand. Just what a forty-three-year-old woman needs, a cute young boy.

A ring of faces, mouths and noses covered with translucent film. "Hello, Allison," Kearney said. "Are you with us?"

"Yes," I said.

"A bit more stimulant," another male voice said. "Local for the scalp."

"Do you want to see the squid?" Kearney said.

"No," I said. A brain-scan squid was a giant cone, vaguely squid-shaped, with cables coming out the cone's tip, the reverse of a biological squid's tentacles, the bottom an indented read head that sucked up against the brain. The whole thing oozes fluids to keep the brain moist and to improve the electrical connection between the brain and the computer. Small probes slide down into the brain to read the chemicals. I'd seen pictures. I didn't want to see the one that did me.

"We're going to map your visual cortex and the speech centers," Kearney said. I felt a needle go into my scalp, first on either side of the ears, then twice to my cheekbones. "Now, we're going to screw in the halo and sit you up."

While the warm, fuzzy boy continued holding my hand, aides strapped me to the operating table which turned into a chair. The chair swung me upright facing a video wall. Another needle to the scalp, then a metal ring with screws descended around my head. I got a screw in each cheekbone, screws in the back of the neck. I felt and heard them crunch bone. Then the surgical team fitted opaque plastic around my numb eyebrows, down by my ears, around the back over my neck screws.

Kearney said, "You'll see your output on the screen. Feedback will help you sharpen the images. Everyone's visual cortex is different, so we'll need you to help us read you. We'll remember that you cooperated."

I tried to nod, but couldn't. Someone was running a catheter tube up my urethra. I took that to mean we'd be here a long time. I tried to move my leg, could have if the hands hadn't held them. Then I could move them, and the warm, fuzzy Amnesty representative covered me with a warmed blanket.

"You'll feel vibrations against your skull. We're using an ultrasonic cutter."

As my skull bones separated, I realized I wasn't worried at all.

"Did she void her bladder?" a voice asked.

"No," my friend from Amnesty said.

"You got the dosage right, then."

"It doesn't just aid in the interrogation, it's a kindness," my buddy said. "Allison, we wouldn't want you to be terrified."

I said, "I'm not." I felt tugging, then heard a sound like torn paper. I was so grateful for the chemicals that kept this from being a nightmare.

Kearney said, "We're going to fit the squid now."

I thought I'd feel the air against my brain, but there was no feeling at all. "I don't feel anything," I said.

"They won't hurt you," my warm, fuzzy boy said.

No, I did feel a fringe of pain, detached skin and flesh from over the skull. My fuzzy boy said, "Let me tell you a story while they're working."

"Sure," I said.

The warm, fuzzy boy's story:

Once upon a time, there was a woman who lived in the bottom of a lake. Perhaps we should say she wasn't quite a woman. She swam up to the surface shimmering like a mirror and saw a fisherman in a boat and fell in love with him. He didn't see her because she hadn't known what falling in love felt like and thought that she'd been frightened. So, she sank back down in the water, but she couldn't forget the fisherman. Sometime later, another time when the surface of the lake glittered like quicksilver, she rose from the bottom of the lake again. The fisherman's boat wasn't there. She felt terribly lonely. *Perhaps,* she said to herself, *I wasn't frightened. Perhaps I was feeling an emotion I'd never felt before.*

So, each time the water surface turned silver, she rose to see if the fisherman was back. On the third day, she saw the boat and rose in front of it to see if the strange emotion would be stranger if she saw him looking at her.

"What are you doing in my lake?" he asked her.

"I was born here," she said.

"I'm the lord of all this land and the waters in my land's hollows and I've never seen you before."

The water woman said, "I hid."

"Why aren't you hiding now?"

"I've been thinking about you since I first saw you. The last time you were fishing."

"Don't lie to me. Where are you from?" the lord said.

"May I come into your boat? I think I can show better than I could tell." The water woman put her hands on the bow of the boat. She wore a dress spun from water spider silk, water spiders still nesting in it. As the lord helped her into the boat, a stickleback ran out of the nest he'd rolled in her dress's hem, all his dorsal spines flared.

"I can see that you're different," the lord said. "Are you dangerous?"

"Are you?" the water woman asked back. "Perhaps danger is what I felt, as I thought I must be afraid. My heart beat so."

"Perhaps I should throw you back and talk to a priest," the lord said.

"I'd like to go with you," the woman said.

"Your teeth are sharp and your skin is cold and there is a dent at the top of your skull, big as a teacup."

The woman didn't know what a teacup was, but she told the lord, "If we keep water in my skull hollow, I can go with you to the priest."

The priest was very upset, but the woman didn't die when the priest emptied her skull hollow and filled it with holy water. So the priest blessed both of them and said he'd say the banns for their marriage.

The woman had never sewn, but the lord's sister taught her. The woman kept a water pitcher with her at all times. The sister said, "I can't imagine a woman growing up anywhere so clumsy with a needle. Except, perhaps, a woman with such sharp teeth as you have. We should file them blunt before you marry my brother."

"Will he love me more?" the woman asked the lady sister of her lord. The lake woman now knew love was what made her heart beat faster and little waves vibrate in the water on top of her skull.

"Yes," said the sister with the file in her hand.

I didn't hear more. My vision whited out. Some time later, I could see. The warm, fuzzy boy said, "I'll finish the story later. You've got to help them now."

Infinite regress of TV screen in front of my eyes. "We've got the visual cortex. Now the memory links."

The warm, fuzzy boy asked, "Allison, can you remember being arrested?"

White glare. I visualized myself standing naked, on the video display. "Okay, that registered lots of places. Try to remember when you made contact with me," Kearney said.

On the monitor he was a small man with sallow skin. I was talking to him. The warm, fuzzy boy squeezed my hands again and said, "Allison, I'll see you when it's over."

The monitor ripped into a fish woman with pike teeth sitting by a red-headed woman with an iron file in her hand. "Aren't you going to finish the story?" I asked.

"When you're finished cooperating with these people," the boy said. His voice was leaving the room.

I saw his face on the monitor. Kearney said, "Allison, try to remember who you spoke to before me."

I was buying the vibrator from the clerk. I exploded like a child bomb, then woke up.

Kearney said, "Don't worry if we tap nightmares. The drugs you've got will mute the emotional load. Now before that?"

The clerk at the store in Picayune. I watched myself, more a sketch than a clearly visualized person, walk back to my car and get in beside Mr. Gun. Mr. Gun was the sharpest image on the monitor, then the survivalists.

"We've mapped that," another voice said. "And speaking of maps, Picayune is on old 59."

"Allison, we're going to take you back up 59. Where did you get on 59?"

On the monitor, I saw Lookout Mountain at Chattanooga. I drove off looking for the aquarium. I watched fish from my memory for a while, then Kearney asked, "Before Chattanooga?"

Joe and I were on the monitor arguing with mountain communards about deep ecology. I looked at Joe, tried to visualize him better. Ah, Joe, I miss you, myself on the video tried to say, but the video wasn't wired to pick up my speech centers.

"Allison, try to keep visualizing what happened in the past, as best you can remember," Kearney said. "Show us more about your friend here. I'm sure you'd like to remember him."

Cascades of Joe and Miriam, the trip down the Colorado, the Pacific Northwest. Kearney said, "That's that damn bitch again."

"Miriam and Joe," I said. I'd always trusted Joe and Miriam, good people.

"Good, Allison," Kearney said. "Someone else also identified Miriam and Joe for us. We're sure we'll catch them soon. What's your intensest memory of these people?"

Hetch Hetchy Dam exploded before it could be closed again. Miriam and Joe lay on the grass laughing. I was up, binoculars over my eyes looking for rangers. "We saved it the second time," Joe was trying to say. We ran through the recovering meadows, laughing.

"We saved Hetch Hetchy," I told Kearney.

"Very good, Allison. Who helped you plan that one?" Kearney asked.

We were sitting in a house in Bolinas, plastique on the table, a computer screen full of data. "Can you remember what was on the screen, Allison?"

The monitor enlarged the screen, showing that I hadn't visualized real character on it. I remembered a bit and some lines turned into clear text: HETCH HETCHY AQUEDUCT. SCOVILLE SECURITY PERSONNEL RECORDS. A photo there was of a man I recognized, one of us who'd infiltrated, who'd never been caught.

"What were the man's numbers, Allison?"

The screen within the screen squirmed, showed a 2 and some hash, then a 56. "Okay, Allison, we'd like you to remember another time that was maybe more dangerous."

I was young, standing against a chainlink fence. "How old here?" Kearney asked.

"Eighteen. I'm getting shot at by police." I couldn't understand why I looked so afraid.

"Eco-action?"

The radio materialized in my hand. "I didn't know what to do with my life then."

Then I visualized Jergen, who saved me and gave me a community and a cause. On screen, then back to me. I got over the fence and ran, the cops who'd shot my compadres back at the store tracking me with sweat tracers, like rattlesnakes slowly follow the infrared tracks of the dying animals they poison. I could run, but I couldn't hide. A back door opened. Jergen grabbed me with one hand and held a spray can in the other. "Sometimes, it pays to know the enemy," he said, spraying away my traces. He rubbed a ball over my sweaty skin and rolled it down the street.

I stood there with the radio. "Why?" Jergen asked.

"We use the parts."

"Bricoleurs," he said. "Shredding the system for parts you can use. I didn't know those gangs let girls play with them."

Behind the screen's reality, Kearney asked, "Can't you get the sound, too."

"Almost," another voice said.

I said, aloud, "I'm a mechanical sex person."

Jergen asked, "Were you going to use the radio to build a better dildo?"

I was angry but afraid—*why?*—to show it. "Street kids can't afford to go to clinics," I said. "Most of us are wanted by the law. But we're not going to give up orgasms."

"Sit down," Jergen said. "The cops won't come here."

"Why not," I said.

"I haven't done anything in a while," Jergen said. "Sit down." He subtly changed into the older Jergen, then the pixels reformed Jergen as I first saw him, a cynical thirty-year-old.

Outside the screen, behind reality, a voice said, "Very good."

"She's not giving us anything more than what we know," another voice said.

So they had busted Jergen before they busted me. On the screen, Jergen gave me soup and sat me down on the couch. "Do you want to tell me your name?"

"Allison, but when I'm forty, I'll be Mattie Higgins."

Behind my head, Kearney's voice said, "Sometime, we have that trouble, memory mixed with fantasy."

Jergen said, "I'm Jergen. Just Jergen. Allison, tell me about how you were almost busted back there."

Or was that Kearney asking? "I wasn't almost busted. They'd have gunned me down as a looter."

Jergen and I were in bed, flesh huddled against flesh. "Masturbation isn't wrong," Jergen said. "It also makes you more sensitive for intercourse."

"AIDS," I said.

"Saliva kills the HIV virus," he said. He moved his head down my body. I didn't do anything for him. I couldn't speak, spasmed, then looked down. The screen showed my breasts, nipples sweaty and flaccid, his head on my belly, eyes dilated, looking back at me.

He said, "I like doing things for women. If we want to do more, I know a medic who doesn't report to the government."

I said, to explain, "I'd never felt protected before."

Kearney sighed. Jergen got up and sat naked on a chair by the kitchen table. He leaned on his elbows and ran his fingers through his hair. "Allison, I'm hiding, too. I've been so lonely."

I was firmly in my body, looking at him from the bed. "Jergen, are you a drug dealer?"

"No."

"What kind of bad guy are you?"

"I'm a good guy. I'm trying to save the planet from the bad guys."

My techno-thief friends thought the Luddies and Illichers were silly, but Jergen wasn't silly. They were the silly ones, thrill seekers going in for bare skin shoplifting, industrial society's human cockroaches, eating away at the edges. Bruce being snide and macho popped up on the screen, frozen in an attitude, then I was back with Jergen, getting recruited.

Getting invited to do good. Within the memory, I visualized Bruce dying in the drug store, packet of orgasm drugs in his fist, body jerking as the open wounds dissolved the drugs into his system. I whirled and ran, my memories shattered.

Be aggressively good. Attack the demons.

The video jerked forward a month. I, in a dress, and Jergen, in a suit, walked by mowed grass and clipped boxwood. We shaved in all the appropriate places, deodorized, and were equipped with fake papers. Jergen was taking me to stink-bomb a polluter's corporate headquarters. "Our toxins aren't anywhere as bad as their toxins," Jergen said, kissing an image of me. My memories watched from overhead as a foreshortened me walked into the bronzed glass building and went to the ladies restroom. I pulled Jergen's bomb out of my purse and flushed it down the toilet. The bomb had a guidance system that would run it in a counter-geotrophic direction. My mind's eye played the diagram of the bomb floating and crawling up the building's sewer lines, then exploding on the executive floor. I left the building and got in the car with Jergen.

"We'll read about it in the papers," he said. "Or not, if they're too embarrassed."

I kissed him, so much better than a kid ganger, my first grown-up lover, taking me out on exciting dates. "Will they know how we did it?"

"The prop and track are biodegradable and the explosion should distort things."

"If one of them sits down on it?"

"It'll be on the floor when it explodes, not in one of the fixtures."

We drove away. What happened wasn't in the papers, but the next group that tried to bring the corporation reminders of its pollutants said the toilets had screens.

Jergen and I laughed with our friends, then Jergen said, "So we take it to their homes."

Jergen and I drove toward Oregon. We passed a sign that said MIN-NEAPOLIS/ST. PAUL. "I'd seen some things that made me think Minneapolis, but I wasn't sure," Kearney's voice said. "Now we know."

"We've got a good mapping," another voice said. "Good traces for most likely relevant memories."

Now without my consciously trying to bring up the memories, I saw Jergen and me firing guns in snow-tipped mountains. Miriam and Joe came over the ridge with a picnic basket. "We're the senators for this place," Joe said.

At nights, Miriam taught me the math and poetry of ecology, the chemistry of polymers, of proteins and of DNA. And my nightmares stopped except for the piddling one where I was supposed to be in class, but hadn't attended for six weeks.

The video showed Miriam and Joe sat on a couch watching videos when Jergen brought me in. "Hi," he said. "This is a friend, a good friend." I was shy around them until we'd spiked the old growth trees with gas bomblets.

Time skipped. Jergen told me, "You can't cooperate even just a little bit. They'll lie to you, make you think your leaders sold you out. Don't imagine that you can trick them. If you're captured, consider yourself dead."

Miriam nodded. This was sometime after we'd come to Seattle. She said, "If you're captured and you get out, escape, especially if you escape, we'll never trust you again."

I heard someone sigh. I couldn't tell whether it was on the screen or behind me, or if I myself sighed.

"Have you seen Jergen?" Miriam was older. I was, too. We'd been a team for more than twelve years, my family. We didn't have children because the planet was too full of them, but both Miriam and I had birth control failures higher than normal.

"No," I said.

"If he's caught . . ." Miriam didn't finish. I stared at her. She said, "Joe and I are leaving. Let's meet again in a year where you first saw us."

If Jergen's captured, if Jergen leads them to me . . . "Did you capture him?" I asked Kearney.

Kearney said, "Let's take her out of the loop now that we're reading directly."

No . . . o . . . o, said my voice. "No," said my voice on the monitor.

"She voided urine," a woman's voice said. "You scared her."

"Allison, it will just be like going to sleep," Kearney said.

"What are you doing to me? I said I'd cooperate. Don't make me go to sleep."

The screen turned to hash. "Jim was right about the worry drug," the woman's voice said. A needle pierced a membrane. Cool things ran in my veins.

Kearney's face was in front of my eyes. "Allison, it would be easier for you not to see what you're remembering."

"Don't rummage through my brain while I'm unconcious."

The fear ebbed away. Watching my memories on video fascinated me. Kearney moved back behind me. "You enjoy remembering your life?"

"Yes," I said. "After I met Jergen."

"Perhaps this will work for us. Make sure you keep that drug in her," Kearney said.

Memories lived on. Miriam and Joe met me on the mountain. After we did Hetch Hetchy, they took me east to meet other people. The world was more crowded, more polluted, more degraded than when we'd begun.

"We need to teach people to use less energy, to use their muscles to make things rather than to work out in expensive gyms," Martin Fox said.

Another man said, "What we really need to do is sterilize people. Overpopulation is the problem. Technological solutions won't work. You can't micromanage the environment."

Martin Fox said, "Sterilize the whole damn planet."

I said, "What can you distribute that won't impact negatively on the environment? It'd damage other life forms."

Martin said, "Put it in people food."

Joe said, "Man we know worked out something that will attack egg and sperm cells, anything with half the normal chromosomes. And it self-destructs in a week, good enough for a city."

Miriam said, "No, Joe, not nanotech."

After that conversation, Miriam and Joe disappeared.

Time skipped again. Martin Fox said, "If we attack the refineries, destroy oil, we can force them to use the last of it. Then we'll have to use less chemical energy."

Behind my head, Kearney said, "Can you fix a date?"

I was about to answer when another voice said, "She wasn't thinking dates when she laid down these memories. It's on a trace straight from the memory of meeting Jergen, see?"

On the screen, a door opened and Jergen pulled me inside. Martin Fox said, "If we attack the refineries . . ."

I said, "Couldn't you ask me when this was?"

"When?" Kearney's voice said.

"Last November."

"Follow all the traces from here," Kearney's voice said.

"Is Martin Fox your infiltrator?" I asked.

Miriam and Joe and I sat at a table, drumming our fingers against the Formica. Joe said, "We need to do something in memory of Jergen."

Miriam got up and set a teakettle in the focus of a sun stove, then opened a window and turned the reflectors so raw sunlight would boil our water.

I asked, "Are you sure he's dead?"

"Nobody's seen him," Joe said. "If he's betrayed us, then we'll all have to stay away from scanners. I think he's more likely to have your retinas than ours, though."

I watched us on the screen, looking for signs that I'd annoyed either Joe or Miriam enough that they would have set me up. They immediately began to frown at me, to whisper at each other.

"Are you reworking this memory?" Kearney asked.

"I've known them for years. Either Martin Fox set me up or they did. But I didn't see them again after Martin Fox proposed sterilizing the human race."

Miriam said, "If you ever disappear, then don't come back. If you miraculously escape custody, we won't trust you."

On the screen, I asked, "Can I trust Martin Fox?"

Joe said, "We've been on operations with Martin. He's reliable, but a little extreme."

Kearney said, "She's confabulating."

I said, "So what's the next operation."

We did Hetch Hetchy and went east. Kearney said, "You're a bit too proud of Hetch Hetchy."

After Miriam and Joe disappeared, Martin Fox said, "We're going to run support for a while. I know it's not as dramatic as doing the actions, but the letter-bombers need a couple levels of cutouts."

Kearney asked, "When was this?"

I tried to remember. "When nanotech and recombinant DNA people were getting hit. Couple years ago."

On the video, I picked up a six-pack from a culvert and walked it over to a kid wearing night-vision goggles. The kid rode away on a recumbent bicycle, his belly in a sling, steering with his hands, the pedals magnetically clamped to his shoes. In infrared, he was a faint light no higher than a dog weaving through green car heat.

The newspapers told about the eighth letter bomb, not the earlier ones.

Martin Fox said, "Miriam and Joe left the country. We think Jergen was captured, but our hacker sources don't tell us anything about you, Allison. We could be fucked. They can tear his head apart by reading his brain."

I said, "I thought you had to cooperate with the squids to have that work."

Martin said, "Watching your own memories can be tremendous fun if you have either an edit button or a chemical lobotomy." He smiled at me as though he was now watching my own interrogation.

Kearney said, "Allison, how did you become Mattie Higgins?"

Martin took me into walk-up cube on East Broadway where a med tech peeled my fingers and lay in the fake prints.

I said to Kearney, "Perhaps Martin Fox decided to get rid of all Jergen's associates."

Kearney said, "So you weren't that valuable."

I said, "Guess not."

"Isn't Fox a lot more violent than Jergen?" Kearney said. "Can't you see that?"

"Did he kill Miriam and Joe, too?" I asked.

Kearney didn't answer. I felt slightly dizzy, then the video showed me picking up the Xhoshiba at a truck stop in the mountains just off I-40. "Did you see anyone, Allison?" Kearney asked.

I looked back at the trucker who'd given me the ride and laughed, said, "I guess my friends are inside, but here's their car. I'll be okay now."

"Aw, well," the trucker said.

Kearney said, "Was he one of you?"

"No," I said while on the screen, I looked around. The other people seemed innocuous. I got in the Xhoshiba and drove down to Asheville and spent the night in a decommissioned chain hotel, now sold to people too poor to get a franchise. They were sympathizers I knew slightly, but the screen didn't register this. I decided not to tell Kearney.

He said, "Trace the people."

My brain threw an image of a party on the screen. The woman who'd own the hotel years later was giggling. Jergen said, "We appreciate your letting us stay here tonight."

"Just don't tell me anything I don't want to know." The woman took us upstairs and showed us to a mattress on the floor. "I'm glad you could come for the party. Less likely anyone would notice strangers at the door."

"Should we come back down?" I said.

"I'm too tired," Jergen said.

I went down and heard our hostess tell another couple, "She's one of the heavies."

I came up to them and put my arms around the couple. "Are you concerned about the environment, too?"

The woman excused herself. I kept holding the couple, remembering. . . .

Machine sex, me with thermoplastic dildos in every orifice, the machine pumping me while my gang cheered. "Beat the bitch." Another woman from another gang lay masturbating under her gang's sex machine. My gloves . . .

"Allison, what more do you remember about the party?" Kearney asked.

"I beat the bitch," I said, trying to remember the orgasm contest and getting a shock, not an image on the monitor. "Wasn't I cute then?" Fuck Kearney, he wanted to know all about me. Here I was, naked and throbbing.

"The party, Allison."

On the screen I was saying to the couple, "I used to be a technophile, but I discovered nature."

"What kind of technophile?" the woman asked. The man squeezed my butt.

"The baddest kind," I said. I remembered the gloves moving the machine. One of the boys wiped my face. Rules were he couldn't touch me below the neck, but he could run his tongue in my ear. Next time, we could have the machine do that, I thought. And up yours, too, Kearney.

"Do you need more information?"

Kearney said, "Let's close her up for now. We've got ID on a couple of the people. Allison, if you can't get off the machine . . ."

My body arched against the machine, muscles spasming. My gang cheered as I collapsed. I heard the other girl moaning, but the dildos read vaginal contractions, nipple turgidity. You couldn't fake orgasm with a machine.

"Allison, we can get you any kind of machine you need," Kearney said. "We're going to put you to sleep now, but from now on, you'll be wired for memories. Also, we didn't get Jergen. He surrendered."

No. I wanted to see more. The drugs they'd given me took away the sliminess I generally felt when I remembered mechanical fucking contests. And I was showing Kearney what a hard-ass bitch I was, throw shit in his eyes.

"Remember to get whatever they've planted in her cervical vertebra," a voice said as I fell asleep, my real-time cunt throbbing as though machines had worked it.

I woke up strapped to a low bed, my head helmeted, the walls, ceiling, and floor around around me padded. My face and neck ached. The blond, fuzzy Amnesty boy sat on the padded floor, barefooted, wearing loose pants and a tunic. He'd tucked one leg under him, the other bent in front. He dangled one hand off the bent knee. His bare feet seemed so appealing.

"Do you remember what happened?" he asked.

"You were telling me a story about filing off my teeth," I said, then I remembered how much I remembered. I'd betrayed Martin Fox, Miriam and Joe, perhaps even Jergen if he still lived. No, Jergen himself surrendered, cooperated. But maybe Kearney lied. Jergen hadn't betrayed me. I threw myself against straps and screamed, "Bastards."

The fuzzy boy said, "You couldn't help it. We had you wired and dosed. Bravery, self-control, none of that mattered."

"Damn Kearney. Jergen would never turn himself in."

"I wasn't at your interrogation."

"I'm tough. I could have handled it all without the anti-anxiety drug. I got to be young again. I saw Jergen again."

But remembering on the screen had been more fun than I could stand now. That had been the anti-anxiety drug. I closed my eyes, remembering how vivid my memories had been on the video monitor. They'd never been that vivid inside my brain. "But you do know that I didn't mean to use a baby nuke, don't you?" I heard my voice pleading, hated it. Why did I want this fuzzy boy to like me?

"Yes, Allison," the fuzzy boy said.

"Do you have a name?" I asked. "Do you have some drug that imprints your prisoners on warm, fuzzy captors?"

"Jim," he said. "I really am from Amnesty."

"Jim, it's your job to be warm and fuzzy, isn't it? I desperately need a friend, or they've given me drugs that make me think I do."

His hand suspended over his bent leg twitched. "What's your job now? Your purpose in living?"

"You didn't answer my question about imprinting. I don't have one. I guess your people can try and execute me now."

"We can give you a reason to keep on living."

"Answer me. Why do I find myself wanting to trust you? It's absolutely abnormal."

"Perhaps not," he said.

"They taped my memories, didn't they? And you watched them later." I remembered what I remembered at the end.

"No," he said.

"Poor Jergen."

Kearney came in then and heard that. "I'd say poor you," Kearney said. "Your friends placed an intermittent loop recorder in your neck, wired for sound an average of every ten minutes, with a randomizer. Storage of three months. They didn't trust you. Perhaps they think you had something to do with Jergen's disappearance."

Jim said, "Leave her alone for now, Captain. She's just had her world collapse."

I said, "You can't tell him anything. He's your boss, isn't he? Jim's not really Amnesty."

Kearney said, "But he is. He enforces the ban on capital punishment."

I said, "So he told me before he drugged me." Jim nodded, touched my cheek gently. I felt like a bitch for a moment, then wondered if I should believe anyone. I was too broken to make up my mind about anything, but mistrusted my desire to believe Jim.

Kearney said, "Jim, I need to explain a few things to Allison about her brain work."

Jim rose from the floor and came over and squeezed my hand. I trembled. He squeezed again and left.

Kearney said, "You don't believe he's with Amnesty."

"Of course, he isn't."

"I wouldn't be vicious with your only advocate if I were you."

"Are you going to formally charge me? I want an attorney."

"Not right now. You're precariously glued together. We've installed an internal squid and processor with a subdermal port. There'll be no external evidence that you're wired. You can read memories by laying the receiving pad over the subdermal. The digitalized signal can penetrate flesh. We can turn on transmission by signalling the processor. So you won't be transmitting all the time, just in case someone else can listen."

At least I wouldn't have open brain holes drawing in infection. I said, "Why shouldn't there be evidence that I'm wired? You can't send me back to the people I'd been working with."

Kearney said, "There are other people."

I thought about asking him to just get it over with and kill me, but knew my asking would just be bravado. "You didn't change me when you had my brain open, did you?"

"Would you know?"

I tried to see if I felt different. If I'd been changed, I couldn't tell. "I'd like to see Jim again."

"He really does work for Amnesty," Kearney said.

I nodded, the helmet making that laborious. I was drugged, perhaps brain-changed, memories stolen, life functionally over.

"He can come back now," Kearney said. He left the room, then Jim came back.

Jim held my hand as I cried. Even as I realized Jim could be the good cop, I needed to trust him. Story of my life, just a human weed looking for a place I fit in. Perhaps I should try to get Kearney to trust me, volunteer to be his informer, get out and disappear. No more actions for any side.

When I'd stopped crying, Jim asked, "Would you rather be charged and tried now?"

"What sentence is likely?"

"Life without parole, but we'd organize to prevent a mental health intervention."

I tried to laugh. "That's already happened."

Jim said, "No, that was a legal interrogation."

"You helped them with the anti-anxiety drug."

Jim said, "Yes and no. Yes, you were more cooperative. No, they would have read your brain anyway, but more traumatically."

"How soon before they unstrap me?"

"I can unstrap you now and help you walk a bit."

"Why do I ache under the eyes?"

"They had to push under your eyes and along the bottom of your skull to get to your hippocampus, where memories live. They tried not to hurt brain tissue, so the probes pushed against the bones." Jim unstrapped me and helped me up, held the helmet until I could balance it on my neck.

"I'm sorry we were so futile," I said.

"I'm sure you had good intentions," he said, easing me around the room. "Do you think you can walk on your own?"

"Why am I in a padded cell?"

"Suicide precautions."

"Amnesty against that, too?"

"We don't think people should be tortured into it."

"I thought you were opposed to torturing people." I shuffled around the padded floor on my own. The pads made for uneasy footing.

"We did everything we could to make the interrogation bearable. You were overwhelmed, but considering that your people sent you out with a baby nuke, Amnesty agreed that the interrogation benefits outweighed your discomfort. But I am sorry."

"I might as well have been raped. I bet they're playing all the sex scenes. . . ."

"Allison, don't worry about that. All irrelevant scenes were edited out. Witnesses certified that the scenes weren't necessary for your defense."

"Witnesses?"

"Other Amnesty officials."

So Jim was telling me he'd only heard about my fifteen-year-old body squirming under a dildo machine, masturbation target during the sex plague years. I'd been breaking bad at Kearney, but now I was disgusted. Naked, dying naked. "So you didn't see me with Jergen?"

"No."

"When I was a kid, the strong form of AIDS still killed people. We got off differently."

"I told you I didn't see any of the tape. I'm your advocate. As a Federal prisoner, you can ask for sexual relief, if that's what's bothering you. Either a surrogate or your regular partner unless he or she is in custody, or you could ask for machine relief."

What about you? Do you give good head? "I hate sex now. It got me born."

"Life without parole," Jim said. "You've confessed, you know. Even if you've never had any homosexual experiences outside, I'd recommend making a life with another prisoner. Amnesty's going to insist that you be allowed out into general population. Making a life for yourself inside seems to be ultimately the most satisfying."

Or I could cooperate with Kearney. "Thanks," I said. "I had some experience with external vibrators."

Jim asked, "Why do you hate people so? Even yourself."

"Why not?" I said. "Humans destroy everything they touch. Look at me. Even when we didn't mean to do that much damage, we do it."

Jim asked, "Do you want to be alone for a while?"

"Alone with the cameras? Why don't I insist you stay?"

Jim said, "Well, I could."

"No, go on. I bet you've got other prisoners to tend."

"Yes, but not at this facility."

"Jim . . ." *Could you tell me if one of them is Jergen? He couldn't have really surrendered. Tell me if anyone in Amnesty knows what happened to him.* Would he be able to tell me? Did I want to know if he couldn't?

"If I go now, I'll be back in four days."

Ask anyway. "Can I find out what happened to Jergen? If he's a prisoner, Amnesty must know."

"Amnesty can't relay information on U.S. system prisoners to other U.S. prisoners. We're your advocate, not your informant."

"Nice to have that clarified," I said. "Okay, go."

So he worked for Amnesty. No one from a child gang ever grew up to work for Amnesty. No drode heads finally found work there.

At least, I thought, I don't have open brain holes. The only person I saw for four days (was it really four days?) was a nurse who checked my vital signs twice a day and gave me pills. My food came by machine. Either my jailers drugged away my nightmares or my demons thought I was in torment enough. No dreams registered.

I asked the monitors, ''Don't I get a trial?''

On the fifth day, or what I thought was the fifth day, Kearney brought in a cat carrier. He wore nose plugs, ear plugs, and gloves. ''Open it,'' he said.

I shook my head. But whatever it was inside the cat carrier buzzed and thrummed. I felt silly refusing to cooperate and opened the carrier.

A foot-tall praying mantis stepped out and cocked its head. Its thorax moved, breathing. *But insects don't breathe like that.* Between *thumms,* I felt uneasy again and looked at Kearney, but the mantis stepped up to me, and thummed again, nibbling my skin delicately. I heard a small hiss, a gas to ease my mind.

''Where did it come from?'' I asked.

''East Coast,'' Kearney said. ''They've reached Atlanta.''

''Recombinant?''

''The lungs and gas transport system are unique.''

''Maybe it's Gaia's revenge, a mantis that tranquilizes humans.'' I took the beautiful insect on my hand and lifted it toward my face. I saw a thousand self-reflections in its compound eyes.

''You can keep it for a few days. We think it will help you recover faster.''

''Thank you,'' I said, enchanted as the mantis nibbled my skin again, not biting deep though it could. I said to it, ''Beautiful insect, I'm sorry we're in jail together.''

Kearney said, ''Good, you've bonded.'' He seemed still able to hear. His ear plugs must shift mantis song frequencies to something less seductive to the human nervous system.

''Kearney, it's a wonderful bug, but I still would like human contact,'' I said. My thoughts flowed faster, as though anxiety had knotted them earlier. The mantis released me. ''Oh, wonder bug, I hope you are natural,'' I told it. Not likely, I realized, but that didn't seem to matter right now. I could see this as a bug from a nightmare, but the bug itself calmed me.

''You bond better with them if you've been isolated for a few days,'' Kearney said. ''They tend to be especially attracted to dole people coming out from read time.''

Even through the mantis charms, I realized the implications of that. Keep them drode heads happy, drugged with bug juice and good vibrations. ''Where were they first seen?''

''New York and Long Island.''

"Any evidence of gene branding?"

"You know about that?"

"We Illichers give each other good educations."

"Brands tampered with, probably from the Rockefeller University people who helixed the street tree silk moths. Or stolen from them."

I leaned back in bed with the mantis still on my hand. "Someone gave it the pheromones, the sounds, and the better lungs."

"Yes. And it eats kibble that's been showing up in ghetto shops."

"Well, why bother about it. Owners couldn't have invented a better insect."

"The tranquilizer tends to make people less anxious. But about 20 percent of drode heads started trying to make their own plans. All of them have had mantises for over three months. Plus, we want this person who tampers with insect genes under control. Insects are very volatile without help, evolving resistances. Now, if a human is unnaturally tampering with insects . . . come on, you're an ecologist. You should hate the implications."

"You're right. I should hate it." But I couldn't. It was Jergen all over again, me feeling three-quarters dead, hating the life I'd been leading, then a door opens and love is on the other side.

"I'll send in mantis kibble with your next meal."

THREE

INSECTS SPIRALLING OUT OF MANHATTAN

*N*ow *we use our enemies to save us,* Dorcas thought as she manipulated her waldo glove. First she'd insert the DNA fragment of redesigned insect lung into a retrovirus. *Insects deserve better than book lungs and spiracles.* She could admit to herself that perhaps she was just playing with insects. *We toy with mantises and they play back to us.*

One of Dorcas's enemies once told her that a non-publishing scientist was an oxymoron. When she told him that she wanted to use science to make neater insects, he said, "You're an engineer, maybe an artist, not a scientist. The world doesn't need neater insects. And we can't afford to give a lab to a bio-enhanced redhead who wants to play."

The viruses were solid crystals floating in front of her eyes, chemically shattered and rebuilt. Dorcas dissolved them and they swirled away, a solution to be oozed into wasp eggs. On the right hand side of the display was a window into the lab that Dorcas checked with periodic nervousness.

Her latest superior and lover, Henry Itaka, PhD, MD, A.Ph.D. (that new degree of academic inflation), rebuilt people. Dorcas, feeling rebuilt people weren't ecologically appropriate, rebuilt insects. The Federal Laboratory Administration hadn't granted them permits to work on either problem. FLA wanted all recombinant projects registered, controlled, and industrially applicable.

(The Rockefeller University security files told the first investigator that the woman in Lab 43, Dorcas Rae, was an adult only child, a Ph.D., and a long time lover of various married men able to offer her postdoctoral fellowships.)

She rarely used technicians in her lab, but if she needed them would get her lover's technicians to do the work. She ordered drode heads for computer connections about half the time, but knew her way around a keyboard, most virtual reality systems, and a couple of programming languages, unusual skills these days.

"You'd make better money in gene-tech," one of her lovers told her. "You don't have the hots for shoving your papers and ideas in other people's faces."

"But . . ." Dorcas couldn't explain that the gene industry monitored its people's time too closely. She preferred being innovative with genetic material too much.

Dorcas lived on what academics call soft money—postdocs, study grants—but never got tenure track positions. She was the junior author of seven papers, the senior author of one, published online in a discussion group chaired by a former lover. Only another woman could take her seriously.

(The first security officer to check her file was male. He didn't copy her file onto his disc, but called up the next file just as Dorcas began changing the cell membranes on the wasp eggs to make them more receptive to the retroviruses.)

Whether working with retroviruses or with chromosomal pieces, Dorcas used electroporation to make the insertions easier. She'd fit tomorrow's eggs with chromosomal pieces. Fewer would take, but they'd be more likely to affect the final product. Every day, she ran off lots of a queen wasp ovary full before doing the tasks Henry assigned her.

Dorcas worried that she was simply creating mosaics with genes that wouldn't bear enough promoter sequences to find expression. If the new genetic material would make a lunged wasp, perhaps that wasp's progeny wouldn't breed true. All transgenes are heterozygotes. Expression is a crap shoot.

Rolling gene dice. A thousand zygote tries to get something that grew up to express the effect Dorcas hoped her transgene would carry.

Dorcas had a strange compassion for the zygotes who failed. She'd been the only survivor of a hundred zygote tries by her parents, their pick of the litter, the best expression of their DNA. They'd turned down rebuilding, not because it was illegal with people—they could have afforded the bribes—but they wanted Dorcas to be their real daughter. And her dad wanted his daughter to be beautiful. Smart was incidental.

After the eggs received the lung DNA, Dorcas ordered the computer to bring in this morning's wasp and lowered the magnification, switching the microscope to ordinary light. A miniature conveyer brought in a queen wasp from a strain already rebuilt with neuroleptic venom and cockroach immunity to insecticides.

We'll be studying war no more, no more, Dorcas hummed.

In Dorcas's field of vision, a needle the size of a broomstick probed between the chitin plates of a wasp the size of a small airplane. Dorcas called for yet lower magnification, moved the needle between two abdominal plates, squeezed the redesigned egg cells into the wasp's ovaries. Then she dosed the wasp's own eggs with the enhanced retrovirus, a "just in case" move. Still blind to outside reality, she pulled her hands out of the waldo gloves and flexed them, high so they wouldn't touch anything on the table. She wore eye cups that would have looked like swim goggles except for the cables feeding from the microscope to the black domes over her eyes.

Dorcas Rae, once a tall skinny kid in transparent braces and red hair, now the heavy side of willowy, still without tenure, an academic gypsy, loved her Klein-bottle logic of using science to attack the ecological bottleneck that human science and technology created.

Lunch time. Dorcas pulled microscope feed lines out of her goggles and the goggles away from her face. After stretching, she put on her UV hat. Before she put the wasp in a vial and the vial in her pocket, Dorcas hit her fooler loop for the lab cameras. *What would they do to me if they caught me stealing DNA sequences?* Dorcas wondered, *Order me to make war bugs? Sell me to industry as a gene hacker drode head? Daddy would protect me, unless he felt I was embarrassing him.* She swallowed chelate pills for the pollutant of the week. The fooler loop edited out the few seconds that Dorcas needed to conceal her insect, but went back to real time with the pills.

Rockefeller University, during the decade when it was really dangerous to be a DNA tweaker, built tunnels into Manhattan subway stations so researchers could come and go without Luddite attacks. Dorcas locked her lab, checked out of Tunnel Five, and rode the walkway across to Lexington Avenue. Blinking, she rose into the sun and walked to Central Park.

Now, for a really big wasp to sting soldiers to sleep. Maybe, this wasp would find a male. Maybe the retrovirus would infect other wasps. Maybe the gene wouldn't be expressed in wasps. The wasp crawled to the edge of the vial. Dorcas looked around to see if anyone was watching. The type of wasp she was rechanging had been designed originally as a house pet, building colored paper nests in room corners, eating mosquitos. The pet company found strains of wild wasps so gentle the people whose houses they'd colonized hadn't thought it worth the insectide to kill them. Then they hired a team that included Dorcas to make the wasps gentler yet, resistant to environmental toxins, and capable of using dyed paper pulp to build their nests. A year later, some drug dealer's gene hacker modified the venom. The drug wasps would sting if their humans forced them.

Tweak the reflexes, the vision, the cascade times for neurotransmitters, and a woman who wanted could make a mean wasp. But this was one of the gentle wasps.

The queen wasp circled Dorcas, buzzing nervously, tilting her abdomen forward. *Why am I being abandoned in the park?* But Dorcas knew the wasp lacked enough neurons to think that. The wasp drifted away from Dorcas, circled a pretzel cart, then flew skyward.

After Dorcas lost sight of her wasp, she walked a bit in Central Park. Slum children gathering silk climbed the trees of heaven looking for cocoons. They stared at Dorcas, suspecting her to be armed, wrapped in Kevlar. One girl looked about ready to be harvested herself, to have her head shaved, dole electrodes put in, turned into a scanning device or a medium-grade data processor. Dorcas herself hadn't redesigned the wild silk moths that spun in the leaves like *Bombyx mori* caterpillars. The work inspired her, though. *What more could insects give us?*

The moth's such a useful insect to have around poor people and weed trees, Dorcas thought. The children surrounded her, but stayed back. *I'm an irritant in a vacuole in the body politic, but a necessary irritant.* She bought a hot dog in a whole wheat bun from a street vendor, then walked back along 63rd Street.

Some poor dole brain lying down with electrodes scanned her security tapes. Dorcas wondered how alert a dole brain would be to the tiny flicker of a fooler loop. How much could a dole person care?

The day was one of those brilliant Manhattan summer days, not too hot, the air so clear Dorcas saw every detail on the old copper roofs. She passed a pet store that sold stick insects, captive-bred endangered centipedes, butterfly eggs, and captive breeding kits.

We're bringing in the fragile ones, so fashionable to be part of the ark movement. Why not make species that can stand up to us? Dorcas herself arked rare fish and one land snail, exchanged juveniles with other arkists, kept pedigrees. *Belonia hasselotti, Betta macrostomata,* antabantoids who evolved to live in low oxygen waters, whose eutrophic waters were drained or filled with hybrid tilapia. She'd asked one of her fellow arkists, "Would descendants of these fish find a natural world to return to? They're evolving now to do well on flake food."

Her friend argued that humans owed the natural world and saving the species mattered, even if they had to be arked across deep space to virgin planets.

Dorcas said, "But funds for space have been cut. Too many people." She also almost said that what we needed was a world where humans had to struggle again, not with each other as now, but with the rest of creation.

With that thought, Dorcas knew she could empower the natural world if she just kept her mouth shut.

The arked endangered species needed teeth, venom, brains.

Dorcas chose insects. She'd already released giant mantises that soothed humans. The dole brains loved them.

She passed under a street light where a group of hornets kept warm through the winter. They moved out of the great paper football when she stopped, looking at her as she looked up at them. She pulled the tip end of her hot dog out of the bun and laid it at the base of the lamp.

The hornets moved their antennae, then one dropped down to the hotdog, then another, and another. Dorcas watched for a minute, then continued toward the University. She went underground at Third Avenue and checked back in.

"Your boss is back," the guard said. "He wondered why you were fooling around with an outside lunch."

"It's a pretty day," Dorcas said. She went back to her office, hung up her coat, took another chelate pill for whatever might have been in the hotdog, and looked for Henry, suddenly feeling anxious. She remembered the hate-filled stare of the adolescent girl, wondered if a dole brain would willfully look for flickers in security tapes.

When Henry put his hand on her shoulder, Dorcas jumped.

She said, "What a weird world we live in."

Henry was part Japanese genetically, whatever that meant, considering that Japan had proved to be a genetic mix of Polynesian, Korean, and Ainu, plus small fractions of Caucasian and African material. His grandfather refused to admit that children he sired on his blue-eyed American wife could be anything other than Japanese. Henry's father married another American woman, as blonde as he could find. Henry came out blue-eyed, a hint of epicanthic folds around them, blonde, and tall. Dorcas, who'd been gangly until she hit her sophomore year, preferred lovers who thought her youth more than made up for her figure. But she was getting older and the lovers younger.

"Why didn't you wait until I got back before having lunch?" he said. She knew he'd been getting a high-security contract. Normally, everyone just interfaced, but high-security types never trusted computer security.

"The planes are always late," Dorcas replied. She felt the blend of lust, envy, and intellectual excitement that marked her attachment to her various mates. But she couldn't tell him what she'd been up to. This, she realized as she took Henry's hand in hers, probably was just as well. Henry wanted to bounce his ideas off her.

"Well, come to my office. I'll send down to the canteen, then we can talk."

When they got to his office, he grabbed her, one hand on her buttocks, the other in her hair. "Missed you. Missed your stimulating conversation." He lifted Dorcas's hair and looked at it again, as if he'd never been convinced that the color was real. The color was real enough even though the number of hair follicles had been augmented and Dorcas's freckles demelanized. A true red-haired beauty was a rare thing, Dorcas's daddy had told her when she knew she'd failed, but her mother had been a good enough provider to have paid for the skin and hair job.

"Women always cheat," her mother had told Dorcas as the pre-op sedatives had begun to work. The red would grow from the roots, from more follicles than Dorcas had been born with.

Now Dorcas told Henry again, "You know my hair's real."

"Yes, the hair is so various in tint, but couldn't your family afford nanoteched follicles? You're always changing in my mind. Each time I come back, I realize I'd forgotten what you really look like," Henry said.

Dorcas suspected he was telling her she needed to lose weight. She said, "Did any of your friends know about any job openings?"

"We got a renewal of our grant, plus a new project. You'll be able to stay on here."

"Where I know the equipment and the genome library, good," Dorcas said. She wondered if she'd spend so much time deepening the ecology with wasp queens and praying mantises if she had her own lab. And how long would this last with Henry? He seemed now to find her convenient, not an object of desire.

"We're getting a domestic containment contract, so if FBI people ask your neighbors . . ." He didn't finish but backed her against a tank in his private ark for endangered Appalachian salamanders and kissed her mouth.

Dorcas opened her mouth and thought, *Maybe this isn't a good time to hack the security system.* She sucked Henry's tongue clean of airplane lunch residues, then pulled back to ask, "Domestic containment?"

"Something against eco-terrorists. Something to monitor the drode heads. Based on military bio agents. They told me we've got some unlicensed insects showing up. Right up your alley," Henry said, his hand sliding up her leg.

"What about my own lab?"

"Money's tight, but . . ."

"What about tenure?"

"You know Rockefeller only grants tenure to lab heads. You need to think like a consultant, lean, mean, and able to switch loyalties for a dollar."

"I thought you were going to ask your friends about a tenure track job for me."

"Oh, Dorcas, what are you, a science slut? Fucking me for job leads? You need to finish that paper on the work you've been doing with wasps."

"Henry, that's not fair."

"The other PhDs from your program should be the ones to give you job leads."

"They hate me because I was beautiful for a decade."

"You could . . . you still are beautiful."

Dorcas hated the stereotype of the sexless woman scientist, hated faculty wives' jealousy, the prigs in her program who quipped that she took her comps on her back. Both as an undergraduate and in grad school, she only fucked people after they'd graded or evaluated her. She never fucked her advisor or any of the guys on her dissertation committee. Dorcas asked Henry, "How is your wife, by the way?"

"She's forgotten every bit of work she did on the human genome project. Some women don't age well."

"I need to get out more, walking. Would the FBI think that was too eccentric?"

"Not for a woman scientist," Henry said. He smiled, Dorcas was sure, at the prospect of her losing weight. Dorcas tried bulimia when she was a teenager, but her braces turned out to be wired to inform on her if she threw up on them. Her family doctor put a shock choker around her throat to make sure she didn't try tickling her throat again. "You're too thin already," both the orthodontist and doctor told her.

Dorcas had a decade and then some as a beauty. Now she'd welcome anorexia, but she was too sane. "Henry, help me," she said, lips at his ear level. She always expected consideration from her men, even after the passion faded.

"I know a great personal trainer," he said. "We could split the cost."

Dorcas wondered if her wasp queen found a mate in Central Park. "I'd love that." She pulled back to look at him.

A hint of anxiety flicked across Henry's face. Dorcas remembered that three out of five of her married lovers dropped her within a year of displaying that facial tic.

On Sunday afternoon, Dorcas visited her mother, Emily, and father, Paul, who lived in a twenty-four-foot motor home now parked in a retirement garage in the Bronx. Since Dorcas had seen them last, Emily had had her face, neck, and arms reskinned and Paul had had his eyeballs re-rounded. Emily still wore her glasses, but otherwise, she looked about Dorcas's age, thirty-four. Dorcas thought she'd run screaming if her mother came out of surgery looking younger than her daughter. Emily, now sixty-five, had been forced into an early retirement at sixty-one. Paul, sixty-seven going on forty, arranged to work quarter-time by modem. Nanomachines scavenged their free radicals, ate plaque out of their veins, but occasionally malfunctioned and cut axons, tangled synapses. The Raes were rich enough to buy youth until their brains went. Then Dorcas would be half as rich as they'd been, death duties taking the other half.

Dorcas said, "I could have interfaced with you easily enough."

Her father said, "I didn't want to virtually see you. You could edit your data before it's up on my screen." Her dad never would use goggles, claimed robbers watched the data lines and broke in on people entranced by computer dreams. He preferred fax.

"Some man was by trying to sell us heroin," her mother said. "Said if your dad liked alcohol, he'd like heroin."

As though reminded, her dad went to his liquor cabinet and pulled out a bottle of clear grain, then added it to a commercial Scotch. "Heroin, oh, wow, let's shoot up and go on the nod. Wow, a nap." He drank down his mix of grain alcohol and Scotch and glared at Dorcas. "You ought to lose weight. Liposuction or nanoscavengers if you don't have the willpower to diet."

"I thought I was supposed to be perfect. I had to have braces as a child and now I get fat."

"Now, Dorcas, you were the best our genes could do. We didn't want a transgenetic child. And you know how difficult it is to guarantee expression.''

''Yes. I'm in the business.''

Paul said, ''If you were in the business end of genetic work you'd be more stable.''

''I'm an academic.''

Her father said, ''No, you're stubborn. But that's true genetic expression for you. I'm stubborn, too. Nanotech, then look for a real job.''

Dorcas didn't trust nanomachines even though they'd given her great hair. She wouldn't put anything in her bloodstream made by the species that put the Nile Perch in Lake Victoria.

''We've agreed that we wouldn't nag her,'' her mother said.

''I always thought you were going to be an ugly cuss, but then you were almost good looking for a while. Why didn't you find a man?''

''Dorcas has a career,'' her mother said.

''You had a career and a child, even if I personally never thought much of the bonsai family concept. The bitch is lazy. She doesn't write her own papers. Postdoctoral, come on, Dorcas, you'd do better teaching high school. If you really refuse to work for industry.''

''People don't teach biology that way anymore. It's all apprentice-ships and interactives.''

''People don't learn right from machines,'' her dad said. ''It's like machine visits.''

''Computers let teachers interact with more students,'' Dorcas said.

''You're both just so stubborn,'' her mother said. ''We haven't seen you since we went west.''

''Isn't it dangerous to be roving around in something this big now?''

''We're armed,'' her father said. ''The human herd needs thinning. We're deputies in Nevada, Louisiana, and Orange County, California.''

''The government elderhostel worker we saw in Tucson suggested traveling in Mexico,'' Emily said.

Elderhostel workers always encouraged more surgery, more nano-machines, drugs, and dangerous hobbies. ''You're looking good, Mother,'' Dorcas said, acknowledging the latest surgery for the first time.

''I feel stiff, but the skin's supposed to supple up in a month or so.''

''Bet Dad approves. You look about my age.''

''I almost died,'' Emily said.

''Emily exaggerates,'' Paul said. ''I'd do anything to make your mother's life more beautiful.''

''So, are you going to Mexico?'' Dorcas asked.

''No, we're planning to ship us off to Asia.''

Dorcas wanted to ask if they expected to find good medical service there, but realized retirees had been wandering away from first-rate hospitals well before elderhostel workers encouraged them to take chances in their free, vigorous years. "I hope you have fun."

"We'll disappear over there while driving through Tibet," her mother said.

"You really might. It's been a war zone for years," Dorcas said. Machines mostly did the fighting now, but occasionally servicemen came home in body bags. The media claimed that the military average deaths weren't affected by the war. Accidental, homicidal, and suicidal deaths for people in their teens and twenties had always been high.

"War is invigorating, just like danger," her dad said. "Good for the economy."

The visit felt over, but Dorcas knew they'd want her to eat with them. "I'd like to get home before dark," she said.

Emily blinked and said, "I understand."

"You worry about us in Asia. What about New York?"

"My work is here," Dorcas said. Her father's disbelief made the work seem trivial. But then she knew he'd approve of her redesigned insects. Having the Feds bust his child would be so embarrassing. "Call me or fax me from Asia."

"Remember," Paul said. "Thieves watch for people sunk in goggle dreams. Don't go virtual at home."

But her parents would sail off to Asia. Somehow, though, old people roving off on adventures made sense. But her parents weren't that old. They still looked like ordinary people. "I've got an old screen somewhere at home."

"Get a new one," her dad said.

"Okay," Dorcas said, wondering if he and his could really distinguish a fooler loop from an on-time visual. Better avoid potential nagging and get a high-resolution screen and camera. It'd make Paul happy. Give in on the little shit and keep on making better insects, Dorcas thought.

Paul said, "You know in the nineteenth and early twentieth centuries, people died in their sixties. Now, it's the prime of life. Work done, bodies tuned, we play."

"I'm happy for you, Dad," Dorcas said, wondering what governments would be left when she was sixty-one. What skin cloning facilities, surgeons? "Well, let me go," she said, using wording that disengaged her from electronic media.

"I'm not holding you. You've got your legs," her father said.

"We'll never be a burden on you," Emily said.

Dorcas nodded and left. Her parents planned to go to a Doctor Death at the first signs of feebleness. Thinking about death doctors and her own parents made her uneasy.

And their bonsai child didn't bear fruit. Dorcas called for a cab. The visit was over except for the waiting, and none of them said anything. Dorcas heard the cab driver buzz and took the elevator down to him.

The driver let her in to his cab and asked, "Folks doing okay?"

"Fine," Dorcas said. The driver looked like he was in his sixties, no surgery, no nanomachines cleaning his blood vessels, no retirement package.

"I hope I can retire someday," he said.

"By the time I retire, Western Civilization will probably be over," Dorcas said.

"I understand that predictions are more about the psychology of the predicter than anything real," the driver said. "You'll be fine. Whole thing been about to collapse since the 1940s."

"It might collapse when I say," Dorcas said. "Too many depressed people building the systems." Dorcas wondered if her grandmother still looked as young as her mother. One child, two parents, four grandparents. Thanks to defective nanomachines, electrical storms fouling computer guidance systems, and thieves from the slums, Dorcas only had one living grandparent by now.

"When I retire, I'll take a chunk of my settlement and get new skin, get myself looking about thirty-eight or forty, touch of grey."

Dorcas wondered if a taxi driver could afford the internal work that remade the body to match the skin. "You're the age of your thoughts."

"Ah, but I have young thoughts," the driver said. He locked the taxi into the navigation grid for the East Side and looked back at Dorcas.

"Modern medicine can't do brains," Dorcas said.

"I'm certified mentally healthy and AIDS-free," the man said.

"I'm not," Dorcas said, half-lying.

"Sorry," the driver said. He didn't say anything more until they reached Dorcas's house on East 19th Street. "I'd have thought you were more uptown," the driver said.

"Didn't inherit a house there," Dorcas said before she realized the driver would have thought she lived in a cube or flat.

"Whole house?" he sighed.

"I rent out rooms," Dorcas lied. She tipped him no more than the preset gratuity and waited until he'd driven away. The block guards nodded at her, and she pressed her palm against the lock plate, then punched out the code that got her through the first door. The second door lock scanned her retina before she could insert the old-fashioned key and get completely off the street.

Rockefeller University installed the security after eco-terrorists kidnapped another postdoc and tried to turn her with a butcher's version of a brain job.

Henry hadn't called. Dorcas went to her fish tanks and fed her Lake Victorian cichlids, noting that she needed to prepare brood tanks for the females holding eggs, checking a brood tank date. That fish needed to be stripped, but she'd do that after she fed everything else. The crippled Peregrine falcon used as an AI sperm donor for Henry's captive breeding project screamed from the aviary. After feeding him, Dorcas checked the three 40-gallon terrariums where she kept fifteen percent of the known world population of Virginia Fringed Mountain Snail, that rarest of Virginia land snails with shells that looked like fossils, coils not sloping left or right, but straight. Since they burrowed and since they were only three millimeters in diameter, Dorcas monitored each tank only once every three years. To keep diseases from spreading, one tank was in the attic, another in the kitchen, the third in Dorcas's second floor study. Arking was like recycling. One had to do it to be a respectable academic.

After feeding the fish and snails, but before she ate, Dorcas took out her baster and caught the brooding female she needed to strip. She dropped the small fish headfirst down the baster, filled it with water from the female's tank, and lowered the baster into an empty fry tank. Squeeze, squeeze. About fifteen babies tumbled out of the mother fish's mouth. Dorcas fed them live baby brine shrimp, then put the mother fish back in her species tank.

Where in the wilds could fish get their babies stripped so they could recover sooner from the ordeal of oral brooding? Dorcas watched the new babies, culled one that had a bent spine, then, finally, microwaved her own dinner.

By midnight, Henry still hadn't called. Dorcas took out the kimono he'd given her, the one that his Japanese great-grandfather gave to his American wife. She dressed in it and pulled out the genome charts for bald-faced hornets, all on fanfolds filled with four letter groups of Gs, Ts, As, and Cs, these letters large and overstruck. Under various groups of large letters, Dorcas could read in small Courier type the commentary on what each sequence did, or was thought to do.

She wondered if she could build a neuroleptic wasp or hornet that would respond to anger. What combination of scents and body language did angry people display? She knew from mid-twentieth-century

Columbia University anthropological work that, cross-culturally, people asked to move a lever in an angry movement moved the lever the same.

The hornets could cause problems at first, stinging to sleep motorists caught in traffic, women angry with their violent husbands. But could a person be violent without being angry? Sociopaths, perhaps.

Maybe humans needed to be engineered to give off a pheromone when they anticipated attacking people. The hornets already attacked when one of their own was damaged.

A pacifist flu? Dorcas decided to check out the chemical paths human emotions took, then went to bed in the kimono even if a Japanese woman would never do such a thing.

Henry finally came by her house in the morning before work, his driver waiting outside in the car. When he saw Dorcas's rumpled kimono, his eyes seemed to frown though his face remained controlled.

"I was thinking of you," she said.

"We're being audited," he said. "The Feds want a full accounting of all DNA sequences we hold."

"That's impossible," she said. "Everyone fakes the exactness."

"And some of us are working off the books for gene-tech firms and surgeons."

Dorcas said, so they understood each other, "Everyone had special projects that might be impossible to fund."

"DNA is also everywhere," Henry said, meaning, *Make sure we've got the right molecular weights of DNA in every sample vial, regardless.*

"Do we have time, or should I get dressed for work?" Dorcas asked.

"Get dressed. I'll drive you," Henry said, meaning his driver would. Henry followed Dorcas to her bedroom. As she put on her day clothes, he smoothed the kimono out on her bed, then folded it.

"Do you wish you were more Japanese?" she asked him.

"I wish you wouldn't sleep in it," he said, not answering. "My wife wears them when she arranges flowers."

Dorcas knew Henry found a real Japanese wife who thought herself to be totally American. Henry must bully her into kimonos. "So, you're not going to be able to moonlight for a while."

Henry said, "They asked who was working with mantises."

Dorcas remembered her mother's words, *Distract men with sex if they question you closely,* and tilted her hips suggestively. "Wasps, not mantises, for that pet company. I've got to feed my creatures before we go, would you help?" She remembered her mother telling her also that men hated the words *could you,* because they all could. *Would you* gave them the option of being gallant.

Henry fed his falcon mice while Dorcas tended the snails, then he fed flake to the adult fish while Dorcas fed the fry fresh-hatched brine shrimp.

"Do you ever have the desire," Henry said, pausing so that Dorcas half expected a kinky sexual request, ". . . the desire to just smash all these tanks, exterminate all the animals we spend so much time tending out of guilt that shouldn't be ours personally?"

Dorcas visualized it and yes, she could see that destroying the arks might give her a tremendous sense of power. "But humans are too powerful already," she answered. If her transgenetic wasps and mantises expressed the sequences she built for them, what she had done would give her more power yet.

"We still die," Henry said.

"Is that what your off-the-books project is about?" Dorcas asked, not caring if security listened now. She visualized herself calling security to tell them what she'd been doing. What would they do to her if she confessed she was empowering insects?

Perhaps they'd put her in a cyberia? She'd die in a roller cage with self-generated dreams in her head. Surrender and forget about fooler loops, bald-faced hornet genome maps, the next postdoc. Or the Feds would want her to work for them. Monitored, doing work other people assigned to her, checking everything with a committee—no, Dorcas didn't think so.

Perhaps I'm in virtual reality now. Dorcas twisted her head quickly, but her visual field didn't streak. Unless she was fooled, this was reality, passing at 80 million polygons per second. Computer research stalled out sometime after the invention of the first really good brain machine interface.

Unless that's what this virtual reality led her to believe. *No, that way lies madness.*

"Are you okay?" Henry asked.

"I wondered if this was real or virtual," Dorcas said.

Henry said, "Have you done anything that could get you sentenced to rehab?"

"No."

"You're a touch more maschocistic than's healthy."

"I'm tired. I should give away some of my species."

"You need a checkup."

"Perhaps I should look for another postdoc?" She hated her whiny tone.

"That's not necessary, yet," Henry said. "And when the time comes, I'll help you."

"I think I'll appreciate that, Henry," Dorcas said, deciding at least part of the reason she'd been gradually sinking at her academic posts. She spent too much time on doing the right things, like arking, and not enough time on the necessary thing, like putting her gorgeous raw data into publishable form. She should write up her redesigned insect lung and the retrovirus that tended to place it in the right sequence into publishable form. One problem, she wasn't registered to work with the DNA she'd used. "Ah, there's so much to do." But if she got permission and published, everyone else could do it, too. And she'd be monitored.

They went down to the car. Henry said, "The car's secure. Do you have anything to hide from the auditors?"

Dorcas leaned back against the seat cushions and said, "I made the big mantises." She felt the earth quit tugging on her, her body drifting in free fall. End of the affair, beginning of the conspiracy.

Henry said, "Why?" He moved away from her, then looked at her, then began patting his knee.

Dorcas wished she had one now to tranquilize Henry. "Because I liked the idea of big mantises tranquilizing humans, playing soothing wing music."

"Dorcas, did you design the new lung?" At least he wasn't bored with her now.

"Yes. They couldn't grow a foot tall without it."

"I must say, they've fit in with the drode head culture. Makes the system more stable to have the drode heads calmer."

"But you wish I hadn't confessed to you. You're my lover. I have to confess to you. Any indiscretions."

Henry sighed as though he'd preferred to have heard about another man. Dorcas felt both naked and in terrific control. He couldn't carry her secret too long without it eating him hollow. Metaphorically. She'd infected him with a meme. But she wouldn't tell him everything. Unless he turned her in soon, he'd have to shelter her without knowing all the details. He'd have to turn her in or conspire to keep her insects secret.

Gotcha, Henry.

I'll either be busted or I won't be alone in this. In ten minutes, they were in the University basement parking garage. Dorcas looked at Henry and pulled her knees together.

"We've got to get ready for the auditors," he said, taking her hand to help her out of the car.

They walked in together, Dorcas behind Henry. She wondered if she'd gone insane to tell him, then seconds later, felt elated, then anxious, anxiously elated, then knew the emotional fibrillations were a sign of something out of whack, but the fact of recognizing her whackiness was a promising symptom. Dorcas needed someone to know she'd done interesting work.

Dorcas went into Lab 43, put on her virtual reality goggles, and began to interact with Desi and Lucy on a reconstruct from old video shows. Give the auditors something to catch.

A wire-frame figure stepped out of the video apartment wall. It moved like Henry, but then another figure stepped out behind him, also wire-frame. "Wasting government time, Dr. Rae?"

"I needed to take a little break."

"Actually, we'd like you to stay right here. We're coming in your office to do inventory on your sequences."

Dorcas saw Lucy shrug. Lucy said, "Why don't we go down and watch Desi give birth to little Ricardo?" The wire-frame figures nodded at her and went back into the wall.

Dorcas said, "Could they do that in your day?"

Lucy said, "I think it will be funny."

Desi couldn't believe this was happening to him, but little Rickie popped out of his mouth when Lucy pressed hard on his stomach.

Dorcas felt a finger rub around her nipple as the bodies outside the goggles put polygraph equipment on her body. "Hi, Henry," she said, pissed that he'd assert his rights to her in front of a Fed, but then treating her so familiarly would make her seem more like Henry's creature. Henry had to inform on her *now,* or he'd be blamed for what she did. A woman whose lover tweaked her nipple in front of a Fed had to be his tool.

"Who's Henry?" Lucy asked.

"He's one of those wire-framed guys who interrupted us," Dorcas said.

"If it wasn't funny," Lucy said, "it's not part of my program."

Letters ran across the bottom of Dorcas's visual field. *How often do you use entertainment programs while on the job?*

"This is the first time in years," Dorcas said.

Are we going to find anything unusual in your DNA inventory?

Dorcas was about to answer *yes* when she realized the polygraph would have read her already.

Are you protecting anyone?

"Why would I protect anyone?"

Are you having an affair with your supervisor?

"I don't believe that's any of your business," Dorcas said. "Lucy, I've got more serious things to deal with now."

"Maybe you should take me home," Lucy said. "I play better when I'm not being interrupted."

The visual field went black. The two wire-frame men materialized. Henry seemed exasperated.

Dorcas said, "I waive employee rights against sexual harassment."

The investigator wire-frame seemed quite pleased. "Are you protecting Henry?" Dorcas knew the investigator was another man and felt quite safe.

"Well, you're reading me. What do you think?"

"You're excited by this."

Well, of course. Dorcas moved her hands to the goggles and uncoupled the feeds, then pulled the goggles off her eyes. Henry and the investigator sat on either side of the polygraphy machine. The investigator looked just like his wire-frame image. Dorcas said, "Do you expect scientists, creative types, to obey the rules like drode heads?"

The investigator said, "It's the law."

The audit so exclusively concentrated on molar weights of DNA that only Henry noticed how many queen wasps were missing.

Henry took Dorcas home that night. "I think everything is okay." The danger seemed to have excited him, too. Dorcas wasn't blackmailing him into continuing with her, just giving him fresh adventures.

"We were missing three micrograms of DNA."

"Destroyed in an L-4 lab. My research assistant took care of the records."

When they checked the ark tanks, Dorcas smelled something foul in one of the Virginia Fringed Mountain Snail tanks. Something had died in the terrarium, probably a third of fifteen percent of the known population. "Oh, shit, Henry," Dorcas said.

"You've got two binocular scopes, don't you? I'll help."

For three hours, they looked through the limestone gravel and soil for live snails, sorting with plastic tweezers. Dorcas wished she and Henry were in bed. She found one live snail, then the dead mouse that polluted the tank. It had probably been poisoned by rodent-control bait that induced quick rotting, then wandered into the tank to die.

"I've got a live one," Henry said.

"Well, at least we tried," Dorcas said.

"What happened to the wasp?" Henry asked.

"She's flying over Central Park, looking for a mate."

"How did you tweak her?"

"I didn't tweak her. I felt sorry for her."

"Dorcas."

"Really."

"They were so concerned with molar weights of DNA," Henry said. "I didn't think I used as much as that, though."

"The mantis lungs were hard to coordinate with the existing growth factors," Dorcas said. "You're sure they're not listening to us?"

"I heard we're going to be under investigation for a while, but, and I know this is sexist, they feel you're my creature."

"From the lips down," Dorcas said. She felt safe. Next year, before Henry got bored with her again, she'd redesign either humans or the bald-faced hornet.

No more live snails. Henry said, "How did the mouse get in?"

"I didn't put the cover glass completely over the tank. Virginia Fringed Mountain Snails don't travel above ground." Technology wasn't the enemy. The human genome with its capacity for excuses and self-delusion was. "So you're looking for a way to make people immortal?"

"Yes," Henry said.

"I think that's a very tempting idea," Dorcas said, her back and neck aching from tension. She'd been bent over way too long.

FOUR

INSECTICIDE

If the mantis hadn't soothed me, I don't know how I could have lived through the first week after surgery. Perhaps it was slaved to respond to my underlying agitation, because it played its wing music all day long, even as it chewed with sideways jaw motions on its kibble.

Down to no one again. Why me? Why couldn't I have been born into a family that kept me, raised me as just another person? I could have been a techie, running scanning people.

Thumm, and I wasn't worried so much. After a week, my head was covered with stubble. I wondered what color my hair would be now. I'd heard about people going grey overnight, but Miriam told me that was a myth. Hospitals had too much to do to redye hair. I felt I looked hideous, bloated under the prison strong dress, face looking vacant or haunted, wrinkles drawing skin down. More of them for sure, my fingers told me.

Now, the insect nibbled my skin as I lay drugged by its chemicals on the padded floor. When the guards, wearing the same ear and nose filters that Kearney wore, brought my plate, the mantis crept up and waved its arms over the food.

Days passed in total light. Cameras behind heavy transparent barriers watched me. I expected that computers compared my moves against a program for expected inmate behavior. I gauged time's passing by my hair.

One time, when the guard brought my food and a box of kibble for the mantis, I touched her wrist. Timidly, I asked, "Please tell me how long I've been here. And where's Jim from Amnesty?" I hated hearing how weak I sounded.

"He's not at this unit now," the guard said, voice muffled behind a breathing mask.

The mantis was to be my only friend. I began to dream about it when I slept, a lesbian mantis chewing at a nipple, jaws squeezing sideways. Then it turned and bit through my skull bones, eating both my nightmares and my good memories. I had no family, no orphanage, no lover named Jergen.

I woke up. While the mantis slept on, I could look at it without the fog of its enchanting sounds and smells.

An insect. A bug. They wanted me to bond with a damn bug. I hated all of them, Martin Fox, Kearney, the parents who kicked me out on a roadside in Ohio, the soothing orphanage personnel easing me into some human Dumpster. Was I born to be confused with tranquilizers?

It began playing its wings, but my own blood pounded in my ears, and I tore its wings off and stomped it, rocking back and forth on the padding covered with bug juices. Dying, it grabbed for me with its chitinous mouth, got my foot in the instep. Its head came off, fastened to my foot.

I grabbed the head and threw it at the cameras.

Kearney came in then, protected against whatever magic the bug might have left in the air. He went up to where I'd thrown the head and pulled out tweezers to pick it up.

"I hate being tranquilized," I said, feeling chilly insect mush and hot blood under my right foot. I stepped away from the wetness, but the blood followed me. My blood. I hadn't realized the mantis bit that hard.

"So, you can resist the insect," Kearney said. "Good. Jergen told us you're really tough. He said you can resist anything."

I didn't know if I believed Jergen told them anything. I said, "I'd feel better about helping you if someone human was half-assed nice to me."

"We'll send in someone like Jim," Kearney said.

"But not that sweet," I said. I'd work for them. I preferred running around on the outside to being in prison. And these insects were nasty. "When I'm more myself, I'd resent a control that reminds me of a social worker or hospital aide."

Kearney manipulated the tweezers, turning the mantis's head, not answering for a second. I wondered if I jolted his expectations and made him change his plans. Now, he seemed to be reviewing the people available to him. "Jergen said if you give us your loyalty, you'd be completely honest with us. Not that you'd always be compliant. But he said you'd need someone who was loyal to you in return."

So did he think he had me with Jergen? I said, "I guess you're too high ranked to work with me directly."

He said, "We need someone you can live with."

"Who can live with me," I said. They didn't trust me not to disappear if they used me as an agent. Why should anyone trust me?

"A half-sweet control, I think that would suit you," Kearney said. He handed me the tweezers holding the mantis, then pulled out his nose plugs and ear muffs.

I said, "The last committment I made to help you was half-hearted compared to now. I hate whoever it was who made the mantis. I'm afraid of how . . . how I look back on what I cared about and it seems like it happened to someone else. But why would you trust me?"

"We need someone who speaks the jargon," Kearney said. "We've also got a good profile on you."

"But if anyone recognizes me?"

"You won't look like you do now. We promised you a prettier body and face, remember?"

I remembered myself naked in a wrinkled body under spotlights. Would Jergen have picked up a forty-three-year-old woman running from the police? "No one I used to know would recognize me?"

"No."

"When does this happen?"

"We're building your nanos now."

"I'm not sure I want to go that way." Every once in a while, nanomachines liquified the body they were supposed to rebuild. Occasionally, they did less lethal damage, fairly frequently ate out the egg cells in ovaries or sperm because those cells had half the chromosomes proper to the human body. Men could grow new sperm. Women, well, we're born with the lifetime supply of eggs. Our group discussed the possibility of sterilizing Manhattan with an ovary-attacking nanobug. Martin Fox had been for it. I remembered the arguments about the risk that our black-market nanobugs might sterilize all the female animals in Manhattan, not just the guilty species.

"Have we done anything to hurt you?" Kearney asked. He smiled and added, "Lately?"

"Will you test them *in vitro*?"

"You'll be okay."

"Maybe you'll give me a nanobug that will liquify me if I get away from you?"

"That's an eco-babble myth. Even if it were true, you're lucky. We assume whoever is making these insects will know to check for nanos. We'll clean them out of you after the change. We wouldn't want anyone to know you've been artificially changed. It wouldn't suit your cover status."

"My cover status?"

"You're going to be labware."

"You're not going to fit me . . ." I thought of drode holes through the skull, infected *dura mater,* mastitus, the short and frequently blanked life of a loser, rendered for fat after the brainworks went back to the state.

"Experimental unit, probe contacts unnecessary. We've already fitted you."

All that running and I still end up a drode head.

"That's worse than being rebuilt by nanos?"

"I could have stayed in the orphanage if I wanted to grow up to be a drode head." This man had cored my brain already. He's seen me naked on masturbation machines. He could be lying to me about nanotraps and leashes. If I refused to cooperate, prison was an option. I was on the Amnesty rolls. "If I won't, I can go to prison, can't I?"

"We'd put you in a cyberia," Kearney said. "We'll exercise you, feed you, and let you think you're committing eco-terrorism twenty-four hours a day."

"Isn't there sleep in cyberspace?" I asked, moving my head quickly to see if this reality streaked.

Kearney said, "The program affects dreams, too. By the way, in the new cyberias, the head servos keep prisoner motions in synch with programming capacity."

What with all the things done to my head, could I ever be free again? I said, "I met a woman who'd been released from a cyberia. She'd seemed permanently confused, telling me that what we called reality came at us at only 80 million polygons per second." I didn't tell Kearney she claimed her cyberspace experiences in the penal program were more real than reality because she'd been purely herself interacting with an accommodating program. In the outer world, other people forced her to be other than herself, but the prison program gave her her very own reality.

This must be reality. Nobody had been particularly accommodating. "Mr. Inquisitor, when do you start with the rebuilding?"

Kearney said, "Your bio-monitors say you're frightened."

I realized then they had me by the memory-reading net. While I'd been worrying about nano-leashes, they'd got me by the brain, like I was a dangerous animal nose-ringed and held at just the right distance with a pole. So much for winning my loyalty. "I bet the net would make the cyberia experience even more real."

"We wouldn't even have to put you in goggles."

Perhaps if I cooperated with them, I'd find a surgeon willing to take a Federal net out of a woman's brain, could escape. I wondered if Kearney knew what I was thinking.

"We know that you are thinking intensely, but the transmitter doesn't have enough bandwidth to read as well as the memory scanning device we had you under."

I suspected Kearney didn't need to read my mind to know what might get me to cooperate. "Whoever's making the insects is our enemy, too."

"Right."

"Martin Fox might order me killed if any eco people recognized me."

"Martin Fox died," Kearney said.

"So he wasn't really an agent provocateur," I said.

Kearney seemed fierce for an instant, his jaw muscles flicking, brows pulled together, then he looked away and said, "No. He was your people."

"We're not all like that," I said.

"Prove it," Kearney said. He smiled as if that would take the sting out of his tone. Probably he'd have preferred to have strangled me in the plane when the nuke went off. We looked at each other a moment, then I huddled up on the padded floor, my back to the padded wall, like a room built of futons, wrapped my arms around my knees and leaned my head down, brow to patellas. Don't forget, I told myself, you're busted and brain-drained. "I have to have some self-respect." That sounded so lame. "Some power."

Kearney sat down beside me and punched me lightly in the bicep. "We're not the country we used to be," he said. "We need to be competitive in this world with other economies, not tearing ourselves into factions."

I lifted my head and said, "How can I not cooperate."

Later that day, a nurse cored my thigh with a large needle and said, "For *in vitro* tests."

"How wonderful you care," I said, but I was quite relieved.

*   *   *

Kearney and a technical sort of guy came in with a small beaker holding millions of nanobugs, each unit so tiny the entire mass quivered like corroded mercury. Kearney said, "They'll do their work, then return to the attractor."

"Do you inject them or am I supposed to drink them?" *About ten cubic centimeters of nanobugs,* I estimated.

"Take some in your mouth. They'll go through the skin there."

"Are they all necessary?" I asked. I remembered some old man who took nitro for his heart this way.

"You don't have to lick the beaker," the tech said. "Just sip a bit of them. It doesn't really matter if you swallow, only it's better not to breach the stomach mucosa. And they'll get to your face quicker."

A Deep Ecologist shouldn't do this, I thought as I took a tiny sip of large molecules. The taste was vaguely metallic. Within seconds, my nose began to feel warm. I swallowed some of the nanobugs, then took another sip from the beaker. Kearney massaged my shoulders.

Would I liquify? Kearney would tell Amnesty that I'd had a nano accident. I couldn't open my jaws for the next sip. The tech pulled down my lower lip and poured the last of the nanobugs through my clenched teeth.

The fluid seeped into me. I was being converted to another person. "How long will it take?" I asked.

Kearney answered, "Two months. We're changing pigmentation, basically, eye color, hair color. Cartilage. Most of how we recognize each other is facial proportions, eyes in relation to ears, to nose. We'll change those."

"Not all the organs."

"No."

"So I'll still be forty-three inside."

"Forty-four," Kearney said. "No, the process won't tamper with your memory."

"You say."

"Allison, haven't I been honest with you all through this?"

"My nose feels warm. And my ears."

"Three-quarters of the bugs go straight for the cartilage," the tech said. Kearny nodded at him and he left.

"Would you want Jim to visit? We can't put you with other people being re-faced because we don't want any of you to be able to identify each other. For the same reason, we can't put you in general prison population. We could put you in a cyberia for duration, but those interactions are never quite natural enough. You need to stay oriented."

"What about my semi-sweet control?"

"Wouldn't you prefer to wait until you look young again?"

"No," I said. "He's got to see me change."

Kearney smiled. I wondered if he'd manipulated me into requesting this. We held our thoughts a beat, then Kearney said, "So he knows who you really are?"

"No, because if he and I don't work, you'll have time to find me a new semi-sweet control."

"Half-sweet," Kearney said. We left my loneliness unconfessed. Jim couldn't be with me every day. He had other prisoners to save.

It all happened so fast. It all happened so slow. The day after I took the nanobugs, Kearney brought me my control, my computer-picked demon lover.

The man came in behind Kearney, not quite as sure of himself as a stud dog when the pen door opens and a bitch falls in. He looked like a young Jergen, but not so obviously that I was insulted. Must be military with a body so stiff, I thought.

Perhaps he wasn't supposed to be my lover, just my control. No, bed. Bed before the body became so much younger.

"Allison, Michael. Lieutenant Mike."

"If you kiss me, I turn into a young princess," I said.

The man seemed to access his files on dealing with women, his face flickering as different options presented themselves. Then the smile of lust and reluctance. Cocksure? Not quite? The lust was more and less than purely sexual. "Do you want that to be part of my job description?" Lieutenant Mike asked.

"I'm a prisoner. I doubt I can write anything into your job description."

Kearney said, "You agreed to work for us. You asked me to bring him to you."

Before I could answer, Lt. Mike said, "She agreed under duress."

"Wow, you're good," I said.

Kearney said, "The job description for controls is that they can sleep with their agents if the control and his supervisor believe it would enhance the working effectiveness of the agent."

I felt naked and ugly. "Can you move me out of this padded cell?"

"Yes," Lt. Mike said although I'd looked at Kearney when I asked.

"Lieutenant Mike, you gonna brain-whip me like he does?"

"No, I'm going to get you moved. We're going to talk about cover identities and about what you were like as a little girl."

"I was an orphan, abandoned in Ohio. That about covers it and I don't want to remember."

"You remember all the time," Lt. Mike said. Kearney moved as if to leave and suddenly I didn't want to be left alone with this young stud control.

"I've got to make the arrangements for the room transfer," Kearney said.

Lt. Mike stayed near the door. We didn't speak to each other until Kearney came back. Since I had nothing to pack, we walked out through white corridors to a different wing of the building. I hated the strong dress, my bare feet, stubbly head and all the people who affected not to look at me.

Kearney unlocked a door. Inside was an apartment, not a cube, but a real multi-room apartment.

"We'll give you something like this when you've caught the gene hacker," Lt. Mike said. "It's got two bedrooms, a study, kitchen, bathroom, communications room."

We walked around. The walls had an oak chair rail running around all of them about three feet from the floor, and oak planks running around the ceiling, both chair rail and planks finished to show the grain, rounded corners, but no fussy routing of lines in them. The kitchen cupboards held all the cooking equipment I'd only read about. Real down comforters covered the beds. I'd always wanted something like this. All the stealing, the eco-terrorism stemmed from this apartment I never could get. Now I could get this if I caught our common enemy, a renegade gene hacker.

I felt cheap. Meanly grateful. I touched a fern hanging from the ceiling by a window. "Which bedroom is mine? Should I look in the closet?"

"The one on your right," Kearney said.

"We'll leave you alone to change," Lt. Mike said.

Under my skin, in my skin, nanobugs repaired my collagen. Would I have to be alone to change? Was the soft down comforter a necessary part of the change, too light to deform my transforming cartilage? I opened the closet carefully, as if my fingernails would curl back if I pushed too hard.

Dresses bought to my measure hung on wooden hangers, hangers that matched the oak room trim. I pulled out one, a wool crepe. Who was it among the eco-terrorists had taught me textiles in her long run from her rich past? First underwear, I told myself, going to the chest of drawers built into the wall. I noticed then that none of the furniture in my bedroom, except for one small chair, could be moved.

Bras, panties, micro-fiber panty hose. I dressed quickly, then brushed my hair. I looked at myself in the mirror. Was it that obvious that I could be bought for a middle-class apartment?

Remember, you can't really close the door on them, I reminded myself. I opened the drapes at what should have been one window and saw mirrors. The mirrors cleared enough to show me the camera behind the glass, then began playing a pastoral scene not quite detailed enough to begin to pass for real.

The other window appeared to be real. Or maybe just better. I tapped it with my index finger. It was polycarbonate or something even more high tech, and unbreakable. Beyond the window, I saw three double fences, high wire topped with razor wire, and robot guns from shoebox size to the size of German shepherds patrolling the plowed ground between the fences.

A robin landed near one of the smaller guns. The turret swiveled, back and forth as though measuring the robin. It didn't fire. The robin pulled a worm out of the plowed ground and flew away.

I wondered if the gun made a mistake or if it really could discriminate between a robin and a robot message pod. Maybe . . .

Maybe nothing. I looked for shoes and found a pair of low-heeled casual shoes. They didn't match the dress, but then I'd been barefoot since I'd been captured.

I went back out to the men. Lt. Mike poured me a drink.

"I can drink alcohol, then?" I asked. The men nodded. Then we sat down in seductive chairs and watched the big screen TV play laser discs of old movies, resting from the conspiracies that opposed and bound us for a few hours, me changing alone.

In the bottom of my head, untouched by either the brain reading net or the nanobugs scavenging my oxidized tissues, was an old argument, "Are we fish or are we something more than primates?"

Jergen said if Jewelfish could talk, they'd have reasons for their dominion over a tank. They're smarter than most fish, take care of their young, have a complex signal system, and are certainly more intelligent than anything else with gills in their shallow weedy home waters.

If humans argue that because we can totally dominate the rest of the universe for our benefit, then we should, that argument, according to Jergen, makes us no better than Jewelfish.

I had another reason to hate people. Brazil began gunning down abandoned children in the late twentieth century and by the middle of my century, the practice spread to Ohio. I was a toxic waste to the system myself, a product of spewing ovarian products all over the landscape.

"A penny for your thoughts," Lt. Mike said.

"I wish you'd come along when I was fifteen," I said.

"No system is perfect," Lt. Mike said. "We all just do our best. You could have told the police about your parents and maybe the court could have helped put your family back together again."

"Same as Jewelfish," I said.

"You're a fish-head?" Lt. Mike said. "I thought Deep Ecology environmentalists were opposed to keeping fish in captivity."

"We only use them as analogies," I said.

"I think we make a big mistake when we demonize each other," Lt. Mike said. "We're both people. We mean to be reasonable and do right."

"I was excluded from your warm, fuzzy world."

"Deep Ecology was never your true movement. They used you. And it wasn't us, it was your parents who abandoned you."

"Martin Fox used me," I said.

"If you hate people, don't you end up using them as tools? Sending them out to die?" Lt. Mike said.

"I don't hate people," I said. "I don't give a damn anymore." I went to the mirror in the living room and stared at my face. I was beginning to look younger, stripped of freeze-dried ideals. I wanted someone to hold me, cuddle me. As had always been the case in my life, I'd have to trade sex for a cuddle. "Hold me?" I wanted to say, but it came out as a question.

Mike came up and held me. I shuddered and he kept holding me, patting me gently on my back. When I cried, he kept holding me, patting my back, just holding me.

"Why didn't my parents do that to me?"

"They didn't know who you were," Mike said. "They were too wrapped up in their own troubles, I'm sure. Since you weren't registered at birth, they must have been living irregularly."

I expected his hands to move to my breasts when we sat down on the couch, but they didn't. This holding seemed both incredibly comforting and ridiculous at the same time. I couldn't as a forty-four-year-old woman be a sexless child getting reassured as to my basic human value. Yet, I was a child right now and fucking me would be rape.

I cried myself to sleep and woke up on the couch wrapped in a quilt, still dressed.

Mike came over with a cup of coffee. "You're unspeakably good," I said, "even the false flaw of offering me coffee when I don't drink coffee."

He looked at the cup and said, "I honestly forgot. I'd actually fixed this for me, but since you were awake . . ."

"Fix me some tea," I said, moving off ready to shower away those silly tears. Then I stopped and said, "Thank you."

Mike sipped on the coffee himself. He nodded. I went on for my shower, wondering if I could burn the nanomachines in my skin or if heat quickened the process.

In back of a nasty car sometime after the third decade of the Third Millenium, my mother had whacked my nose crooked, so slightly it was only visible when I looked. The nanotech machines had begun to rebuild my nose. I could see the change already.

I dried off with the blower and patted off the remaining water, wiped the mist from the mirror and looked at my nose again. It was straight, longer. Was I imagining that the nano-machines had wound my cheek bones closer together?

When I was dressed, I used eyeliner to make the nose look as it had before, then cleaned off the false shadows.

They'd given me eyeliner, I realized only after I'd used it to make my nose look crooked again. Did drode heads use eyeliner? I'd avoided looking too closely at them.

When I came out, I asked, "Do female drode heads use makeup?"

"When they can get it," Mike said. "They're human beings, after all. They can't afford reworking so they do what they can to look good."

Suddenly, I wondered how old Mike really was? "Are you going to wait until I'm good-looking before you fuck me?"

"If you really want sex with me, I'll sleep with you."

"Ooh, that's right cold."

"Don't be embarrassed about last night."

I couldn't answer him. He handed me a cup of tea with just the right amount of sugar. I didn't trust myself to say anything further right then, so drank my tea. He microwaved frozen omelettes and made a sauce for them with fresh tomatillos and coriander right in the blender. Perhaps he was more than a lieutenant. He could be as old as my father, but rebuilt.

I managed to say, "Thank you."

Probably not as old as my father. After breakfast, I swept the tomatillo husks off the counter and put them in the composting bin.

Soon, I became a bit bored. Mike taught me how to play tennis in a Quonset hut. I ran on an indoor track. Industrial exercise, Jergen used to call anything done indoors or with machines.

Mike was unnaturally patient for someone naturally young.

"Most of our work was in the west," I said to Mike. "We were fighting lawless people."

"Who told you they were lawless?"

"I found cyanide guns set out."

"You know ranchers put them there?"

I remembered the man standing in the back of his pickup, a dead deer at his feet, a syringe in his hand, injecting poison. Jergen shot him as he dropped the syringe and reached for a rifle. "The newspapers told about a prominent rancher murdered in the back of his pickup. He was setting out a ten-eighty bait. I thought no one could legally make ten-eighty."

"When did this happen?"

"Back when. He was pulling a rifle on us."

"How did you know it was ten-eighty?"

"We fed some to a rat. The rat died. We waited three days, then fed the rat to a cat. The cat died. The cat poisoned . . ."

"So, you aren't adverse to animal experimentation when it suits your purposes."

"I guess we should have caught another rancher and fed it to him," I said.

Steve said, "We're not asking you to go against your principles. The man making these insects is as much a danger to your cause as ours."

"A real ecological saboteur," I said. I imagined the guy in his lab, smiling a twisted smile under his rebuilt eyes, having been born the kind of nerd who'd need glasses if it hadn't been for his parents' money. "Person has to be removed from real life for sending out giant tranquilizing mantises against the already passive drode heads."

What happens, I wondered, after we get this mad scientist? Will the Feds really let me walk away? "Mike, why do you keep asking me what I really believe?"

"I want to understand you better."

"To control me better."

"Yes, but that's not all of it."

I fantasized bringing him to my side. I knew better, but the fantasy made me smile slightly.

By now, I was younger yet. I threw up every morning as though I was pregnant. My body thought it must be growing an alternate self. The routine—working out in the gym, walking inside the fences with Mike.

One week, a punctuation. Two nurses, one a prison nurse from my time in the strong dress, came to the apartment jail with a lump of plastic and metal hollowed nose-shaped inside. "It'll guide the nano-machines," the prison nurse said. "You'll breathe through two tubes."

The other nurse said, "We'll glue it to you with electro-setting glue, no straps that might slip."

An orderly wheeled in an ultrasound machine with a narrow probe. *That goes up my nostrils,* I realized. Funny to be so queasy about this nose work when the Feds had had my brain open, under a squid. "Does the ultrasound repel the nanomachines?" I asked.

The team didn't answer, but moved the nose void over my own nose. One breathing tube up one nostril, the ultrasound probe up the other.

"A cunt-hair to the right," the prison nurse said.

I felt both the tube and the probe press against the left side of my nostrils. I felt as though I was being smothered. Mike reached for my hand and held it until they'd gotten the nose form settled and set. Then they pulled out the probe and fitted both breathing tubes with rubber stops.

After the nurses and tech left, Mike gave me a backrub. I tried to remind myself that they were still playing Good Cop, Bad Cop.

"We'll need to register your new appearance with Amnesty when we're done. You met Jim, of course."

"When I was older," I said.

Later that week, a surgeon and two nurses came in and used old-fashioned laser surgery to raise my ears. The plastic bandage looked like my own skin. No, lighter than my own skin had been. So this was the pigment change.

In two weeks, the nurses peeled the nose form off my face. I now had a high narrow nose. Two days after that, Mike brought me a coat after I dressed in the morning. "We're going out," he said. He pulled out a cloth hat, a high-fashion variant of a turban, that would cover my short hair.

"Out?"

"To a little town nearby. I thought you might like to get out around other people." They'd turned me into a high WASP pixie.

"You trust me enough?" I pulled the hat on down to my relocated ears.

"We've got your head wired, remember?"

I nodded, then asked, "Is it a real little town?"

"It's a training site, but we provide free housing to the extras and they've got real jobs outside the agencies, so it's also a real enough town. But don't tell anyone I told you."

I wondered what my own life would have been like if I'd known I could get free housing for playing a townsperson in a Federal cop training town. ''Do you help the extras find jobs?''

''I don't think so, but I don't know for sure.''

''Seems like a great place to . . .'' I was about to say *put federal protected witnesses,* but thought I ought not to seem so curious. ''. . . live. Protected by trainee cops and all.''

Mike nodded. I noticed that he didn't catch my hesitation, then counted the barriers between me and the outside—the door to the apartment, the door to the unit, the car door.

Kearney was driving. He looked back at me as I continued counting gates: the gate to the compound, the several gates to the three fences I'd seen from my window. We were processed out by eyeball, retina, the net in my head. Then, five miles through pine forest, another set of three fences, separate gatehouses offset from each other. Concrete and steel tank barriers like giant jacks forced the car to wiggle through them.

Nine barriers. At the first of the outer three gates, I bent my head so the Army uniformed people could read my identity off my neural net, then Mike and Kearney pushed their eyes into black goggles for retina scans. At the second gate, a woman in an Air Force captain's uniform put the black goggles on me. At the third gate, even though these gates were only about 100 to 200 yards apart, two men and three women in plainclothes checked my fingerprints, my retinas, my brain net, and took photographs and a sample of the nanomachines that were still rebuilding me.

One of the women drove the car we'd been in back toward the compound. Kearney said, ''Wait,'' then walked toward another car beyond the gatehouse. I stood as far away from the others as seemed possible. When I moved a bit farther than I should have, the two men edged closer to me. Prisoner.

Kearney scanned the car, pulled out an Uzi, checked it, put it under his suit jacket, then nodded. Mike then said, ''Let's go.''

As I got into the car, I smiled slightly at the two men who'd been uneasy when I stepped away.

Mike said, ''You counted the doors and gates, didn't you?''

I didn't say anything, just huddled in the corner of the seat and door. The car drove through another gate more conventionally manned, then pulled out onto a four-lane highway going through scrub oaks and pine trees. The roadsides were white. Sand. I saw a house after a few minutes, an ordinary-seeming brick-facaded house with a child's tricycle in the front yard with a sand driveway. The car passed more houses, a strip mall, some big development on the left, sand showing where machines moved away the grass and trees. The weather seemed too cold for Texas or Georgia. I began remembering where I'd seen State Route 211.

The government couldn't own all of this. I thought it was too early for them to trust me. My brainwork had details they hadn't explained.

"We have a surprise for you," Mike said.

"I'm terminally jaded," I said. The driver pulled off at the exit for Pinehurst. "We're in North Carolina, then. I thought we were somewhere in Georgia or Texas."

We passed a hodgepodge of Gothic, Tudor, and hacienda replica houses on acre plots, then the driver turned again. On the right, I saw apartments surrounded by golf courses, men playing in the cold. The older apartments were two-story units with cantilevered balconies and bays. The newer apartments were five-story units. Kearney pulled up to one of the older units.

I don't know how I guessed then, but I knew they had Jergen. I was glad not to be so surprised, then, when Lt. Mike and Kearney walked me up to a Christmas-wreathed door. Real evergreen Christmas wreath, I noted, not Jergen's style at all.

The man who answered the door didn't look like Jergen until I saw the hands. They'd done his camouflage with surgery, no nanotech at all. But his hands had aged, not changed. When we followed him inside, he went to a counter and sat on a stool, leaned on his elbows and moved his hands randomly over the counter, tapping a bit with his nails, then sliding one hand over the other. He didn't look back at me, so they'd told him who I was. His height, his ways of moving were the same. I remembered a bootleg virtual reality rig my teenaged gang used. One recognized one's hot-suited friends in whatever virtual body. I wondered if anyone would spot my moves in this rebuilt body.

"Jergen, it's me, Allison," I said. I looked at Lt. Mike and smiled very slightly.

Lt. Mike said, "I believe you told us that you made retina scans and memorized them. We've got the equipment."

Jergen said, "How did you recognize me?"

"I used to play in virtual reality," I said. "You learn to recognize people by their move style. And you've still got the same hands."

"They told me they did a tree-read on you and confirmed what I'd told them. Since I surrendered, they let me shield one person. I shielded you. I hoped without me, you'd drift out of the Movement to something else. What happened to Joe and Miriam?"

"They surfaced briefly to get me in touch with Martin Fox, then vanished again. You might as well've turned me in, Jergen. Nobody quite trusted me after you left, but maybe that was the plan. Leave one person untouched, not wanted, and the group goes rancid with paranoia."

"I was hoping that without me . . ."

"Pretty damn vain of you, I'd say. You cooperated?" Somehow, also, I knew that he had, that he hadn't been wired up, hooked to a video, and drugged.

"I was tired," Jergen said. "I'm sorry, Allison."

"I went on years without you. Miriam and Joe were as much an influence on me as you were. You were tired of what? Of the movement? Of me?"

"I wasn't sure Joe and Miriam cared about ecology so much as doing damage to the industrial system. They never gave us retina scans. The money people, the anonymous sympathizers, sent them."

I said, "The movement worked for me, Jergen. I'd have been dead without you, but the movement kept me alive after you abandoned me. Orphanages, kid gangs, aging eco-terrorists, now the Feds—all keeping me alive."

Lt. Mike said, "He saved your life twice."

I wanted to say, *Jergen?* They'd finally surprised me. I found a chair behind Jergen's back and sat down.

Jergen turned his head slightly, but didn't turn around to face me. He said, "When I heard what you'd tried to do, I felt that you were my Frankenstein's monster."

"Well, now I really am an artificial beast."

"You believed everything I told you, everything all my friends told you. I wasn't so sure, myself. And I was tired."

"You said that already. I bored you with my parrot chatter back of what you told me were your principles. Principles you'd die for."

"I also told you that once busted, never trusted. Allison, shit, Allison. I'm sorry, but I've asked them to give you a chance." He nodded at Mike and Kearney.

I thought back, wondering if he'd always been an agent, then realized I was being paranoid. He should have taken me with him, but shit. "Tired?"

He finally turned around on his stool. "Tired of feeling guilty when people died. Of not feeling part of the real world, always with people who agreed with me, never talking to people who disagreed with me."

"There's quite a gap between eco-activist and federal collaborator."

Jergen said, "The government isn't the boogy-man."

"Do you have a mantis?" I asked, wondering if some insect tranquilized him to this state.

"No, I have a wife now, two children."

"You bastard," I said, forgetting Lt. Mike. "But then I knew that door wreath wasn't your style."

"Didn't you agree to be interrogated with the squid?" Lt. Mike said. "Did you ask for a semi-sweet control?"

"I didn't want to die," I said. "But I didn't arrange to be busted."

Jergen said, "Ultimately, the cause wasn't that important to you, either."

"When you walked away, you left a vacuum for people like Martin Fox."

"Martin Fox was inevitable."

"Did you help them catch him?"

"Good grief, yes. Allie, the man was a mad bomber. He destroyed half the Gulf Coast."

"I thought we were just blowing a refinery." I stood up and asked, "Where's the bathroom?"

Jergen pointed to a door on the left. The toilet, sink, and tub were surrounded by philodendrons and orchids. I could have escaped through the greenhouse, if the glass, plastic, or polycarbonate would have shattered, if I'd tried. I didn't imagine the try would get me anywhere useful, so turned back to the horrors bubbling in my brain.

Nets. Ideas. Tree-routes to base concepts. The government fought pollution but not enough. The insect I killed was a gene-tech biosphere contaminant.

Hold that thought, I told my strange new face. I emptied my bladder into the ecological non-flushing toilet. *The philodendrons and orchids will eat tonight.*

I went back out and asked, "Even if you surrendered, why didn't the government do something to you? I never heard of an eco-warrior going on trial. Why not?"

Jergen said, slipping me out some comfort, "The government doesn't want to spread the word on how things are done. Open trials give the spectators ideas. And I married one of my interrogators. You're not in the hands of heartless people."

"If I'd have insisted on being tried, would I have been?" I said. "But Amnesty had me on their books."

"Amnesty can't say much if you tried to escape. Or complain if you were so violent, the prison put you in a cyberia."

I could try to escape. I imagined they had forty-plus ways of catching me. "I'm glad I didn't try the greenhouse," I said.

"Oh, Allison, don't even joke about it," Jergen said. "The government isn't the bad guys. *We* were the bad guys."

"Out west, I thought everyone was the bad guys. Nobody obeyed the law."

Lt. Mike said, "People who saved the Montana coyotes were media stars working on private land trusts."

Jergen said, "Allison, even now, busted and brain-rigged, you're trying to be hard-assed."

Kearney looked at me and smiled like he'd be pleased if I gave him an excuse to use the Uzi under his suit. I started remembering what fearing death was like. Then I resented that they would scare me into working for them.

Miriam and Joe were still out there. Lt. Mike said, "Allison, remember the mantis."

Jergen said, "You had a psychotropic mantis?"

"I was recovering from surgery," I said. "When I got to the point where I hated being sedated, I killed it."

Kearney said, "You could have asked me to take it away."

"Would you have?"

"Allison, they're humans just like us," Jergen said. "Most of what we did just bonded us together as outlaws. You stole electronics as a teenager to make you part of a gang. Then I saved you from the cops and you did what you had to do to fit in with me and my people."

I wanted to flare back, *I've grown since you left me,* but saying that seemed immature. Everything he said was true, good little Allison trying to find a place for herself in the human weed community. But I couldn't just turn my head over to the government. No, wait, I had done that. "Is my life permanently blighted? Once busted, never trusted. Not by anyone."

Whoops, that sounded more juvenile than *I've grown since you left me.*

Kearney said, "To quote the classics, 'Walking on water wasn't built in a day.' Let's go have lunch. I know a Mex place in Southern Pines."

I watched Jergen, knowing he hated to eat in restaurants. He seemed as uneasy as ever, a true foible rationalized, perhaps, into a political position.

Jergen said, "I'll stay here."

Lt. Mike said, "Come with us. Government's treat."

I knew Mike knew Jergen hated eating in restaurants, hated big parties. *He'd turned his agoraphobia into a political movement,* I realized. Drugs calmed phobics these days. Had the government which so kindly didn't kill Jergen left him with his phobia to hold him to his wife and his apartment surrounded by golfers? I said, "He hates restaurants. Why don't you send for takeout?"

"Allison, don't make an issue of it. I'll go," Jergen said. He stood up and stretched, yawned, and then got his coat out of a closet by the door. I saw a flash of tiny technicolored parkas and a fur coat.

Momma worked. Daddy was a househusband, but the kiddies didn't know Daddy used to be a bad guy, so they'd been whisked away, not through the cold but probably across the entranceway, before I arrived with my keepers.

The interrogator wife went to work in her other coat.

The house sizes shrank between Pinehurst and Southern Pines. We drove from the rich town streaked with apartments for horse grooms, clerks, and government informants to the middle class town for shop and restaurant owners, mill executives, and the better-off sorts of craftsmen. Developers in the late twentieth century turned horse farms into subdivisions, complete with the old training tracks and stables, stables now mini-storage units.

The land of olivewood spoons and ceramic teapots with polished stone lids passed into the land of replica crystalware and double silver plate. Magnolias and railroad tracks split the Southern Pines business district. I felt Jergen's body heat, looked at him. He had his eyes closed.

"It's worse, then?" I said.

"Seeing you . . . I don't know. It's a bit embarrassing."

Had I been younger, I would have been insulted, but I thought I understood. "So you think we were wrong, then. Not just Martin Fox, but us."

"I would have been as bad as Martin Fox if I'd stayed in the game."

We pulled in to a parking place under the magnolias, by the train station. I'd been about to ask Jergen what he meant, but we were in public now. Perhaps asking wasn't a good idea. I'd lost my privacy whoever was around.

Lt. Mike asked, "Are you okay, Sam?"

Sam was Jergen. He nodded. We went inside and sat down between two tables filled with Special Forces people drinking Mexican beer and eating beef and chicken fajitas.

I wondered if they'd come to intimidate me. One of them looked over at our table, bent forward to whisper to his sergeant. They both laughed.

Were turbans old fashioned? Were they a drode head fashion? Jergen flinched slightly and stared at his plate. I remembered, with pity and self-contempt, when I took him so seriously. I stared back at the table, smiled slightly when the Special Forces enlisted guy looked back at me.

Jergen said, "I'll have the chicken fajitas and a Dos Equis."

I liked the look of the fajitas on their steel oval pans, but wasn't used to eating meat. "Refried beans, cheese enchilada, and rice. A beer, Dos Equis would be okay."

Mike and Kearney also ordered beer and fajitas. I felt sure that the troops on the flanking tables knew Jergen, knew the situation with me. I said, "Jergen, what do you know about strategy games?"

Everyone heard me. Mike nodded slightly. Jergen said, "They give me a drug for the phobia and I run in them."

"You're training people in catching us?"

"You'll do it, too," Lt. Mike said. "It's good preparation for when you go out."

"I thought you were going to use me to find the person making mantises." Fuck the secrecy, we were surrounded by people who'd have gunned me down for shoplifting.

"Are you really going to cooperate with us?" Kearney said.

I wondered if anyone inside the restaurant was a real civilian. No, these civilians would be most willing to play civilians in the strategy games in this place. Ecology-killing golf links with their herbicides, insecticides, and fungicides were the main growth industry.

"I'll help you catch the person making the insects," I said. "I don't trust you enough to fake running."

"We'll get Jim from Amnesty to witness," Captain Mike said.

"Why?" I said.

The waiter brought the fajitas sizzling on their metal servers. Jergen's fork clattered against the tray. I reached for his hand and gripped it, a thing I'd done in the past which seemed to soothe him then. In the past, I'd thought he'd been anxious or excited about the actions we'd been about to run. No, he was damned ordinary agoraphobic. He pushed my hand away and reached for the beer.

Lt. Mike said, "Funny, you didn't remember his agoraphobia when you remembered him in interrogation."

Jergen looked over at me, beer can rim between his teeth, and rolled his lips inward, then swallowed more beer.

I said, "So, reading memories out of a brain doesn't give you everything."

"We could get everything out, but a lot of what we get from deep probes never happened. Trash and wishful thinking," Lt. Mike said. "And you were cooperating with us."

Were.

"You obviously think we're still the bad guys," Kearney said. "I don't think that matters for training exercises, but we do need to know that you'll cooperate with us when you're operating outside."

"I said I'd help you. I cooperated with the interrogation."

Jergen said, "She's always been honest."

Kearney said, "She stole. She fucked machines in sex shows."

Jergen said, "When she gives you her word."

Kearney said, "She lies to enemies. If we're still the enemies, she'll lie to us. To you, too, if she thinks you went over for the wrong reasons."

"What will practicing capture prove?" I asked. I'd at least know how good they were. If I could get away . . .

. . . with a net in my head, yeah. Could someone in the hacker underground help me? Shit, I could always pass for a runaway drode head, sell access to the black side . . .

. . . if I didn't run into federal infiltrators. But then if I got away during practice and they caught me later, wasn't that still part of the practice exercise?

"I want Jim to witness," I said. "Promise you won't kill me. Promise Jergen and Jim you won't."

The three tables of men smiled. Jergen said, "It will be painful. Emotionally, not physically."

"Shut up, Sam," Kearney said. I remembered Jergen was now Sam.

A brain fuck. But I'd recovered enough from surgery and was getting very bored. "I'd do anything to get out of the apartment," I said.

Jergen winced and closed his eyes. He opened them to reach for his beer. The waiter brought a second one. No, a third. I sat back in my chair wondering why I hadn't noticed Jergen's weaknesses earlier, even why I hadn't noticed when he got the second beer minutes earlier.

I reached for my first beer and sipped it, then finished off my vegetarian fare with no further conversation until we'd all finished. I reached for a strip of beef that one of the men had left on his plate. Nobody commented on that either. I could like beef, but I'd have to work to it gradually. I'd eaten meat as a street kid—stray pigeons and dogs—but when I'd had to eat a whole hamburger as a cover in my early thirties, I'd gotten diarrhea.

After we left Jergen at his apartment, I asked, "Why don't you treat his phobia?"

Mike said, "He doesn't want us to. He thinks he deserves it."

I almost said, *he was only doing what he thought was right.* I did say, "I've killed a couple of people, too, and I don't feel that guilty. They were killing the planet."

"And besides, they were breaking national regulations on using poison on public range. And they threatened to kill you."

"You weren't going after them," I said. "You were going after us."

Mike said, "We treat them the same way we treat you. They talk about their sources and stay clean, we leave them alone. Public trials spread too much information."

"What if they don't stay clean after the first warning?"

"Depends," Mike said.

"I wish we could have closed trials like the Brits," Kearney said. "Make life a lot safer."

I said, "Whatever, if I play in your games, you could kill me."

Kearney said, "I could shoot you right now."

"What's the point of having me play a terrorist for you?"

"It's a training exercise," Mike said.

"It's an artificial one. We ranged over the whole country, into Canada and Mexico. I can't tap into those sources either as my old self or my new one. Unless you've rebuilt me to look like someone specific." The thought was chilling. Someone else, a beginner, probably, not someone in the permanent underground, died so I, with considerably more experience, much more guilty in Federal eyes, could replace her.

Kearney said, "No. We're training on some new equipment."

"Am I supposed to surrender when your guys spot me? Or can I try to run?"

Lt. Mike said, "Try to run. Try to fight us off. The point of the exercise is taking people alive."

Kearney said, "Try your very best to get away."

I said, "There's a catch."

Kearney said, "If you don't cooperate with us and refuse to run, then we'll transfer you back to the padded cell and give you a mantis in a cage you can't destroy with your bare hands."

Lt. Mike said, "She's agreed to play with us. Sam said she keeps her word."

I said, "What if I get away?"

Kearney said, "Jergen got away for a month once. Jergen called us to come get him."

So, I was to practice running to train me in evasion in case I had to use it against my former colleagues. The first time went like this. The referee in his colonel's uniform said, "The ground rules are that you will not be deliberately killed or injured. When hit with the pink dye, you will immediately stop. You will have a blue dye pistol. Do not discharge it at a range closer than ten feet. Don't fire at the referees. Keep the goggles on.''

Military paintball, I thought. I ditched the goggles. Who but targets would wear them?

I got whacked the first time by the little old lady who opened her door and said, ''come this way,'' when I was running from troops. I put my hand on the soda can she offered me and it exploded. I was screaming at her when a referee came in and said, ''You're dyed pink. You're dead.''

''It's in my eyes, damn, it's in my eyes.''

The second time: I had contacts to protect my eyes, not the so-obvious goggles. Three guys pinned me down inside an empty warehouse. We all knew if we moved to fire, we'd become targets. I stayed put, expecting to be rushed at any minute. I'd get at least one of them before they got me.

We waited. My legs began to tingle from being sat on. My bladder seemed ready to burst. I shuffled to deeper cover and peed. I heard them pissing.

A referee came in and began yelling at them, ''You'd let some terrorist take you out with a suicide rig while you wait. Rush the bitch, you spineless mothers.''

From behind my barricade, I yelled, ''I don't have a suicide rig. And, it's only dye.''

They rushed me. I shot the referee. What could they do, reduce me in rank?

He pulled a dye pistol from one of the guys and shot me between the eyes. For a second, it was almost like getting killed. The world went black. I felt my sphincters go slack. The referee washed the paint off. I had a lump like a third eye growing under the skin.

After I cleaned up and changed from slacks and a sweater into a wool skirted suit, the troops bought me a beer in the Mexican restaurant and tried to feed me meat.

I said to the referee, ''I've got nanomachines inside. What if you'd broken one of them?''

The referee said, ''Don't shoot referees.''

I said to Mike on the way back to the apartment, ''As long as I have nanotech inside me, I couldn't really run. When do you take it out?''

''We can take them out tonight,'' Mike said.

''But I'm not completely changed,'' I said.

"Did you think we'd make you completely young again?"

I realized I thought they'd take me back to the time when I first met Jergen. If I could have been taken back to eight, I could have started over again.

About ten that night, Kearney came to the apartment with a medic. "You might be more comfortable on a bed," the medic told me. Mike and Kearney looked at each other, nodding little cop nods.

We went in my room. I took off my suit jacket and lay down on the bed. Kearney rolled my blouse sleeve up. The medic attached a large suction cup to my arm and said, "You need to be asleep for this."

"I'd rather not."

"You don't have any choice," Kearney said. He and Mike looked like they were about to pin me down.

I said, "Okay, already."

The medic slid the needle into my vein inside the elbow. I wondered if they'd gossip about me over my unconscious body, then fell asleep as the suction cup on my left forearm tightened.

I was alone in the room when I woke up. Where the nanomachines came through, the skin was bruised.

The third running exercise was more real. I had a three day head start and leads from the civilians playing terrorist sympathizers. I began looking for my own connections, not as an eco-warrior, but as a Klanswoman. Connections to that other underground would exist here, I suspected.

In Aberdeen, I found a man, Mr. Etheridge, who understood that the Army frequently used captured agitators for training. He wasn't Klan, but rather on the dog-fight circuit.

"When they seize our dogs, they put medic trainees to shooting them," Mr. Etheridge told me as we sat talking on the bench looking at the Rockfish Aberdeen freight station. "A dog goes down fighting, it's in his nature. But to get shot, treated, then killed to see if the medic did a good job, why that's an insult to the dogs. They're game."

"I'm game, too," I said. "Getting a bit wearing paying for my attitudes, though, being used as a exercise target."

"Where you say you're from?"

"Ohio. Orphan from Ohio."

"Dangerous thing, being an orphan these days."

"Yeah."

"I can't help you."

I understood that could either be never, or not directly. "I understand. It's good to talk to someone even if you're going to report what we said to a referee.''

"If they ask, I'll tell them I couldn't help you. Been out of the business statute of limitations times.''

I said, "I understand perfectly. It's not so bad being the fox in a drag hunt. They've promised not to kill me.''

"Wouldn't you'd be better off getting killed in your real game? Before you got got, were you were fighting for real?''

Um. "Just talking, you know.''

He said, "Had some game dogs once. Animal rights people cut them loose, but they ended up on surgical tables just the same as if they'd been seized.''

I didn't know quite what to say, but fighting dogs, even if bred to insanity, do cooperate in the fighting business. I tried to imagine what one felt like, immobilized, stuffed with painkillers, shot, treated, killed. I got a bit too empathetic.

"Well, I'm sorry that I can't help you. Been nice talking to someone who didn't go all disgusted about the dog fighting. I miss my sport.''

I remember thinking dog-fighting people were cruel dumb fucks who'd probably pollute and exterminate as bad as any if they only had power to do so. "I'm glad I could listen. Now, I've got to run, so to speak.''

"You looking for a job while you're being a drag fox?''

"Yeah, I'm supposed to make this look authentic.''

"Be around this summer?''

"Probably not.''

"Pity, they're looking for a clerk to run the concessions at the lake.''

I asked, "Where does the train go?''

"Sunny Point. You couldn't get on that train, though. It's most heavily guarded, being a munitions train.''

I found a job at a fast food place, working nights, and gave Mr. Etheridge as a reference. A teenaged boy came in one day and traced the word, *dogs,* in water on the counter.

When I followed him out, a gang of teenagers grabbed me and shoved me into a car trunk. I screamed like the whole thing was real.

The car took me to an abandoned sand pit. As the army car headlights approached, a man pulled me down into a tunnel illuminated by cold-light sticks.

"What were you?'' he asked.

"I wanted the United States to be the way it should be,'' I said. "Population no more than 100 million and that's probably ten times long-term carrying capacity.''

"Maybe I should throw you back to the dogs?"

"I was an eco-warrior. Maybe you should."

"We got common cause in one thing," he said.

"What?"

"They don't try us proper in court and let us tell our side of it."

I said, "Open court, we'd just give each other ideas."

"I hate your kind. On a normal day, I'd slit your bitch throat, but . . ."

"Tell them I told you I was an eco-terrorist and you dumped me down the road somewhere."

"They got a tracer on you?"

"Net in my head."

"Tell you that'd broadcast?"

"Yes."

"Dumb bitch." He turned on a machine near by and watched lights run through series of diodes. "I bet I know this game."

"Tell me."

"They're training you. You know what you'd do if you did get away?"

"Find some quiet lie, make a fake life, and crawl in until I get old."

He said, "Could you? You might as well stay with them, then."

"You're one of them, aren't you?"

He pulled off his cap, parted his hair with his fingers and showed me a drode hole scar, then moved the fingers and showed me another in case I'd thought the first scar was a wound. "Not hardly, babe."

I said, "Could you hack . . . ?"

"No, I just got away. People do, you know. You can live a quiet lie if you don't fuss, you don't sell your net time. I scavenge, hunt some, grow patches of herb and vegetables on land the owners don't seem to be using."

"What did you do?"

"Got born the wrong time, I reckon."

"Can I get away? Or are you going to shoot me blue?"

"Maybe you can get away. Maybe you really want to die, or to work for whoever's selling you the most excitement and the best excuses to not face that you crave the danger rush."

"They said if I did get away, they'd pick me up eventually. Jergen got away for a month. Sam? Did you help a man named Sam?"

"Never help anybody. You go back to them, you call Mr. Etheridge, you understand. So I can find another quiet hole. Mr. Etheridge, he just talked to lot of people about you."

"Being a drode head's that bad?"

"Man sleeps enough without losing months to people using him to read handwriting. Being looked down on's no fun, either. If we're useful, it shouldn't be welfare, it should be work."

"They don't use you, they use some of the brain's faculties."

"Come on, sugar, and street kids should be gunned down for stealing and jacking machines?"

I said, "If I got away, really, I can't imagine that I'd turn myself in. But I wouldn't go back to being an eco-warrior."

"If you believe in it, why not?"

I couldn't say I told him that to pacify whoever might be listening or whoever he might report to. "Because I'm tired, that's why."

"Running takes energy," the man said.

"I've got the energy," I said. "Besides they promised me even if I ran as hard as I could, they won't gun me down in the recapture."

"You planning to surrender?"

"No," I said, feeling bolder than I'd felt in years.

"Can you ride a bicycle?" the man asked.

"Yes," I said.

"Here's the ticket to San Francisco the government had for Mr. Etheridge to give you. And some money."

Woops, my heart and diaphragm squeezed double. So Mr. Etheridge was a plant. The Feds probably laughed at me this very minute. I took the ticket and the money, feeling utterly silly.

"And here's the key to a bicycle locked at Dallas–Fort Worth. I got a bicycle here if you can ride good."

"What's the daily range for a bicycle?"

"You're young. You motivated enough, you can get to the ocean. Hell, across the country if you're willing to steal." He took me deeper down into his tunnel and pulled a tarp off an open-framed bicycle, tubes and an exposed saddle, not an enclosed recumbent at all. I'd seen some adults who rode open-framed bikes for sport.

"They'll be able to see me."

"You'll be wearing a helmet, glasses, and bike clothes, all of which been stolen long ago," the man said.

I was about to ask him how did I know he wasn't working for the Feds, too. But what was the point? Running for real was just as good for training purposes. If they lured me with false contacts, so what? They could get me off a bicycle real easily, not like I'd stolen a car.

"Could you bring it to town?"

"You got to go from here in the morning."

The man had a small cookstove and a sack of welfare grade bean-and-wheat flour. He made a mush, flavored it with kale and onions, then found me a sleeping bag. "Bike's got bags to it," he said. "Nice racks for riding with touring gear."

"What would you do if you were me?" I asked between spoonfuls of mush.

"Go somewhere the opposite of the Raleigh–Durham airport, head for the beach, maybe. You could make the ocean in two days, one if you ride good."

"Bicycling."

"It's very ecological," the man said. He wiped out his pot and rinsed it with water from a plastic five-gallon bottle.

I laughed. "When's the ticket for?"

"February second. You can change the times for twenty-five dollars each."

"What is today's date?"

"About January twenty-sixth," the man said.

"I could sell the ticket, couldn't I?"

"Oh, yeah. They want you to have lots of options."

" 'They' is the Feds?"

The old man nodded.

I said, "You work for them, too."

"Some people Mr. Etheridge feels genuinely sorry for, he tries to get them to people like me for advice. Most of you targets give up and play the Feds' game."

"Did you escape?"

He said, "You know, if you gonna leave, you ought leave early, take Route 211 down south and ask for directions as if you're lost."

"Let me have the key to the bicycle in Dallas," I said. "Just in case."

All night, I leaned up on my elbow or lay on my back, awake, wondering if by some chance, I could escape, truly.

I expected somewhere to cross the Federal Zone of Influence, but the eastern part of North Carolina was conservative to the coast. I reached Whiteville by the end of the day and camped at Lake Waccamaw State Park, careful to pay for the campsite with the change I'd gotten when I'd bought lunch at Red Springs and asked directions.

Probably a meaningless gesture—all along my route, storekeepers could have other marked bills waiting for me. I expected the Feds would take me when I was too tired to move further, but I got my tent up and a night's sleep without anything happening. The next day, I left my tent up and rode along the lake, remembering ecology lessons about its endemic fish. Surrounding the rare fish was the banal ugliness of lakeshore buildings and trailer camps.

Now, for a design decision. I could go down to the North Carolina coast in less than a day, or I could turn into South Carolina, find someone at Myrtle Beach who'd buy my airplane ticket, and go back to Ohio to try to pick up my old gang connections.

Or sell the ticket and go to California anyway. But if I was being closely tracked, then if I used the old gang signals, I'd lead the Feds to other people.

First, I'd sell the ticket. When I had that money, I could plan what came next. I could throw coins and take a random walk. The ocean at Myrtle Beach wasn't that different from the ocean in Brunswick County, I thought as I looked at a gas station map.

I bought a North Carolina fishing license with one of the Federal bills, then headed for Little River, planned to poach a sleep off the road.

Little River was a small seaport for game fishing. I scavenged some guts out of a garbage barrel and caught crabs, no South Carolina fishing license, but then I was so close to North Carolina I could claim I'd not noticed I'd crossed a state line.

"What you doing?" a teenaged boy asked as I brought the crabs back to my bicycle.

"Fishing."

"You camping out?"

"No, I'm not. I plan to check in a motel."

He smiled. I got back on the bike and rode for ten miles before I trusted that he hadn't followed me.

I should have asked if he wanted to buy a fuck or watch me with a vibrator. Diseases? None of the veneral diseases now was 100 percent lethal. The Feds would cure me when they caught me.

Or not. Commercial sex was still a gambler's way.

I pulled way off the road and cooked my crabs, wishing I'd stolen a handgun, even one that shot red paint.

The dark threatened some thinking out: the Feds couldn't catch Miriam and Joe. Or had Miriam and Joe been informants? Why hadn't the Feds emptied Jergen's head as they had mine? Why did they let him keep me secret? I knew I wasn't an informer, but if the Feds were hunting Miriam and Joe, but not me, then I sure looked like an informant. I hoped the Feds thought I was too insignificant—minor player, a name in other people's files. Jergen disappears. His girlfriend isn't being chased. If I'd known Jergen had turned himself in, I would have wished he'd tipped me off somehow so I could have just disappeared, not gone back to Miriam and Joe.

The next day, I was in Myrtle Beach, looking through the fringe community for the right bulletin board to advertise my ticket. I found one in a New Age restaurant. Before I wrote the card, I pulled out the ticket and noticed that it was a round-trip, like I was going to fly of my own accord back to North Carolina.

All the easier to sell, though. I wrote on the card that I'd be back for lunch on the 30th, but before I'd got to the door, I heard a voice, "Hey, you with the ticket to Frisco."

I turned around. Everyone in the restaurant was looking at me. The guy who yelled came up. He wore black clothes, a turtleneck sweater and cords, but he looked military, too exercised and held together to be a real New Ager. I almost ran, but decided his money would be real enough. "Yes, and you can change the days for another twenty-five dollars coming or going."

He looked at the tickets, pulled out his billfold, paid me. I doubted, somehow, that he was planning to desert.

With the money I got I went out and bought travelers checks with most of it, a motel room at winter rates for the week with the rest. The motel parking lot was full of incongruous cars, either wrecks about to be abandoned in ditches or stretch limos with matt black fenders. As I figured, the clerk checking me in didn't question my story about my ID being in the mail.

For two days, I rode the bicycle around, fully loaded, as though I'd be headed away at any second, but went back to my motel room at night, behind a lock.

The second night a motel clerk, a tense boy, came by. "We'd like to see your identification card. You said friends were mailing it to you."

"Where I'm ending up, not here. I was afraid I'd lose it on the road."

"I don't believe you," the clerk said.

"So," I said. "The motel would be in trouble for not insisting to see my ID the first day."

"I guess people can tell what kind of motel this is," the boy said. "Well, we don't want trouble here."

"What kind of motel is it?" I said. "Maybe I better leave."

"You looking for work?"

"Non-sexual. Maybe sexual if the money's right."

"We thought about selling you to a guy in New Orleans when you first came in, but there's people watching you."

"Thanks."

"You make us nervous. We're refunding you. Go away."

"You could keep the money if I could borrow one of those delivery junkers."

"Could I have the bicycle?"

"Hey, kid, you could bonk me over the head and call the Feds."

"Is the bicycle stolen?"

"I suppose."

He wrote on a piece of the motel's stationery, holding the paper against the mirror so it didn't imprint on anything. *If I get you a car, could you meet me down at the Pavilion in an hour and give me the bike and $150?*

I went to the mirror and wiped it, up and down, signalling *thief yes.* "Sorry, we couldn't come to terms. I'll be leaving in the morning. Thanks for not bopping me over the head."

"De nada," the boy said.

It's just a replay of the last time, I found myself thinking, *a long run for nothing.*

But now I could move forward at speed. I wondered what would have happened if I'd been kidnapped and shipped to a brothel.

I made the trade down at the Pavilion, let the boy ride my bags down to the car, then strolled around by the screaming machines for a while before heading for the car, if he really had given me real keys to an active car.

Life's dangerous for unconnected women. Except for the year after Jergen disappeared, I'd never been alone. Even then, I had ecology contacts, sympathizers who let me sleep in the backs of bookstores, sweep, cook in their restaurants, babysit.

Fuck. Yeah, that, too.

I thought about all the people I'd suspected of not quite being committed, the people who like to talk firemouth, but who'd never do an action themselves. All in favor of them, you know, but the job or family didn't leave them enough time to participate.

Those people. I remembered a couple in Berkeley. Yes. If they weren't around, then Berkeley was full of eco-warrior would-bes. I turned the key in the ignition. Yes, bring those suckers a nice visit from Mr. Kearney and Lt. Mike. Radicalize them, or scare them away from even expressing a rad sentiment. Either way, they'd be improved.

The key worked. So, I drove and didn't try to lose the helicopters, the grey cars studded with microwave antennas, the truck that didn't pass me for fifty miles. But somewhere around Kansas, the sky was empty and no grey cars were around. I ate the greasy bean burgers of trucker's stops, played the machines in Elko under the nose of hand-gunning pit bosses and people who were probably disguised as hand-gunning pit bosses.

Found a mirrored whorehouse in a legal county, and discussed work-ing with the manager. "Not madam," she said. "That's for really tacky operations. We consider what we do a service."

"I don't have a legal ID," I said.

"We can't use you," she said.

"Is there anyone who could?" I asked.

"I wouldn't know of anyone who hires outlaw girls," she said. "If you don't leave now, I'm calling the cops."

I left. Outlaw girl, I could always go back to exhibitions and stealing. The sex shops had different brands of synthetic jissom than they'd had when I was a teen ganger—oh, fake prostate juice with all the right chemicals, amazing what's in semen besides the little sperms. I bought some for nostalgia's sake, plus a tube of hand job lotion for guys, all the high tech chemicals that make masturbation fully satisfactory. After Jergen, I never cared about making masturbation my central sex act.

Refrigerate after opening, the synthetic jissom bottle said.

When I found a refrigerator, I supposed I would. I felt older than forty-four, aware of the younger civilians, the people not in on the game, watching me, smiling.

I thought about calling the local FBI office and arranging for a flight back to my apartment jail. The car waited in the desert night, gambling lights reflected off its windows.

I got in and drove to a rest stop where I slept for a few hours, then drove up the Sierras the next day. Good car for a junker, I thought. People filled the Sierras, even in dead winter, the snow pushed back from the road, the skiers coming in with their bright industrial product skis and parkas—various hardened oils, fibers in resin, spun carbon, laying smears across virgin snow.

I left my own mess—the fake jissom bottle stuck in the refrigerating snow.

Then down to the foothills, at three acres per house where the gov-ernment didn't own the land. I stopped at Jackson and wondered if I knew anyone here, if anyone had a trap-door to a mine hole I could disappear down, become the hermit sage of Amador County.

But these weren't the people I wanted to get in trouble.

I did eat lunch in a crafter's restaurant, though, watching the people I could have become. They talked about their gardens, their clients, the levels of *giardia* and *E. coli* in the water they tapped from the irrigation canals. Lake Tahoe skiers shat in their water.

Down from there, I drove across the agricultural valley, the Delta like the other Delta. Fear hit me. I pulled off the road at a reststop and waited to be busted. The truck that had been following me since Jackson went flying on down the Interstate.

I slumped down in the seat and slept again. Where was my Federal tail? If I'd thought I could really get away, I'd have gone to Cincinnati or Louisville. *Please, where are you, Mike?* I was too tired to drive that far back east.

I left the car with the keys in it at the BART station at Orinda and bought a ticket, a new-style plastic one, laser-coded for station of purchase, amount of purchase, and date of purchase. The ticket went void in five days, but any remaining amount could be applied to a new ticket.

Meaning, someone was hacking BART tickets big time. I smiled to see evidence of other outlaws in the system, then took the BART toward Berkeley and got off at Rockridge when I spotted its funky-looking neighborhood.

I found a public-access computer and scrolled through the messages. A Dr. Karen, whose offices were on Shattuck Avenue, was looking for drode heads to do a sociological study, would pay five dollars an interview.

Yeah, in Berkeley, even the drode heads were on the net. Probably paid for by the city. And wasn't I a drode head? I wrote the number down and scrolled on further. Stopped again when I saw an ad for a woman looking for a live-in baby sitter.

Some people don't want daycare with multiple children, all possibly infectious. Other people don't want to be drode heads. So they meet each other. One has her job. The other's job is the first woman's children.

I called the woman, Mrs. George Reese, looking for a live-in sitter. She gave me directions to her house up in the hills, but then said, "I could meet you downtown."

"I can get up there," I said. "I'll take a bus as far as it goes, then walk."

"No, I'd better come pick you up."

"Lady, I've already got directions to your house."

"Oh," she said. "I'm sorry."

I went up to Mrs. Reese's house, a large sprawling glass and chrome gizmo stuck up on pilings like it really wanted to move to Los Angeles. She came out with a two-year-old girl child on her hip and said, "I work at home, but Lucinda really wants my attention, all the time." The woman wore a long silk dress covered to the knees by a sleeveless peasant coat in handspun wool. She was shod in buffalo-hide sandals with wool socks knitted out of the same wool as her coat.

I said, "I don't have any references. I don't have any ID. I used to be in the ecology movement. If any of that's a problem, then I'll be on my way."

"Have you ever taken care of children before?"

"No."

"Could you learn?"

The kid obviously bit. "What are you offering me?"

"You'll live in, get our meals, take care of Lucy during the day while I'm working. We'll feed you, shelter you. My husband's a lawyer. You can be his client."

"No cash?"

"How can we pay you if you don't have an ID? You'd never be able to get a bank account in the Bay Area without ID. The banks are very strict."

"They're still making the folding stuff, aren't they?"

"I appreciate your honesty. Lucinda needs someone tough and honest. We've been giving to the Sierra Club for years, so I understand about ecology."

Probably not with a house like that, I thought. What she really needs is someone too desperate to complain to the state employment office about sub-minimal pay and poor working conditions. "Lady, I need fifteen dollars a week over and above room and board." That would be less than what she'd pay on the open market.

"But if you rented a room in this neighborhood, it would cost three times minimum wage."

"Maybe twice minimum wage, but I wouldn't be subject to midnight calls. I could have my own friends over."

"Well, you could have your own friends over, as long as you weren't noisy and didn't bring in undesirables."

"I hope you find someone."

She said, "You won't find many people willing to take in an undocumented stranger. Are you sure you were an ecology person? I know some of the people around here."

"Fifteen dollars a week. I'm going to get busted eventually. So the Feds will know you weren't willing to pay me the minimum." I lifted my eyebrows at her, bounced them, and smiled.

"If you agree to fifteen dollars a week, then you'd have to sign a waiver of minimum wage."

"If the kid bites, I'm not staying."

Mrs. Ethyl Reese wasn't really working at home. I'd call what she did a rich girl's hobby. She wove peasant coats and place mats and all sorts of things like that. Little Lucinda loved to crawl under the loom and stand up suddenly, breaking warp threads. She did it again when Ethyl showed me her looms and spinning wheels. "Momma," she said, throwing her hands out.

I said, "Lucinda, your momma hired me to beat you up if you do that again."

"You can't hit her," Ethyl said.

"But I can pick her up and hold her in the air," I said.

"No," Lucinda said, not quite so pre-verbal that she didn't understand *hit, hold.*

"Yes," I said.

"Just as long as you don't hit her," Ethyl said. I wondered how many sitters had quit already. "I suppose you need to get your things."

Lucinda ran to her mother, waved her little arms. Ethyl picked her up, and Lucinda turned around to glare at me.

I said, "I just have the clothes I'm standing in. I don't suppose you know of a free clothes closet."

"The safest one you could go to would be the one run by the Episcopal Church," Ethyl said.

If the momma knew that much but still couldn't keep help, then the child was a true monster. "I guess you couldn't drive me."

"I'd be happy to drive you."

So the monster's momma had a nice captive wanted person to work for her. If Mrs. Reese decided she needed to find a new hire, she'd simply call the police and say she found her diamond broach hidden in my clothes. But I knew I could prove my side of the story. Brain records don't lie.

I couldn't have found a better person to get into trouble. I said, "I've got to have some time off."

"It's not like taking care of Lucy is a strenuous job." Little Lucy crawled over me heading toward the backseat where she began jumping up and down on the cushions.

"I think after I cook your dinner, I'll be going out. I'll come back at ten. That should be all right. Then you can take care of your daughter on the weekends. I'll make some microwave casseroles."

"George and I plan to go away weekends. We've got a good house security program, but it can't keep Lucinda out of trouble."

No wonder she wasn't too scruplous about hiring an outlaw.

"Can I take little Lucy downtown with me then?"

"Why do you need to go downtown?"

"Because I'll go stir-crazy if I sit all the time around your house."

"You've already got the evening off. You could even come in as late as midnight. The house has a good screening program. I'll introduce you to it."

Ethyl watched me as I foraged through the abandoned clothes bin, looking for pants and blouses that would fit but weren't too worn. I looked at her and figured we were about the same size, so why couldn't she lend me some of her clothes? But no, I had to look like the help. After I picked out a couple pairs of pants and various tops, Ethyl made a contribution to the church fund.

"I don't think you have to do that," I said.

"It's a good gesture," Ethyl said.

"If it doesn't come out of my weekly stipend."

For a minute, I thought she was going to pull the money back out of the box, but she merely looked miffed. Little Lucy began to run and shriek. Momma looked at me. I grabbed Lucy and carried her and the new clothes in a wadded mess to the car.

Lucy managed to tear up one of the bras before we got home. I didn't hit her.

Retina, handprint, blood sample. The house hesitated as though suspicious, then logged me as an inhabitant.

Please, oh, please, Kearney and Mike, pick me up now. I wondered if the person looking for drode heads could do evening interviews.

After being shown the place, I fixed a meal of sorts. "Don't you know how to cook?" Ethyl asked.

"Vegetarian," I said.

"You've never cooked steaks before?"

"I didn't believe in steaks."

Lucy took this moment to smear peas through her hair. "We could send you for cooking lessons," Ethyl said, "but you'll have to pass a probationary period first."

Her husband, a man who looked like he ate fatty meats regularly, came in about eight. Lucy seemed thrilled to see him and obeyed when he took her to her room to put her to sleep for the night. About nine, he came out. Ethyl said, "The new sitter. She cooks vegetarian."

"Does she have references?"

"No."

"Undocumented?"

"Yes," I said.

"You might have not told me that," George said. "But I prefer honest help. And I like my steaks rare, warm inside but still bloody."

"I've never cooked steaks before," I said.

"Jesus, what are you? An eco freak?"

"Yes," I said.

He looked at his wife and smiled. If I got out of line, they'd turn me in.

"Your wife said she'd pay me fifteen dollars a week on top of room and board and that I'd have evenings off, but that I'd take care of Lucy weekends when you went away."

George looked like he thought his wife was a bad bargainer. "We'll get some video tapes on proper service. You do know how to operate a video, don't you?"

My brain plays itself on video if the connections are made, I thought, but I simply nodded.

"You're a runaway drode head," George said. "No other kind of woman would have such short hair."

"You got it," I said.

"Better you work here than lie around collecting my tax dollars."

I remembered the man in the sandpit, the escaped drode head. "I always wanted to work, sir, but not as a drode head."

"Drode heads don't work. We use brain capacity they could never tap on their own."

"Well, I'm working for you now, sir, so we can both be happy."

"Are your electrodes still active?"

"It was an experimental net, sir." *No, you can't get free net access through me,* I decided. "Besides, I had a hacker fry the connections when I ran."

"Did you steal research property?"

"I suppose you might think that, but I didn't volunteer for anything other than simple drode holes."

"Hackers sometimes lie to drode heads about turning off the equipment. I'll bring in some equipment from the office. We can open the ports again."

"I didn't have ports. It was a new system that projected through skin. You'd need the matching read-head."

"Bummer."

"Actually, sir, I'm on a training exercise. If you'd like, you could call the Feds and ask to be routed through to the training facility near Pinehurst, North Carolina. Ask to speak to a Captain Kearney. Tell them Allison wants to know if the rules change after a month."

George forked his grey steak, looked at his wife. He finally said, "Do you need this job?"

I said, "For the purposes of the training exercise, I need a job."

"A woman can get better money than by babysitting."

"The licensed brothels want ID."

Ethyl pulled her lips tight and looked away from me. George said, "I can arrange to hack your head, edit out your working for us."

"Why don't you think about all this when I'm out this evening?"

Ethyl said, "You've got to clean up first."

After I cleaned up, I left the house and called from a public phone. Dr. Karen did have night hours. I said, "I've got an experimental subdermal rig. Are you interested in talking to me, or just plain drode heads?"

"I think you should come right now," Dr. Karen, a voice that could be either male or female, said. Perhaps this would be my bust, but I wondered if George and Ethyl would tell the house to forget me by the time I got back. I needed five dollars. Dr. Karen gave me the address of his/her office on Shattuck, a third-floor office.

I was only four blocks away when I saw a mantis, but managed to keep it together until I got to Dr. Karen's office.

Dr. Karen matched his or her voice, male or female, I couldn't tell. Three definite males in brighter-than-usual business suits were also in the room. They had white contacts over their irises, fake blind stares. One of them parted his coat, exposing wide suspenders. I looked at more electronic equipment than I'd seen since Kearney put the squid on my naked brain. Some of it was dusty, some looked like the three guys just brought it in. I looked at their suits again and realized they were exaggerations of real business suits, not quite right. The white eyes wiped any individual sense I could have of them. Their hair was slicked down and darkened. I could never identify them.

"Allison? Is that your real name?"

"Yes."

"Your phenotype doesn't match any known records. Can we do a DNA scan?"

"I was changed by nanotech. I don't know if that would affect the DNA or not. I'm an escaped witness."

One of the boys in business suits sat down at a keyboard and flurried his fingers over it.

Dr. Karen turned to another screen. "One Allison was supposed to have died in an atomic explosion in Louisiana."

"I was supposed to, but the Feds pulled me out. You have eco contacts?"

"When you said you were an escaped witness, we set up a serious evasion program. We have managed to evade the Feds in the past. I'd like to put you in play."

"Can you find me a place to live? I thought I had a child care job, but they thought I was just a regular drode head when they hired me.''

Dr. Karen said, ''Better put her on satellite and use serious worm medicine.''

A second suit sat down and entered data with a pen pad.

''Can I get a look at my file? I'd like to know if people are watching me now.''

''I don't think so,'' one of the three guys said.

''No,'' Dr. Karen said. ''And go back tonight. They may prefer to pretend to have contacted the Feds and will tell you that no one ever heard of you.''

I asked, ''Can you check their long distance phone records?'' but no one replied. One of the guys shoved fiber optic cable against his white contact lenses, like really long leeches dangling from his eyeballs.

Dr. Karen scraped inside my cheek for squamous cells, ''better than blood cells for full DNA,'' and ran the scan. ''You almost appear to be who you say you are, but alive, not dead. Nanotech alterations could account for the discrepancies.''

I said, ''I guess I'm too hot to hack.''

Dr. Karen smiled, seeming for a second more like a woman. She/he said, ''No one is too hot to hack.''

''Could I have more than five dollars then?'' I asked.

''You agreed to five dollars.''

''I agreed to an interview, a sociological interview for five dollars. I can jam your hacking.''

''Full audiovisual display capacities?''

''Yes,'' I said.

''Subdermal squid? My dear, yes, I think we could pay you twenty-five dollars to take a look at that.''

The guy with the fiber optics attached said, ''A look through that.''

''Why do you guys do this?''

Dr. Karen seemed about to correct me on the sex, but pursed her lips—I was beginning to see Dr. Karen as female—and said, ''We believe curiosity is humanity's highest attribute. Knowledge should move. If we want to know, we should know.''

I'd heard hackers scavenged information to sell to pay for more curious explorations. The eco people went to them occasionally, but never trusted machine heads. ''How long will it take? I've got to be back at the Reeses by midnight.''

Dr. Karen said, ''Perhaps you shouldn't remember coming here.''

''Time to play with the snakes,'' the white-eyed guy with fingers on the keyboard said. The third guy dripped some fluid into the fiber optic guy's eyes. I thought goggles would have worked better, would have allowed him to blink, but fiber optic leads to the contacts floating over the eyeballs certainly threw a tougher image.

"We'll have to shave your head," Dr. Karen said, "but we'll throw in a human hair wig for free."

Then I went blank.

"Hi," a voice said. "You're new here."

"Who are you?"

"I think I'm the Roanoke sewage treatment plant this week, except I'm also supposed to be looking for you. Sometimes I target bombs into Tibet."

I asked, "Where am I?"

"In the system. I'm one of the people who's been looking for you."

"Do the people monitoring me hear us talking?"

"I don't think anyone knows I can find my own private spaces in here."

"Roanoke, you're Eastern Standard Time, right? What time is it?"

"I think it's after midnight, but if I went where the data was, I wouldn't remember."

"You're a drode head?"

"Yes."

"You hacked your own system?"

"I started remembering a bit and found a way to go away from the bugs."

"Bugs?"

Bugs—an emanation of beetles, not a word, not an image, an electronic gestalt of squirming hard shells, bugs making crazy. A visual of a mantis walked in through the electronic dark, calming the man gestalt, eating the other bugs. I felt my electric self tremble. Another nightmare victim.

"Don't you like mantises?" the mantis said in the drode head's voice.

"No," I said. "I feel about mantises the way you feel about hallie bugs." I didn't know I knew about hallie bugs.

"Allison, you're leaking data I don't think I want to know. I can't quite figure out where you are. I'm going for help."

I felt the voice retreat. "Wait."

Another voice said, "Ghost in the machine." The voice seemed to be in my real ears.

In my mind's ear, the male voice said, "I saw what you did to that mantis."

"Willie, are you going to help them track me down?" I said, not knowing quite how I knew his name.

The voice outside said, ''Flip us. It's a trace.''

I dreamed of headless mantis males fucking me. When I woke up, Dr. Karen was on top of me, me naked. It had a penis, thrust it hard into my cunt, then saw my eyes looking back.

''Such erotic content,'' he said. ''I couldn't resist and I didn't think you'd mind.'' His hand wiggled over to a switch. I tried to shove him away. ''If you do mind, then . . .''

Blackness again. Mantises. I thought I was screaming.

When I woke up this time, the office was completely empty except for my clothes, twenty-five dollars, the wig, and a note saying, *For what we got, twenty-five was worth it. See you around, Allison.* Dr. Karen hadn't been a woman turned man, nor a epicene man, but rather a teenaged boy claiming age with the degree, the sociology scam. A rutty, nasty teenaged boy. All of them rutty teenaged boys. I realized that only now, found the toilet, threw up, washed between my legs, threw up again.

Did Willie see that? Did the Feds? I screamed, ''Kearney, if you're listening, you bastard, why didn't you get me out of that?'' Willie said he was leaving to get help.

The walls absorbed my screams. Too late for any other office people to be around. Perhaps the nasty boys listened to me.

Even though the sun was coming up, I went back to the Reeses. The house let me in.

George saw me first.

''Don't you touch me,'' I said.

''I wouldn't,'' he said. ''Some people prey on drode heads, catch them in the fugue state. Didn't you know about them?''

I shook my head. George said, ''You're safer if you go out with Ethyl or stay in the house. I've heard about hackers getting escaped drode heads.''

''Yes,'' I said. ''You're not going to hack me.''

''I wouldn't. I'm an honorable man. We won't fire you, but we'd appreciate it if you guard yourself a bit more carefully.''

''Did you call the Feds?''

''Why should we want to turn you in? Lucinda needs a babysitter we can trust. You've been honest.''

Ethyl came out then with Lucinda. They both stared at me, then George led them away, to explain, to make excuses. I didn't even know where my room was, what to do next. The family came back out. George kissed Ethyl and went out the door. Lucinda came over and poked me in the legs, giggling. Ethyl said, ''Looks like you could get some sleep. We're going to let you have the morning off.''

My room was over the garage, an all-in-one unit like a jail cell with tub, sink, and toilet standing exposed in the room.

Lucinda giggled. Ethyl said, ''I'll call you for lunch.''

''Thanks,'' I said, somewhat grateful, ashamed of what I'd gotten done to me, how little I knew about my new condition.

After they left me, I washed and washed, took the wig off, scrubbed the naked scalp, then lay belly down on the bed, afraid to sleep.

Mantises and bugs. Nasty teenaged rich kids. The Feds had not been so brutal. Or had the Feds put the kids up to it?

I thought about calling the Feds. Must have been Army Intelligence that had me. But as soon as I thought that, I felt stupid and childish. Here I was, finally, where the orphanage wanted me to go, working daycare for rich people. Maybe the Feds didn't care. They could leave me taking care of little Lucinda until little Lucinda got her own computer to fit my neural net. I'd end up drooling under the wires, a scanning device for a Stanford University student.

Raped and abused. All my life and it's come to this. *Kearney, Mike, why didn't you find me?*

I fell asleep and dreamed of gunning down the Reeses and the boy hackers. Kearney told me I'd been a fool. I woke up just as I began to understand I was dreaming, but the feeling of being a fool didn't go away. And this damned dream stayed with me, too.

It was noon, duty time. I dressed, and, still in hiding, cooked lunch in my wig. I felt like I bled under it, but I only sweated. Cheap drode head polyester wig.

FIVE

WILLIE CUT AND DRIED

The mantis sat on Willie's knees, nibbling a katydid. Trying not to disturb the mantis, Willie felt in his pocket for the money he'd been saving from selling his plasma. Behind the house, the fields in their terraces lay dormant, but he'd heard that the company who owned the farm had thought about putting the fields to a winter crop. Willie didn't much like the idea, having to hear the automatic tractors all year round.

He'd thought once about stealing parts from the machines built into the terrace walls, but hadn't. That was before he had the mantis.

A memory. Memories running together. A woman's voice. Looking for a brain pattern.

He'd found the brain pattern, but he hadn't. He'd found the brain pattern but hadn't told the people operating him that he had. Hackers drove him out before he could figure where he was.

Maybe. Maybe that's what the people operating him wanted him to believe, he thought.

The mantis spread its wings and sprayed him with more juice to stop his knees from moving so much. Willie had heard somewhere that people had tiny nostrils inside their air-breathing ones, little holes that soaked up pheromones. The mantis made good pheromones.

Willie turned the mantis so it sat on his left thigh. It bopped out with an arm, cutting his thumb slightly, then trilled its wings with his agitation. He felt a twinge of anger—might be big, but it was still a damn bug—but the mantis calmed him down.

"She hated you," Willie said.

The mantis felt cold and began climbing up Willie, shivering slightly. Willie took her inside and put her back in her tank under the heat lamp.

He remembered the woman's terror. War materials being moved, hunting a brain pattern. He wondered if his memories from the times under the electrodes were real, or distortions like bug hallucinations.

Wars fought by machines. Brain patterns ran. Wasps put tiny humans in their nests. A voice that sounded like his target brain pattern screamed.

Willie wondered how he got his dream of doing something. The mantis should have cured him of that, but maybe what the bug gave him stimulated him as well as calmed him.

Time to sell the junk he'd smuggled back from Tibet on his first tour of duty. Then he'd have to find a keyboard hacker.

Maybe his dream was impossible. Maybe the mantis was curing him slowly of his bug horrors. Willie bent over the mantis's tank and breathed in deeply, then went to see his art stuff.

Down in the cellar, Willie pulled his first idol from a box filled with moldy shoes, sweat-rankled socks, and old canning jars full of black slimed peaches.

He brushed it off with a soft, new paintbrush like he'd seen archaeologists do on Public Television, then pulled on his wig and best clothes and rode his bicycle into Stuart, parked it, and used his welfare pass to get a train to Danville. He had to wait until the paying passengers got on, then the intercom announced eleven spots for pass carriers.

At Danville, he switched to the East Coast maglev, standing room only for pass carriers, but he only had an hour and a half to the Outer D.C. Belt. The Capitol District commuter trains only accepted welfare passes between eight P.M. and midnight, so Willie had to buy a pass. Riding into Alexandria, he felt conspicuous even in his best clothes until he spotted a couple of other drode heads among the commuting bosses. Maybe he should transfer to a city where oddball money was easier to come by?

Too far from home. Willie wished he'd brought his mantis. He felt hopeless. Bugs kept moving around the corners of his vision. But under his arm, he had the first Buddha.

What did he think he was doing? The man in Old Town would call the police, would cheat him.

No, Willie told himself, *I've done okay until now. The man in Old*

Town has as much to lose as I do, maybe more. I used to be able to handle things real well. Willie tried to remember what that was like, back in the Army on the Tibetan Plateau.

All he could remember is that he used to manage real well. He couldn't remember how he'd done it, though.

He got off in Alexandria at the King Street Station and remembered the number and street the bloodsucker woman in the Stuart plasma clinic gave him.

The address was for a used bookstore. Willie went inside, the Buddha in its paper bag under his left arm. A man who either didn't have the money for nano-rejuvenation or who believed his purposes were better served by looking fifty came out. He was grey haired, somewhat fleshy in the face, with slight jowls and loose flesh over his eyelids.

Willie said, "I'm Jubbie Carter. I'm told Mr. Wilson is expecting me."

"I'm Jones. Mr. Wilson is no longer with us," the man said in a voice that sounded like a New Yorker. "You have something you'd like me to appraise. Do you have a bill of sale for it?"

"I left it at the house," Willie said as he'd been told to say. "I'll mail it to you, but we can write one up here with my address and all."

"As long as it isn't listed as stolen merchandise, I'll be happy for you to mail me your purchase receipt later." Wilson reached out for the paper bag, pulled it off the statue, sat the statue down by a computer.

"I got it in Tibet," Willie said. "When I was in the service." He realized he'd said more than Jones needed to know. But then the girl at the plasma parlor could give Jones the same story.

Jones pulled out a camera, scanned the sculpture into the computer, then said, "Computer, scan, compare, quiet report."

"What databases?" Willie said. He'd bought this sculpture, but some of the others were loot.

"Interpol, North American, Japanese, other countries that are in a position to fuss." Jones smiled.

The computer screen flickered impossibly fast, then cleared. NOT STOLEN.

Then AUTOMATIC REQUEST FOR POTENTIAL OFFERS: TWO.

"You know already you can sell it?" Willie asked.

"Perhaps. Two's not an impressive number."

"How many Tibetan buddhas are there for sale?" Willie asked.

Jones looked at his fleshy lids half closing his eyes. "How many Americans were in Tibet during the war? How much of Tibet didn't get looted?"

"I thought it was a particularly good-looking statue," Willie said, "even if it don't got lots of jewels and gold plate."

"I'd appraise it at sixty dollars. If you want me to sell it, I'd have to deduct 20 percent as a commission."

"Could you make it an even fifty?"

"Should I write you a check?"

"No." Willie knew then he'd get cheated.

"Well, then for cash, I'd have to make it forty-five dollars."

Willie used his welfare pass to get to D.C., so the trip only cost him the D.C. transit fare. "I'd like you to waive the cash discount in the future." He sounded in his own ears like his captain.

"If I'm able to sell this piece, I'll consider dropping the cash discount," Jones said. "Automatic offers aren't sure things. People could have forgotten to purge their request files." He opened a drawer, pushing back his tweed jacket so Willie could see the gun in his belt. Thick fingers counted out the money, a five-dollar coin, two twenty-dollar bills.

Willie got an erection. He could afford a whore. Then his vision went dim with bugs in the corners.

Jones said, "I see you're very excited to have some cash. I'm sure you'll need more soon."

Willie said, "I'll manage."

"If you would like to do further business with me, please call me collect," Jones said. "I'll deduct half from any possible sale, take the loss if we can't sell your property."

"Thank you," Willie said, not feeling particularly grateful. But he now had almost a hundred dollars between this and the money back in Virginia. He put the two bills in the pouch on his belt and the coin in his front pocket, the one he'd sewn up with new cloth.

He started to worry about city thieves, but nobody would expect a drode head to have so much money.

At the maglev station, he had to wait because the train already had its quota of free riders, even standing. He bought a sandwich out of the five-dollar coin, heard people standing behind him muttering about freeloaders, then got on the next train with his welfare pass. Willie got a seat this time all the way through the dark to Danville.

If he had the scanning computer and the access codes to the stolen art system and the computerized art bids, he could offer his pieces directly to the buyers. He knew he was cheated by Mr. Jones. The bitch in the plasma shop wouldn't do him any good for a direct contact, but perhaps the hacker who'd gotten busted with him when Willie tried to sell his contacts might know someone who knew someone.

At the Stuart station, Willie left his bike locked and went to the little late night fritter place where he'd met his hacker the first time.

His friend wasn't there, but Willie spotted a friend of the local hackers named Little Red. Little Red was a nanotech damage case worth $10 million. He never talked about anything. When the small hacker units in the county were all busted, Little Red wasn't among them. But Little Red didn't testify against them either. Little Red, who'd been eighteen when he got frizzled, was now a tiny thirty-something guy. The company's settlement for shriveling up his legs and spine, Little Red told everyone, was just the cost of doing business. The company offered a free rebuild instead, but neither Little Red nor the local jury wanted to settle for that. Little Red could get rebuilt whenever he'd trust nanotech again, but he'd get to keep his $10 million.

From under his feedstore cap, Little Red watched Willie come in. He nodded at Willie, then turned back to his deep fried pig's ears. Being only about four feet tall, Little Red could make a meal out of what would have been another man's snack.

The man behind the counter looked at Willie and sighed. No tip from this one. "Can I help you?"

Willie knew he could get veggie fried things for stamps, but decided he wanted to buy real food. He leaned over the counter and said, "Couple of tacos."

The counter man said, "Can you pay real money?"

Willie pulled out the change from his five, then decided he was close enough to home and pulled out one of the twenties. He must have been leaning over the counter pretty fiercely because the counterman backed away and looked at where the defense module must be.

Willie leaned back and put the twenty in yet another pocket, worrying slightly that he might forget all the pockets he'd spread his money through.

"Willie, that's not a whole lot of money," Little Red said. He talked to Willie's reflection in the mirror on the wall over the cookers.

"I sold something I bought in Tibet and found out about an entire system of scanning art to see if it's stolen, of computerized bids for pieces."

Little Red gnawed on the gristle part of a pig's ear. Willie wondered if he'd surprised Little Red. Little Red said, "You need money, Willie. Have you thought about suing the Army? Didn't they promise you an education?"

"I could have gotten one I don't remember," Willie said. "The bugs messed me up considerable."

"Or sue them for not treating you better," Little Red said.

"I'm a drode head. You don't do anything, either, do you, Little Red, other than play with the money you got for being messed up? Didn't stop the nanotech company."

" 'Cost of doing business.' "

"We could both be doing better than this," Willie said. "But we're lazy Appalachians."

"This isn't Appalachia," the counterman said with some anger, perhaps, Willie thought, as much for not being included in the conversation as for the regional slur.

Little Red said, "No, Appalachia starts uptown. We're in cracker country."

Willie said, "I'd have put better use to ten million dollars."

Little Red put his pig's ear down and turned to Willie, not talking to the mirrored Willie, but looking directly at the real man. "God, Willie, that's downright nasty. What happened to you?"

"I got cheated today."

"You been getting cheated for a ton of years. Why's it a problem now?"

"I think the mantis pheromones are counteracting the war bug terror."

"Well, Willie, see you around. You paying off the bitch in the plasma parlor?"

Willie felt his face turn hot. He wouldn't look at Little Red direct or in the mirror.

"Well, tonight you insulted me," Little Red said, getting off his stool and patting Willie on the back. "Maybe you can work up to bigger things." Little Red squeezed Willie's shoulders and hobbled out on his shoes of different heights, his crooked spine covered in a leather jacket.

Willie worried that Little Red stole his money, but felt something stuck in his belt.

He finished his tacos quickly against closing time, then went back to his bike, flipped the generator on, and rode home before trying to read Little Red's message.

On a napkin, Little Red wrote down a phone number, 555-6676-9. Willie threw the number in his disguised walnut cupboard and went to feed his mantis.

The mantis made him glad, easy with the world, but Willie realized, floating in its love, that what he felt now didn't just come from the mantis.

Welfare wanted him for sessions in the morning, but he'd be free again in two weeks. First free day he'd do it.

In two weeks, all he remembered of his time under was searching for the brain pattern again, but not finding it. And no one rifled his memories. And no one had broken into his house. Odd, Willie thought as he dialed 555-6676-9, that he'd never remembered being audited, but now he remembered that he hadn't been audited.

He heard a voice and tried to speak, but the voice, one he didn't recognize, didn't appear to have ears attached. It said, "Willie, ride up Route 8 and call me again at the phone booth at the Parkway."

Willie rode his bicycle up Floyd Mountain. His knees ached, he pushed the bike a lot, but he finally got up. No way he could get home by dark. He saw the phone booth at the Blue Ridge Parkway and dialed 555-6676-9 again, wondering if he should have dialed 703 first because what had been a local call in Patrick wouldn't be a local call here. But the phone rang, another recorded voice answered and asked Willie to wait for a phone call.

No sooner than Willie hung up than the phone rang. A live woman said, "Willie, we'll pick you up."

Willie wondered if this had all been a ruse to get him away from his house so Little Red could send robbers after his Tibetan sculptures. "Okay."

An electric van glittering with photovoltaic panels pulled out from behind the abandoned motel. Little Red called out, "Willie, come on."

Willie wheeled his bicycle over. Hands hauled it up, and Willie followed his bike into the van. He sat down beside the battery compartment and said, "You can run it off batteries, too?"

"We use as much sun as we can get," the van driver, the woman from the recorded message, said.

"These are very expensive," Willie said.

The woman smiled at Little Red. Little Red said, "Willie, we're both rich. Got it the same way."

The woman said, "Not quite the same way, Willie. Little Red is a nanotech disaster. I'm a chemical spill."

" 'Cost of doing business,' " Willie said. He looked at the woman, wondering where her damage was. Nothing was visibly wrong with her other than she was too skinny.

Little Red said, "Willie, leave the irony to us."

Willie said, "Chemical spill, what's wrong with you?"

"My child died. I'm sterile."

"Dead child's sort of bad, but most women have to pay to get sterile. Except drode heads," Willie said.

"Red, Willie wasn't being ironic," the woman said. "He sincerely believes that what happened to us and to him was the cost of doing business.''

''If I'd worked at it harder, I could have fought off the hallie bugs. The people turned me into a drode head made better use of me than I could make for myself. At least, just after the Army.''

''Jesus, Willie,'' Little Red said. ''You really believe that, we'll take you back down the mountain.''

Willie said, ''I was knotted up with terror. If I got a hardon, 'scuse me, ma'am, I saw bugs. Women made me feel like bugs were crawling on me. The government made me unscared.''

The woman said, ''They lobotomized you. They have you tranquilized by an insect now.''

''My mantis eats other bugs. She's a good insect.''

Little Red said, ''He's just running a program. He's really as pissed as we are.''

Willie said, ''I'm going to work out a plan.''

The woman started the electric van, and they drove into Floyd by the signs to the Genuine Twentieth Century Hippie Village and the Beds and Breakfasts lodges with parking lots full of expensive electric and gas cars, no junkers there.

The van pulled off down a dirt road and went through rhododendron scrub to a clearing studded with photovoltaic panels, grids, electric cookers, and three geodesic domes with stove pipe sticking out their tops.

Little Red said, ''Laurel, looks good.''

''We can move it all in seven vans.''

Willie said, ''The domes, too?''

''Yeah, but we'd have to buy new waterproofing tape for between the panels,'' Laurel said.

''What are you?'' Willie said.

''Industrial accident gypsies,'' Laurel said. An ancient woman, tinier than Little Red, hobbled out. She had flippers instead of arms.

For an instant, Willie wondered if she had survived from the thalidomide damage in the mid-twentieth century. She seemed ancient enough, but only nanotech could have kept anyone alive that long.

''Thalidomide?'' Willie asked. Then he wondered how he knew about thalidomide.

The tiny old woman said, ''Yes.'' She had what Willie thought of as a Mexican accent.

Willie said, ''God, you must be very old.''

''Not so old, Willie,'' Laurel said. ''Some places sold thalidomide over the counter into the late nineties.''

Willie felt coldly stupid, then smarter than he should have been, confused. He wanted to have his own plan. Now, these people picked him up and put him into their plan, like a chess piece.

Willie didn't know he knew anything about chess. But then he knew how to spell *pheromone*. "So, what do you want from me?"

Little Red said, "Your memories of the last couple times under the hood."

"I've got locks on."

"We won't use the electrode holes," the tiny woman with seal flippers told him. "We'll pick up the signals from around them."

Willie said, "You've got a squid?" He'd heard squids worked best against bare brains.

Laurel said, "It's not that kind of squid and besides you've been modified to output to electrodes."

"They'll audit me eventually. I've gone to Washington on my pass. I'll make other trips there if I can't find a better way to sell my Tibetan things."

"They won't find a thing," Laurel said.

"You're going to wipe my memories."

Little Red said, "We can do that without chemicals."

"Post-hypnotic suggestion," the little Hispanic woman said.

Laurel said, "Or we can set his memories to wipe before an audit, but trust him until then. Why do you want money?"

"So I can get off the dole."

"What if I told you they don't want you off the dole. Someone would have to develop true artificial intelligence to get from a computer what they get from you linked with a computer. And the brighter you are, the better they can use you."

Willie thought Laurel was being a trifle intense for a woman. "I'm just one drode head. Surely they can spare me."

"What if you had enough money? Do you have a plan?" Little Red asked.

"If I had enough money, I'd come up with a plan," Willie said. "Can we quit standing around arguing and go inside? I thought you wanted to know about the program for art bids."

The Hispanic woman said, "A program for art bids?"

Little Red nodded.

Laurel said, "Why don't we just hack that today, see if we can get the bidding up on some of Willie's Tibetan art."

"I've got to be home tonight," Willie said. "To take care of my mantis."

Little Red said, "Willie, we don't use unwilling links, so if all you want is better prices for your loot, then we'll try to help you. But we think we can help you with that plan.''

''It wouldn't be my plan,'' Willie said.

''Do you remember audits?'' the Hispanic woman asked.

''I'm remembering more and more,'' Willie said.

Laurel said, ''Do you like remembering?''

''Yes,'' Willie said. ''Otherwise, I've lost half my life to the fugues.''

''I might try to find another way to block the audit than tampering with your memories, then,'' Laurel said. She opened the door to the closest geodesic dome. Willie went up some stairs to the interior floor. The space was weird, a circle, almost, about 16 feet across, stuffed with electronic gear. Willie recognized the squid immediately—a black cone that looked like some visual cross between a de-tentacled biological squid and a dunce cap, with a three-inch cable coming off the top. He could imagine it sucking a brain and shuddered.

Now he had to sit under it. ''I'm going to be screwed,'' he said.

The Hispanic woman said, ''You've already been fucked. What's a screwing?''

Willie sat down in the chair under the squid. Laurel taped over his drode holes and then spread jelly over his head. Her fingers felt kind, then condescending.

As the squid dropped onto Willie's head, Little Red asked, ''Willie, what do you remember about the fence in Washington?''

He remembered that the fence was in Alexandria, not the District. ''It was off King Street in Old Town, Alexandria.'' He knew he wasn't walking into the shop again, but he reheard his conversation with Jones along with the click of a keyboard. When Willie got to the memories of Jones speaking to activate the computer, the memories slowed down, went backward, played again.

Laurel's voice said, ''Voice-activated. We can do a normal synthy of Jones's voice.''

From under the hood, Willie asked, ''What's that?''

''Obviously the computer would recognize Jones's voice. But it would also have to recognize a tape. So we have to modify the voice.''

Little Red said, ''There may be other signals. Let's look for a mouse.''

Willie backed up and began again. He looked harder at Jones's hands than he ever remembered doing.

''Will I remember this?''

''Do you want to?''

"Dunno." He hung in the scene while Laurel, the Hispanic woman, and Little Red tried to see how they'd get into Jones's system.

Willie, being idle, thought about the brain pattern he'd been looking for. Laurel said, "Hey, Willie, cut it out. We don't need to know that."

The Hispanic woman said, "I remember that pattern."

Little Red said, "Laurel, when did we decide to be that scrupulous?"

Then Willie started not to remember Laurel's voice. He and Little Red sat in the restaurant in Stuart talking about the ball game.

Little Red told Willie, "The point of the ball game is winning. Attachment to the players isn't the important thing. If we could find better players, they'd be on our team instead of the folks we've been playing with."

Willie wondered if they were really discussing ball. He knew they weren't really in the restaurant.

The next morning, Willie woke up in a sleeping bag. Laurel said, "Willie, are you really that sexually dysfunctional because of the hallie bugs? You seem lonely for women."

He looked up at her, saw her eyes, and said, "I don't want to be a pity fuck."

"Do you mind if I sit down by you?"

Willie said, "Okay. But I've got to get back to my mantis." As soon as he said that, he felt weird, like he'd mated with an insect.

Laurel said, "Willie, you should be getting compensation for war-related injuries, not treated like a welfare case."

"I need to get back to my mantis," Willie said. He wanted to be alone if he was going to feel this weird.

"We'll drive you."

"Aren't you afraid of being seen with me?"

"Your masters don't care that much about what you're doing. Besides, we've had people watching your house ever since you talked to Little Red. That Jones could have had his girl in Stuart let him know when you went under the wires in Roanoke again. We just made sure that someone was always around. Favor to you."

"I have to sell the stuff. I didn't want to sell it all at once." Willie wondered what these people did, really. "Seems pretty strange you watching my house for me when I was under the wires." He got up out of the sleeping bag, pissed in their composting toilet, washed his face, loaded his bike in back of the van, and climbed in beside Laurel.

Little Red popped up a seat in the middle and pushed it real far forward so he could lean against the front seat. "Willie, we'd like to replay your next session under the wires."

Laurel started the van. Willie asked, "Why?"

Little Red told him, "You found the brain pattern of an old friend of ours who supposedly died in Southern Louisiana when a refinery blew up."

Laurel said, "She didn't know us personally though."

Little Red leaned back in the van and didn't say anything more.

Willie said, "She was a drode head and she was getting hacked and raped by some white-eyed boys."

Laurel said, "We'll take your art now, sell it for you, either through the net you saw or other ways. Maybe not sell it, but pay you fair value for it. But we'd like to find out more about this woman."

"They rebuilt her, I think," Willie said. "You'd never recognize her. I don't think I'm the only one looking for her, either. She disappeared during a training exercise, but I'm not supposed to know that much."

Laurel said, "Loba can recognize any brain pattern, any retina scan, the personal body style. Harder to change the personal body style than the retinas."

Loba must be the Hispanic woman, Willie figured. He knew her name meant bitch wolf in Spanish. Willie said, "She's sort of run away from the Feds, but she sort of hasn't. I was confused."

When the van pulled in beside Willie's house, he saw a fully enclosed recumbent bicycle tilt to upright by the old falling-down barn across the street. It looked like a fiberglass bullet, but so black it seemed to absorb light. The windscreen was opaque, hardly distinguishable from the body of the cowling. Feet moved the thing to the road, then disappeared under the cowling to pedal away.

Laurel said, "Willie, could you put your mantis in an enclosed space? Like a gallon jar with a lid?"

"I've got her a tank. I could put plastic over it, but maybe she'd smother."

Little Red asked, "How big is she?"

"Maybe a foot since her last molt."

"Can you tell us where the things are, then take her outside?" Laurel asked.

"She's not going to addict you so quick," Willie said. "I can leave her for whole days."

Little Red sighed. "Go check her. We can wear nose plugs."

"We'll still hear her," Laurel said.

"Why are you so upset?" Willie said.

"We don't know where they come from," Laurel said. "We tried to see what the Feds knew and they've got it narrowed down to a couple of labs. Some recombinant DNA lab is doing pirate work.''

"Maybe they just mutated,'' Willie said. "I'll put her in the bathroom and put a wet towel under the door.''

Laurel helped Willie get his bike out from the van, then waited at the door. Willie saw an almost invisible membrane tear away when he pulled the screen door back. Remembering booby traps, he wanted to scream and duck, but Laurel rubbed the door jamb with her hand, then spun the membrane into a thread between her fingers.

"Ours,'' she said. "We got it off before you came home from Roanoke.''

Willie went in and found the mantis waiting in the dining room for him. It had pushed the tank cover aside and gone foraging for spiders and cockroaches, judging from the husks it left on the dining room table. It raised its arms toward him—spiders and roaches weren't enough. Willie lured it to his forearm with a mantis kibble and walked with it perched on his wrist to the bathroom. He opened the tub tap just a little so water would drip, then set the mantis down on the tub edge.

Waves of happiness washed over Willie. He had new friends, an adventure, a mantis. First laying down a few more kibbles, he remembered to wet the towel and sealed the mantis in the bathroom.

The air outside the bathroom seemed lonely. Willie walked back to the door and said, "You can come in now.''

The nose filters made Little Red and Laurel look like pigs. Willie wondered if he should be hanging with such people. He let them in anyway. They followed him in to the dining room. Little Red stared at the walnut cupboard under its cheap paint. He asked, "Why the paint?''

"Underneath's walnut. Too valuable for a drode head to own,'' Willie said. "I was supposed to sell all my assets that weren't utilitarian.''

"That's a linen table cloth,'' Laurel said. She went close enough to see the mantis's dinner remains and stepped back. "The mantis runs loose?''

"She pushed the tank cover aside,'' Willie said. "Mostly she eats kibble, but she gets insects from time to time. That's why I could stand to have her around. She kills dangerous bugs.''

"Oh, I feel better already,'' Little Red said. "So, let's see what you've got that you want to sell.''

Laurel asked, "Where did you get a linen table cloth?''

"Been in my family long as the walnut cupboard. Got a chest of linen made back in the 1890s.'' Willie saw that Laurel didn't approve of mantises eating on linen, but then he didn't understand why she was so squeamish. Willie unlocked the closet that lead to the space between the ceiling and the rafters that wasn't quite an attic. "In the summer, I don't go up because of wasps," he said. "You have to climb up the shelves and then go through the trap door."

Willie began climbing. Little Red followed him. They got all itchy from fiberglass insulation. Glass wool ran up under their fingernails as they pulled various curios out from where Willie had buried them.

"Damn," Little Red muttered.

The biggest pieces were in the basement in the old water tank. Mantis gas settled down by the bathroom water pipes, so by the time Willie and Little Red finished getting the big pieces out, they were both laughing.

"You gonna put the tank together again?" Little Red asked.

"No, gonna leave it like I burglarized myself," Willie said. Both of them held onto the standing Buddha and laughed.

"Mantis tranquilizer goes in through the lungs, doesn't it?" Little Red said.

"You lose lot of the effect if you don't take it by nose. Goes in the little gizmo inside the nose that picks up sex pheromones. Guess I should have caulked better," Willie said. "It's not so bad, is it?"

"Mantis usually give off this much?"

"Must be pissed, getting locked up in the bathroom like a bad feist dog," Willie said. Little Red shook his head for some reason. Willie wondered if Little Red knew what a feist dog was, sure he did, coming from the country where men keep the little rat-and-ankle-gnawers.

They heard wingcase music and paused for an instant before continuing up with the Buddha.

Laurel had cleaned off the dining room table while they were gone. "How come they don't put other people in with you?"

"Veterans get to keep their houses."

"This is your house?" Little Willie asked. "You've got title to it?"

"Why, yes," Willie said. He felt proud. "The country does well by its veterans."

Laurel said, "They let you keep your house."

Willie didn't know what precisely in her voice made him feel foolish. Little Red said, "Amazing all it takes to make someone happy."

Willie said, "How much are you going to give me for the Tibetan stuff?"

Laurel and Little Red unwrapped all the different artifacts and lined them up on the dining room table. Willie wondered if Laurel would clean up this mess the way she cleaned up after the mantis.

Little Red said, "We'll give you half of what we get for them, or seven thousand dollars right now. But how would you account for it?"

"Jones gave me sixty dollars for one of them," Willie said, lying slightly. "You're not a better deal."

Laurel said, "Willie, we won't cheat you."

Little Red said, "And we'll add a bonus if you let us read you."

"How will you give me the seven thousand dollars?"

"You'd prefer that to a share in the sales?" Laurel asked.

Little Red said, "He doesn't want to see us again."

Laurel asked, "You want the money in cash?"

"Well, I can't hardly take it in something I've got to explain."

Little Red said, "We'll give you ten thousand dollars on a traveler's card. If you let us read you."

"I don't know." Willie wondered if getting money had been all there was to his plan. Scrounging around for the little bits extra, having a dream in his head to make him think he had a goal. Now, confronted with $10,000, he realized he didn't even have a way to keep it safe. Today, it might be his $7,000 to $10,000. Tomorrow, anyone could take it away. If he enrolled in a study program, someone might wonder where a welfare drode head got $7,000 in cash. He could pick up five, ten, even fifty from time to time. No one expected drode heads to be honest, and the law didn't mind as long as you kept the theft petty. But serious money? Willie asked, "How much do training institutes check where the money came from?"

Laurel said, "Willie, what is it you want to do?"

Little Red said, "He wants to feel like he's not just another drode head."

Willie said, "I'm not just another drode head."

Laurel said, "There's no such thing as just a drode head."

Willie remembered the men who put the war machines together. He said, "I could learn electronics and fuel cell maintenance."

Laurel said, "Anything legitimate, you'll have to give them test scores, references. And are you going in with the drode holes or a cheap wig?"

Little Red added, "Nice wig goes for around six hundred dollars. Operation for the drode hole would cost you most of what we're offering."

Laurel said, "Or you could let us invest the money for you, come in, let us read you. Then, after a year, we'll take you with us."

Little Red asked, "Have you discussed this with anyone else, Laurel?"

Laurel said, "It's been discussed."

Little Red said, "He's not one of us."

Laurel stepped over to Willie and took his head in her hands, whipped off Willie's wig, and bent Willie's neck to point the drode holes at Little Red. "You want to tell me he's not industry-damaged?"

"Sure, but he didn't sue."

"They said what I faced was a hazard of war. I couldn't sue." Willie twisted his head out of Laurel's hands.

Little Red said, "I'm not happy. Willie, if you trust me, I can give you fifty bucks a week for three years. You'll have some extra, but not so much as to attract attention. If you get robbed one week, you'll still have more fifties to come."

Willie picked his wig up off the floor and said, "Laurel, you're a bitch. Now I've got to sterilize it."

Laurel said, "I still want to hear what you plan to do."

"Why should I tell you? If you can't protect your friends better than to get them raped and fucked over, shit . . ."

Little Red said, "My offer still stands."

Laurel said, "But we want to help our friend. Eventually, you'll get a brain infection. You won't live to see sixty. The Feds are working out better links, subdermals, but you won't get one. You've been used up."

"I didn't realize I'd come into money this fast."

"If anyone audits your daily memories for this period, you're going to forget we helped you with the art and discussed this. I can say I've got so much and you've got so little that I decided to help you out."

"How am I going to account for my stuff being missing?"

"You'll remember that it was stolen."

Willie realized they could have stolen it for real. But they hadn't. He remembered the brain pattern, the contact with the woman. "Give me time to decide."

Little Red said, "We've got to take the stuff with us now."

Willie knew Little Red thought he was a loser who'd thought the world had been fair to him because he got to keep his house. "I'll take the fifty dollars a week, but out of half of what you sell the stuff for." He stopped, wondering if the house was worth killing a drode head for. "If I help you, will you take the drode out when you take me with you?"

Laurel said, "We'll do our best to help you. Now, I've got to rework the memory lock before we leave today, so come back out to the van." As they walked to the van, she continued, "After you've come back from Roanoke, spend some time before talking to Little Red. We don't need the information instantly. Don't establish a pattern."

Willie sat down under the squid and got to remember what they'd agreed on when he walked away. If he was audited, the memories would dive, but he'd remember again when he saw Little Red. Right now, Willie both trusted Laurel and wondered if Laurel ran a brain program that made him trust her.

Walking back to the house, Willie felt like he'd been shot and was now dead, but the body didn't know it yet. The old Willie died under the squid, but then a man couldn't live for a house and an insect.

Willie hunted for the brain pattern the next time he was under the wires, but she wasn't online.

When he got back to his house, the walnut cupboard was gone, leaving a clean triangle of pine boards covered with things that had been in the cupboard. Willie stared at the old letters, farm ledgers, and broken dishes piled on the floor and wondered how he'd held onto the cupboard this long.

The mantis crept out from under the plastic covered sofa to greet him. One wing was broken, sticking off at right angles to her body. She tried to move it.

"Hell, baby, you'll have to wait to next molt to sing to me," Willie told her. He found scissors and clipped the wing at the break. It oozed bug juice at the veins, then the juice hardened. He could remember the deal he made with Laurel and Little Red. He hadn't been audited. Once they had his stuff, they'd stopped watching his house. That pissed him off, but they had saved his stuff long enough. Now he wished he'd sold them the walnut cupboard, too.

The thieves came in wearing nose plugs, but they couldn't afford not to hear. They broke the mantis's song wing. Willie visualized big men in ski masks, nose filters white in the gloom. The plasma center bitch told Jones where he lived.

Still, Willie went back to the plasma center because he never quite believed Little Red would continue to pay up. An audit would send Willie's memory of the deal way down and how'd he know what Laurel did would make the memory come back? Everyone cheated Willie. He would try to cheat them back. He knew the plasma center bitch set him up, but he'd have to spend time finding a new plasma center that wouldn't report him.

The plasma center bitch asked, "What more do you have to sell Jones?"

"Got robbed," Willie said. "Tell Jones he owes me for the walnut cupboard and I didn't appreciate him hurting my mantis, either."

The bitch said, "Welfare people not supposed to have equity over thirty dollars in furniture. Welfare people not supposed to be selling plasma either.''

She sat him down in a different chair, one rigged to go manual. Willie pulled his arm away from her needle. She was looking at him like he was dead and didn't know it yet. ''Chair's broke today, so I gotta do your plasma in the machine in back,'' she said. ''So we're using an old chair.''

Willie realized she'd planned to fuck him with wrong type red blood cells in the return, shock him out. The mechanical chairs always gave you back your own cells, type O-positive for Willie, but mistakes could be mixed with a general centrifuge.

''I'd better not sell, then,'' Willie said.

''Better never try to sell plasma anywhere,'' the bitch said. ''Nobody gives a fuck about people who sell plasma illegally.''

''You doing me a favor telling me there's a blacklist.'' Willie left and walked over to the restaurant where Little Red held court.

Willie said, ''I nearly got killed over a walnut cupboard.''

Little Red said, ''Willie, order whatever you want to, my treat.''

Willie said, ''Good of you. I ain't gonna sell my blood no more.''

Little Red looked as if he were about to ask Willie why he'd sell plasma now, but he just closed his mouth, shrugged his crooked shoulders and bought Willie a Mexican pizza.

That night, Laurel read Willie in the restaurant's upstairs room. Willie woke up with fifty dollars in his pocket.

When Willie walked down the stairs into the restaurant, the counterman looked up from the glasses he was washing and grinned big and sexual, like Willie screwed Laurel.

A year of this, then Willie would become yet another person. He'd saved his life today, though now he realized he'd been stupid to go back to the plasma center, stupider to ask to be paid for the walnut cupboard.

At home again, he cleaned very carefully around his drode holes.

SIX

BABY BREAKDOWN

I spent the next week about ready to look for a mantis. Baby Lucinda squalled and bit every morning when her mother went into her weaving room, but I quickly learned to take her out for a walk, pushing a stroller with the other undocumented workers. I wasn't the only one with a cheap wig.

No mantises had come this far west yet.

I stayed off Shattuck Avenue, off the bulletin boards, worried that the hackers knew where I lived and would try to get me again.

Some time later, George Reese said, "You look better."

"Thanks," I said, wondering if he planned to make me feel worse.

"The child seems to like you."

"She stopped biting after Wednesday." I looked down at the crescent of baby teeth in the web of my right hand. Once she realized I could pick her up and hold her off the floor indefinitely, and would every time she bit, she stopped.

"So far," George said.

I said, "You haven't turned me in, have you?"

"No. Do you want to be turned in?"

I didn't answer.

"What were you running from?"

"My former principles, maybe." I felt slightly guilty that I wasn't grateful to George for providing me with a home, understanding after I'd gotten myself screwed.

"You should hire me to be your lawyer," George said. "I have some criminal practice," George said.

"So . . . let me see . . . if I hire you as a lawyer, then whatever I tell you is privileged information, right? So they can't bust you for harboring me? Or can they?"

"And you would be working for me to pay your fees."

"Do you do a lot of immigration cases?"

"Perhaps I have," George said.

I doubted he could play with the Feds quite so neatly. "So, how do I hire you?"

He pulled out a contract that would take five dollars a week out of my salary forever.

I said, "What you're really doing is reducing my wages." On the other hand, five dollars a week would almost be worth it to see him realize what he'd thought was a simple runaway turned out to be a fugitive terrorist who'd run out of an informant training session.

He said, "Is the money so important to you?"

"I like having options."

"There's always prison, isn't there?"

"No, actually not. I'd agreed to work for . . ."

He put his hand over my mouth and said, "I can't hear this unless after you sign the contract."

As soon as he pulled his hand away from my mouth, I said, "Feds. You heard it."

"Fine. Would you like to leave now? I'll have to fire you for failing to show proper ID."

Well, I'd had my bravado moment. The streets were mean. I had only the money the hackers gave me for making myself available. The baby hadn't bit in a few days. I could live with this.

I signed the contract, rolled my new fake prints on it. Reese said, "I don't suppose I'll find you on any Census records."

"No, I'm a rebuild."

"So, how did the Feds turn you?"

"I was supposed to go up with a mini-nuke in southern Louisiana, but they rescued me. They didn't mean to rescue me. I agreed to go hunting for them, someone who was making big seductive mantises. Improving insect lungs, giving them pheromones that tranquilized humans, fucking with insect neurotransmitters. Seemed like we had common cause, going after some mad scientist. Then, I was doing these training exercises on evasion. So far, they haven't caught me. They swore to Amnesty that they wouldn't gun me down.''

''I see. As your lawyer, I could call the Federal Bureau of Investigation and arrange a surrender. But if this is a training exercise, why not see how long it takes for your trainers to find you?''

Yeah, and maybe the Feds got a kick out of seeing me raped by hackers and living as a babysitter. ''The people training me were military. Somewhere north of Camp Mackall, I think, in North Carolina, east of Fort Bragg.''

''Did you intend to go up in the mini-nuke explosion?''

''No. I didn't know a mini-nuke was in the car.''

He said, ''Do you want me to arrange a surrender?''

''Oh, damn, I don't know.'' Shit, for all I knew, he could be another part of my training exercise. The hackers yet another. Bastards. Or was I being paranoid? *'Is what we faced a conspiracy or just sets of unlinked actions based on what most of our opponents believe in?'* Who'd said that, Jergen or Joe? ''Maybe you're one of them, too.''

''Have you considered the possibility that I could represent eco-terrorists?''

''You could. But you don't call them eco-warriors or eco-defenders, so I rather doubt it.''

''Allison, you could agree to take a scan to prove you didn't deliberately set the nuke.''

''I've done that already.''

''Your people must have suspected you could be unreliable.''

''Guy who recruited me works for the Feds now.'' *Thanks a ton, Jergen, for not putting me on the hunt list, too.*

George shrugged slightly, lips twitching in an echo of the shoulder movement.

I said, ''Damn, thanks a lot.'' I was feeling angry again, happy to have that emotion back. Me, against the world. Of course, the world would win, but I'd be damned memorable.

''Do you think you can continue to take care of Lucinda in the house? I don't want you outside with her if there's a chance you might be busted violently. Are you going to stand calmly when they come to get you?''

''They swore they wouldn't.'' Stand calmly, not struggle? Make sure they got Lucinda back to the house? Hell, I didn't know.

''Do you want me to call Amnesty and tell their lawyers where you are?''

''Is that safe?''

"They're lawyers."

I laughed. "Sure, if I'm gunned down, let's have Amnesty protest. Lucinda's going to start biting me again if I don't take her for walks."

"You're good with her. You'll find a way to pacify her."

I thought about letting his daughter chew on his skull. "You're advising me to continue the training exercise, then?"

"I don't see why not," George said.

I couldn't stand this life forever. If they haven't caught me in another month, I'd turn myself in. "Thanks. Now, you know I'm not a serial baby-killer."

"Or a thief."

I didn't tell him I had been one. We nodded at each other, him putting the contract away, me leaving a poorer woman, but weirdly relieved to have told someone.

The next day Ethyl went out, leaving me and Lucinda in the house. When she came back, she gave me a real human hair wig. Behind her eyes, my story seemed to be playing—nukes and rape. George had told her I was pitiful, not dangerous. Oh, pity, I hate you, I thought a second before I decided to be grateful. We recycled the hacker's wig through a polyester bottle shredder.

Lucinda bit me when she found out I wouldn't take her outside anymore. I found that pushing her around the house in her stroller was an adequate substitute. If I pushed fast. I could also balance her on my feet, me on my back holding her hands in mine, and throw her onto a sofa—leg lifts with child. She giggled down at me and screamed with delight as I hurled her through the air.

Here I was, in a new body looking thirty-five at the oldest, stubbly head, in a house constantly disintegrating around me: baby shit, vomit, coffee grounds, textiles turning into lint and rags, dust settling, fermenting garbage in the worm bin, fruit flies looking for leftover apple cider in the bottles in the recycling bin. Every morning, I pulled off Lucinda's messy diapers, put them in a pail for the laundry service. During the day, most of the time, she used the toilet.

Like other people concerned about saving the pieces of a disintegrating ecosystem, the Reeses maintained an endangered species—a greenhouse orchid. Their yard was a Xeriscape. They did not waste water rinsing out the bottles they'd recycle, either.

Were these the people I wanted to be when I grew up? Lucinda ran shrieking into the greenhouse and pulled down three slabs covered with orchids and tried to eat the pseudobulbs. She looked up from the fat, swollen leaf stem she'd bitten into and said, "No."

I felt the orchids would have been safer in an intact Indonesian rainforest, but extinction is forever. I took the orchids away from Lucinda, wondering if George would notice the baby bites on them.

At lunch, I said, "I'm sorry. Lucinda got into the greenhouse today. She pulled down some plants."

George said, "Orchids are used to having primates and other mammals run over them."

Ethyl said, "She could have been poisoned."

George said, "They're not toxic."

Lucinda said, "Daddy, Momma, Ah-ah, no."

Once they figured Lucinda called me Ah-ah, George and Ethyl called me Ah-ah, too.

"Are we going to miss Ah-ah when she goes away?" George asked Lucinda.

"Ah-ah go?" Lucinda asked back.

I remembered a cat who also decided it was the center of the universe, with less evidence. I said, "Allison will probably leave someday. Big men will come take her away."

Ethyl said, "If they show up, you'll have to go outside to deal with them."

"Ah-ah's going to bring in the fruit now," George said.

Lucinda watched intently as I peeled a banana for her. She probably figured it was a pseudobulb and if she'd only had the peeling concept that morning, she could have gotten to what was good to eat in an orchid. She reached for the banana, said, "Ah-ah, me do."

I gave her another banana, but her fingers were too weak to pull back the peel. I cut up the first banana and put a few of the slices on her plate.

George and Ethyl didn't watch. They were talking about machine war somewhere, maybe Asia.

"Ah-ah, do you think Lucinda's learning to talk on time?" George asked as I picked up the fruit peel and cores for the worm bin.

Don't make an issue of the name, I told myself. "I don't know."

"You've taken care of children before?" Ethyl asked.

"No."

"How did you get out of that? Since you weren't really a drode head."

I almost said, *I ate them,* answered, "The ecologists I knew didn't believe in having children. Sometimes, I wished we weren't the top predator on the planet, had something that would get enough of us so that we could be humans full out and leave the finer details of ecological maintenance to the ecosphere.''

''We're only having one,'' George said. ''But I have clients who've had more. And a welfare rights organization is pushing to allow welfare women to have more than two children.''

''Why? Are we running low on drode heads?''

Ethyl said, ''We're compassionate people. If children are a comfort to welfare mothers, then perhaps we should allow them to reproduce more freely.''

''We're like coyotes. We're stress breeders. We need an efficient predator who tranquilizes most of us before it kills a select few.'' Perhaps that wouldn't be enough.

George said, ''How did this get started?''

I said, ''You asked me if Lucinda was learning to talk on schedule. I said I didn't know. Why should I know?''

''Child care is commonly available work.''

Unspoken was *for people like you.* On the other hand, I thought as I fed the worms in the composting bin, they were trying to make me an expert in something, allow me my competence. As I went back to clear the plates from the table, I said, ''I don't remember when I learned to talk. I didn't go to the orphanage until I was eight.''

None of them said anything. The two adults were busy trying to figure out how to fit me into their conceptions of themselves as good people.

Had Jergen said, ''People who see themselves as good can be ruthlessly brutal to anyone who opposes them''? Or had that been Kearney? Both my sides—eco-radical and military—seemed more realistic to me than this exploitive liberal couple sitting while I cleared their plates.

They kept Lucinda with them in the media room while I washed the dishes in the grey water system. The bitten orchids would get the microscopic food scraps.

Things could be worse. The orchids could be extinct. I could be ashes floating in the Gulf of Mexico.

If the ecosphere is trying to put runaway stress breeders back in balance with the rest of the planet, how will she do it?

Worrying worries itself out. One day, Lucinda and I took a nap against the heat-storage wall behind glass on the south side of her home. We'd brought in a feather bed and a down-filled comforter. Trombe wall, I remembered from my ecology lessons. We were so warm, we didn't need the comforter. Lucinda's warm body curled against me. To her, this must seem like hiding, a secret place south of the Trombe wall, behind windows suspended over the hill's slope. I wondered if I dared to fall asleep, breaking the windows would be so easy.

Winter turned to spring through that one clear day. Lucinda was the reality cats imitated, a human baby needing love and cuddles, a human woman finding power and value in that need. Was Lucinda really so awful?

I tried to remember my mother cuddling me.

What was so wrong about a house full of Trombe walls, greenhouses, and worm bins perched on an earthquake hill?

I tried to imagine the present-day population of California housed in Miwok bark-slab cone houses, those slab-walled teepees I'd seen in a museum exhibit. Fifty million people would have to heat with wood, all the women out grinding acorns. We'd exterminate the trees. And the pollution would be terrible, millions of pounds of fly ash, carbon monoxide, phenols.

Did Lucinda's mother have to let other women do this cuddling by the Trombe wall, to avoid being tempted into yet another child? Micromanaging the ecosphere is so unnatural. Evolution led us to freefall whoopie with the machines.

Could I stay here and let this child substitute for what I had aborted, what my mother gave away?

Lucinda asleep was so very tempting. Jergen's wife had two children.

But I knew Lucinda well enough to know not to fall asleep. I propped myself up on one elbow and watched traffic in the streets below. All present vehicles from the lowliest open frame bike to the most luxurious of natural gas autos fought entropy, were engineered by law to last at least twenty years.

We were better than we used to be, but . . .

You can get used to anything. Jergen had told me that, not Kearney, and I'd thought he meant me in particular, not any human being.

I wanted to refute him before I sank into this role forever.

Ethyl said, "When she was first born, when the sun shone, I took her to the front of the Trombe wall and nursed her."

In space above ground, the Miocene female apes nursed babies that led to us.

But ultimately, the innate patterns weren't enough compensation. I was bored, edgy. Could I love this baby? Should I run farther? Where was the person who could teach me how to operate as a runaway drode head? Had the orphanage, the hacker rapists, and the good liberals sucked out my brains? On my day off, I called Fort Bragg and asked for a Captain Kearney at a training base north of Pinehurst.

They got the public phone number and asked me to wait. I stood exposed by the phone, waiting for the hunters to come down on me. *Should have called Amnesty first,* I supposed.

Why was I doing this? Answer, the military had the bigger gang. I was bored. I hated being tempted by a baby.

The phone rang. I picked up. Kearney asked, "Allison, why are you calling?"

"Why haven't you picked me up by now?"

"So, you're in California. We haven't noticed an increase in eco-crimes." He both sounded like he was joking and like he was concerned. Had I really gotten away? Was this call really stupid? Kearney said, "What have you been doing?"

"Babysitting for a lawyer. I'm his client, so he can pay me less and all that."

Kearney said, "Do you want to stay there?"

Revenge. "Kearney, I got hacked and raped by some teenage jerks. I'm going nuts from boredom. I don't really expect you poured thousands of dollars into my head to leave me on the streets as a babysitter."

"We could bill your lawyer for your modifications. Allison, why did you call?"

"Kearney, when I remember mottos and sayings, I can't remember whether you told them to me or Jergen." I looked around me but saw nothing that looked like quickly-approaching Feds. A woman looked at me, but if no one had looked at me, considering how worked up I was getting, I'd have been sure Kearney had his people in place. "Kearney, what is the real purpose of this training exercise? To see if I really wanted to get away, back to the ecological life?"

"Perhaps," he said.

"Damn, Kearney, I really don't want to be a babysitter for the rest of my life. And I want these guys who hacked me and raped me."

"We saw that in a probe, but we couldn't trace it." So Kearney hadn't been able to find me. I'd just given myself away. I felt like an absolute idiot. Then Kearney said, "You want us to bust those guys?"

Yeah. I pounded my fist on the wall. "Yeah."

"They can't go to trial."

"Oh, man, I don't want them to go to trial." What I wanted was their white eye lenses covered with blood, their cocks skinned and balls crushed.

Kearney didn't say anything for a moment. "What did they look like?"

"Fake businessmen with white eyes. Cables against the eyecovers. Young guy who pretended to be old, pretended to be a sociologist."

Kearney said, "O . . . kay. Yes, we think we know who that might be. Yes, interesting by-catch here."

"Kearney, when are you going to pick me up?"

"Who are you working for?"

"Lawyer named George Reese."

"Stay put for a while. We've got a few days to check out the boys and set things up. Then Mike and I will come get you. We'll let you see the bust."

"You mean I'm not surrounded by people already."

"Allison, you called me."

"Yeah, I did. What of it? I couldn't stand the waiting."

"What if you'd really gotten away?"

"So, did I? I sure didn't escape a job the orphanage suggested to me."

"All that's important is that you called me."

I felt at that point as though I'd been pinned in the searchlight again, stripped naked, grabbed. "You want to hear it? Fine. I'm busted down deep to the bone now. I crave to work for you."

"Give me the number where you work. We'll call you when we've set up the hacker raid."

"555-6788." I tried to hang up the phone, but it missed the cradle. I fumbled it back in place, and walked down the street, feeling numb. I doubled back a few times to see if I'd been followed, but they could be working relays on me, one follower per block.

I'd busted myself.

"Yesterday, I called my control officers," I told George and Ethyl as I served the family breakfast.

"I wish you'd let me do that for you," George said. "After all, I'm your lawyer."

"They're letting me stay until you find someone else," I said, not really sure I should tell a lawyer that the Feds planned a lethal bust on the hackers. I looked forward to seeing hacker blood. "Why don't you go through an agency and get someone legal this time?"

"I have good instincts for the right people," Ethyl said.

I worried that the hackers might run if they noticed my job had come open. They'd never bothered to come after me. I didn't know whether or not they knew where I worked, if they'd bothered to hack me for that, or if humiliating me once was enough. Maybe the trace scared them off?

George said, ''What did you tell them about me?''

''I said I was your client.''

''Military intelligence?''

''I got routed through Fort Bragg.''

Ethyl cut through her tofu so fast the fork clicked the plate. Lucinda didn't say anything, just looked from adult face to adult face.

The rain seemed unclear as to whether it was heavy mist or falling drops. But then it was like Berkeley to call weather mist, as if admitting it rained as much as it did would dissolve all the metaphysics that held the town together. I called the day rainy when the Reeses let me open the door to Kearney and Mike.

Mike said, ''We brought you a change of clothes. God, that looks like a real human hair wig.''

''My boss-lady bought it for me.'' This was extremely awkward. I felt like I'd been a bad girl and was now sorry. I also felt like a fool. ''Come in. The Reeses reprogrammed the house tonight to let in two men if I verify them. House, verify these two men for tonight.''

The house voice asked them to put their palms against the palm plate. Kearney and Mike did. I wondered if I'd been shifting from foot to foot ever since I answered the door.

Mike said, ''How are you?''

''You want me to be honest? Half of me wants to be kicking and screaming.''

Kearney asked, ''Are you sure you want to see us bust them? It will be a replay of what we did to Martin Fox.''

''Why didn't Jergen turn me in?''

Kearney said, ''We got his cooperation by letting him leave one person unidentified. He explained a little about you, though.''

''He nearly got me killed for that favor,'' I said.

Leaving the guys in the living room, I took the clothes into a bathroom and unwrapped a package of subdued natural fibers: tweed suit, long silk undershift, bra, cotton panties, leather shoes with real leather sock linings. The only synthetics of the lot were the pantyhose and raincoat, both of microfiber. No, in the raincoat's folds, I found a rainhat, also microfiber. Rain-repellent, cloth like a fine poplin with a slightly greasy feel, the coat and hat looked like something Ethyl might wear on an average day out.

I wondered if the Feds had tracers in these clothes. I laughed out loud. They'd gotten inside my skull.

The clothes closet trash stayed wadded on the floor while I put the wig back on. Ethyl could deal with the charity rags. Ethyl's wig I'd keep. *Fuck, she bought me the wig. I ought to be more considerate than to leave clothes for her to pick up.* I took the second-hand store clothes to the washer. Mike followed me. He said, "We could buy you a new wig."

"It looks like a good wig to me."

"You don't have any bad associations with it?"

"The hackers left me with a twenty-dollar bill and a cheap polyester wig. Ethyl bought me this one."

"I'm sorry. You're good at evasion, but I guess you didn't know the drode head/hacker problem. We should have taught you more."

"What is the problem? Is it like between open-frame cyclists and country dogs, real serious for bike riders, but nobody knows his dog crashes bikes when he's at work?"

"Yeah." If Mike knew that problem, he'd ridden open-framed bikes. I could get to like my control.

"Ready?" Kearney asked. "Realize what we're going to do?"

"Yeah."

"You could stay in the car."

"I want to make sure it's them," I said.

Kearney said, "Don't identify with them."

"I'm with you now. I called you, didn't I?" I was anxious to get this over with. I didn't want anybody walking around thinking how he'd raped me, how stupid I'd been.

Mike pulled out a regular FM pocket radio and turned to the Pacifica station. Static noises clued him. "We're meeting up with the other units in Oakland. They've rented a warehouse and are advertising for actors."

I wondered how this could be the same hackers, but didn't ask. Mike said, "This is the Bay Area. Lots of non-working actors are dole people. Or you might say, lots of Bay Area dole people are wannabes of various persuasions."

As we got in the car, Kearney said, "I've heard they're thinking of making actors drode heads. They'd get more consistent performances."

I said, "Or the studios could just use computer stimulations."

Mike said, "Whatever, your hackers find all sorts of ingenious ways to get drode-head women."

Kearney said, "We've found out how they break the drode locks."

I asked, "Do I have drode locks?"

"You're a different system entirely," Kearney said. "If I'd have been them, I'd have run my fake interview and put you back on the street. But hackers are so arrogant."

"They did hack your rig in my brain," I said.

We pulled up at a warehouse with huge bronze propellers stacked in the yard. Mike said, "If you don't want to wait in the car, you need a different jacket for this." He went to the trunk and pulled out a bulletproof jacket with a ceramic heart insert. I hung my suit jacket on a hanger in the backseat and put on the other jacket.

Kearney said, "You could get hurt."

"I know. But I need to see."

Mike said, "Point him out to me. I'll take care of him." He pulled out a long-barreled pistol with a laser sight. "Everyone will be trying for head shots."

I said, "If they know we're coming tonight."

"Hackers don't hack without body armor," Kearney said.

I'd never heard that. Kill those hackers before they spew their secrets and mine in public trial. We left the car hidden behind the marine propeller warehouse. Kearney went out first, his coat flapping. Mike watched him, then said, "Let's go, but we don't want to catch up with him. Other teams will converge at the site."

I wasn't going to feel clean until I saw the little freak dead. "Mike, I want to get that bastard."

"I'll kill him," Mike said. If he'd said, *I'll kill him because of what he did to you,* I'd have felt manipulated and doubly used. Mike would have seemed cheap, but the way he said what he did seemed almost like *I'll kill him cleanly. You'd torture him.*

Mike stopped and hugged me, reminding me bitterly of how eco-warriors hugged before and after monkey-wrenching. He checked his watch. We stayed plastered body to body for a few moments longer, then he said, "Now," and we ran to a warehouse where men knocked the office door down with a pneumatic sledge.

The building itself seemed to say, "Everyone on the floor, hands behind your back. Anyone moves, we shoot." Bam, we were in, running. I smelled medicine in the air, and fuck-or-kill lust hammering in my cunt. Testosterone. Or an analog that worked as an aerosol. The raiders and hackers hammered into violence on testosterone, ignoring surrender.

Two lights pinned a slight teenager, aging his face with cross-shadows. He looked caught in lust. "That's him."

"Bitch." The boy fired at me, bullet clanging against the heart shield. I went down, furious and bruised, sliding sideways to get my head under cover. But even laser sights need steady hands, and the boy couldn't paint a point. Mike lifted his gun slowly, moving his own light dot up the boy's body. At the throat, Mike squeezed a redder line from clavicles to jawbone, skipped, and finished with a shot between the eyes.

Kearney brought up a live white-eyed hacker, dressed in black, fake bohemian this time, not businessman. The hacker was crying. He looked all of eleven.

Mike said, "If it's okay with you, Allison, we'd like to see if this one will tell us how they did what they did."

I said, "Are the others all dead?" The rest of our team went through the bodies on the floor, cuffing them all with disposable cuffs. The surviving drode heads could go home. "How many other hackers were here?"

"We got five."

"I don't remember more than four, counting the fake doctor." I walked over to the fake Dr. Karen's body and rolled it over with my new real leather shoes. Yes. I looked at Mike. He'd killed for me. Yes.

The baby hacker said, "I'd just joined them."

Kearney said, "I don't think he's old enough to rape, either."

I started to kneel by Karen's body, but Mike came over and stopped me. "It's done. Are you hurt?"

"Bruised," I said. I kept thinking, *Mike killed my rapist.* I knew he hadn't done it for me. In fact, if I looked at the incident more callously, he'd done it to me. But my ovaries were thrilled. *Mike killed my rapist.*

As we walked back to the car, I asked Mike, "Will you turn the baby hacker the way you turned me?"

Mike said, "It was an emotional night, wasn't it?"

"Logically . . ." I couldn't tell him that emotionally, I felt like part of the team now: Kearney, Mike, me, bonded by revenge killing. They'd got Martin Fox, now my rapist. But logically, I was still someone they'd turned, not someone who'd grown up on their team.

I also realized I was more bruised than I thought I was. "Oh, man, he got me over the ceramic shield." We sat in the car, waiting for Kearney. About fifteen minutes later, he climbed in the driver's seat and said, "Allison, you okay?"

"Bruised."

"You want us to stop at a hospital? You could have broken ribs."

"I just want to sleep for a few days."

"Mike, look at her when we get to the hotel. Let me know if we need a medic."

We had a suite at the hotel, two bedrooms. Mike took me into one with twin beds, eased my flak jacket off with trembling hands, then helped me pull the shift off. I couldn't raise my arms over my head.

The bra opened in front. Mike touched gently, pressing. "Maybe a rib's broken, but you're not concave. Your breasts cushioned the blow."

I laughed through the incredible sexual tension. "What do you recommend?"

"We'll take a few days off, maybe go to the Sierras. As your control officer, I recommend light hiking at first, then maybe some boulder problems to get your pecs back."

"Yeah, I rock-climb a little," I said. I loved to see guys climbing, their fannies bunching, thighs sweaty, hands white with chalk dust, their vulnerability when they got themselves in danger.

He fastened my bra back up and helped me into a shift. "I'll get you an ice pack."

"I'm tired enough to fall asleep through the pain."

"You'll wake up fast enough if you try to roll on your side," he said. He took a cover off the other bed and covered me, then turned off the lights and left me alone in the bedroom.

For a few moments, I lay under the covers, listening to Kearney's voice and Mike's. Their murmurs made me feel safe enough to fall asleep.

In the morning, I stood minutes under a hot shower, feeling clean for the first time in months. When I came back in the bedroom, I found an open suitcase on my bed. "Do you need help?" Mike asked beyond the door.

"I'll manage." I pulled on a sports bra, then found a blouse that unbuttoned down the front, then pants and silk socks. Moving around loosened up the stiff muscles.

When I came out of the bedroom, Mike handed me an aspirin and a glass of orange juice. Kearney sat in a chair, staring out the window at Coit Tower.

I said, "I guess I'm a sucker for getting rescued."

Kearney turned and looked at me. His lips flattened, pulled back. A smile? A grimace? *Don't you like working with me, Kearney?*

Mike put his hand on my shoulder and turned me toward breakfast. "You look so much more relaxed," he said, lifting metal hoods off plates of eggs, sausage, tofu, hashbrowns, and rice and corn porridges.

"I don't feel like a prisoner now," I said, but that wasn't entirely true.

Kearney said, "He's right. You do seem more relaxed."

I said, "I didn't make contact with anyone in the ecology movement, if that's what's worrying you."

Kearney came over to join us, making a plate for himself from the egg and sausage dishes. He said, "Allison, what happens if someone else rescues you sometime later? Would you just go along with them, find yet another cause?"

Shit. I knew I wasn't gutless, but didn't I have principles? "Kearney, aren't we making common cause against someone who's screwing up the environment?"

Kearney said, "Allison, if we had more time, I'd try to teach you patience, consistency."

I said, "Kearney, you might be right. Maybe I like to do things with a gang, find a social context for being outrageous. But I called you. You brought Mike. Mike killed my rapist. If I wanted to be paranoid, I'd wonder if you set me up for rape, but nobody volunteers to get gunned down to impress a defector. So don't get paranoid about me, okay?"

"You didn't defect," Kearney said.

I looked at Mike as though he'd defend me. He kept eating as though he hadn't heard a word. "What is the point of making me feel shitty about myself?"

"Are you really with us now? At least for this operation?" Kearney asked.

"Yes, I want to get the freak who sends out brain-flattening mantises."

Mike said, "Kearney, we do deserve a few days' leave."

Kearney nodded. I ladled myself a bowl of corn porridge and crumbled a sausage link into it. I tried not to cry, didn't even understand precisely why my eyes were tearing up. Mike looked at me, looked at Kearney. Mike said, "She's okay."

I said, "Don't leave me out." Hardly my own voice, too soft, too high-pitched. Coming out like my mother's voice shocked me, and the tears just rolled. Mike put his left hand over his mouth, thumb against his nose, fingers curled down over the right lip corner, and looked at me. He looked at Kearney. I wouldn't look at Kearney. I said, my voice again too soft, "I want . . . I wish . . ."

Mike said, "Go ahead and cry, Allison. It has been rough."

I ran into the bedroom and cried until I gagged on my tears. Mike came in and patted my back. I said, in my normal voice, "God, I'm embarrassed."

"Don't be. You've been through a lot."

"Kearney doesn't trust me." I felt tears rising again. Utterly disgusting if I cried because Kearney didn't trust me.

Mike stopped patting my back for a few beats, then began again. "Kearney doesn't like running breakaway tests. But you did call us."

I rolled over, my tear ducts finally under control. "Oo-u, my bullet bruise."

Kearney came to the door, leaned against the door frame. "Is she okay?"

"Ask me, Kearney. I can talk."

"Are you okay?"

"I am okay. I got away from you and I came back, didn't I?"

He clicked his tongue off the roof of his mouth, then looked at Mike. I got up and washed my face with cold water, made wads of wet toilet paper to put over my eyes when I lay back down. I said, "I supposed you had some nanomachine in me that would bring me down with excruciating pain if I hadn't called in another month."

Mike said, "All that really matters is that you came back to us of your own free will."

Kearney said, "I'm going to arrange our leave. How well do you climb, Allison?"

"When I was in shape, low Class Fives. I don't know what I'm going to be like now. Prison stole my form."

Kearney said, "Oh, I don't think so, Allison. I'll book us time on a Yosemite climbing wall." He picked up a phone and called Bass.

I said, "Yosemite's going to be ice-climbs only this time of the year. Or cross-country skiing." My bruised muscles couldn't take that.

Kearney said to the phone, "What climbs are available in Yosemite tomorrow through the next week?"

The machine must have echoed my information. Kearney said, "What indoor walls in the L.A. area would be available next weekend?" He listened to the machine, then said, "Yes, book three climbers on Class Five to Five Point Two climbs for Agora Hills Rec Mall next weekend." He turned to us and said, "They also have an indoor trail if we can't get time on an outdoor trail." He turned to the phone again and said, "Before the weekend, what Southern California trail time is open?"

Mike said, "We're here. We could do Mount Tam."

Kearney said, "We don't have a record for her doing anything in . . ." He stopped. He was right. I'd never spent much time in Southern California. Earthquakes could protect the ecosphere there.

I said, "I've never been on an indoor trail. Is it a virtual reality trail, or would we walk through real air?"

Kearney said, "Okay, book us for four days of hiking at Agora Hills Recreation Mall, with a day afterward for climbs."

We'd always sneered, my fellow eco-warriors and me, at indoor/outdoor recreation, but I wanted Kearney to seem less nervous about me. And I couldn't be tempted into running again. The Feds could control all the exits. Besides, I'd never been able to afford a rec mall before and I was curious.

The mall, a mile and a half long, ten stories high, loomed over the other buildings in the area. The outside looked as though some giant had cut slices of El Capitan, Seneca Rocks, and other famous climbing walls, and made them into building veneer. All of the building was covered with climbers, supreme advertising visible from the freeway. We parked in the underground garage and took an elevator to the forecourt.

Looking more like a real mall, the forecourt was filled with restaurants and branches of Gucci, L. L. Bean, and Orvis. Behind the forecourt I saw the entrance gates. Tennis, swimming, and weightrooms in the basement, a velodrome on the roof. I walked up to a diagram of the hiking trails. They'd folded them through the building so that the mileage was staggering. Besides the outdoor climbing walls, we could climb on rope-length climbs throughout the building.

The only thing that appeared to be missing was loose rock at the climbs' bases. Oh, well, talus mainly served to sprain ankles, and the mall couldn't afford the insurance.

I wondered what the lighting bill was. Some of the trails were advertised as caving experiences, so they didn't get the full-spectrum fluorescents and hologram walls that the fake-outdoor trails got.

I said, "This is insane."

Mike said, "It spares the real wilderness."

The trail guide told us that we'd see three species of cave fish in the caves, four species of endangered butterflies and their host plants on the Coastal Trail, and a Pacific Northwest rainforest complete with salamanders and banana slugs. Real, not virtual or holograms.

I said, "If it spares the real wilderness."

Kearney said, "It's more like a zoo, okay, but extinction is forever, and this way the animals pay their own way."

"I won't say more. I agreed to come."

Kearney picked up fanny packs with snacks, water bottles, and a sweater. We wouldn't carry sleeping bags or a tent. No stove. Nothing for the evening meal. I put my pack around my waist and entered our trail head between Kearney and Mike. We'd hike to our campsite, where little robots in the walls would pop out to supply us.

The air inside the mall was purer than the air we'd been driving through. We went into a tunnel of plants, walking on what looked like real dirt and rock.

Kearney kicked a rock overhanging a too-round cavity. "It's an earthquake shelter," he said. "The pod supposedly could resist the building collapsing on it."

Every fifty feet, I saw some clever way to disguise earthquake protection. Wonderful clever apes that we were, the pods gave the hike a subliminal thrill. We weren't just mall walking. We were exploring our human-ness in earthquake country. The walk was inside us, the plants and animals imported by us to entertain us.

The campsite had all our night supplies. Mike and Kearney checked to see if the tent had been set up properly while I found the small hatch for the food and cookstove and the larger hatch for the campsite's earthquake pod. In a strange way, I felt I'd come home again, to the machines.

Mike said, "I suppose this annoys you, Allison."

"No, it's like walking around in the collective mind of Southern California. When I was a kid, I loved malls."

Kearney said, "It is a mall, really, isn't it?" He pulled his sleeping bag out of the tent. "If you want, we can call for a movie. The screen is on the ceiling."

"Why not?" I said.

Kearney said, "Allison, you're full of surprises." He didn't sound too happy. He said to the air, "Movie menu."

The plants around the ceiling faded, only holograms. The ceiling screen flashed scenes and titles of the movies that we could watch instead of constellations. I said, "Anything that's not a nature flick."

We watched an ancient movie about a German submarine. I thought the Germans had been our enemies in that war, but here they were suffering like heros.

After the captain died, I lay back, thinking of how a person had to have some status in the world to care about things like honor and name. Maybe not, the guys I knew who stole for a living cared tremendously about their reps. I thought at one time I'd like being the best sex display on the machines. I said, "Who shoots me if I don't work out?"

Kearney said, "I do."

I sat up and looked at him. He sat up, too. Mike stayed on his back, looking from one of us to the other, and back, as if he was watching another movie.

I said, "Nice to have that cleared up. And if I work out, and we get your mad scientist, what next?"

Mike said, "A house, me if you want, kids if you want. Passes to RecAmerica malls everywhere. A job. We can train you quickly through the head set."

I wondered what they'd offer the mad scientist. No, that one would die. Couldn't afford to have hackers taking notes on improving bugs.

In the night a skunk tried to steal our food. I woke up to the scuffling, Kearney about to grab it. The machine voice said, in a high pitched excited girl's voice, "No, it's not descented."

Part of the interior adventure was having a fully intact skunk steal breakfast. I started giggling like a fool. The lights brightened.

An old hand at this drama, the obese skunk looked up at us, then returned calmly to his meal before waddling off.

Later in the day, Kearney said, "They've got a griz in here, but the path is optional and we'd have to sign a waiver."

I said, "I don't believe it."

Mike said, "I've read about her. They bring in semen from the Bronx Zoo when she's in heat."

Kearney said, "I don't want to see the bear."

Oh, well. We hiked on, did a cave with a swim, goggles waiting for us at water's edge. The cave fish, lateral lines jolted, swam for cover. I stopped at a handhold for a second and saw tiny crustaceans and snails eating a film off the artificial limestone. The filter hummed gently in the background.

By noon the third day, we'd reached the velodrome.

The velodrome was under an air-conditioned bubble on the roof. Kearney bought us tickets so we could sit in the bleachers eating hot dogs and watching bicyclists in skintight shorts circle and pose on fixed geared open machines. Some balanced their machines at almost full stop, moving backward and forward, pedals not moving completely around in either direction.

I said, "What happens to them if the big one hits?"

Mike said, "They're on top. They can ride off the rubble."

Kearney said, "No, they'd probably die."

I said, "We'll only have a day to get back," then realized we were only six stories up, just a short walk if we did it on staircases.

Kearney said, "We're going to go back on a route that has some rock scrambling on it. I thought we'd see how your shoulder muscles recovered."

I flashed on Kearney with his fingers up my snatch, feeling for a suicide kit. Having Kearney along inhibited me with Mike. Putting my hands on the bleacher seat in front of me, I tried a mini-pushup. ''They're better, but I'd better stick to climbs that don't require a lot of upper body strength.''

Kearney said, ''If you like, we'll give you a pass to a rec mall in New Jersey. Keep you from being too bored on your off-weeks.''

''Bored?''

''Time to think about your assignment. You'll be under the wire in shifts of two weeks, two weeks off. You're going to be aware of what's happening when you're under the wire because we want you to be able to react quickly if the insect hacker figures out what you are. We're not sending you in to die. But, then you're going to have to have some cerebral cut-outs because you'd go nuts just lying there for hours on end, processing data. Still, you'll need a violent activity outlet. We're going to arrange that you win a free membership. Drode heads love to win stuff. The government and companies that use them sponsor raffles. And you'll have a transportation pass on a seat-available basis just like a real drode head.''

Mike said, ''We've got to introduce you to drode head culture when we get back. I'm sorry we didn't sooner.'' He sounded apologetic, but he could have faked it.

I shrugged, leaned forward, and tested my chest muscles again, then said, ''I almost could have stayed with Lucinda. Odd.''

Neither of them said anything. Kearney ordered us each a beer before we began our descent to the next campsite and the hike to the climbing walls outside.

''If you've only got one shot at El Capitan, you practice here until you know what you're doing,'' Mike said as we waited to be assigned a wall. ''And your experience at the real face is enhanced because the park's not crowded with several thousand other people.''

Maybe this was Mike's joy, rock climbing. I said, ''There are some real climbs in the East, Mike, if you're really into this. We could go up to the Gunks, down to Seneca Rocks.''

Mike said, ''Drode heads can't afford East Coast climbing time.''

Kearney got our tickets and led us to the north face of the building. I didn't recognize the mountain, but it looked like artifical conglomerate, smooth fist-sized stream pebbles in a matrix of sandstone turned to quartzite. Kearney pushed buttons at a waist-high display and three top ropes dropped from ledges and the roof. One rope reached us, the others reached only to higher ledges between us and the roof.

A human guide came out with our climbing harnesses and rock shoes.

''No,'' I said, ''I'll just watch.''

Kearney waved. A pair of guys in chinos and tee shirts split off from the crowd and came up to us.

I said, "Don't you trust me?"

Kearney said, "I'm too tired to want to worry about it." The guide clipped a mike to the top of his shirt, then fitted Mike.

Mike said, "Do you really like watching other people climb?"

"Yes, especially if they're guys."

One of the guys in chinos handed me a pair of binoculars.

They went up the first climb without a fall. In another fifteen minutes, Kearney and Mike rejoined us. They looked a bit bored.

Mike said, "Can we do one without top ropes?"

The guide said, "You'll have to sign another waiver and put down a five-hundred-dollar deposit."

Kearney flashed some ID at the guide. The guide nodded, *okay, you guys don't need that,* and fished in his equipment bag. He pulled out a belay plate and locking carabiner. "We've got two Class Five Point Three climbs and one Class Five Point Six set up for belays. Bomb-proof belay stands."

Mike said, "We'll take the Class Five Point Six. I'll lead."

Kearney looked at Mike as if calculating their relative weights. The guide ran the biner and belay plate through a scanner, to see if they were sound, then rigged Kearney to catch.

I was sorry now that I hadn't at least tried the top-roped climb. The top ropes retracted. The guide pushed some buttons on the controls. A line of white light resembling the printed route lines in climbing guides ran up the building. I looked at the line through the binoculars. It resolved into dots of river cobble turned electric. The guide said, "After you get off the ground, the belay stands are here, here, and here." The face flashed dashes of green across the white line.

I said, "Isn't making this so safe and predictable a subversion of the very reason to climb?"

Kearney said, "Obviously, Allison, this is a surrogate adventure."

On belay.

Climbing.

At the second pitch, after Kearney hitched himself in and propped his legs against the belay foot braces, Mike started climbing again.

The earth swayed a tiny bit. A microscopic earthquake tumbled Mike off the wall. Kearney caught him.

But Mike hit the wall hard enough to bleed. I put up the glasses and watched Mike's face, his eyes squeezed shut, his lip and chin cut. Kearney lowered him to the belay point. Behind Kearney, a square of the rockface pulled back.

The guide said to me, "Do you think he'll want to finish his climb?"

"That was an earthquake, wasn't it?"

"A little one. Maybe a Richter three. It must have startled him. Maintenance says nothing happened inside."

I wondered how many people ducked into the earthquake pods. "What about the guys inside?"

"The building's so long, it dampens the waves. Probably only noticed it here and on the south wall," the guide said.

In the circle of binocular light, Mike stood up and stared at his right hand. He must have caught the wall with it. His nose also bled. He seemed to be saying something. Kearney unhooked from belay and stood up, too. They went in through the square hole by the belay point.

One of the other guys said, "Pity about the earthquake. Mike's a better climber than that."

The other guy said, "Universe is out to get us."

I thought, *now we're both bruised, me by hackers, him by Momma Gaia herself.*

The guide said, "If you like, we can meet them in the infirmary."

The infirmary was behind an unmarked door by the food court. The people inside hadn't noticed the quake at all. Maybe all of Southern California should be put in long flexible buildings, headed north on granite floats.

In a few thousand years, they'd be in Oregon. What we now call Oregon.

Mike sat on an examination table, his left hand holding a sterile dressing against his nose. The physician spread the injured right hand on a plate, then wheeled a scanner up. Mike looked at me and said, "I generally don't come off Five Sixes."

"We had a little earthquake," I said.

The physician said, "Can you remove your shirt?"

Mike could, with a bit of help. His right shoulder was bruised, too. I'd never seen him this close to naked before. I hoped he had no broken bones in his right hand.

Kearney looked across Mike's body at me. I couldn't read his eyes, but I began to be embarrassed to be looking into them. I looked at Mike's hand.

The physician said, "Nothing's broken. I'll tape your wrist and give you painkillers."

I couldn't look at Kearney, or the other guards. I watched Mike's face. He seemed pale, trying to hide the hurt. *Oh, men.*

Kearney said, "We've got a hotel room for tonight."

Mike said, "It doesn't hurt that much."

I felt like we were breathing in unison, Mike and I. Kearney said, "I'll go get the car."

Wounded guys, yes. Wounded women are too vulnerable. Just nakedness makes us helpless, open to fingers, cocks, plans of eggs and sperms. A guy's skin doesn't have voids to the interior unless it's broken. A woman with broken skin is scarred, sexually damaged, but not a guy.

I was going to fuck Mike tonight if he was at all able. Now I said, "Is your nose okay?"

He pulled the dressing away and said, "I'm just bruised."

The physician said, "Lie down and I'll check that." He washed Mike's nose carefully, then greased a probe, pushed it in one nostril, then the other. "Light doesn't show anything serious. I'll try ultrasound."

Mike said, "I'll get it checked when I get back to the base."

The physician poked around Mike's shoulder, then said, "You waived liability. Who do I bill?"

Mike reached for his wallet and showed the doctor his ID. The doctor scanned the ID with another light wand.

That night, Kearney left Mike and me in the motel alone between nine and whenever. As soon as the boss was gone, I asked Mike, "Do you need a massage?"

"A careful one," Mike said.

We examined each other's bruises. Mine were fading, a yellow under the skin. We breathed at each other, hands careful. We had sex gingerly, the threat of getting so emotionally ripped we'd lose control and hurt each other an added excitement.

In the morning, Kearney woke us up. He gave me a hard look, to the face only, then said, "Mike, is everything okay?"

Mike smiled, carefully. "Yes."

Kearney grunted and left us. Before Mike dressed, I ran my tongue around the bruise on his shoulder.

He said, "So it took an earthquake?"

"Kearney expected this, didn't he?"

"Not the earthquake. But we both knew you had to make the first overtures." Mike let me help him put his shirt on. He flinched slightly when I touched his shoulder. I almost said, *You look good in bruises,* but sensed that would come across too kinky this morning.

Mike said, "Heroes are often injured before they triumph."

I thought, *So he sees himself, not me, as the hero of this adventure.* "You're the control officer, so you must be the hero, right?"

"Right."

"You're not that injured. Maybe this will turn out to be a comedy."
Ah, fuck, why had I said that? Mike turned away from me and, despite
his bruises, got his shoes on, laces tied. If this was a comedy, then was
I the fool?

At breakfast, Kearney said, "Enough fun. We're headed back east
to put you in place."

"Training first," Mike said.

"The training will be a real drode head orientation," Kearney said.
Machines and I always got along when I was a kid.

SEVEN

ADULT CHILD, PART TWO

The second week in May, Dorcas got a fax photo at her house from her father. He and her mother sat crosslegged in front of their mobile home, a wide muddy river behind them, the light dim. Hanging from the top of the motor home was a huge catfish, lashed to the luggage carrier but dangling to its tires. Across the bottom, her father had scribbled, *Crossing the Mekong this morning.*

Her mother looked younger than ever, but wary. Her father grinned, one hand thrust back against the catfish's head. Another fax came through—the fish had wiggled. Fresh faxes. Dorcas took off her shoes and wondered how the Feds were coming on their DNA audit, if this was a usual audit or if she'd failed to edit the brands out of the DNA she'd used for the mantises. Welfare was assigning her lab a new drode head. This one had been fitted, the welfare office said, with a new model subdermal pickup, one that picked up more brain activity without putting the drode head to additional infection risk.

Dorcas had never heard of subdermal pickups before. Henry told Dorcas that the drode head was part of the audit. Oh, well, she'd be wise to slow down making insects for a while. *Let's see how the mantises and the neuroleptic wasps fare.*

A third fax came through her machine. Dorcas looked at the photos more closely. In the background, across the river, was an industrial plant covered with Japanese and Vietnamese characters. Dorcas faxed them back, *I've only seen photos of those catfish dried before.* If her parents got killed, she'd find out within the hour if their robot monitor could connect to a modem. Everywhere in the world was around the corner from a fax office these days. Everyone could bounce transmissions to a satellite.

In the next three faxes, Oriental women cut into the fish. Her father held up one vertebra without ribs while her mother looked at what the women were doing to a chunk of fish on a charcoal braiser. Dorcas wondered how many photos he didn't send, discarding them as unbalanced or showing grim expressions on Vietnamese faces, perhaps other American tourists.

Dorcas faxed another scribbled note, *It's the largest catfish species in the world.* She wondered if it was endangered.

Her father wrote over the next fax photo, *We're going to fly-fish for Asian arrowana next. Preservation should pay for itself.*

And some people hunt people, Dorcas thought. She waited by the fax machine to see if her parents had more to show her, but in ten minutes, nothing more came through. She then microwaved her dinner. A drode head could be hunting her. Dorcas felt that was weird, like being bitten by a fax machine suddenly gone concious.

Perhaps the drode head was only a conduit, not a concious hunter. Perhaps Henry was the target. Henry should be.

Dorcas was curious, though. How did the Feds recruit a drode head for undercover work?

In the morning, Dorcas called for the new drode head. Allie, new or fake model, came in, wearing polyester slacks and tunic, but a real human hair wig. Dorcas wondered how a drode head got such a wig. Allie took off her wig and looked at the helmet and read couch. Dorcas noticed that she had scars on her hands, broken fingernails.

"What do you do when you're not here?"

"I climb at a rec mall in New Jersey. I won a pass."

Dorcas had a former lover who had a permanent ten A.M. to two P.M. Saturday pass to the Gunks, climbing cliffs near New Paltz. She'd gone with him once, passing two rec malls on the way up. "I've never been to a rec mall."

"I didn't until the lottery," the drode head said.

Dorcas said, "Have you ever gone climbing in free air?"

"Why do you ask?"

"I just wondered."

"You need to chat with a drode head you're going to lay out unconcious after the chat?"

Dorcas felt bold. "Are you part of the DNA audit?" She wondered
if the Feds knew Henry found out about the audit or if they'd told him
they were auditing the labs.

"What DNA audit?" If Allie was a psychopath, not just someone too
dumb to earn her own living, she could beat a lie detector, voice stress
analyzer and all. Dorcas realized what she should have done was to have
gotten the drode head under the reading helmet, then hacked her.

No, the Feds would wonder why. Dorcas should get someone else
to hack Allie's system. "You seem different than the other drode heads.
. . . Should I have used that word?"

"It's what the State made me, isn't it? I use the word myself."

"Well, it's rather crude, don't you think? I'm a little unsure how to
use your system. How much access do I have?"

"If you're real curious about drode head life, I'll throw up me and
my lover."

"You have a lover?"

"Yeah. We lead ordinary lives when we're not paralyzed in a reading hood."

"What do you mean, ordinary?"

"Like we cook, clean house, ride around on the subways on a space-
available basis. Go climbing. Go to Coney Island."

"Yes, you get free unlimited transportation passes."

"Bull. It's space-available. You just hear it's unlimited because the
system wants you to hassle drode heads for being freeloaders."

"Aren't you being a bit paranoid?"

"I know what my pass is. I know what you just said about thinking
it was unlimited. Someone lied to you."

Dorcas said, "Henry said he thought you were part of the audit."

"I'm not. Why would I lie?"

"How would you know? You aren't supposed to remember."

"New equipment. Some things leak through. Actually, other drode
heads tell me it's not that uncommon. We don't remember real accu-
rately, you understand, but we get images here and there. More with
me. Because of the new equipment."

"How did you get to be the one used for this new equipment?"

"Unluck of the draw, I guess."

"How did you manage your electrodes before?"

"Didn't have them before. This is a post-prison gig."

"Oh." Allie was a sociopath, then. "How long did it take you to
get caught?"

"Years," Allie said. "You want action video memories? I could
make you virtually me."

"I think you're part of the audit."

"What's this audit?"

"They're checking the DNA stores to see if we've used some we've not accounted for."

"When you can just make it fresh from any tissue sample, some gene breakers, and a splicing computer, only I understand it's not just as simple as snip and paste. The bits got to work in synergy. Maybe they're trying to see who acts nervous, Dr. Professor."

"I'm just Dr. Rae. Not a real professor. How did you learn this?"

"Someone taught me. If you don't keep getting postdocs, you could end up under the wire, too."

Dorcas said, "I have independent money."

"So, do you want me to lie down and entertain you? You got work for me? Or am I a guinea pig for liberal guilt?"

"What were you in prison for?"

"The badger game."

"What?"

"Whoring illegal, really just pretending to be an unlicensed whore, then ripping off the fool johns."

"People generally only go to unlicensed whores for . . ." *rough trade*. Dorcas stopped her tongue in time.

"Well, me and mine were meaner than they'd expected. You could learn from me about handling men."

Dorcas resented that. "I knew some of you were unemployable for other reasons than stupidity."

"We are employed. You don't admit it. We come too cheap."

"I should report you to Welfare."

"Do that. Or put me under the wire so I don't have to be here talking to your face."

Dorcas realized if she didn't come across like a guilty liberal, she'd come across like the one nervous about the audit. "I've always been curious. I'm sorry if I pried."

"Hey, we both got ahead for being promising and cute. I got caught. You got your position. Under Henry, right."

"How do you know about Henry?"

"Everyone knows."

"You're very brazen, but I do have a post-doctoral position and you did get busted."

"Like to humilitate drode heads? You can have me limp and down anytime you say."

"I feel like I ought to see you as people, but it's hard."

"Why?"

"I've been using you as terminal links since I was a kid."

"You plural? We're not all alike."

Dorcas felt like a guilty liberal. She sighed a little. "Does it hurt?"

"Scanning? A little claustrophobic, but I loaded a few movies before I came in. You won't need my whole brain."

"You're the first drode head I've really talked to. Maybe exposed electrode connectors made me squeamish." Dorcas felt that neatly combined liberal guilt with a need to know more about this woman. "Can we chat more?"

"Sure, anytime."

"How did you get started in the badger game?"

"It was a family tradition. My brothers were the screaming husband and his friends."

"I didn't know families like that still existed in America."

"Lots of things still exist in America you don't get on the news nets."

"I'm going to do a literature search. You want to lie down?"

"Not particularly, but as I said, I brought a few good movies."

Dorcas resented that she didn't get the drode head's entire cerebral function. But no one did. Drode heads kept their concious personalities for off-duty. "Slide under," she told Allie. *I've never known a drode head's history before. Hardly even their names.*

Allie slid into the helmet. Dorcas activated the circuits in the helmet and watched Allie's body go limp. *Motor cortex out, involuntary breathing muscles still going, like dream sleep. Poor tough bitch, to come to this.* Dorcas said to the unconcious but processing ears. "I want a literature search of all projects involving attempts to prolong human life from last year on. Look especially for projects that disappeared."

Let's get Henry in trouble.

Allie's voice said, "You don't need to worry about me now. I'm safe." She sounded tender.

"What?"

"What?" Allie's voice sounded flattened, a voice from the computer/brain complex, not a personal voice at all. "Ah, Willie." Allie was behind her voice now. "I've got work to do. I'm sure you do, too."

"Allie, did you hear me?" Dorcas said.

Allie spoke in an uncanny imitation of Dorcas's voice, "I want a literature search of all projects involving attempts to prolong human life from last year on. Look especially for projects that disappeared."

The voice shifted back to the affectless one. "Printout or media storage?"

"Allie, who were you talking to?"

"Allison isn't here now. She's in the visual cortex with a movie."

"Who was Allison talking to?"

"Willie."

"Who's Willie?"

"Allison controls access to that file."

"Okay. Will Allison remember this?"

"Allison got bored and went to a movie."

Agh. "Okay, load the scan on a write-overable. I'll take it home and read it later."

The disc drive whirred.

Dorcas pulled the disc out and slid it into her wallet. She loaded a laser disc into another slot and said, "Copy Allison's movie."

"Allison's movie is copy-protected. Its title is *Another Callie and Lelia Rescue.* You may rent it at any Masters of Video store."

Dorcas said, "Could you search for three reviews of the movie, preferably *New York Times*?"

"Unauthorized use of computer time for non-research projects must be paid for by researcher."

Dorcas slotted her credit card into the helmet. "And print out the reviews."

"Turn on printer."

Dorcas said, "Turn on printer." She wondered why the machine couldn't turn itself on, then realized how the drode heads could abuse their systems if that was possible.

Another Callie and Lelia Rescue

NEW YORKER MINIREVIEWS: In the spirit of director Silva Purcell's earlier woman's weepie, *Callie and Lelia,* the eponymous heroines find another wounded male to tend. More shots of beautiful tough women with guns and the wounded male they save, tend, and set free. If you like this kind of thing, it's the kind of thing you like. NEW YORK TIMES: One wishes these women would have the sense to drive off the edge of the Grand Canyon in the 20th Century tradition of women's buddy films. Instead, they rescue a sensitive poet being mistakenly stomped for homosexuality by ugly drode heads. Their wounded pet recovers, screws them both, and drives away into the sunset while our heroines look for yet another male to rescue for Callie and Lelia Three, which one cynically assumes

will be made if this flick is as successful as the first Callie and
Lelia movie. Available on media as of January 1.

MS. MAGAZINE: We hate to admit this, but American women have
a sadistic side, with movies like this appealing to all of us who
fantasize about the open and vulnerable male as a care object.
Director Purcell takes this fantasy to its ultimate, the male, bleeding like a sacrificial object to testosterone poisoning fulfills our
need to have our men reduced to childhood. But bleeding? In the
subtler forms of this trope, the male is psychologically wounded,
is frequently the point-of-view character. His women help him
recover his balance, but he's the center of the female audience's
attention. In late 20th Century films, the wounding became more
physical, bleeding blondes all over the video stores. Women
should not find pleasure in seeing themselves as intact defenders
of damaged fellow humans. This merely reverses the sexual po-
larities, doesn't eliminate the inherent cruelty of reducing intact,
functioning adults to passivity.

Dorcas thought she needed to see the movie and that Allie needed to
see the reviews. She said, "Print another copy. Log all future time to
the university."

Allie's flat voice said, "If it's valid research."

"Literature search. Henry Itaka's publications." Dorcas shoved the
disc with the earlier literature search back into the small disc slot. "Add
it to the small disc."

The drive whirred.

"What is Allie looking for?"

"Allie is with the movie and cannot answer that question."

Is the target me or Henry? Dorcas knew she couldn't ask that without setting off alarms in the whole system. The Feds could be after
both of them. "Literature search: Recombinant work with insects,
publications in the last year."

Was it her imagination or had Allie's muscles tightened, lost their
slackness? "Allie, are you back from the movie?"

The disc drive whirred. *If I kill her, they'll know it's me.* Dorcas
realized Allie wasn't tied down, wasn't socketed to the helmet. Could
be watching through the building security system, could come out from
under the helmet fighting. *I probably can't kill her.*

"Allie, would you like a mantis? One of the big ones? They might
make you feel better."

Damn, I'm pushing it. Damn, damn, damn.

Allie, personality in the voice, said, "No, I had one already."

"What happened to it?"

"I tore its head off. I hate being tranquilized."

"Allie, what are you here for?"

"Slot card for non-research related inquiries." Allie was gone again.

Dorcas stared down at Allie's limp body. She tried not to look at the scanning cameras. *Damn, and what have I told them?*

As much as she's told me. She said, "Open grants search. Biological insecticides."

I'm telling them more. She pulled out her credit card, and said, "General reporting search and literature search. The large neurologically reactive mantises."

Am I self-destructive or what?

Fifty-five major grants for biological insecticides, including ten specifically for mantises with cockroach gene enhancements. Only five articles in the popular press about the mantises.

"I'd like copies of the complete proposals for grants three, fourteen, thirty-seven, and forty-five." Include one grant going against the mantises.

If you hesitate now, they'll know you're responsible. Dorcas wanted a court record search of trials of researchers who'd abused their facilities, but not through this drode head. Maybe the Feds were scanning many labs? Maybe this drode head was only a prototype for a newer model?

Maybe if Dorcas knew more about the drode head's off-time life, she could find a safer way to kill her there. Or hack her.

"Slot another disc."

Dorcas slotted another disc. "I want to look at the grant applications at home," she said, trembling slightly when she heard how her voice sounded. Stress analyzers would have her. Maybe she should play guilty liberal again? She turned off the interface. Allie slid out of the helmet without Dorcas's help and looked at her with aware eyes. "Allison?"

"What?"

"Help me get over my bigotry about drode heads. And I copied some reviews of your movie." Dorcas handed Allie the paper.

"If you were a drode head, you'd understand the appeal of my movie," Allie said.

"Where do you have your rec pass?"

"Out in Jersey, some recycled dump."

"When do you go?"

"When I can get out," Allison said. "You know your boyfriend played nasty games with his drode heads when they were female. Welfare doesn't send him women anymore."

"He said he thought male brains processed faster."

"Bastard wants to make rich people immortal, doesn't he?"

"Yes. It would be ecologically incorrect."

"You are a cute little girl, aren't you?"

Dorcas almost said, *but I don't spend hours limp while other people use my brain as a scanning device.* "Do other drode heads feel like you do?"

"Most of them were never independent operators," Allie said. She looked at the wall clock and said, "You didn't spend much time logged on."

"I was looking for some grants to apply for. You put the information on a disc for me. Thanks."

Allie waved her hands in front of her face as though shooing Dorcas off. "Really, you hate to think of yourself as a bigot. Bet you considered getting me a mantis and all that, pet for the poor drode head."

"You don't want one?"

"Yeah, yeah, shit. Did I tell you . . ."

"Who's Willie?"

"A friend. We meet on the net. He's another drode head somewhere survived enough to learn ways around the system."

"Like you?"

"Shit, if I weren't in the system, I'd be an undocumented babysitter. Sorry if I bitched on you."

Dorcas wondered if the movie had provided enough vicarious power to relax Allie. "Well, it was your first day here. I'm sure you were a little nervous."

Allie put her hands over her face and said, "I hate being helpless."

Dorcas realized it was unusual for a drode head to be able to read texts. "You can read?"

"Oh, yeah. Thing prisoners do for each other. Helps pass the time."

"Did you have any other options besides the badger game?"

"The badger game worked for years."

"You'd get old eventually."

"Then I'd be the mama screaming for the husband and brothers to stop. My mama never got caught."

"I thought prison was supposed to rehabilitate people."

"I'm rehabilitated. I don't con guys anymore."

Dorcas said, "I'll see you tomorrow."

"You think you'll get one of those grants?"

"I generally get one out of eight that I apply for. Henry will be the recipient of record, senior author, et cetera. You know how that goes."

"Nope, but it sounds rotten to me, lab wife." Allie saluted Dorcas as though the postdoc was an officer and went out the door. "See you tomorrow."

Dorcas pushed a light pen against her desk, her fingers sliding down the pen, then turning the pen over, sliding down, turning the pen over. She hoped Henry would come over to her house so they could talk in private. Perhaps the Feds bugged her house. They could write words on their bodies.

But she should call Welfare to complain. Dorcas never met such an aggressive drode head in her life. She picked up the phone and asked to be connected to the local Welfare office.

"Welfare, East Side Manhattan."

"This is Dr. Dorcas Rae. You've sent us a new drode head named Allison. The one with the experimental pickup. I'm getting too much personality."

"Dr. Rae, we'll debug Allison. She's just through indoctrination."

"She told me she was a sociopath."

"Well, yes, but she's nonviolent toward women."

"You normally don't send female drode heads to this lab."

"We've alerted Dr. Itaka. Give the woman a few days to settle down, remind Dr. Itaka she won't be attached physically to the machine."

"I'd like a different drode head. You're normally quite cooperative."

"We're testing Dr. Itaka to see if he's recovered from his idiosyncrasy."

Dorcas wondered if Allie would pull herself out of the helmet and tear Henry's dick off if he raised that polyester tunic. "Why don't you tell Henry that she's not attached to the helmet?"

"We've told Dr. Itaka that he should not molest this woman."

Dorcas wondered why Henry hadn't mentioned that to her. "Thanks."

"We'll talk to Allie and modify her if necessary."

"Thanks."

EIGHT

THE POST-DEATH SYNDROME

She made me," I said. "She knows I'm not a real drode head." Lying on my back after being in the read hood made me claustrophobic, so I mounted Mike, pushing against him with my hands, grinding pelvis to pelvis, not really aroused, feeling him inside me also less than aroused. I would rather have hit him than this. "She knew I was an agent. I was trying to save things, so why did you keep flashing messages to me on the movie screen?"

He put his hands on my bald head. "Let's stop this. You aren't interested in sex. You're mad at me. Let's go for a walk."

I let him drop out and said, "Fuck it, Mike." I pulled on pants, a sports bra, a sweatshirt, the human hair wig Ethyl Reese bought me in Berkeley. Welfare issued me a loft. Who lived there before, I didn't know, but I suspected that my loft, like the neat apartment on the military base, was a material seduction. Slot Mike in the loft, put my favorite foods in the refrigerator and freezer, my favorite plants in the windows, and I'd home in after my day as a data processing unit. Space in Manhattan cost plenty, but these days I tended toward claustrophobia. My head could decompress in a loft. The Feds knew what drode heads craved.

"Do you know how frustrating it is to decide to work for the Feds and have the target make me the very first day?'' I asked Mike when I was dressed.

''I'm here for you. We can discuss it.''

''Control officer.''

''We knew it would be difficult. If you hadn't gotten yourself raped, the helmet would be a little less traumatic, but, hey, you could be dead.''

''The helmet's not traumatic. It's not being able to fool some dumb bitch stuck in continuous postdocs. So, what do you think?''

''We need to scan all labs more often. Bet both doctors Dorcas and Henry use Federal materials and grants on pirate projects.''

''Yes, but it isn't your butt lying down muscle-locked. It's like having nightmares without being able to wake up when I wanna. And I'm not forgetting.''

''See, your prior experiences do aggravate your concern.''

''She could kill me.''

''You'd come out from under the helmet fighting.''

''I didn't in Berkeley.''

Mike didn't answer.

A large hornet droned against the loft glass, bumping, backing off, bumping. Mike and I stopped and looked at it.

''What is that?'' I asked Mike of the hornet.

''I don't know. Some of them carry modified venoms. Maybe it's a drug dealer's carrier gone astray.''

''Manhattan's nuts. People buying and selling pet bugs. Whole neighborhoods of drode heads. Why aren't we living in a drode head neighborhood? Don't you think this will make Dorcas suspicious?''

''Allison, these first days are hard, I know.''

Mike seemed excessively calm, which put me in an anxiety spiral. ''But she made me as an agent. Somehow they knew about the audit. Your security sucks.''

''If she really made you, then pretend to side with her. Tell her the cover story is a lie. Tell her the truth.''

And get gunned down with doctors Rae and Itaka? I should be numb to dying, I'd had so many near deaths. But, no, I wanted to have my own nice apartment, my control lover. ''I want to make her feel guilty.''

''About what?''

''About the way she sees drode heads.''

''Look, Allison, you're not like most drode heads. Most of them are reasonably contented with their lives. We don't let people abuse them. I shot the hacker who raped you.''

Yeah, Mike, but not in time. "I don't like going in and being made as a plant the first day. Then getting some lecture from you when I do what I can to save the situation. I didn't want her to know I knew she knew. Now you're insisting that I shouldn't be anxious."

"She complained about you. Are you sure you're not being a bit abrasive?"

"She knew she had to complain, otherwise we'd know she suspects."

The odd hornet went away. I walked to the back of the loft, fifty-five feet from the window and squatted with my back against the wall, facing the space in front of the window. Mike came over and squatted about five feet away.

"Yeah, Mike, give me space."

"You want to go camping your next free period?"

"Outside or inside?"

"Or have you ever been sailing?"

"No, I never got involved with the whale rescue people." What was this, my interrogation?

"We could sail out from City Island, go to Montauk. I can get us a sloop." He sounded wistful.

Shit, he really liked sailing. "You must want to go sailing."

"Yes."

"And I won't get claustrophobic in some little cabin?"

"The view will make up for it."

"You miss sailing, Mike?"

He looked over at me as though afraid I'd want to deny him a pleasure. "If you don't want to, it's okay. But there's lots of space around a boat."

I was a mean bitch, but I didn't like feeling like a mean bitch all the time. "Okay, Mike, arrange it."

"I was an Olympian sailor," he said. Took me a few seconds to figure out what he was talking about, commercial sports not being all that critical for eco-warriors.

"Gives us both something to look forward to," I said. "So let's go for a walk now." Maybe Mike found monitoring me tedious, fucking me a chore. Old Mike was a controlled control officer, except for that moment when he proposed a sailing holiday.

We took the elevator down to the lobby and walked down to the Staten Island Ferry, then walked along the Battery toward a saxophone's jazz. An old man played under a streetlight, no open instrument case, no sign that he wanted money. Eyes closed, he just played.

Then I saw the cheap wig. A drode head played saxophone while the Hudson flowed to the ocean, bearing ships full of sewage over sturgeon.

We stayed until his eyes opened, focused on my wig and Mike's own hair. The drode head pulled the saxophone out of his mouth and said, "Excuse me, folks, but I wasn't playing for you."

Mike said, "We appreciate it anyway."

"You appreciate whatever you want, don't you?" the drode head said.

I said, "Mike, let's go on, so the man can play alone."

"Sorry," Mike said. After we'd gone fifty feet uptown, we heard the saxophone playing a dirge behind our backs.

"Mike, how often will someone with a job live with a drode head?"

"It's fairly common in Manhattan. Among liberals. But mostly drode heads do marry each other."

"Shave your head, then. Get a cheap wig. We'll be less conspicuous. Or do you explain me to the neighbors as an off-the-books servant?"

"We rented the loft because we thought it would be easier for you. Most agents serving as pseudo-drode heads need space between sessions." Mike said. "But if you really want, I'll have us moved into a welfare neighborhood."

"It's okay, Mike. I just don't like having screwed up so much. I haven't done anything right since . . ." Since New Orleans? Since I was eight?

Ever?

Mike put his arm around me and we walked a looping walk together as though we were stoned or drunk, just being silly like kids who weren't in danger of getting gunned down. We moved uptown. Mike seemed to know where we were going, so I just held on to him, which was rather fun.

We stopped in a bar. Mike had found one filled with a mix of drode heads and working people. One man who didn't bother with a wig was saying, "The Feds provide the garret, the part-time job, what more does a painter need?"

I said to Mike, "Does anyone leave the dole?"

Mike said, "Some of these people are real painters." He steered me up to the bar where a live bartender mixed our drinks. Robots don't have the judgement necessary to handle all of a bar's possible problems.

We couldn't talk about my mission in public. I wondered if Mike brought me here to shut me up, or if he had a non-trig side, bit of an artiste, perhaps. Mike asked, "So, do you like New York?"

I said, "I never lived here before. Closest I came was the Catskills."

"You're from Ohio?"

Ohio—hopeless place for me. "My earliest memories are of factories and scrub pines and oaks. River locked in between dams and factories. People making pilgrimages to various healers and preachers. Cops shooting at us. My Ohio. I don't know if I was born there or not, just most of my memories came from there. My parents drove me across a bridge to Louisville for the Derby. That's my earliest memory, going to the Kentucky Derby."

"You know, all these people you think should have helped you, they're only people. Like you."

I said, "But their parents didn't dump them on the street at age eight." Not a damn civics lecture, Mike, I was beginning to have fun.

"Someone took you to the orphanage. The orphanage fed you, educated you. And I am glad we didn't just lock you in prison for the rest of your life. I'm here for you, Allison."

"No, no, no, I took myself to the orphanage." I smiled at Mike like I'd made a joke, wondering if now I knew too much to live for a court date. Probably. "What do you think happens next?"

"You go back to work tomorrow."

As we walked home, I said, "You monitored the entire session?"

"Yes. Who's Willie?"

"One of the drode heads you had looking for me while I was in Berkeley. He found me when I was getting raped. He was worried about me and got space in the system to come looking."

"Oh," Mike said. "But we used ex-military guys with security clearances to look for you. Well, I worry about you, too, Allison. I can't help everyone who might need it, but I can help you." He opened the door to our building.

I pushed the elevator button and said, "I bet you say that to all your spies."

He said, "Your main bad guys were those parents who abandoned you. And Martin Fox."

"I wondered if they really abandoned me or if they'd left me in the park to get over my tantrum. Maybe they were planning to come back for me and I abandoned them?"

"Allison, I don't know why you need to think that. They could have looked for you. There's no record of anyone trying to find you."

"But I wasn't registered at birth. They were outlaws of some kind."

"So, what kind of parents were they?"

As we got off the elevator, I said, "I don't remember."

Next day, I went into work and played ashamed in front of Dr. Dorcas. I said, "I'm sorry I was so rude yesterday."

"Welfare said you were new at this."

I'd heard that Welfare told her I'd be reconditioned if I gave her further grief, but I didn't say anything, just took off my wig, slid under the hood, and began to watch a movie.

A man slid into a seat beside me. He said, "Don't say anything. You tell them I found you yesterday? Just nod."

I nodded. The movie screen went blank. The man had plastic caps over his drode holes. He looked intensely Appalachian, high cheekbones, thin long nose, thousand-yard stare. If he had security clearances, but was a drode head, he had to be a war casualty.

"Yes, I got hit by hallie bugs," he said. Of course, he could read my mind, we were both inside each other's minds.

"In my private space," the man said. "Are you really okay? Friends of Jergen's want to know."

"Jergen turned state's evidence. Are these friends of Jergen's also friends of Martin Fox's?"

"What are you hunting for?"

Don't think about the mission. I tried to walk away from this man, but he caught up with me.

"Are you going to report me to Mike?"

"Shit, how can I *not* report you to Mike. He's reading me right now. I told him that you'd found me in Berkeley, then again here."

"No, today, as far as he knows you're at the movies. It's very easy to fake someone being at the movies. Easier to fake than being blanked."

A woman with no arms joined us. "I'm Loba, we helped you in the past through Joe and Miriam. Perhaps we can help you now. How happy are you to be working for the Federals now?" She looked Hispanic. Somehow I knew the real woman was small even though in her projection, she looked quite tall.

"They'll audit me. They'll know about you."

"But this will register as your dream tonight. What's so dangerous about the insects?"

How dare they give me dreams. I didn't need more nightmares. "They're an unlawful gene-hack by someone at Rockefeller University, probably funded through a misappropriation of Federal grant money."

Suddenly, we were back in the movie theatre, but watching my capture and interrogation on the screen. Shit, and I couldn't wake up even to be paralyzed and terrified. "Not like Jergen then, not a volunteer. But you don't want to die," Loba said.

"The insects are an ecological hazard," I said. "I haven't sold out completely."

The man, who I knew to be Willie, said, "I love my mantis. She's made me more confident."

I said, "The Feds say drode heads who have mantises become more ambitious. But I hate being drugged, manipulated." The screen showed me killing mine. "Loba, when Jergen turned himself in, you abandoned me. Martin Fox planned to kill me. What was I to do?" I wondered what they'd do to me. I still didn't want to die.

"So what, you're afraid of dying. But we haven't decided what to do with you yet," Loba said, answering my thought, not my willing question. I was back alone in my movie threatre. The screen was playing final credits. Mike subtitled across the bottom, *She's been talking out loud while you were at the movies. She isn't quite sure what you are.*

For a horrible instant, I wondered if Mike knew about the people who'd stolen me away from my movie, but realized he was talking about Dorcas Rae.

I said, "Why don't you just blank me? I'm a bit tired of the movies."

Play possum, why not? I expected a strange dream tonight, and being concious of time passing with people plotting in chronoflow was nerve-wracking.

The last subtitle was *You're right. It would be better.*

I should have asked for this sooner. It wasn't like an unremembered nightmare at all. In the next instant, I was sitting up on the read couch, my wig on, drinking tea. Dorcas must have given it to me before I came back completely. I understood real drode heads spent the entire two weeks they were on in fugue states, even if they weren't under the helmet for all that.

Dorcas saw me look at her and said, "Oh, hi, you back now?"

"I won't know until the end of the two weeks, will I?" I drank the tea. She'd done it the way I usually ask for it, enough sugar to crystallize at the bottom, no lemon or milk. I'd told her even if I didn't remember telling her. I felt naked and helpless again. Maybe the fugue wasn't such a good idea after all. I wondered if Willie and Loba out on the net could kill me with lethal programming or if that was a myth. Dorcas, maybe, would get the blame. But on her own, she could kill me with subtle poisons or malfunctioning nanotech, make it look like an accident. Or Mike could just shoot me. I suspected that lethal programming was a hacker's myth, but the other risks were real enough.

Dorcas said, "I'm sorry if I got you in trouble."

"I guess I deserved it," I said, eating the sugar out of the bottom of the cup.

Maybe the between-sessions fugue was a blessing, like forgetting nightmares. With it, a drode head only went down once into oblivion every month. I suspected my rig was experimental, indeed.

Shit. Maybe Dorcas had no secrets. Maybe the Feds turned me over to Welfare for real?

I finished the tea and wondered if Dorcas expected me to wash the teacups. She put her cup in a stainless steel dishwasher, no, probably a labware washer. I did the same and said, "I wish humans could be kinder to each other," half meaning it, half throwing it out to see how Dorcas reacted.

Dorcas said, "What we need is to be blended back into the ecosphere again, to be just another species among others, not the top consumer."

"How can a human do that?" Perhaps I was on the wrong side here. "I feel like I'm blended into the draft animal population myself, or into the machines."

"Perhaps you're not part of the problem. You welfare people live low on the food chain. If you didn't travel so much . . ."

"The transportation pass? We only get free space when it's available." I thought I'd told her this already.

"Perhaps we all should be more like drode heads," Dorcas said. "Did you consume a lot as a badger game thief?"

My, my, my, drode-headism as environmental stress reducer, I thought. "We had to be careful not to flaunt it."

"What would you like to have that you don't have now?"

"Twenty thousand acres of wilderness with a truly wild grizzly in it," I said, looking at the wall clock. "Shit, five o'clock. I'll have to wait." No point in leaving until the subway crowds thinned out. My pass wasn't good for peak times.

Dorcas said, "I never knew you couldn't ride during rush hours. None of my other drode heads told me this. What did they do if I let them out during rush hours?"

"Nobody knows. The average model's fugued out. Mill around? Go to a special drode head waiting room at Penn Station and just sit? Whatever, they don't remember."

"Some of you won't wear wigs."

"I heard about that in orientation," I said. "It means *eye-fuck hair-heads.*"

Dorcas said, "Would you really want twenty thousand acres of wilderness with a truly wild grizzly in it?"

"Yes," I said, wondering how the Feds would read their audit of this moment. I remembered seeing the last San Juan mother grizzly who would have taught her cubs to avoid humans, to only kill wild things, not men-tainted cattle and sheep. Trappers sent her to a captive breeding program. Her children haunt rec malls.

"Isn't the badger game urban?" Dorcas asked.

"Aren't cities wildernesses for humans?" I countered. "Men are wolves to men."

Dorcas said, "There's no true wilderness now. What we call wilderness existed because we like some of our garden shaggy. No place on earth can resist us."

I said, "We've got technofixes for everything, even for wild humans like I was."

Dorcas said, "Ah," but didn't say anything further for a while. Then she said, "I could get you a mantis, if you like. One of the big ones."

"If you fix it with stimulants, not tranquilizers," I said.

"What's wrong with the present ones?"

I said, "I hate being tranquilized. I tore the head off the one the Feds tried to give me in rehab." I thought I'd told her this already. She obviously didn't listen to drode heads when she made conversation with them, first she'd forgotten about the transit passes, then she'd forgotten I told her this. Or had I? Perhaps I hadn't.

"Yes, now I remember. You told me when you were under the wire. I thought you might have been lying. The Feds are giving them out in rehab?"

"You know, it takes me two passes to make an impression on you. Yes, the Feds brought me one to keep me calm after they busted and wired me. Otherwise I'd have been hysterical for days. You gonna listen to me or you gonna make conversation with a drode head and spend half your mind being satisfied with your liberality?"

"I'm sorry."

"Forget it. I'm obviously a sociopath and the head rig at least makes me useful to the community and all that."

"Allie, is what happened to you why you find wounded guy rescue movies so attractive?"

"Shit, I tell you something when I'm here and you don't listen. When I'm under, you sneak looks at my movies and try to analyze me."

Dorcas pulled her chin back like she was expecting me to hit her. I looked at the clock. Ten after five. Another five minutes, and I might get space on the subway, or I could walk home. Did the hackers we killed in Berkeley have friends in Manhattan? Dorcas said, ''You'd like to leave, wouldn't you? Too far to walk?''

''I'm afraid some guy will play the badger game on me in reverse. I'm a drode head with an expensive wig.''

''We could share a taxi. I'll pay for it.''

Shit, she'd see the loft and wonder what the fuck was going on. No, she'd just see the outside of the building, an industrial building converted to dwelling spaces downtown—store those industrial flesh components in old factory buildings. ''Why not?''

''You think I'll be shocked at where you live?''

''I've got a normal boyfriend. An artist.''

''Is he nice?''

''His trust fund keeps him from being a drode head. Otherwise . . .''

She seemed pissed when I said that, and quickly asked, ''Whose place is it?''

''His.''

Dorcas Rae had a whole house. We drove by it and she pointed it out, then went west and down town. ''How did you find a rich boyfriend?'' She sure was blowing her money on curiosity and this cabfare.

''I actually completed some tricks in my day,'' I said. We pulled up in front of the building. I saw Mike at the window and waved up at him, wondered if he'd signal me through the net in my brain, but no, he just waved. I waved back and got my keys out. ''I'd invite you up, but he hates thinking about what I do for a living.''

''That's okay.'' Dorcas sat in the taxi while I unlocked the front entrance door. The cab pulled away before I got upstairs.

Mike said, ''What was that all about?''

''Dorcas paid for a cab.''

''How's it going?''

''She's finally starting to listen to me. I don't know if she trusts me more or less. Were they supposed to know about the DNA audit?''

''No, but security for you is different from security for a standard audit. If they ask their source in the Lab Practices Bureau, that person won't know about you.''

Turning on lukewarm water first, I took off my wig and leaned my head under the kitchen tap. Rinse that sense of failure right out. Cool that hot brain.

Mike came up behind me and began massaging my neck muscles, then, gently, my scalp. The ever-faithful hunting bitch had returned to her loving master. What he was doing felt good to my body, no matter what the brain's attitude. I said, "She asked me what I wanted if I could have anything at all. I want twenty thousand acres of wilderness with a real wild grizzly in it."

His fingers paused, then continued their soft circles on my wet head. "That really is what you want, isn't it?"

"She pointed out that humans had eliminated true wilderness from the planet. Nothing could stop us if we didn't want to stop."

"Don't you think it speaks well of humans that we did spare some wilderness?"

"We only spared it because it entertains us," I said.

Mike's fingers shifted to my neck muscles, digging the tension out. Oh, subversive tension. He said, "A little more than a week and you'll be off."

"For a little less than three weeks," I said, pulling down a towel and drying my naked head. Mike sat down beside me, gave me a little hug, and turned on the TV to a football game.

I laughed at that domestic cliche—hug woman, watch ball game. I said, "She's the one who designed the insects." Saying it out loud made me more sure.

Mike's head tracked a bit slowly away from the game. "Why do you say this? Could be Itaka. Could be someone who traded material with a Rockefeller researcher, someone at another lab."

I said, "Dunno precisely. But making mantises to calm people down seems like a female thing to do. And she keeps offering me one of my own. Twice, even after I told her I tore the head off mine."

"Um," Mike turned his attention back to the game, then, during a commercial, looked back at me. "We've got to have proof before we can act."

"What will you do?"

"We haven't decided yet." Evasive eyes darted to the left, then came back around to help the face tool up an earnest, honest look.

"What's proof?" I asked.

The game came back on, but Mike, with a grimace, kept most of his attention on me. "She's got to either use you to work on a gene design project for an unauthorized modification, or she's got to tell you she designs the insects and you then follow through on verification, get a story about how she redid the mantis lung, whether the sequences are transferrable to other insects. Try to get her to show you the steps."

"I guess what you really wanted was for her to use my link in a design project."

"Then we've got to be sure she's not protecting Itaka."

I said, "See if he wants to turn her in," and let him return to his ball game. I found a CD I wanted to listen to, plugged in earphones, sat with my back to the wall, and listened to Bach's "Goldberg Variations." No one I'd ever met since my parents abandoned me ever believed I found Bach on my own.

NINE

AEROSOLS AND GESTALTS

Dorcas Rae got another of the new model drode heads when Allie went on break. Normal people didn't use the term break, they said their drode heads were on or off. Funny, Dorcas thought, I'm almost seeing it her way. Being under the read hood is her work. We force work out of people who'd otherwise be useless, Dorcas thought, but Allie's limp body speaking impersonally at her made Dorcas uncomfortable. If she hadn't talked to Allie, if Allie hadn't come back to herself after the sessions, Dorcas could feel better.

The new drode head, fortunately, wasn't a talker, probably born to a Welfare family. Having another drode head relaxed Dorcas, just another impersonal pair of eyes and vocal cords, looking for patterns in the data. If this drode head watched a movie while Dorcas used his visual, she didn't know about it. Dorcas suddenly wondered how was that done anyway? Did the visual cortex timeshare between the drode's personality and Dorcas's commands?

She was sitting beside the drode head, scanning for information on how insects read their visual data when Henry came in. He sat down on another chair and said, "It really is a new system. A couple of labs have them, and the designer published a paper on the system in *Welfare Management and Medical Practices.*"

Dorcas didn't see that proved the new drode heads weren't part of an audit, but then any Federal agency could read a drode head after the fact. Any timesharing on a Federal System—well, the IRS and the various Federal regulatory systems said they didn't access data transactions without a warrant, but Dorcas wondered how one could know. And if hackers hacked your system and Feds captured the hacked material, of course, they had a warrant.

"Do you know any way to erase memory of retrieval and analysis from a drode head?"

Henry waved his hands as if the drode head was listening. Dorcas realized he could be listening, or listened through.

How do I get a wasp to recognize human anger? How do I design a system without a computer-generated model wasp? Dorcas knew wasps reacted when creatures injured wasps, most likely to an aerosol pheromone. She wondered if the pathway could be adapted to adrenalin and testosterone. Dogs supposedly could smell fear, but testing proved the cuing was largely visual.

"Have you got a problem?" Henry asked.

"I wish sometime I had the wiring for direct computer access." And rarely, but sometimes, Dorcas wondered if she wouldn't be happier as a drode head.

"You can always use a virtual rig. Retina painting gives about the same feel, I've heard."

"But virtual is slower."

"Maybe this procedure will be safe enough." Henry waved at the man whose head was inside the helmet.

"Maybe this has always been a way to keep track of how we spend our grants," Dorcas said.

Henry said, "Are you interested in coming over tonight?"

"For your wife's party? Henry, I don't think so."

"If you don't come, people will talk."

"I think you want to gloat at both of us."

"Dorcas, I'm proud of you both."

Dorcas remembered that Allie called her a lab wife. She didn't reply to Henry for a few moments, but signed out of the system instead. The drode head pulled himself out of the helmet, sat up, and blinked at them.

"I'm through for the day," Dorcas told him.

He didn't speak, just nodded and looked for his coat. Dorcas had moved it while he was under and got it for him. Henry didn't speak, either, just watched until the drode head left. Dorcas said, "I don't have a gift for her."

Henry said, "She'd appreciate flowers, I think."

Dorcas didn't think much about Henry's Japanese-American wife. She was Henry's rebuke to his grandfather's people who didn't really believe he could be Japanese. Dorcas wondered if the wife took Henry's Orientalismo seriously, or if she didn't care who Henry slept with as long as she was the legal wife. Because the Wife brought Henry children who looked almost genuinely Oriental, Dorcas knew she shouldn't even fantasize about breaking up the marriage. "I suppose I could bring ikibana shears for a more substantial gift."

"The flower trimmers, not the heavy shears. She's always losing flower trimmers and shears, but I bought a box of shears last time I was in Japan."

"Does she really like ikibana?" Dorcas ran a fantasy through her visual cortex, Henry's wife, in a kimono, stabbed Dorcas with the flower scissors. Or snipped Dorcas's jugular. Dorcas saw herself dying in Henry's arms. Or alone in a corner while all the other partygoers concocted a story to protect the Wife. Flower scissors, wouldn't the Wife know then that Dorcas and Henry were lovers? No, all she'd know was that Dorcas and Henry talked about her.

"Of course, she likes ikibana, she's Japanese."

But then, Dorcas wondered, why is she always losing the scissors and shears? "Flower scissors, I'll come."

"Good," Henry said. "That means all the lab postdocs and professors are coming."

Coup for you, Dorcas thought. How much madder should people get before her wasps stung them unconcious? Dorcas wished she could run an aerosol analysis now, her anger just under the threshold. What was she giving off that would trigger wasps?

Perhaps, she should modify people, have them give off the pheromone that drew wasp attacks when they got too angry. What was too angry?

Dorcas went downtown to an orchid and ikibana shop on Varick St. She realized she was near Allie's loft and went by, curious as to what the wild drode head did in her time off.

The bells to the various floors weren't marked. Dorcas stood looking, trying to figure what floor Allie pointed to. A man came out of the building. Dorcas asked, "Which loft belongs to a man living with a drode head?"

"I'll give him a message. Who's looking?"

"Dr. Dorcas Rae. Actually . . ." Dorcas almost said, *It's the drode head I'm looking for,* but somehow this sounded too quirky, somewhat perverse. *More perverse than buying sharp edges for your lover's wife?* "I'll try back later. Just say Dr. Rae called."

"They're off sailing," the man said.

"Sailing?" Dorcas could imagine a drode head in a recreation mall. She couldn't imagine a drode head sailing. Sodium and chloride ions could corrode the connections, but then, the new system didn't expose the connections. Sailing drode heads. She wondered if they could be connected to the sails through a computer, adjust the rigging as the wind pressed sensors on the main sail, the jib. One person could run a schooner, perhaps, with the right sensors and computer. "I suppose a drode head could make that easier."

The man smiled and said, "I'll tell him you just stopped by."

"I . . . sure."

Henry's wife had a Japanese name, but never used it, preferring to be called Mary. Even Henry complied, and the house only looked Japanese in the Style Memphis, industrial metals with bast fiber cushions, flower arrangements in stainless steel pots that seemed vaguely medical. Mary answered the door herself, looking young after her second child and first nanotech rejuvenation.

Dorcas came inside carefully, the wrapped flower scissors against her midriff. She thrust them out at Mary who said, "So glad you could come. Henry says your work is quite good."

"Thanks." Dorcas wondered how long she'd have to stay to be polite.

Mary smiled and took the present off to a stack of presents on the dining room table. She told Dorcas, "Drinks in the kitchen."

Dorcas went in to the kitchen and saw Henry making drinks. He smiled at her and the men standing around him also smiled, *Wow, what a guy with his wife and mistress in the same house.*

"Gin," Dorcas said. It seems cheap enough.

"We've got some genuine juniper gin," Henry said.

"Okay," Dorcas said. Henry handed her a glass of white spirits which she knocked back in one slug. The liquor tasted of red cedar.

Henry said, "George has gotten a tenure-track job at Minnesota."

Dorcas couldn't remember which other postdoc was George, but a guy who'd always volunteered to escort visiting professors smiled and nodded.

George said, "They're giving me my own lab. I'm bringing one of my grants."

"Hope you don't freeze your balls off," Dorcas said. Had Henry suggested that she not apply? Or had he made dismissive noises?

George said, "I knew I ought to be in a tenure-track job or in industrial research before I'd done too many postdocs. One can't afford to do too many. Industry's nervous if you look too eager to be an academic and our colleagues tend to wonder if a scientist doesn't get on with his career. If this hadn't come along, I was going over to private industry.''

Dorcas said, ''But it did,'' and left them talking in the kitchen. Just after she turned back, she heard a burst of laughter and knew she'd amused them.

But they don't know what I really do. I'm the Mantis Mother.

Dorcas wandered around the house and discovered that Henry and Mary didn't keep any endangered species at home. She now felt put-upon that Henry boarded his sperm-donor Peregrine with her.

Mary found Dorcas in the master bedroom. Dorcas cringed, expecting a confrontation. Mary smiled and said, ''Women like you are so good for Henry.''

Dorcas would have rather been stabbed. ''Should I stay until you open your presents?''

''Guests come and go. If you have other friends to see, I can thank you for your present now.''

''You're welcome,'' Dorcas said. She went downstairs and put on her coat, walked out into the spring night. Her life, not just the evening, felt wasted. No point in saving herself from the street now, Dorcas walked home.

It was spring. Time to make insects. Perhaps the solution wasn't a particular wasp, but lots of them, neuroleptic, addictive, brighter than average, more pesticide resistant. Modify the egg too, so that bigger wasps could come out of them.

Solution to what—human nastiness, of course. Dorcas felt a different adrenalin surge through her, thrill of the object of a chase. If the Feds caught her, she'd have to turn on her own designs. Perhaps they'd kill her, but Dorcas planned to offer to betray her insects. She could get her own lab.

Dorcas thought she couldn't lose.

TEN

INDUSTRIAL DESPAIR AND ACCIDENTS

Willie sat on his front porch with his mantis on his knee, hardly aware of the wind twitching the maples overhead. He wondered if he should be involved with the industrial accidents people at all. How would he sign off welfare if he wanted to? He could talk to his social worker, explain that he'd met people who'd offered to help. If they asked who offered to help . . . he couldn't betray Little Red. His mantis tried to comfort him, but the tranquilizer made him bolder, calmer but bolder.

I wasn't always like this, Willie thought, running his finger down the mantis's wings. He'd joined the army for adventure, got that craving flayed from him. The Feds were hunting the gene hacker who'd made him this mantis, but other gene hackers made the hallucination bugs and the war machines. Nobody hunted them down.

The real war, inside a man's head, went on. Nanotanks prowled his bloodstream, search-and-destroy teams rappelled down his bronchial tubes, ideas that were mere waves of electric potential spied on other ideas, a mash of them in the brain.

Outside, Willie rocked on his front porch in drode head calm. Inside, he raged despite the mantis, or perhaps, because he had been jittery timid and now he was çalmly angry thanks to the mantis juice.

The industrial accident gypsies would use him and leave. Willie supposed they wanted to find out who the insect hacker was. He'd found the Feds' plant. She trusted Willie, sort of. If she could discover who made the insects, if the gypsies could beat the Feds to the hacker, then they'd have their own uses for better insects. Would they leave Willie on welfare when they disappeared?

If the Feds thought he'd tipped off the hacker, helped her get away, he'd be busted. Maybe because he was a vet, they might keep him alive. Or maybe because he'd broken security, they'd throw him in a hallucination bug cyberia. He had a security clearance, that was supposed to make him trustworthy. He'd skinned his cock for his country, but his country expected him to stay trustworthy, trusting.

The mantis kept him from panicking. Willie put the mantis back indoors and rode his bike to Stuart, looking for Little Red.

Laurel pulled the gypsy van up beside him and said, "Get in."

"Why?"

"We need to talk."

"I want to talk to Little Red."

"I'll take you to him."

Willie braked and loaded the bike in the van. He got in beside Laurel and said, "I've been thinking. Do you plan to leave me behind?"

"We can't do that," Laurel said. "We think you ought to join us now. Loba thinks you could work at the informer better in real time, not over the net." She turned the van off and drove through woodlands, not straight for Stuart. "But I've argued that you should go back to your ordinary life. And that we leave Allie alone. So when I say 'we,' I don't mean me."

"I feel sorry for Allie."

"Well, yes, but she could have suicided rather than agreed to work with the Feds."

"Is that the solution you recommend to your own people?"

"Willie, we didn't realize what we were getting you into."

"What's that supposed to mean? I wanted a change."

"You're not really one of us."

"Little Red thinks so."

"Willie, we might have to nanosculpt you."

"Could turn me into a heap of jelly by accident, then."

"We don't use people as tools."

"Oh, really."

Laurel said, "We're debating whether the insects make a good attack on industrial society or if they're part of the problem."

"Allie thinks it's the woman scientist."

"Is this woman a renegade we can use?"

"Use as a tool, Laurel?"

"We feel responsible for you. You could live with friends in New York. But Welfare would wonder why you go to New York so often."

"Hell, Laurel, lots of us go to New York or San Francisco whenever we can. Lots of ways to pick up spare money that way, only my head is locked up. I wouldn't be going that often. I can make contact with Allison in less than a trip or two."

"And do what?"

"Have her bring the insect woman to me."

"What if she decides to turn the hacker over to the Feds?"

"Hacker's giving powers to the non-human. If Nature could take care of herself, you think we'd need eco-freaks and industrial saboteurs?"

"We should sculpt you."

"No, just give me friends to stay with when I'm in the city. I'll bring my own foodstamps and the mantis."

"You can't travel with the mantis."

"Seen some spray advertised lets you carry them around without having the scent tranquilize everyone. Too expensive for Welfare people, but you could get some for me."

"Willie."

"I've always wanted to go to New York and remember it. I think I was shipped out of there on the way to Tibet, but I didn't see enough to get a good impression."

"Willie, we could offer you refuge, now, if you'd let us resculpt you."

"Can't change the brain patterns, can you, and leave me myself?"

"No."

"So, they know me by my brain waves, not my face. Who remembers a drode head's face?"

"Willie, we could merge you with someone else, split the difference. But there are risks."

"I don't wannna be half dead, half in someone else's skull."

Laurel didn't say anything more for a couple of miles. Willie understood that if he'd agreed to that, they would have half killed him without any further qualms. The rule was, *You can't use other people as tools, but if they volunteer, all bets are off.* He was repelled and excited at the same time. Being a drode head was half death, too.

Then, "Okay, Willie, Little Red will strike up a conversation with you. He'll suggest some people who are curious about drode heads in New York, give you an address, wrong apartment. The real apartment is in the building, but you'll ring the wrong bell. You'll ask for Loba. She'll meet you in the lobby. I'll see you there.''

''You're moving to New York?''

''It's easier than having you know more of our faces,'' Laurel said.

''I could shoplift the spray.''

''Don't you have some money from the art we sold?''

Willie grinned. ''Shit, the spray would be a business expense for you.''

''Buy it yourself, Willie.''

''I'm going to be on starting next week. Want me to say hi to Allie for you?''

''Don't. We don't know quite how you're working the system to program these hidie-holes, but eventually, you'll be audited.''

''They had bunches of us ex-soldiers looking for that girl. Why would they think I did anything? I'm an old hacked-out drode head, slacked out with a mantis, poor old Willie with locks on.''

''Willie, you've never traveled much before.''

''Think they keep tabs on all of us? You know who they got to do it? Drode heads. Think we're all so automatic?''

''I know there's a drode head subculture.''

''It's like the olden days' secretaries. Most of us feel inferior and grateful for any handouts, but we stopped getting you coffee.''

''But most of you aren't conscious.''

''We don't remember. Most of us, yeah, but amazing how many of us are allowed to correct for data slop.'' Willie thought he'd said too much to someone who wasn't herself a drode head.

Laurel said, ''The hacker keys in data on a private machine. She wouldn't do work on a public system.''

''But she's got to fish data out of public systems from time to time. Why don't we approach Allie's scientist directly? If she's making the insects, we tell her to run with us because the Feds are a day away.''

''No, Willie. If she isn't the one, or if she's got other plans, we've told the Feds we exist. She could trade us for herself. The Feds would love such a deal.''

''I think this woman would love to work with us.''

''Us? Yeah, Willie.''

''I'll have tacos tomorrow for lunch, then I'm going to be back under for two weeks.''

''I'm curious. Who takes care of your mantis when you're gone?''

''Automatic feeder.''

Laurel stopped the van in Stuart and helped Willie with the bicycle. He asked, ''Couldn't I ride to New York with you?''

"No, Willie, because we're going to stay for a while and you're going to go back to your read head after the two weeks off are up."

Willie realized they'd want to discuss him in the van. He wasn't one of them. He'd never sued the people who damaged him.

ELEVEN

BECOMING A DRODE HEAD

I didn't instantly become a cultural drode head just because computers could scan my head and exchange data with me through VR goggles. Sometimes, I wanted to know the culture of what I'd become. Was there a drode head resistance? I'd fought the world that made drode heads all my life. I sure hadn't planned on being a cooperative drode head.

What Mike offered me next was his most serious seduction—respite, a rocking boat. When we sailed out from City Island, except for Mike, my life on land disappeared.

We put on hooded wetsuits against the cold water and set off under motor through the wide channel between Hart Island and Hewlett Point, putting the little islands on our left. I looked behind us and saw bridges and city, the forested chunks of Pelham Bay Park. Then Mike switched off the motor and taught me how to handle the rope that controlled the small sail with no boom in front of the main sail. "Sheet, not a rope," he said. "Jib sheet." He controlled the main sail sheet and the tiller himself. Sailing was like climbing, the one who knows the most leads.

We maneuvered up the Connecticut coast, anchored in the suburbs for the night. The next day we stopped for lunch at a yacht club in Guilford, the marshes protected down to the shore, the coastline studded with pilings that had once been docks. Ducks and geese flew over us, around us. I watched a mute swan drown a native duck.

"Mute swans mate for life," Mike said.

"They're supposed to be in Europe," I said.

Other than that moment, I wasn't anything but a woman with her lover on a boat. Mike was right about the space around us making up for the cramped cabin, but I wanted to leave the Sound, go out to the ocean, keep moving.

But finally, a week was enough for a first sail. When we could see City Island and the Throgs Neck Bridge, Mike switched on the outboard motor.

"I've got another week," I said.

"Your woman scientist dropped by the loft while we were sailing," Mike said. "The water will get warmer."

"Everyone wants to go sailing when it's warm," I said.

"We could get away from them on the ocean," Mike said. "You did good for a first-time sailor."

"I've climbed before. Both are rope handling."

Mike looked at me funny, but we were fast approaching the boat's berth. Mike gave me the boathook and yelled over the motor, "Go to the bow. Pick up the buoy line."

I fumbled it, and Mike had to reverse and fuss. Next pass, I caught the line. Mike cut the engine and came forward. He said, "Keep us from banging into the fenders."

Fenders? Right, the bumpers on the dock. We fussed the boat back into where we'd found it tied up, then sat apart for a few seconds to catch our breaths and settle our tempers.

"Did you like it, overall?" Mike asked me.

"Yeah, except coming back. Don't yell at me like that."

"I'm sorry."

I went back into the cabin and got my duffle bag, then Mike came down for his. As we changed into street clothes, I said, "You've got a radio on board."

"Yes," Mike said.

I realized he'd have to, both for boating news and for military communications. "Well, it's nice that the wet suits have hoods, but in warmer weather, it's going to look odd, sailing with a bald woman. I don't think a wig's going to do in the slop."

"Maybe by then, you can grow your hair back."

My eyes teared up. The body has reasons the mind doesn't want to think about. I pressed my face with my left hand until I felt more under control. "So you're not going to kill me after this mission's over."

"I couldn't kill you."

"Kearney?"

"If we don't keep faith with people who work for us, then how will we get new informants? You're working for us because your people didn't keep faith with you."

"Thanks, Mike." Maybe there would be a time after this, a life of being the female equivalent of Jergen, married to Mike, playing war and insurrection games, living by a golf course. Sometimes, I can't stand the bitch the world beat me into becoming. Give up the suspicions, roll out to suburbia on a backwash of trust.

"But you have to keep the faith with us," Mike said.

As the sun began to set, we got a taxi back to the loft. I fell asleep halfway through Midtown, the buildings a jolt after the Sound's marshes. I dreamed myself back to the Pacific Northwest, a wilderness a day's hike to the center, trails folded through it for weeks, the original hiker's maze that inspired the recreation malls.

Nature, the non-human, would never have control of the world again. I'd never have control of my life again. Mike was kind, but that was calculated even if Mike was naturally kind. The only wildernesses that survived were human wildernesses: Manhattan, Mexico City. We were our own predators.

As the elevator took us up to the loft, I said, "You think I'm right about Dorcas?"

"Dorcas?"

"The woman postdoc I work for."

"She's never been an open drode head sympathizer."

"Maybe I should tell her I wasn't a fake whore, really, but rather a convicted eco-terrorist?"

Mike said, "That could be too obvious." He went to the bar cabinet and poured us both brandies. "Are you hungry?" he asked.

"Why don't we get something delivered?"

"Pizza? African? Chinese?"

I remembered my little African car. "Groundnut soup with spinach."

"Lots of chiles?"

"They didn't have chiles pre-Columbian." The world was one human stew: Lebanese food in Yucatan, Mexicans using stir-fry as inspiration for fajitas, American corn in Italian porridge and Chinese soup, hot peppers in Indian curries. "Since I can't undo 1492, with moderate chiles, then."

He ordered me peanut soup and a rice-and-beef dish for himself, but I fell asleep before it arrived and microwaved it hot again for breakfast. I said, "What should I do next?"

"Perhaps you should do what other drode heads do."

"But I'm not a typical drode head," I said.

"You said she made you. If you don't seem more like a real drode head, what we did to try to convince the Rockefeller U people that the new models weren't part of the audit won't work. We've put other new models in various research labs. But the others behave like real drode heads. A few of them are retrofits. You shouldn't seem too different."

"I want to tell her I was an eco-terrorist."

"Then how do you explain me?"

"Being an eco-terrorist doesn't keep me from also having been a whore."

"Allison, don't make things too complicated."

"Okay, but I've got to have ecological leanings to bring her out."

"That's okay," Mike said. "But you need to be more like a real drode head. If she made the mantises for drode heads, then she's got a social theory about drode heads."

"You do think it's her, don't you?"

"We thought it was Henry, but we found out what he's doing. He's trying to work out a way to get humans transferred to computers without killing the human who's crossing."

"Is that illegal?"

"It's ecologically incorrect," Mike said. "Perfect immortality for only part of the population could cause riots. People put up with differences in status because of different responsibilities, but if the rich lived forever and the poor died, then how long would the poor put up with that? Dying equalizes us. We're all oil and ash in the end."

Yeah, but a drode head corpse has its borrowed equipment dissected out. I said, "Interesting couple."

"The wife thinks Dorcas is a joke," Mike said. "Dorcas does all her own endangered species maintenance, plus Henry's. So Henry's got more time to further his career."

"How did you find that out?" I asked.

Mike said, "We got a job for one of Henry's other postdocs and he jabbered like an old lady."

I said, "Amazing what a person does for a job." Poor bitch, now I had to feel sorry for her.

Hanging with drode heads didn't take much doing. While my immediate building only contained me, about two blocks away, drode heads had established a beachhead in a former co-op, renting from the original tenants. I wondered if the owners got a tax break for renting to Welfare people, but the immediate task was to begin riding home with them after work. Since I had been raped by a drode-head predator, I certainly was nervous enough to seem sincerely looking for folks to come downtown with.

Drode heads congregated in a supermarket that took food stamps without being snotty about it. I suspected that the supermarket gave coin change, not scrip, but uncovering that wasn't my mission. The supermarket offered free coffee. I said to the other bald people hanging around the coffee machine, "I'm new here."

A woman who looked about twenty asked, "Where do you live?"

"In a loft on Hester."

"How?" the woman asked.

"A friend who saw me out of prison. I don't think it's going to last a whole lot longer."

"You fuck a hair-head?"

"Yes, but I was fucking him when I was a hair-head myself."

A man joined us and asked, "What do you want?"

"I'm looking for people to ride downtown with. Just after I went through orientation, I got raped by some sleaze who advertised he wanted to talk to drode heads for research."

Two more drode heads came up and listened while getting themselves free coffee. I felt like this was a more critical test of my cover than when I ran it by Dr. Dorcas.

"Where you working?" the man who first joined us asked.

"Rockefeller University," I said, suddenly uneasy.

"You don't have drode holes. One of those experimental systems?"

"Yeah," I said. "Cut a bit of time off my sentence to take it." I felt like a whore for real.

"Shit," the man said. "Hope they can retrofit. Open holes are a bitch to tend."

I said, "New system's working out fine in me. And I have heard about retrofits."

They all looked at me as though I'd won the lottery, then the woman said, "If nobody in your building lives downtown, you might want to walk over to Fifty-seventh and Third. I work in the Windermere Gallery."

The man said, "We'll find some other people."

They were concerned about me. I felt ashamed to be fooling them. But then, I was a drode head and got time off for cooperating, so I hadn't lied to them too hard, had I?

I stopped wearing my wig.

When I went to the Windermere Gallery, I found out that the woman I'd met was an exhibit there, naked, no, covered in a plastic skin that imitated flesh and fed her movements into a virtual reality rig. She wore a helmet on that looked like a mantis's head, transmitters antennas, radio controlled woman. The cartoon world she walked in showed up on a video display eight by twelve feet. A salesman came up to me about to tell me all about the control panel when he saw that I was bald.

"We're going home together," I said. "When is she off duty?"

"You don't have holes," the man said.

"New system," I said.

"Could we do a remote pickup?" the man said. He walked over to the control panel and sent the drode-head woman walking back into the offices.

I said, "I certainly hope not. Will she know who I am?"

"I don't know about the fugue state."

"I don't have fugue states often myself."

"She seems to know what's going on, but she doesn't remember anything during the two weeks she comes here. I have some artists who are looking for new model drode heads. I'll call your Welfare office. Same as Marcia's, right?"

Marcia. I hadn't remembered the drode head's name, or maybe I hadn't bothered to ask. "I don't think I can be reassigned. I'm working at Rockefeller University. The Welfare office wanted to really test my system on science stuff."

"You don't work," the man said. "You're a drode head."

I said, "Before I was a drode head, I used to eat men alive." Marcia came out then and tugged at my elbow.

When we got to the street, she said, "Don't argue with them."

"Sorry if it makes life difficult for you."

"You're not wearing your wig."

"No, you don't wear yours all the time either."

"Mine's so obvious. Yours looks good enough to be real hair."

I said, "It is real hair. You want it?"

"Your lover would be furious."

I said, "I don't think so. I'll tell him I lost it and he'll buy me another one. Hell, if I'm a drode head, I ought to look like a drode head."

"We all keep our holes covered with adhesive patches, you know."

"I'll put adhesive patches where I should have holes, then. Shit, will he call Welfare to try to get me? I think he's a hacker rapist. You looked naked."

Marcia said, "I'm glad I won't remember you said this."

At the subway stop, we gathered around with other drode heads until the paying computers cleared, then boarded for downtown. I wondered if the fugue state came from the system or from the organism, a self-blinding to keep the insults from piling up in memory. Then I realized I hadn't remembered anything about my work today with Dorcas.

Willie hadn't been there, though. Perhaps our two weeks weren't synchronized.

That night, I dreamed of insects, many different insects, smarter and bigger than naturally evolved insects, insects walking humans on leashes, insects operating on humans stung to sleep. Mike held me as I floundered out of nightmare's paralysis. "Do you know what I was working on today?"

"Dorcas was doing a scan of grants in human DNA work," Mike said. "Looking for adrenal and testicular information. Didn't seem to have anything to do with insects."

The landscape in my dreams had been beautiful, I remembered now, manicured by insects. Dorcas today reminded me of something familiar, only I didn't have time to remember before I went under the reading hood. Now I tried to think. Yes, she reminded me of Jergen the week before he disappeared.

I said, "I fugued out during the sessions today."

Mike said, "You asked me to do it. Don't worry. I'm monitoring what's going on."

"Why do people fugue out?"

"The information they process doesn't make sense to the brain, so the brain, the daily personality, doesn't remember it. That's the best theory. Sort of like infancy memory loss."

I almost told him, *I think it's the trauma of having your personality overwhelmed, plus the daily insults from hair-heads.* "Mike, a guy at the Windermere Gallery said he was going to call my Welfare Office to see about getting me assigned to an artist. Don't let this happen."

Mike said, "Not even to protect your cover?"

"Find a better way to protect my cover than that."

Mike ran his hands over my head and said, "We will. Go back to sleep now."

I closed my eyes, but I didn't trust him as much as I had when we went sailing, as much as I needed to trust a man before I turned my life over to him. He'd sent me out to the drode heads. Had he known what he'd sent me out to find? Was this his way of being cruel or was he stupid?

"Roll over and I'll give you a backrub."

"I'm so vulnerable under the hood."

"I'm always watching. I'd get you out in no time."

I let him massage me and fell back into my dreams. A mantis soothed me. Not a nightmare, this time. I apologized to it for the mantis I'd killed.

The drode heads were like pale copies of people, so inoffensive I had to surpress the urge to abuse them. We went around in a group, though one of the drode heads transferred to Manhattan said that country drode heads tended to be more integrated into the rest of life as poor kin to hair-heads.

I realized Mike didn't know what he'd done to send me to them, but Kearney, watching at the edges, must have wondered if Mike had lost his mind, because Mike, obviously under orders, said, "Don't get too close to the drode heads. You're not one of them really."

"Right," I said. Mike wouldn't shoot me, but he'd let Kearney know the instant I defected. I wished Mike needed me, really, as Jergen needed me to buffer him against his agoraphobia. I'd been too coarsened to notice something subtle like a phobia and flexible enough to have compensated without realizing what had been going on. Mike only needed me for a promotion, to prove he was a good case officer. And he wasn't enough of a case officer to know that I really shouldn't have been sent to take a closer look at the drode heads.

I wished he'd been my perfect control, wise, bittersweet, then, seconds later, I was glad he wasn't. If he'd had been perfect, then I would have been convinced that the way the world had treated me was justified. I hated Mike's explanation that the world was full of people as fucked as I was, but of all the people I'd offered my alligence to, only Kearney seemed to be perfectly in control. And he was ready to kill me the instant I wavered. My cunt was born to have his hand up it as though I was his puppet.

Hollow inside.

Lucky for Mike, the drode heads weren't organized. I felt like stomping them into a protest movement, but no, they were already overstomped, so I drifted with them between sessions under the hood. The Welfare Office and Mike kept me out of the art gallery, and I got Marcia to meet me downstairs when she finished displaying at the Windermere.

Then someone tapped me on the shoulder at the grocery store that catered to drode heads and said, "Allison? I'm Willie."

"Willie?"

"Willie. I found you when the hackers had you."

"What are you doing here?"

"I was concerned about you." Willie looked like the subdued drode head lost to the quirky insane side of his personality. "You're working for Dorcas Rae."

I wondered how long this would take to get back to Kearney. "I'm assigned to Rockefeller University. I'm living with a guy who reports back to the guy who busted me."

Willie looked as though he and the Brazilian woman from the internal movie theatre had more questions they wanted to ask me, but he drifted back through the store.

I went home and wondered if I'd just lost even more control of my life. Well, the first forty years had been interesting, fun even since I got thrills from being an uncaught fighting underdog.

When I got home, I didn't mention Willie to Mike. After dinner, I lay with my bald head in his lap as we listened to Charlie Mingus. Mike stroked my head gently as if the baldness was erotic. I finally said, "Drode heads are so dreary. This weekend, can I go to the rec mall alone?" I wanted to get away from them all, but in a monitored space, protected by camera eyes. The country within a hundred miles of Manhattan is too infested with people. If I'd had a hint of an active drode head underground, something more than the one or two isolated drode heads hiding out in the social margins and the minority who refused to wear wigs in public, I'd have rebelled, but my brain belonged to the Feds now. They were the meanest guys in my social universe now.

Mike said, "Let us know if anyone approaches you."

I paused, then asked, "Approaches me at the mall?"

"Yes."

"Mike, I feel like I'm drowning. If you need real proof, I've got to get Dorcas to brag, to do something."

"We need to turn her. She's too expensively trained to just kill."

In the morning, I stuck my brain through the hood and into a theatre. Loba spoke to me from the screen, saying, "Allison, we can help you."

I said, "Against the Feds. Against Martin Fox's friends. Where's Willie?"

Loba said, "He's creating this security space."

"Let me finish my work for the Feds, then rescue me before they decide I'm too weird to live."

"We want you to find out how Dorcas Rae makes her insects, to see if she'd work for us. We think her insects fit our program quite well."

"What is your program?"

"We're a homeostatic control unit. If the industrial machines create monsters, we monsters get more freedom to act. If the technicians stop the industrial accidents, we don't get funded. We provide an ecological balance.''

Other than maybe she was mad, Loba hadn't told me much of anything. ''How do the insects fit in?''

''The eco-terrorism depends too much on people. We already know that people aren't reliable.''

''But these are people-made insects.''

''People started them, but they will be successful or not on their own. They'll challenge people to fight them, even, perhaps, to cooperate with them.'' Loba's arms turned into little short nubs with fingers. I knew those were images of her true flesh arms. ''Thalidomide?''

''Yes.''

''Can you tell me who you represent?''

''Industrial accident victims.''

''You could get legal compensation for the damages.''

Loba said, ''We did.''

I figured it out now. ''Your group funded the radical ecology people, didn't you? You knew me from then.''

''Yes.''

''I could turn you into the Feds and they would love me forever.'' I could, I could.

''But we're the group you've spent your life searching for.''

''Can you save me from the Feds?'' I shouldn't have asked that. She could lie to me. The Feds could lie to me. I wondered how it would feel to have Kearney actually kill me. He'd come so close before. I imagined my corpse at Kearney's feet, flaccid, eyes open and drying out. I'd been virtually dead since he'd pinned me with the searchlights. Could the dead body feel rot?

''Whoever you work for, you've got to get Dorcas to trust you.''

''Ah, yes, ma'am.'' The next step was simple, then the decision tree sprouted wildly. I died in most of the branches.

''We'll stay in touch,'' Loba said. She faded from the screen under groups of four letters. DNA code, I realized, for a virus.

Another world waited. *Aprés moi, les moches.*

Dorcas said that. *After me, the flies.*

Then I ran an assembler, but the data drained out onto the floor. ''In case anyone is listening,'' Dorcas said.

I wanted to tell her that erasing me was evidence, but my body lay slack on the read table.

Finally, I came to myself sitting up, sweating. A wasp in a jar buzzed angrily. Dorcas, both hands wrapped around the glass, moved the trapped wasp in circles, then toward me, away. Angry. I, too, was angry.

I said, "So you do work with insects."

"Collaborating with them," Dorcas said. "Will I live to get home?"

I wondered what was in the wasp's sting. "I don't care, and I don't really know."

"The wasp can tell if you're lying or not."

"But I'm telling you, I don't care enough about people to report you, whatever you're doing."

"You were a professional liar before. That's what the badger game is, a professional lie."

"I was busted, but I wasn't what I said I was. I spiked trees."

"Would they sentence you to that for spiking trees?"

"Well, yes. I had to defend myself a couple of times."

"You've killed people?"

"I didn't stay for a medic." I was defending Jergen, not really murdering people.

"Wouldn't you have rather been stung to sleep?" Dorcas said. She turned the jar's lid.

"No, don't, please," I said, really scared now. The wasp seemed to be calmer.

"If I could go to the Feds, would they give me a tenured position or kill me?"

"I'm not connected with the Feds." If I got mad, the wasp would react.

"You said I was just a lab wife. You were right. If I went to the Feds, they'd pardon me, give me a lab, and dictate everything I did for the rest of my life."

"What are you going to do about it?"

"I'm going to help the insects as fast as I can before something happens to me."

Loba needs to snatch her right now, I thought. I said, "I might be able to contact some of my old friends."

"DNA recombinant labs are very expensive," Dorcas said. She uncapped the wasp's jar. The wasp crawled out onto her hand. It was larger than the biggest hornet I'd ever seen, but slim like a wasp. It breathed. My skin crinkled in goosebumps. My body thought a wasp breathing was too eerie.

Dorcas said, "If you trust her, she won't sting you."

"How many are there?"

"Who's asking?" Dorcas said. She gently manuevered the jar lid to recapture the wasp.

"I don't need to know," I said. If the insects worked, humans could be humans again, without unnatural self-control, without having to turn part of our own population into the non-human. "But you've got enemies."

"Were you really one of those ecological Luddites?"

"Yes."

"What I'm doing is tampering monsterously with the ecology, so maybe you really hate me."

"The wasp didn't think so, did it? Can I go now? I've got to pick up a friend."

"I want to talk more about this," Dorcas said.

"Sure. Does Henry, Dr. Itaka know?"

"He wants to make people immortal. I hate the idea."

I said, "Don't tell anyone anything. I'll be back Monday."

"I need to have someone to talk to," Dorcas said. I suspected that now she'd confessed, I wouldn't be able to shut her up. Keeping my eyes on the wasp in the jar, I backed out, picked up Marcia at the Windermere, and went home.

Mike wasn't in. Probably busting Dorcas, I thought. I decided I might as well go on to the rec mall and loaded a day pack with the clothes I'd need for the weekend. Two nice things about rec malls: instant security and freedom from large backpacks. I scribbled a note for Mike, pulled on a cap, and got back on the subway. At the George Washington Bridge bus station I had to wait around for pass card space on the bus. The bus station was noisy, clattering cups, people walking around in bicycle shoes with plastic cleats, other hikers with various sizes of packs, ropes, clanking carabiners, and chocks. Some people were headed to the rec malls; others were going to hike in open air. I wondered if any of us sitting here besides me had spiked trees.

A bus with pass space came in about nine P.M. I hoped that I could hike to a camping space before midnight, wasn't quite sure what I'd do if the mall was full. Go home? Through the night?

Where had my nerve gone?

About five people got out at the rec mall. It was longer than three football stadiums, smaller than the Southern California mall, maybe a few stories taller. We all hiked in from the bus station to the forecourt.

"Lighted or moonlight?" the scheduling computer asked. "Willing to be assigned to a group?

I punched *moonlight, yes*. The computer asked for other singles willing to share a space. Two people, one man, one woman with long black hair, came forward. I wondered if either or both were with the Feds, but I was beginning to get sleepy.

The guy had the decency to look nervous. The machine issued us each a map marked with our campsites. "You are not required to walk together," it told us.

But we did go in together. "You're on Welfare, aren't you?" the guy said.

"Yes," I said. "The state has lotteries to give us little perks."

"The people I work for want to put me on Welfare," he said. "Does it hurt?"

I said, "Make sure they give you the subdermal model."

The woman didn't say anything, just pushed her hair back, her left hand spread between the index finger and all the others.

The man asked, "Have either of you ever hiked to the Appalachian Trail?"

The long-haired woman said, "I heard it was dangerous to women and gay guys until you were about fifty miles from Manhattan."

I said, "Heard the same."

The man said, "You can take a bus up to a trail crossing in the Catskills, from there it's not so bad. When I have my vacation, I think I'll do that."

Poor bastard would get lots of opportunities to hike if they put him on Welfare. I said, "I've got a hair-head boyfriend. He takes me sailing when I'm not working."

The woman said, "Hair-head? Working?"

"Yeah, that's what we call you. And that's what we call the time when we're connected to computers."

"You don't work," she said.

"If we've got it so easy, you wanna volunteer for Welfare?"

The man said, "So Welfare doesn't lobotomize you."

Perhaps that explained why so many of the drode heads seemed like copies of people. "My rig's experimental," I said. "I'm not like most drode heads."

We hiked on through real plants and holograms until we reached the campsite. The supply and tent-setting machines were just rolling back into the walls. They'd give us a large three-room tent, but had left the sleeping bags in stuff sacks by the picnic table.

We looked at each other and all slept alone. In the morning, I saw the cougar option trail. "Is the cougar real?"

The dark-haired woman said as though I was stupid, "No, it's a puppet. Too many crazies coming from the city to risk a real cougar."

"I still want to see it," I said. I left them and went toward the cougar preserve. Fifteen minutes later, in the trail ahead, I saw a steel door hanging in the air between two rock faces. Up close the polycarbonate

surround was obvious, smudged by a large cat paws and nose. I signed
the release and went in to see how a robot cougar compared to the real
cats I'd seen in Western wildernesses.

The door said, "Get in quick before the cat comes." I pushed my hand
against the control plate, leaving fingerprints, and entered. The trail
turned at right angles and a cougar loped up, not a stalking charge, then
paused about thirty feet from me. Her tail rose like a house cat's, curled
over to one side. If this was a robot, the swollen teats were authenticity-
overkill.

Kearney said, "Pretty, isn't she?" He was sitting on a long tree limb
over the trail, looking like he could drop on the cougar, break her neck.

I said, "I thought she was supposed to be a robot."

"Not quite a robot. Did you have anything to report?"

"Can this cougar be tapped?"

Kearney said, "Why do you ask?"

What to say? How much longer would I live? The cat could cover it
up. I wondered if the rig in my brain would snag in her teeth or poison
her.

Tell some of it. "I was tapped."

"You were tapped? You disappeared offline for five minutes."

"Yes. I don't know by who, but Dorcas is the one making the insects.
She wants a lab, tenured track position." The cougar came over and
rubbed her body against my leg. I rubbed her head behind her ears.

Kearney said, "Did you tell her what you were?"

"I went to the second level cover, told her I was a busted eco-freak.
Didn't tell her you guys could listen in."

"Tapped by your old friends?"

"No," I said, realizing seconds later that Loba told me they'd been behind the eco-warriors. The cougar looked up at me with half-lidded eyes.
"Dorcas had a wasp. It reacted when I was scared angry."

Kearney didn't speak, just leaned forward on the tree limb, his legs
wrapped around it. The cougar looked up at him and lashed her tail
slightly. Should I deliver Loba and all her crew to Kearney? I looked at
the cat, wondering if anyone controlled it.

"Please, Kearney, I've done what you asked."

"Have you?"

"Yes."

"Allison, who's behind Dorcas?"

"Nobody."

"You sure."

"Kearney, no, I'm not sure." I could save myself, tell him about the consortium that wanted Dorcas and her equipment. "But she's got access to everything she needs for the work right there at Rockefeller, doesn't she? And if she worked for you, you'd watch her every move."

"Our profile on you is so good we knew you'd come to see the cat," Kearney said. "You're predictable, Allison."

If he had an accurate profile, he'd have known not to try to humiliate me. But then I didn't want to say, *I left a note for Mike where I was going. You had fifteen minutes to trace me once I told my companions I was going to see the cougar.* "Kearney, do you like squashing me like a bug?"

"Strange choice of simile," Kearney said. "When were you planning to report to us?"

"I thought you were reading me all along, listening to what I heard."

Kearney said, "We wanted your full cooperation. You went out of the loop for five minutes. What happened?"

"I don't remember. Kearney, if you're going to kill me, do it and be done. Quit bullying me." If he hadn't bullied me, I might have given him Loba. But not now, I wouldn't, not consciously. I'd thought that while Mike could be dumb, Kearney was brilliant, but was he really?

"We want you back for a full reading."

Loba said she'd read like a dream. Could I trust her? My head went to the best technicians. "Now?"

The cougar began pushing against my legs, herding me toward the steel door. Kearney jumped down from the tree limb and walked behind us. I asked, "Is it trained?"

"It's a robot."

"No, I don't think so," I said. "I can't imagine why anyone would build a lactating robot."

"Doesn't matter," Kearney said, but the cat looked back at him. I wondered if cougars played with people who were afraid of them. Housecats certainly did. Kearney moved his hand. Cougar kitty was trained to gestures, obviously then.

"Here, kitty, kitty," I said. She was obviously well-fed and lonely. Motherhood hormones made her affectionate. Maybe she wouldn't trust males so much now either? I rubbed her ears.

"Allison, whatever the thing is, it doesn't go through the door with us."

"I'm supposed to meet some people tonight at our campsite."

"The machine will tell them you were reassigned." Kearney gestured again at the cougar. Pure cat, busy getting her ears rubbed, she ignored him.

"I could shoot both of you."

"Kearney, quit being so melodramatic. We'll let you out of the door first." I wondered how many generations of cougars bred in captivity lead to this big kitty.

"A robot would have obeyed the hand signals," Kearney said. The cougar turned her head at the sound of his voice. He signaled for her to go back. She wanted through the door.

I had to smile. Kearney pulled a cellular phone out of his hip pocket, spoke the number, and said, "Send something to take care of this cat. Why did you tell me it was a robot?"

I wondered what the answer was. Perhaps city people might feel freer to torment a real cat but would fear machine retaliation. *Don't mess with the machine kitty, it's got cousins in all sorts of shapes can put you straight down.*

Two footlocker-sized robots came out of the wall, rolling on tracks like miniature tanks. The cat decided getting through the door wasn't worth it. She darted back toward the dogleg in the trail.

"Now," Kearney said, motioning toward the door.

We walked out. The door closed behind us, the robots rolled back into the walls. I said, "I guess if a man's had his hand up a woman's cunt, he never will take her seriously."

"We didn't have a matron with us, Allison, when we caught you at the bomb site. Did someone approached you, someone from the old days?"

Pawn, I was just a damn pawn. "Kearney, I don't want to go back to Rockefeller." I suspected I was a pawn for the ecologists, too, knocked off the board about a year and a half ago when Loba and her friends weren't paying attention.

"Have we lied to you since you agreed to work with us?"

We left the trail section for the forecourt shops and restaurants. Mike, looking anxious, was waiting in front of an Italian restaurant.

I said, "He didn't kill me yet."

We went inside the restaurant. Not many patrons at 10:30 on a Saturday morning. Kearney said, "Allison says it's Dorcas Rae, but Rae's screwed her way from postdoc to postdoc, so I wonder."

Can't take a woman seriously if lots of men have had their hands up her vagina. "Maybe her bosses screwed her because she was so bright and they wanted to put the sexual whammy to her to get her ideas."

A waiter in the Italian restaurant seated us and handed us menus. Kearney said, "The question now is does she have help."

I was supposed to feel part of the team again, eating *osso bucco* at government expense. Sitting with two hair-heads made me feel sleazy.

I'd learned the drode heads' dos and don'ts. When not working, a decent drode head avoided the hair-heads. I said, "So far, only insects."

Mike said, "What is she trying to do?"

I said, "She's working for the insects. Even before her, they could hold their own against us better than any vertebrate and most other invertebrates. If you're looking for allies against us, they're the best bet. I think she hates people."

Kearney said, "But I remember what you did to the mantis."

Mike said, "Empowering insects. That seems like a particularly female thing to do."

Every waiter in the restaurant works for the Feds, I realized, or has been replaced by a Fed for this morning's little chat. As empty as it was, the restaurant hummed with background chatter, but when we stopped talking, a waiter came to take our order.

I ordered octopus.

After the meal, we left the restaurant. I thought I saw Willie but wasn't sure whether I saw him for real or if I'd just been wishing he'd been around. Outside, a grey limo with a microwave antenna on the trunk pulled out of the parking lot and stopped at the curb in front of us.

I wished the guardian robots worked for me. Mike got in first, then me. Kearney popped up a jump seat and sat facing us. He said, "Someone contacted you through the net, whether or not you remember. We're going to put you back on and see who comes to watch."

I said, "Dorcas nearly made me. Why don't you let me continue on schedule, go back when I'm scheduled to go back?"

Kearney said, "But you told me you didn't want to go back to Rockefeller University."

"I don't." I looked out the window at the industrial hazards lands, the superhighways looped on steel intestines dangling in the polluted air. "But if I'm suddenly back online during my time off, then they'll suspect a trap."

Kearney said, "You're probably right. We're going to read you on a secure machine. If we like the read, Mike, can you take her back out on the Sound for the rest of her time off?"

"I'll have to call my friend," Mike said.

"We'll rent you a boat," Kearney said.

I said, "Rent something big enough for ocean sailing." Perhaps I could get to Willie, get his friends to rescue me. What could his friends do?

Kearney said, "No, we'll have men watching from both sides of the Sound."

Mike said, "We could use the coastal monitor system."

But first they'd do a complete read, on private equipment unlinked to even the central power grids, much less the network. "The read will be clean," I said, "Why don't you trust me enough to let me go ocean sailing? You can watch by satellite."

Mike, an obvious blue water man, was tempted. Kearney said, "If the read proves you lied . . ."

I understood I wouldn't wake up. The body might continue to move, but the personality would be gone, a mock woman to catch bugs with.

The limousine pulled up to a building on Cuonties Slip down by the water. I walked through the nineteenth century facade into a hall padded in brown soundproofing. Kearney steered me into a room with a read-head couch, a computer, a wall that was all computer monitor, and a tray set up with vials of pharmaceuticals and disposable needles. I didn't look closely at the drugs. Mike stood at the door and said, "I'll get the technicians."

I stopped remembering from there, short-term memory caught in blackness.

TWELVE

REALITY IS ANOTHER ESCAPE

Willie caught his mantis trying to reach the loft's fire escape several times. She found a crack in the glass and pried at it with her front legs, then drummed against the glass, flicking out with the praying legs. The other people in the loft avoided Willie when he tried to keep her away from the crack. Although she was restless, she gave off less and less, then finally none of the pheromone that tranquilized humans.

Then one day, Willie caught her eating the head of another mantis while the beheaded male body humped her. His mantis couldn't get through the hole she'd finally broken at the crack, but the male could. Willie wondered how the male mantis's owner detoxed from the mantis tranquilizer. His must have switched over to her own species's attractor. Standing over the two mantises, Willie felt a mix of revulsion and pity for the male. For his mantis, he was grateful for what he'd had and for the gradual reduction of the tranquilizer. Impregnated by the dead male, she'd now lay eggs, probably die. Ordinary mantises died after laying eggs, but perhaps this extraordinary one wouldn't.

But perhaps she should. In the male's thrusts, he remembered what bugs made him do to his own cock.

The female mantis finished eating the male's head, then looked at Willie and thrummed.

He didn't care what the Industrial Accidents Consortium thought, he had to find the woman who designed the mantises and ask her if they bred true.

Maybe I'm on the wrong side, Willie thought, but then he wondered who really welcomed him to their side.

He went to the main part of the loft and said, "My mantis broke through the cracked glass and let a male in. Why didn't anyone stop her?"

"We didn't notice," Laurel said. She and Loba were sitting with earphones on, listening to some digital tap, keyboarded in, reading a screen. Willie wondered why they didn't use him. But the system might recognize him by the software he had in him. His link was adapted to his brain.

Willie stood watching the women keyboard. He wondered if he ought to do something for his mantis, but he couldn't face her right now. He pulled on his drode head wig and left the loft. If he rode the subway, Welfare would have a record of where he went. He'd walk up to Rockefeller University and no one would be the wiser.

He went to the front door and asked the woman sitting behind the clear barricade, "I'm here to speak to Dr. Rae." Why not?

The woman looked startled, then glanced over at a man standing by a monitor further protected by the barrier than she was. The receptionist asked, "What business do you have with Dr. Rae?"

"Tell her Allison's friend Willie is here." What that would mean to Dr. Rae, Willie had no idea. Willie felt prickles of interest emanating off the man's eyeballs. He lifted off his cheap wig and bared his skull at the hairheads.

"Where is your Welfare office?" the man asked.

"Roanoke, Virginia, but I'm visiting New York, friends of friends." Willie believed that his mantis would die after she laid her eggs. One stage in his life would die with her. He'd been addicted to mantises, but his would be kind enough to detox him easy if she died slowly after laying eggs. He'd been revolted by her fucking, but perhaps he did crave that tranquilizing gas. If she died, would she breed true?

"I could go see her at home," Willie said, having no idea where Dr. Rae lived. He should have asked Allison if she knew, or Laurel in the real time.

"How do you know where she lives?" the receptionist said.

Willie hazarded a guess, "I keep the same endangered species she does."

The man said, "You don't keep endangered species. You keep a mantis."

Willie said, "Can I see her?"

The man tapped into his monitor, then nodded at the receptionist. She spoke into a communicator, then said, "She isn't here."

"Fuck," Willie said. He knew the man would go now to wherever Dorcas Rae lived, or call someone to check. "Well, she did say she might go home and wait for me there." He decided to walk back downtown to the loft on Hester Street.

Oh, lordie, lordie, what have I done?

Then he realized, looking into a shop window full of suits and shoes he'd never be able to afford, that a woman was following him. Willie wondered if she had perverse designs on him or if she was Dr. Rae. Did Dr. Rae have designs on him? Willie looked further behind the woman, then back at her. She was wearing a wig like a drode head, but her clothes were too fine.

He kept walking, then stopped to look back through a shop window reflection again. The woman was still there. Willie felt old combat training reflexes shift through his body, rehearsing the blows, tweaking the nerves running the muscles.

He kept walking downtown, but didn't want to show her where the loft was. And they could be trailed by shifting teams. He went down to the supermarket where he'd seen Allison. Two drode head women, one wearing a real human hair wig, faded out of the store. They knew the woman following Willie wasn't one of them. Hair-heads disguised as drode heads were bad news.

Willie turned to the woman and said, "You followed me."

"Why were you asking about Dr. Rae?"

Willie looked at her a long while, then said, "I've got this mantis. She's mated with another big mantis. Will she die when she lays eggs?" A real agent wouldn't come up to him like this. Willie knew this was the insect maker herself, Dr. Dorcas Rae.

"You're Willie," the woman said. "Why did you come here?"

"Friends want to know what you're capable of."

"Why are you harrassing me?"

"Man was already watching you. They want the mantis maker real bad."

"Who is Allison?"

"She's cooperating with the Feds to get out of a sabotage bombing. I brought the problem to the attention of another group."

"Oh, shit."

"Dr. Rae, you ought not to go home."

"You bastard. You tipped them off that it was me."

"The Feds want to be really sure. If they're sure, they'll kill you.

My group might have a better option, but I've got to find a place to leave you for now. First, you've got to get shaved and real Welfare clothes.'' Inside Willie's head, he kept thinking, *My mantis's dying, but I can get another one. My mantis is dying, but the bitch deserves it.* ''Stay in the bathroom here. Sit up on a toilet so no one can see your legs. I'll be back.''

Turn her in and maybe the Feds would fix my head all the way. Yeah, they'd probably nano-cook me into jelly, just to make sure I never talked.

When Willie got back to the loft, Laurel said, ''Willie, Allison's having trouble.''

''I've got Dr. Rae stashed somewheres safe.''

''What? Why in the world?'' Loba and Laurel looked at him.

''I need some female drode head clothes and a razor. She's got a wig already, but it's all puffy from hair.''

''Willie, she could be infiltrating us. Allison, too. Trade us for whatever they did, the Feds would go for it,'' Laurel said. ''They don't suspect we exist.''

Little Red came in, limping as usual from his crooked spine. ''What's up?''

''Willie contacted Dr. Rae,'' Laurel said.

''Pretty damn undisciplined, Willie,'' Little Red said.

Laurel said, ''The police are looking for her now. She's supposedly under the influence of an experimental drug.''

Little Red said, ''Anyone trained on her will recognize her even in Welfare drag.''

Willie said, ''Shit, you mean I should just let them have her?''

Loba said, ''She makes great insects.''

Laurel said, ''We don't have to explain everything to her. We didn't to Jergen.''

''What about Allison?''

Laurel didn't say anything, but ducked her head. Little Red explained, ''They pulled her from a rec mall in New Jersey. We hope the contact reads as a dream, but if not, they'll fry her before she's out of fugue. Willie, we need Dr. Rae. Allison, well, we can't afford to trust her.''

''We do feel guilty,'' Laurel said. ''We'd planned to rescue her . . .''

''. . . if she wanted to be rescued,'' Loba interjected.

''She's been treated awful,'' Willie said. ''You fucked with her. The Feds fucked with her. Hackers fucked her.''

Little Red told Willie, ''We can't make everything straight. We've got a plan you can use to help Dr. Rae. Laurel, I think we should.''

Loba nodded. Laurel moved some boxes holding geodesic dome panels, then found a suitcase and pulled out a shift, hose, and rubber shoes. She said, "With this shift, it won't matter what size Dr. Rae is. Bring her down to the ferry. If we don't pick you up in fifteen minutes, take the next ferry to Staten Island and ride back and forth all night if you have to." Laurel found a shopping bag, put the clothes in it, and handed it to Willie.

He took the bag and asked, "They don't implant trackers in the scientists, do they?"

"If they do, we can pick up electromagnetic bursts," Loba said. "We'll scan her when we pick her up."

Little Red went over to look at the screen in front of Laurel. He said, "Go finish the job, Willie."

"How do I know you'll take care of me if you won't take care of Allison?"

Laurel said, "Willie has a point."

"We'll talk about it, Willie," Loba said. "First bring us Dr. Rae. You've forced everyone's hand. Perhaps we should have gotten you another mantis."

"No, I don't want to bring you someone if you're going to kill me or do my memory damage. I've been damaged enough." *And thank you very much for that crack about mantises.*

"Willie, we trust you. Allison's a more complicated creature," Loba said.

"Only because she's been more complicatedly damaged."

"Willie, don't mess with me," Little Red said. "Bring the woman hacker in and we'll talk about doing something in exchange for Allison."

Loba and Laurel nodded. Unified team, Willie thought. He left, hoping Dr. Rae was still waiting in the grocery. At the grocery, he ran into the woman named Marcia, friend of Allison's. "What is that woman hair-head in the toilet to us?" Marcia asked.

"A vast change," Willie said. "Anyone prowling around? She put her feet down or what? Can you buy me a razor? Go in and give her this stuff. Allie would seriously appreciate it." He found a dollar coin and handed it to the woman.

The woman said, "If Allie says so, maybe."

"Here's another coin," Willie said.

"How you been getting those?"

"I sold my gun collection. Please."

"Gonna love shaving a hair-head." The woman drifted off, bought a razor and some other knickknacks, looking at Willie's distorted re-

flection in the bull's-eye mirrors. Willie wondered if the grocer preferred the non-electric to something his customers might shift current
out of doing a bit of black time, renting out the drode holes.

Willie suspected shaving a woman's head would take at least as long
as shaving stubble from between the electrodes. He'd always wondered
why Welfare didn't depilate its clients, but then a man would know
the caseworkers never expected anyone could get off the dole except
by brain infection. Leaving follicles gave a drode head hope.

Twenty minutes. He went to the register and said, "Tell the women
I'll be back in a bit. I've got to check on something uptown of here."

And so, Willie walked downtown and around, thinking about his
mantis and the changes he'd been through. Other reflexes, other training
came back to Willie. He checked for tails, but knew he'd never spot
the switching kind, or the smaller machines. Could be a mechanical
pigeon watched him.

He swung back a little uptown of the grocery, looked for cars with
microwave antennas, or variable tint windows. Then, he saw Marcia
and Dorcas Rae come out. Marcia said, "If someone's looking for two
people, they might not be looking for three."

Willie visualized a mob of drode heads walking down to the ferry.
"You get me together a little mob of us, we'll confuse them. We could
take the ferry back and forth, talking."

Dr. Rae said, "What if she's audited?"

Marcia said, "I'm an artist's puppet. What data can I trade away?"

"We're just drode heads going for a walk, in numbers for safety,"
Willie said. But, besides confusing anyone looking for two or three
drode heads, one a fake, this would confuse Laurel and Loba. Oh, well.
Willie could spot either of them quick enough if the windows weren't
on deep tint.

"I've got to tell my parents something," Dr. Rae said. "I worry
about them. They'll worry about me."

"Not now," Willie said. He took Dr. Rae's elbow, guided her like
he'd been guided when he was freaked. Marcia talked to a few other
drode heads, so while they didn't have the grand procession Willie'd
imagined, they had five of them, all walking around in full personality,
none fugued out.

Dr. Rae seemed like she was, though. Did she not believe what was
happening to her was real or did people like her not face the same
consequences for what they did that people like Allison faced? Dr. Rae
said, "But if I turn myself into the Feds, I could get my own lab."

Willie said, "We'll give you a lab, too."

Willie didn't expect they'd actually take the ferry tonight. He was right. The van pulled up beside them and Laurel said, "We've got room for two in, if anyone wants a lift."

Dr. Rae's eyes looked huge, scared blue almost black. Willie wondered if she had freckles on her newly bald scalp or if getting them would take sunshine. He said, "I'd be curious and my woman friend here." He still had Dr. Rae by the right elbow.

Laurel said, "Your other friends won't be ticked?"

"No, they're just walking the same way. We're not together in other than the drode head way, safety in numbers and all that."

"Hop in, then," Laurel said. She took Dr. Rae's other elbow. Willie let go and opened the side door and saw the geodesic dome crates packed in already. Laurel and the drode head named Marcia pushed and pulled Dr. Rae in after him.

"Hi, Dr. Rae," Laurel said. "We're friends of yours, we think. Willie, your mantis finished her egg case."

"Dead?"

Laurel asked, "What's supposed to happen to the giant mantises after they lay eggs, Dr. Rae?"

"Well, they live for a couple of years before they're fully mature. I didn't arrange for multiple ovulations, so I suspect they'll die once their ovaries are mature unless what I did affected other parts of the genome."

Willie went glum. "You gotta do better than that."

Laurel said, "Tell us what you need to keep working. We can steal it."

Dr. Rae said, "I think security is tighter than you imagine."

Laurel said, "We'll get you what you need."

Willie said, "And now we've got to get Allison."

"Where is Allison? Was she really an eco-terrorist? I told her . . . shit, it's out of my control, isn't it?"

"She told the Feds you were the insect maker, but she was only guessing," Loba said. "But the guys running her thought you might have been covering for someone else."

Willie began to wonder if he'd joined the wrong team. "Allison's been captured, brain-scanned, offered suicide. She was strapped down and she thought they'd killed her, but they kept her alive on a respirator. I dunno. I feel a little sorry for her."

Dr. Rae said, "Who does she really want to work for?"

Loba said, "Willie, did she tell you that while you were sneaking around together on the net?"

Laurel said, "We are going to have enough problems with this one. What if Allison had been working for the Feds from Jergen's time?"

"I like Allison," Willie said. "Rescue her. I can read her."

All this time, the truck was headed uptown, then into the Bronx.

Loba said, "They've put her in a fugue and Mike's taking her sailing."

Dr. Rae asked, "You can bug the Feds?"

"In a normal's mind, an armless woman is a disarmed woman," Loba said.

"Nanotech could grow you new arms. My parents stay young that way," Dr. Rae said.

"Perhaps having arms might be a good disguise, someday," Loba said. "But some of my friends were scarred by nanotech."

Willie said, "What are we going to do for Allison?"

Laurel said, "Let the Feds have her."

Dr. Rae said, "She used to work for you? What happened?"

Loba said, "The man we'd made contact with disappeared, informed for the Feds, but didn't give them Allison. Allison contacted our people later. We put her in another eco-terrorist group and withdrew our people, watched to see what would happen to them. The new leader, also suspicious of her, sent her to Louisiana with a baby nuke."

Laurel said, "The Feds killed him for resisting arrest. That's probably what would have happened to you, Dr. Rae."

"I don't think so. I could have agreed to work for them."

Loba said, "I think they have enough gene hackers."

Willie realized he couldn't go home again. Well, he had gotten out of his rut. Then he realized neither Loba nor Laurel trusted Dr. Rae, but they were going to scare her into working for them.

Dr. Rae said, "If Willie can read her, then why not rescue her, read her? If she's really working for the Feds, then you could . . ." She couldn't quite think of what, Willie realized.

But Loba could. "If she couldn't identify us, then we could feed her back to the Feds. But she can identify us. Willie, could you put false memories in her head, edit her?"

Dr. Rae knew her neurochemistry. "You could keep her on continuous short-term memory. A number of drugs will do that, plus a little selective brain damage."

Willie said, "So you let Allison take chances for you, kept her in the dark about who was funding the eco-warriors, now you want to feed her back to the Feds." He looked at Dr. Rae, like, *Do you think these people rescued you for good?*

Loba sat still for a while. Neither she nor Laurel spoke until the van was well out in Westchester County. Then, Loba asked as though she needed to change the subject, "Why did you build the mantises?"

"To see if I could. To make life easier for the drode heads."

Willie felt Dr. Rae was lying.

Loba asked further, "Were you doing anything more? On systems for controlling human aggression, perhaps? Or overpopulation? Insects for pollution control?"

"Yes."

Loba asked, "Why?"

"I was mad."

"Are you still?" Loba asked.

"Nobody takes me seriously, so I was mad and I could get away with all sorts of pirate projects."

Loba said, "Why did you sleep with your bosses?"

"What has that to do with anything? They could keep that from interfering with their evaluations of my work."

Loba said, "They told you this?"

Willie said, "Dr. Rae, guys never fairly evaluate women they've successfully lied to."

"I want out. You're kidnapping me."

Loba said, "If you want, we can deliver you to the Feds and witness that you didn't resist arrest."

Willie said, "I'd feel a lot better if you rescued Allison. Bet Dr. Rae would feel a bit better, too. I said I'd read her."

Loba said to Dr. Rae, "Did you get along with Allison?"

"I felt sorry for her," Dr. Rae said. "How do I know I can trust you?"

Loba said, "We can fund your insect projects. We like them. The Feds don't. We'll let you do your own projects as long as you teach us recombinant DNA work."

"Will I ever be able to walk around like a normal human being again?"

"With modifications," Loba said. "The Feds might gun you down now if they can't catch us. At this point, they don't know we exist."

Dr. Rae asked, "Willie, why should they rescue Allison?"

"Because I won't trust them if they throw their friends away. How did the mantis work?"

"The pheromones enhance beta-endorphin production and also tend to be depressants like alcohol. I was trying for a bliss effect. The wing music has some psychological impact also. Are you having withdrawal problems?"

"My mantis took me off gradually when she must have been switching to her own sex pheromones. Allison killed her mantis," Willie said.

"But it helped her survive surgical brain scanning. You people owe her something."

Dr. Rae said, "I guess I would trust you more if you didn't throw Allison away."

Loba said, "Willie, would you be willing to see her die if she reads out as a complete traitor? If she's decided to turn us in?"

Willie felt like Loba was asking a lot of him. He almost whined, *But I'm only a fucked-up drode head.* No, he'd gotten beyond that now. "Yes."

Loba said, "We'll need to borrow a special submarine."

THIRTEEN

WHAT PITY DOES TO SOME WOMEN

I came up talking to Mike on a thirty-foot sailboat trimmed in teak and brass. I'd passed the brain scan, maybe. Whatever I'd been saying deteriorated between fugue state and the instant I took over my tongue. I wore a bikini and a bathing cap.

"Good, you're back," Mike said. "Frankly, we're concerned about your dreams."

"What dreams?" And why now?

"The one where you talk to the woman in the theatre," Mike said.

I tried remembering, could bring vaguely to mind some dreams I'd had about people I'd talked to at a movie house. But these dreams were nothing like my nightmares. "Yeah, I guess I have some resentments."

Mike said, "That's understandable."

From the state of my body, I realized he'd been fucking me minutes ago while I was in a fugue state. "How do you know when I'm fugued?" I asked.

"You tend to be more childlike, less intense about being in control," Mike said. "More trusting. I wish you could be like that when you were fully conscious. Life would be easier for you."

I knew why I felt loving toward him and hated him at the same time that I wanted to curl up in his arms. "Did you do this to Jergen?"

"What?"

"Not you, personally, but the woman Jergen married." It stopped being a question by the time I finished speaking. Of course, imprint a captive on a mate.

Mike said, "Rock with the boat. I'll get you some tea."

We were out in the ocean, the shore invisible. Mike had gotten his way. I looked to see what was watching us, but I couldn't see the satellites in the sky, the planes at 80,000 feet, the submarine that might be circling below, listening by hydrophone through the hull, by air-mike disguised as floating trash.

Mike came up with tea and said, "Where are they taking Dorcas Rae?"

I had no idea what he was talking about. "Didn't you pick her up? Who's this 'they?' "

"Drode heads got her, we think. What did drode heads think of the mantis designer?"

"We never talked about the mantises," I said.

"Who's Willie?" Mike asked.

"He was the drode head connection when you guys were looking for me. When I was in Berkeley. He's ex-Army with a security clearance."

"Does he have imperfect fugues?"

"Imperfect fugues?"

"Memories from the times under. Like you can have." *Can, but didn't this time.*

From a non-dream I was just beginning to remember, Loba said something about Willie being part of the technoscape to his users. I lied. "I don't know." I sipped at the tea to give my face something to do while Mike stared at me.

Mike said, "When we picked you up in Louisiana, your own crew considered you expendable. We saved your life. We're still offering you new chances."

"To be the tame deer in a faked chase," I said. I wanted to say, *I'm sorry I'm resisting you, Mike. I will cooperate body and soul.* I couldn't believe I wanted to say it. Mike was warm, loving, utterly trustworthy, not the man who'd kill me, but he'd screwed me while I was fugued childlike. I absolutely wanted to trust Mike. But I'd even had reservations about Jergen, tiny ones. Absolute trust wasn't like me.

"Woman, I really care what happens to you," Mike said.

"Did they drug imprint you, too? Or is it an ego thing, winning me completely over? I've been cooperating with you to catch someone who's messing with the environment. I can't declare all my life before forty completely invalid."

"You're not forty anymore," Mike said. "You've got a chance to reach forty again, with a whole different life. We could make you even younger."

"Mike, I really want to throw myself in your arms and weep for you to show me the right way. But that's so unlike me that I figure you guys drugged me or reprogrammed me, or something, so I'm here, drinking tea, getting pissed off. I told you who was making the insects. You didn't want to believe I knew she made me for an agent, that the way I handled it made her feel enough guilty about what she'd given drode heads that she decided she might be wrong."

"But who financed you when you were out spiking trees and wrecking mining machines?"

"Jergen had money, I guess. Or Joe and Miriam." Why wasn't I curious about that? Did someone else play post-hypnotics with me? Or had I been so angry I didn't care where the money came from? I felt like I was tripping over wires in my own head. "Fuck all of you."

"You've got to trust someone. We're the most powerful set of players."

I pulled off the bathing cap and let the wind play over my baldness. True enough. "But the most powerful people I knew as a child threw me out of a car when I was eight."

"Allison, your government has laws against child abandonment. You refused to cooperate with the police."

I said, "My mother could throw away something she nursed, but I couldn't betray my momma." I began crying.

He looked away, hands working the tiller and main sail sheet, then he said, "I apologize for trying to manipulate you while you were fugued."

"Mike, I'm your job. Manipulating me unfairly is part of your craft."

He shifted the sail, then said, "Do you want to help me with the jib?"

"Not really."

He wrapped the main sail rope around a cleat, then raised the jib. I took the jib sheet anyway. He took the tiller again, and unwound the main sheet. We nodded at each other, and began to cooperate on the business of making airfoils out of polyester canvas.

A small motorboat passed us on what felt like the shore side. I remembered hearing that some drode heads used their transportation passes to get otherwise-unrented boats at Coney Island and went out for tuna. Share-fishing—the people who did it gave half the catch to the boat owners. What did they do with the fish they kept, transport them back by subway?

Mike listened to the transceiver buried in his ear, the only sign of it his eyes' inward focus and his head tilting to the right. Then he smiled at me, turned the boat slightly so we headed away from the motorboat.

I adjusted the jib. ''What's the deal? You gonna take me sailing until I'm all yours, or what?''

''Amnesty knew you surrendered, but someone's reactivated your file, and the New York representative wants us to produce you. Was Amnesty tipped by the people who snatched Dr. Rae?''

''Probably. But I'm only deducing it, not knowing it. And if Kearney shows up, I'll jump overboard, save you the trauma of seeing him kill me.'' I jerked the jib sheet, then let it out so loose the sail popped in the wind.

''Allison, aren't you overreacting?''

''Shit, I've been born and abandoned, rescued and abandoned, raped by hacker dicks and Kearney's fingers. You fucked me while I was fugued, so maybe that's another rape. Am I overreacting?''

''I'm sorry. You know, you're my first agent. I'm a very new case officer, really.''

''No, I think you're a lying nanotech oldie. Not inexperienced, just callous.''

Mike straightened up and wrinkled his lips, as though I'd hit him. He said, ''I am new. I need some advice.''

''Shit, call Kearney. He'll come fix me for you. Pull all my brains out and install a computer or something.'' Maybe they could do that. Why ever did I want to stay alive? I'd been dead since I was born.

Without saying another word, Mike tied off the rudder and dropped the sails, then went below. He came back up and sat down at the tiller, but didn't do anything. We drifted.

I heard the motor before seeing the cutter. The cutter, an unmarked fifty-five-footer like a Coast Guard dope catcher, swung around us, dropping a Zodiac which came at us like a motorized condom waiting to be unrolled.

I said, ''So you called for the bad cop?''

Mike said, ''I wanted this to be so nice.''

''Moral of this story is don't put attitudes and emotions in an agent's head she wouldn't be able to come up with on her own. Makes her suspicious.'' I'd asked them to kill me once and they didn't do it. Maybe they would now.

The cutter turned back, perhaps not wanting to attract too much attention to our boat. Who besides the Feds might have satellites? The

Zodiac came at us, rubber bladders twisting. I could make out Kearney, standing with a gun in his hand.

Mike sat with his hands between his knees, head bent down slightly. Kearney's Zodiac pilot swung up beside the sailboat stern and Kearney holstered his gun and came up the swimmers' ladder.

He said, "Allison, quit trying to jerk Mike's chain. You say one instant you're cooperating. Another, you're acting like you want us to kill you."

"Mike said Amnesty reopened my case."

Kearney didn't react, but Mike flinched. "Allison, what if we slipped up and let someone rescue you?"

"Kearney, make this fool apologize for trying to get me to imprint on him."

Mike said, "Allison, I think I said I was sorry. I just wanted what's best for you, what would make it easier. You'd be happier, trust me, if you gave up the hard bitch attitudes."

Kearney said, "Ever occur to you that he might be imprinted on you? He's honestly and earnestly trying to win you over."

I said, "Imprint Mike on me? You were that stupid?"

Then the Zodiac pilot said, "Fuck."

A large shape rose in the water, a submerged Viking longboat, no, an oared submarine. The Zodiac popped, the pilot disappeared down what looked like a giant vacuum cleaner hose.

Then we heard a "thwuck" against the sailboat hull. Kearney pulled his gun and aimed it at me. The sleazy little bastard was going to get to kill me after all.

I said, "But didn't you plan this?"

"What?"

"Aren't you using me for bait? You've got your fish. Bring in all the crap you've got to protect the coast."

Mike shook his head. He went down to the cabin and came up surrounded by two thin women in projectile-resistant cloth and motorized exoskeletons. Behind them, the woman from my non-dreams used tiny fingers on stub arms to prop herself against the mast. Her foot moved like a hand to draw something from an ankle holster. A short muzzle pivoted inside a tiny housing topped with a wide-angle lens.

Loba and the projectile muzzle moved slowly, but Kearney seemed too amazed by the spectacle to shoot either me or the woman. The gismo muzzle stopped pivoting, fired, pivoted as though panning, fired again, a head shot.

Kearney's gun hand convulsed, shooting the deck. As Kearney's body fell, Mike dived off the boat.

I yelled, "Motherfuckers. All of you are motherfuckers." I kicked Kearney in the head, then stomped the hand he'd used to search me. "Fuckers." Then I looked more closely at my rescuers. The fake dreams gave me friends who looked like demons.

The woman with the tiny arms used her toes to reholster what must have been a gun. I couldn't understand how she aimed it, holding it in her toes, but Kearney was dead enough.

I said, "How did you pull the trigger?"

"It doesn't have a trigger," she said. "It fires when it reads the preprogrammed target. We knew Kearney would be here."

I said, "Oh."

One of the tall women in the exoskeleton pointed to Mike in the water and asked, "What do you want us to do about him?" Both women had bones too thin to support them.

Then Miriam and Joe came up and I thought I understood completely now. From my dream that must have been a buried memory I remembered the seal-armed woman's name, Loba. Joe said, "Allison, do you want to shoot him yourself?"

Mike pulled a tab and his vest inflated. He'd killed my rapist. He'd been my control lover. He paddled like crazy in the water, but faced the boat, staring at me. Joe handed me a revolver with laser sights.

I put the light bead on Mike's forehead. He almost seemed to feel it, twisted his head. "Allison, I'm not the bad guy."

I said, "He was kind to me when they were jerking me around by my brain. He thought I'd be happier if I let myself trust people."

And shot him. Pity kills.

The body jerked, blood oozing out of the hole between his eyes, but he didn't bleed a lot. He died without having to worry about it much. And I couldn't unkill him. I wondered if Kearney would have been as quick in killing me. "Don't mind me," I mumbled before I began wailing sensory and emotional overload hysterics.

Miriam and Joe took my arms and lead me down the steel tube into the submarine. One of the powered girls must have been rowing, because the oars were all slaved to a central mechanism. Now the girls in exoskeletons pushed most of the oars out of their holders, through the gasketed oarlocks, and screwed covers over the oar holes. Then the submarine dived and crawled for days on rubber treads. At obstructions, the powered girls used the four remaining oars to walk or swim the submarine over, lifting off the bottom. We spent almost two weeks doing that quiet creep.

I spent the first day and a half lying on a bunk wondering who the fuck I'd joined this time, refusing to sleep to keep the dreams away.

Mike and Kearney waited for me in the back of my brain. Everyone left me alone, which was fine because I'd have torn anyone's head off for condescending to sympathize. Then I got hungry enough to sit up. I felt dizzy and guilty for shooting Mike. Food would cure the dizziness. If I hadn't killed Mike, how could these people trust me? They'd think I was rescue-bait.

Trust was my problem.

I got further up and asked the general air, "Where's the galley? The head?"

Loba was closest, looking at ocean bottom charts. She bent slightly at the hips and pointed with one foot toward the rear of the submarine. I got up, lurching to the uneven motion of the crawling vehicle. Loba seemed steadier on one foot for that second of pointing than I was on two. She put her foot down and said, "We have microwave packets, but ask security before using. Otherwise, try something canned."

I said, "I had to kill him or fall completely in with him."

Loba said, "Obviously, he wasn't the nastiest person you dealt with."

"No, he wasn't."

"Then I'm glad you have regrets."

Well. I went back, found the head, pissed, holding myself down on the lurching toilet. Could my urine be identified, I wondered as I wiped my hands on a packet towelette. I waited for a few seconds of steady forward motion before I stood. The submarine rolled almost smoothly as I found the galley. Miriam and Joe were eating cold sandwiches, Joe listening to something in his left ear. I suspected that meant we couldn't use a microwave source, but asked, "Can I have hot food?"

"Not now," Joe said. "They're pinging us." The submarine slowed down, rose slightly, then lurched across what felt like a boulder field. I flopped down into a chair. Miriam pushed a half sandwich across the table to me.

I said, "I saw Jergen while I was captured."

Joe said, "So he cut a deal that he'd betray methods but not all the people he worked with."

I said, "I wish he'd betrayed me." I wanted to know if they'd been eco-warriors, primarily, or if they'd been these people. "Most of these people look damaged."

Joe said, "Sometimes it doesn't show. Or it's been sort of repaired."

If I began asking questions, then they might wonder whether I'd tried to turn in everyone, too. Actually, I had. "Jergen's eidetic for retina patterns," I said.

Miriam said, "You were planning to cooperate fully when they read you. We need to read you again."

I said, "When they caught me, I thought I would rather die. Kearney, the guy Loba shot, proved to me that I really would prefer to live. He stuck me with the curare needle and let me pass out, but kept me alive on a respirator."

Miriam looked at Joe. He said, "We've got someone who can read you. We're going deep, to the motivation level."

I felt sick to my stomach, not just from the lurching. My head ached. I said, "I understand," and bit into my sandwich. Then I said, "Mike pitied me."

No one else dared pity me.

In eight or nine more days, we surfaced in a fog bank, put on a disguise superstructure with Angolan registry, and went up on hydrofoils. I wondered then how the boat was powered.

I asked Loba, the woman who'd shot Kearney, "What if a satellite spots us rising?"

"Fortunately, the satellites transmit digital data, not analog. We've painted in a boat crossing the Atlantic, and found a convenient fog bank so we don't have to match exactly."

"How did you break the encryption?" The encryptions must be changed daily, if not hourly.

Loba said, "We have our ways."

"Where are we going?"

"To pick up Mr. Hunsucker and Dr. Rae," Loba said.

"Who?"

"Willie. He was very concerned about you."

"I hate being a pity object."

"You will find Willie more convenient than that," Loba said. "He felt if we didn't keep faith with you, then we might not keep faith with him. The idea of not having a side to trust made Dr. Rae hysterical."

I said, "I also hate being an object lesson."

"Would you have preferred to died at Kearney's hands? You will stay below when we're stopped by the customs agents."

I must have looked upset, because she laughed and said, "Don't worry, they're corrupt. We have an agreement that they'll take off some of our contraband and pass us through as a sealed boat. After all, South Carolina would be a Third World state, the poor worse off than than in Brazil or Mexico, if it weren't connected to the United States. Still poor enough to encourage officials to take little bites." Loba grinned.

"They know we bring in drugs, but what but drugs would keep their peach-pickers docile?"

"Drode head peach-pickers?"

"A person must be conscious to know a ripe peach from one merely partly colored," Loba said. "Same as you cannot replace a hamburger fryer with a machine."

I said, "I thought they did all agriculture by machine."

"No, for some things—stabbing veins, picking tobacco, picking strawberries, breaking rich ladies' horses—the brain, eyes, and hand must work directly."

"And people fear becoming drode heads, so they do it cheap," I said.

"Yes, but you must go below now. I hear the customs boat coming. We'll be in Charleston tonight."

"All sorts of Feds there," I said.

"Yes, but we need a port able to unload our cargo," Loba said. "And we will all turn mulatto, as dark as is believable with our various noses, shortly after landing. You can become quite dark. We've merely borrowed the boat. The owners will reclaim it, we've already covered the appropriate bribes."

I wondered what cargo.

By the time we got to Charleston, we had inspection papers. The harbor was a motley place: mostly African ships ranging from decent Ghanaian-built freighters and tankers to ancient patched ships from the South African mothballed navy, to Euro lux-goods container ships, and oil tankers. I wondered if the Louisiana coast was too contaminated for ships to come in to New Orleans, or if this was normal. Beside the commercial traffic, the military ships and submarines looked hyper-trig, frantically clean. Fort Sumter was now used as an agricultural quarantine site—who would want to make a memorial to the War for Slavery when most of the port's business came from Africa?

We left the weird submarine-turned-hydrofoil and walked off something like an airport's boarding tunnel, no gangplanks here. Five large boxes came with us in the second van driven by the girls who needed the motorized exoskeletons to walk.

I said, "Can't you have them rebuilt with nanotech?"

"Nanotech did that to them," Loba said. "They collect two million a year as long as they're like that. The company is always ready to rebuild them."

I said, "Did you all get settlements?"

"You are bright," Loba said. "But do you want to know this?"

I said, "I don't need to know."

We spent five days in a voudoun temple turning dark. The mambo, who talked a lot with Loba, said, "Some of you must look Arabic, perhaps Ethiopian, but I don't think you want all the same shade, right?"

Loba, who was now darker than quadroon, nodded. I said, "Can you make me completely black?"

The mambo said, "Your nose lacks enough flare for pure African."

The two bird-boned girls put on mechanical support skins several orders of magnitude less startling than their motorized exoskeletons. I realized, looking at them without the framework, that they'd originally been darker. They bid us goodbye, and merged with the crowd outside the temple.

The mambo finally got my skin color exactly to suit her. Miriam and Joe looked Ethiopian. Loba put artificial limbs on over her stumps. They looked almost real, but didn't quite match her present skin color. The mambo made adjustments and sent us on our way.

The trip felt like it bisected my prior selves, the ley lines that lead from this fate to that. One self drove to New Orleans, the one escaped to California from a military camp in North Carolina. "The Feds say the people here are conservative," I said. "They trust them. They play war games with them."

"The Feds are arrogant. You had help in getting away. The locals are not so docile."

"You mean they didn't know where I was in California?"

"No, but they didn't search for you then as diligently as they do now."

We changed vans five times, taking old Federal 178 up from Charleston. I never saw the other van drivers. For lunch, we pulled into a small town with a strip mall, all built behind a parking lot, exposed to the hot South Carolina summer. The luncheonette had air-conditioning, various grades of powerless people in baseball caps, some women in synthetics, children beside them, still looking hopeful. Some of the pure whites among them looked like they wanted to be racist, but we might represent an African firm with uranium money, oil, chrome, agricultural produce to be cooked into rayon, paper, or synthetic fuel. Maybe we'd buy something from them—peaches, cotton, tree fiber, computer experts.

The waitress, however, wished we'd all die before she had to serve us. She was a wiry woman of interdeterminate race—Native American, white, black, Arab trader from the coast either back in Africa centuries ago or fifty years back here, some Syrian from Charleston's foray out into the hinterlands. She looked at us as a woman might who's learned strangers wreck a woman's contentment.

A sheriff's car pulled up. Two deputies got out, one lighter than the other, but neither pure white, both pure American. "Hi, Louise," one said to the waitress, "wish they'd all rot."

The other one said, "Feds and those tree-spiking scum both." The two deputies looked at us, then at Louise.

Louise said, "Never can get peace for all the stirring up. The Feds invented those folks to keep up their jobs."

Loba said, "Who are the Feds looking for?" when obviously it was us. She opened her purse with an artificial hand and pulled out her wallet.

"We don't care," one deputy said. "Nobody did nothing in my jurisdiction."

Loba checked to see what she had in her wallet. "I think we have enough for four chicken dinners," she said.

"Where you from?" Louise asked.

"Brazil," Loba said. "But my father was an American."

"Feds are looking for a light-skinned drode head, but I can't figure what harm drode heads can do," the first deputy said. "Ain't but one of you growing out hair and she's not half light-skinned enough."

"Snap your fingers, Brazil," the other deputy said.

Loba snapped her fingers, the sound slightly off, but then I was listening, not watching.

Miriam and Joe sat like they were just too road tired to get into this.

"I hate agitators and Feds both," Louise said. "Running back and forth across the country fucking people over for causes."

I felt that everyone in the room agreed. After centuries of being whipped poor with idealism, these people decided anyone trying to sell them a cause was evil. Even fighting for themselves, the various eyes said, was a waste of time. Someone else would make money off them, forever. Abandoned children would raid them. The Feds would bust all their cockfights and gambling joints unless they promised to cooperate in Federal anti-crime schemes. Their senators would give tax breaks to foreign corporations and give them the costs of the improved roads, the additional schools, the additional fiber-optic cables the locals couldn't get on except as drode heads. They themselves would spend decades paying off their new masters.

They also knew we were the ones the Feds were chasing, but turning us in was too much like getting involved. Louise shoveled frozen chicken and sliced potatoes into the microwave, then into the fryer. The people started talking then, to each other.

When we got back in the van, I said, "I thought . . ."

Joe said, "If the Feds didn't have us on breaking one of the Ten Commandments, the locals weren't going to give a damn."

Loba said, "The deputies got a good look at our money. We'll be searched up the road if we don't contribute to their community center fund."

Before we left the county, another set of deputies stopped us. Loba, who could drive now that she'd put on her artificial arms, looked down at the deputy.

He said, "We could use some help finding the people the Feds are looking for."

Loba opened her purse again and handed him several hundred-dollar bills. "We will arrange a larger fund transfer later to your school board. It won't be conspicuous, but we'll send more every year for a while. Some people we know might want to give a grant for a public access fiber-optic cable."

The deputy folded her money and said, "Thank you, ma'am."

After we started up again, I said, "So, will local deputies hold us up for ransom every county we go through?"

"No, a county like that doesn't want to share. If the next county holds us up, then this county knows it would be out a fiber-optic cable, probably even the donation to the school board."

I asked, "Why the school board?"

"If the money actually gets used for education, it will serve them." Loba didn't sound like that was likely. "If the most important people, who generally run schools in places like this, keep the money, then we've paid off another state senator."

"Another state senator?"

Joe said, "South Carolina is run by state senators. Can't start a business, expand city limits, without getting a state senator's approval."

Loba said, "This is a very pragmatic state. The rich wish to stay rich. Whatever's necessary, they'll do. Undereducating the poor works quite well."

Joe said, "Our state senator here takes it in drugs. We gave him a front junkie, so he isn't registered."

"Where does idealism come in?" I asked.

Loba said, "We're angry. We take revenge. There is no idealism. Not even the poorest take payment in idealism any longer."

I said, "I did."

"Are you sure?"

Was I?

Joe said, "You wanted to learn. You wanted power. And, baby, it was always obvious you wanted revenge."

Miriam nodded.

I said, "So much for ecology? Next come the insects?"

Miriam said, "You'll still get to travel."

The estate was an old house, built in 1840, sold to a regional historical society in the early 1960s, sold to the Senator around the turn of the century when he was nanofixed. The Senator promised to open the house to the public when he was in Washington, but renovations kept it closed most of the time.

His front junkie was a blonde woman who seemed to recognize Loba even with arms. She had pupils surgically, not pharmaceutically, pinned, contracted to tiny black dots, and wore visual enhancer glasses indoors. "I'm Sue. Come this way," she said, leading us into the historical display part of the house."

Loba read a plaque and asked, "Did the family really adopt their slaves?"

"Little alternative myth developed in the last part of the 1990s," Sue said. "I seriously doubt it, but by then, the mostly whites invited the mulatto kin to join them for family reunions, so, these little white lies made the get-together run smoother."

We walked around like tourists while Miriam and Joe checked security, then we had our own family reunion in the slave quarters right behind the house.

Willie was waiting for me by the read helmet. He looked embarrassed. Dorcas was next door, checking the equipment Loba brought her from Charleston. We had to move everything with mechs since Loba didn't want to expose more humans.

I wanted to stay with Dorcas, but Loba and Joe said, "It's time."

Willie said, "We can keep you from remembering, if that would be a blessing."

"Will I wake up if you don't like the reading?"

Joe said, "We can work with all sorts of motivations, but we can't work with someone who plans to betray us." *No, you won't wake up if we don't like the reading,* second threat this month.

I said, "I don't plan to betray you, but I guess you've got to see that for sure."

Loba said, "We don't anticipate that you plan consciously to betray us now. We want to know if you might need to later, from guilt or masochism." Joe loaded a junkie-issue syringe.

I said, "I'm tired of having other people use my brain."

Loba said, "You hate not knowing what's going on." Joe pushed the needle home. They lay me down on one of the read couches as I went limp.

I didn't remember precisely what Willie read, but felt rage, loss, self-pity, ugly little girl screaming by the roadside while the future whizzed by laughing. My worst nightmares told me they'd be with me forever. Loba and the power girls stalked them into corners where, wearing Kearney's face and Mike's body, they gibbered.

The nightmare didn't break for hours, vicious enough to throw me out of sleep if I'd been in natural sleep.

I ended seeing myself as a lethally nasty piece of work, but I woke up. Loba handed me a cup of soup and said, "Eventually, the Feds will get us. But we will have gotten the insects out."

Joe said, "We won't let them take you alive."

Willie said, "You're as wounded as I am."

I said, "Is that pity?"

Willie said, "We can help each other. Is that too much sympathy?"

I remembered something from the scan. In the middle of my worst machine-induced nightmare, where Kearney pulled my skull apart and turned tiny, walking in my brain forever, a virtual Willie offered me his left breast, a small newly grown one, the right breast only a male nipple. Willie's fantasy or mine? I'd sucked the virtual tit and felt safe. Now I ran my fingers around my lips, wondering if I'd pursed my flesh lips for that fantasy male nipple. Did Loba and Joe watch this? I looked around, but didn't see any video screens. "You didn't watch?" I asked.

"Willie talked to us," Loba said.

I was relieved, but felt my lips tingle slightly. I drank the rest of the soup and said, "So whatever my deep motivations are, I don't need to know them?"

Loba said, "You always wanted to belong, but not to the people who hurt you. We've been your people before. We educated you, rescued you."

"But you don't entirely trust me," I said.

Joe said, "You hate being predictable. And we are sorry about Martin Fox."

"And the Feds won't rest until they kill us all, no deposit, no return."

"Yes," Willie said. "We'll be like soldiers forever."

I knew that was terrible for him. I wanted to be able to protect him. I wanted him to grow that breast and nurse me from it.

Willie said, "I thought you were impossibly hard-edged until I saw your dreams."

"Can you make them stop?" I said.

"You have to learn from them," Miriam said.

Loba said, "Dorcas needs lab assistants. We've got software for you."

Willie helped me up off the couch. I felt wrung out, but safe for now. The most powerful beast on the planet had challengers now. *Go, insects, go.*

We went into the next room and saw Dorcas checking out the DNA sequencer.

She looked at us and said, "Loba brought me feral mantises."

Willie said, "We better get to work. We never know how much time we have."

We lay down again under our hoods and began to design wasps with hostility to human anger and neuroleptic stings. Then crop-tending bugs, plowers, harvesters, and guardians, to reduce human stress even further.

Dorcas said, "And better petroleum flies."

Loba asked, "What's the common factor?"

I said, "Humans are stress-breeders, so we've got to make them happy about losing power. If we rely on something other than ourselves, then we have to cooperate more with the natural world. Humans are also lazy. Bugs that till the soil and don't just steal from us will make us Nature's dependents."

Willie said, "Sharing power."

Loba looked dubious, but went away. When we broke for dinner, she wore templates for arm-building nanotech machines. I said, "I thought you hated the machine world."

Loba said, "We hate it and use it, just like all other humans."

Joe said, "We can't stay here more than a couple days. Laurel's coming with Little Red so we can pack and move on."

Miriam said, "Make some nice wasp for the Senator."

We left him a wasp egg calculated to provide his favorite drug without a front junkie. Sue let a nanomachine unpin her pupil muscles and left with us.

The Senator died in a freak car accident a couple of weeks after we left, we heard on the news. Also, new Welfare clients in New York sued the system to get the new holeless net systems. We never heard any more about us over public news, the Feds not wanting to advertise their failures.

Teach them Feds to be so clever.

FOURTEEN

DOWN A STRANGLED RIVER

Dorcas decided the closest analog to the group's mode of operations was to army ants. She was the queen producing eggs. Then, while the eggs went through diapause and earlier hatches pupated, the group would pack its geodesic domes and move on, carrying eggs and pupae in the backs of buses, limos, and vans, across the South, through North Carolina, Tennessee.

The group gave Dorcas everything she'd ever wanted as a researcher: equipment, materials, all the DNA Loba's friends could steal, her two computer-enhanced lab technicians, her human-brain-enhanced teraflop computer. She didn't have to publish, didn't have to even teach graduate students, much less undergraduates. And nobody asked her to make recommendations on other people's grant proposals or to publish. She *couldn't* publish. Dorcas giggled. All she could do was applied science. Insect engineering. Invertebrate art.

As winter set in, the group reached Davenport, Iowa. Dorcas looked at the Mississippi caught between flood walls and asked Loba, "What do we do now?"

Loba said, "After Willie and Allison distribute the last batch of the little wasps, we head downstream."

Dorcas designed a wonderful wasp that responded to sulfur dioxides. Pollute, and it stung anything warm-blooded near a sulfur dioxide source. Dorcas almost gave it the large size of her earlier neuroleptic wasps, but Loba suggested a tiny social creature, a blend of bee and hornet. Dorcas decided that her large wasps could be easily spotted, followed in the air. This baby was smaller than a honeybee, with the pesticide resistance of Manhattan cockroaches and a sting that made humans intensely happy but unable to drive or operate heavy machinery. The group felt happiness undermined humans better than anything else.

Allison suggested releasing the little wasps away from pollution sources so they could multiply before they reached humankind. Every national and state forest in Tennessee, Kentucky, Ohio, and Illinois had some.

The real challenge was still the neuroleptic wasp that could sting to sleep people whose violence was breaking through. Dorcas wanted that wasp to be perfect, not to respond to any common anger.

But Willie asked, ''Do people who start wars have anger, or is it just the bastards getting ripped by machines and hallucination bugs who get mad?''

If only Dorcas had a lover, her situation would be perfect. Willie's experience with the hallie bugs made him an unsatisfactory lover. Dorcas tried, but erections terrified him. She knew Allison still worked on Willie, but emotional cripples made Dorcas uneasy.

Meanwhile, Loba grew two perfect arms. Loba with arms seemed less threatening than Loba without.

Later, the morning after they'd reached Davenport, Loba went out before the others woke. She came back and said, ''I've rented us barges,'' Loba said. Now, she limped. Dorcas wondered if the Brazilian woman could allow herself a truly normal body. ''We can see the damage Allison's bomb did as we head down to Mexico. Then to Brazil and Venezuela. Many black flies in the jungle, if not so many human-sucking mosquitos. You'll find lots of good genetic material.''

''Are we coming back to the States?'' Dorcas asked. She found she missed sex more than she missed Henry or any of her earlier lovers, which surprised her. But now, watching the Mississippi roll between its levees, trees bare, gas and battery recharge stations visible, Dorcas remembered her parents' faxes from the Mekong. Perhaps they could go to release insects in Asia, then she could look for her parents. Her parents would be pissed if they knew what she was doing, of course, but Dorcas could pretend she was involved in secret war games. Of course, she was, but on what her parents would consider the wrong side.

Of course. She could arrange to meet them in New Orleans.

Loba said, "Hard for you to leave who you were?"

"I wasn't much, a lab wife."

"Don't play tough with me. Why don't you make an insect to take your mind off the men?"

"Whatever do you mean?"

"Miriam could have cut your heart out over Joe."

"What kind of yuppizoidal possessive crap is that? Does she own him?"

"Yes, they own each other."

"But I'm the scientist here."

"Allison could make you a machine."

"I don't miss it that much," Dorcas said. She was glad she'd arranged a special meeting code with her parents, a personal ad on *The American Times* net.

Or she could trace them through the American Association of Retired Persons, but that might trip a back-trace.

Loba said, "We'll meet the barges at Hannibal."

Willie and Allison plugged into the navigation system, maps and sonar to show where the Mississippi main channel was this week. The barges began drifting. Loba took Dorcas's arm and led her back to the next vehicle.

Dorcas was surprised to see read helmets and what looked like a newer version of her computer. "I thought all my stuff was on the barges." Dorcas asked.

"We've been acquiring duplicate equipment," Loba said.

Dorcas wondered how long it would be before they acquired a duplicate gene hacker. "So now, we're going down the Mississippi." Various people did this every year, the aquatic equivalent of hiking the Pacific Crest or Appalachian Trails. Dorcas had always wanted to bisect America through its industrial midsection. She wished they could have started at the head of navigation in Minnesota, but this was much more than she'd even expected to have time to do.

At Hannibal, a restored nineteenth-century town laced with monorails and tramlines, Allison and Willie, in very good wigs, toured the Mark Twain sites. Loba met them as though they were strangers. Allison invited Loba and her friend to join them on the barges for dinner.

After dinner, they cast off again. Willie ran the first barge and towed the second. On the Illinois side, red and blue lights flashed on abandoned smokestacks. Dorcas realized this pollution had stopped before her time, but newer pollution continued, chemical factory drains, smokestacks that ran only in rainy weather to disguise their plumes. The river doubled when the Missouri hit it. The barge stopped for each lock. Big steel gates closed around them, water swirled out, then the big steel lock gates groaned open and dropped them to the next level. Now, the eastern shore showed outlines of windowless buildings processing industrial secrets, backlit by streetlights and rail lines.

The barges passed under a brightly lit bridge. Between it and the next bridge floated a mini-mall, neon under plastic. Attached to the land by gangways, with windows down on the water sides, steel and aluminum hulled fast food joints sold krill, soyaburgers. Behind the floating fast food joints and riverboats-converted-to-casinos, Dorcas saw an old cathedral and an old courthouse, both land-bound buildings losing their dignity to the events on the river.

Beyond the second bridge, the Arch glistened above its flood lights, more fast food barges moored to the river steps. Loba said, "We pick up some food here, why not?"

The two barges pulled up beside a floating Chinese takeout place. Loba ordered kung po chicken, seven orders. The waiter at the window smiled and handed seven bags back to her almost as fast as she'd given the order. Dorcas wondered how badly the steam table or heat lamp damaged the servings.

"Okay, let's move," Loba spoke to the bridge. Willie manuevered both barges back into mainstream. They passed the landing and steps up to the Arch.

Loba and Dorcas stood by the side railing looking at the city levees and the buildings glowing behind them. Dorcas asked, "Can we as a species sustain that, those flood walls, that energy consumption? But when it goes, something marvelous goes. I couldn't have made the insects to defend the planet without that civilization."

Loba said, "But without that civilization, the planet wouldn't have needed your insects. We're the defective by-catch of that civilization's chase for the perfect."

"You and the others. We're funded by industrial accident settlements, aren't we?"

"You, too. The planet speaks through you, whether you understand the message or not."

Dorcas knew the Gaia hypothesis in any incarnation. "Never grant purpose to the universe. Or a planet. Things just happen."

Loba said, "I suppose. Ah, St. Louis, you wanted to be Chicago, you wanted to be New York."

Dorcas said, "I applied for a job at Washington University once."

"What happened?"

"They didn't hire me. Said I hadn't published enough senior author papers."

Loba said, "I've never understood this American mania for training people the system can't absorb."

St. Louis extended lights and bridges for miles, reflections dancing on the surface, then the barges floated off over darker water.

When they stopped at Memphis, a mantis boarded them. It was as large as anything from Dorcas's lab-spawned generation, but not quite as chemically charming. Willie said, "We have a mascot."

Dorcas asked, "Why did they lose the pheromone tranquilizer?"

"Probably it attracted things perfectly capable of loving what they ate," Loba said.

Dorcas said, "But birds don't have senses of smell." Then she realized the mantises were big enough to feed a cat, help feed a coyote. "Yeah, they'd be vulnerable when they molted. I should have had the chemicals shut down then."

Willie took the mantis up on his hand. He said, "But it's still nice. I don't need the tranquilizers now."

Dorcas said, "But you're still phobic of erections and small bugs."

Willie turned slightly toward Allison, then shrugged.

Dorcas spent the rest of the time working again, submerging herself in science, wondering what she could do with jungle insect genomes. She could give them torpor and hibernation, perhaps finding pesticide resistance superior to even Manhattan cockroaches. The desert and high Mexican mountains had always been the barrier between the rainforest insects and the civilization that created small tropics in concrete and steel, stacked higher than rainforests, heated and cooled to match Pliocene savannas. Dorcas would help these insects over the barriers.

Memphis crawled with agents of all descriptions. Loba limped off the lead barge to begin to deal with them. She came back and opened her hand in Dorcas's face. In her hand was a vial four inches long and an inch and a half in diameter. Inside the vial was a grub. "Yours?"

Dorcas looked closely at the grub. "I never worked with beetles. What does it do?"

"It aborts women. It tastes quite good."

"Steam engine time for insects," Dorcas said. She felt miffed that she wasn't the only one, but then this other hacker meant that she was not the Fed's only target. "Do you plan to locate this person, too?"

"There was a bombing in Davis, a letter bomb mailed to a DNA researcher who had a guard to open his mail, but the guard was a Federal agent who neglected to open this letter. None of our friends knew anything about the researcher until after the bombing."

Dorcas said, "What would they do if they caught me?"

"They'd offer you life if you let them do the full brain scan, what they did to Allison. Then they might send you back to us. We can't take you back if you disappear for more than a few hours. They'd want you to make mantises that never helped anyone rediscover ambition."

Dorcas asked, "Would you come hunting for me?"

"No."

Dorcas enjoyed her new life, but if it ever became tedious, she could just leave. She took the vial off Loba's hand. "You say women eat these? What if they're not pregnant?"

"I've heard the worm gives pleasure."

Dorcas opened the vial and ate part of the grub to see what it tasted like. She needed to eat it all. In twenty minutes, she was slumped against the superstructure, a female wringing her womb empty in wrong-way orgasms. The air touched her over and over, most knowing and intimate air. Loba passed her several times, looking down, then going on about her business.

Loba came back and said, "Are you through now?"

Her uterus twitched back on its ligaments. Dorcas looked up and said, "It will work quite nicely to cut back human numbers."

Loba said, "Trucks are coming to off-load us."

Dorcas stumbled to her feet. She was astonished to find that she was fully dressed.

Loba said, "Remind me not to try that."

Dorcas realized the insect orgasm was scary, now that it was over. "An aphrodisiac that really works." Only a man would want to design an insect that left women so out of control.

"You'd push a man out. Rupture his dick."

"And what it would do for childbirth," Dorcas said.

Loba said, "The worm doesn't have that reputation on the streets. I wondered if it would bring men to orgasm. Perhaps Willie could try it."

Later that afternoon, Dorcas found a dockside kiosk that accessed *The American Times*. She asked Loba, "Can I see something on *American Times*? You can see me from the street."

"I'll come in with you. What are you looking for?"

Dorcas didn't answer, but hypertexted to the want-ads from the last two months.

Ruthie, we've found the papers on your Rottweiler, Black Brock. Her parents were looking for her. Dorcas picked up a message pad and stylus.

Loba grabbed her hand and said, "What?"

"My parents are looking for me. Can't I tell them I'm okay. We've got a code. Daddy was always ready for complete social chaos.''

"No.''

"Do you think the Feds would have approached them?''

"Of course. Your parents could trade you to the Feds, get a nanotech rejuvenation and start a whole new family.''

"They are nanotech rejuvenated already,'' Dorcas said.

"Would it please them to know you're an outlaw gene hacker? They're not going to do you any favors.''

Surrogate momma Loba spank and humiliate, too. "I'm their gourmet child,'' Dorcas said. "Their bonsai family.''

"For a woman with a PhD, you are being stupid.''

"Okay, I won't let them know I'm okay. They'll worry about me.''

"I'm sure,'' Loba said.

Dorcas asked Willie to put the prearranged code on the net. Loba perhaps knew and decided to let Dorcas, her star gene hacker, have a little leeway.

Willie and Allison stayed behind in Memphis.

FIFTEEN

FURTHER INDICATIONS OF THE ECOSPHERE

Mike came to my dreams with his shot head. He told me how I'd be better off if I had married him. "Do something for Willie," he said before he faded and the tone of the dream changed from nightmare to just REM sleep. I tried to sleep with Willie while we were somewhere in Tennessee, camping out with flasks of insect larvae eating through our culture material.

He was eager enough until he got an erection, then he immediately went soft and rolled off me. He lay trembling beside me. "You remind me of hallie bugs," he said.

"Thanks a lot," I said.

"I always wanted a woman, but I thought I didn't have money enough for a whore."

"Always found a way not to," I said, juices curdling inside me.

"I could have fucked to death," he said. I looked more closely. He was crying.

"Oh, Willie," I said. I sat up.

"I thought I was . . . I had fucking down pat once."

I wondered if I could coax Willie into trusting his dick again. "Is cuddling safe?"

"I could grow a tit, like we did in the machine, do something for you. The virtual you loved that a lot."

The virtual me, the flesh me, the face I controlled—which was real? "Willie, when does the fear hit?"

"I thought I wanted a woman. I thought I wanted to come up with a plan. I'm doomed now. We're going to get gunned down eventually. Dorcas thinks she can change her mind and live, but ain't no way now, even for her."

I knew he avoided the larvae flasks. How could he take working for insects if he was so afraid of anything that reminded him of hallie bugs?

"Willie, let me try to help you." I wondered if he'd mind being pitied as much as I did. No, I wasn't pitying him, I was being compassionate.

"I thought they'd fix me," he said. "But they just muffled the fear."

"Did the mantis help?" Laurel brought us the egg case Willie's mantis had laid in New York before she died, but Dorcas told us it wouldn't hatch for months.

"If we could take out all those memories," Willie said. "In both of us."

I felt strange. We could edit all his memories, at least the major connections between sexual arousal and terror. But we'd have to trust nanotech machines to cut and nip in the brain. My memories would have to stay to remind me how nasty life was.

I felt bewildered by my feelings toward Willie—irritation, compassion, and a strong desire to be the woman who fixed him.

In Memphis, Loba brought Dorcas a beetle grub which laid her down on the deck in orgasms. Willie couldn't look. I found him staring off the stern, his hands over the rail twitching.

"Is it that bad?"

"It's the same damn thing, isn't it? A hallie bug."

"We can ask when she's done."

"Why did I get involved with you people?"

"I'm glad you're saying that to me, Willie. You ought to be careful around the others."

"They abandoned you once. You trust them now?"

"I'm happier than I've ever been," I said. Miriam told me to look at my hands when I had nightmares, get control of the dream, realize all the dream characters came from my own brain. I was the Mike with the bloody hole exposing our brains.

Monsters invaded the planet, but I made them good guys even though the boss monster tried very hard to shift them back to the bad mode. My child self found Loba in a dream, then Willie. We attacked a terrifying cola bottle and threw it down between stair railings.

Kearney, taller than life, burst through my door with two little short men on either side of him.

Rape. I woke up laughing, the symbolism was so obvious.

Willie sat beside me, asking, "Allison, are you all right?"

"I just had a symbolic nightmare about rape. Willie, I want us both to be all right. After your body learns it won't damage itself with orgasms anymore, perhaps you'll be okay. Let's try the worm, a tiny bit."

"I can't believe you want to do this to me."

"Willie, I want you to be whole." I wanted to really help someone else. People had always done to me. Hurt or helped, I'd always felt powerless. Not even the guns really helped.

"Bug of the bugs that bit me."

At lunch the third day, after Willie went into town alone, with one of Loba's friends discreetly following him, we all discussed it.

"Memphis has isolation tanks for rent," Miriam said. "That would eliminate any possible friction."

Joe said, "It would be permanent if he hurt himself this time."

When Willie came back, I said, "Willie, please let us try to reverse the conditioning. You were only hurt with hallie bugs once, weren't you?"

"I've adjusted to being fucked up," he said. "Besides . . ."

"Are you a coward?" I asked. "We'll suspend you in salt brine. You can't possibly hurt yourself."

"God, I'm with you people," Willie said. "You want to experiment on me?"

"Wouldn't it be nice to enjoy sex again?" I put my hand on his leg. I'd never delayed gratification so long before.

Joe said, "Jesus, Allison."

Willie said, "Let me see if I can even bring myself to look at one."

Loba made a call and came back to say, "One of the whorehouses rents isolation space and virtual suits for perversions live women refuse to handle."

"No, it's more than that," Joe said. "Some guys just want to be alone after sex."

Loba drove on with Dorcas, leaving Miriam and Joe to bring us back from whatever happened. I began to wonder if I was bullying Willie. I asked him, "You really want to try?"

He said, "Then I could cuddle you out of your nightmares."

"Oh, Willie."

The whorehouse sold worms, so after we paid the couple who ran the house, we were all set.

Willie crawled in the tank naked, his dick and balls tight against his body. Joe said, "I can't watch this," and left the room.

Miriam said, "Should I go, too?"

Willie said, "Stay, I'm scared." I felt rebuked, as though I scared him. I probably did, though, insisting that he recover his sexuality. We left the top hatch open so we could talk to him. Sensory deprivation wasn't in order here. I sat by his head and stroked his face, remembering the boys who'd watched me in my teenaged machines.

"Don't show me the worm," Willie said. "Don't even give it to me. Let me just rest in here."

I said, "Can we give you just a little bit blended in milk. You won't see it."

Miriam said, "Allison, why is this so important?"

I said, "I want to heal him. Before I was always the worst injured one."

Willie said, "You lucky *I* don't shoot people for pitying me."

Miriam said, "He's terrified."

Let him look close at his own damn nightmare. I said, "Might as well go all the way, Willie."

"Don't show me."

"In milk," I said.

"Let Miriam mix the dose," Willie said.

Miriam went to the whorehouse kitchen and came back with milk stained light brown. Willie closed his eyes and tasted the milk, out of her hand, not mine.

"It's got sugar in it," he said. "And liquor."

"To cut the taste," Miriam said.

"Wasn't the taste of bugs messed me up," Willie said. He sipped so slowly I wanted to grab him and pour it down his throat.

We waited for a half hour. He got an erection, gasped, sweated all over his head where it was above the salt solution, lost the erection. "Is this worth it?" he asked.

I said, "The Feds took this away from you, Willie. You won't be yourself until you're fully functional as a human being."

Willie said, "But you don't even like human beings."

Miriam said, "If we truly hated human beings, there'd be none left by now."

"No, I'm talking to Allison."

"I go from hating them to hating myself, Willie. I want to love someone all the way. Mike . . . Mike, I think he was partially right in that I needed to trust someone, but I need to have my brains together, I need . . . someone like me."

"Okay, I'm trying. Let's go for it." He looked like he was ready to die. I wondered if I looked like this while Kearney played with my lethal needle.

Miriam mixed a stronger dose, then left me alone with him. I held his hand while he came. I felt like I was rebirthing him, healing him of sexual trauma. Men so rarely suffered sexual trauma that I felt a twinge of regret that this might work.

"Enough for today?" I asked.

He nodded, the Epsom solution sloshing around his chin. I opened the bottom hatch and helped him out.

He said, "It felt like the other bug. But not as long, not as intense. Without hallucinations. So bugs took it. Bugs will give it back."

I wanted to take him to bed now, but sensed he wasn't ready. Yet. He turned away from me to dress, then said, "I'm hungry."

We ate fajitas while the latest Ghanaian band wailed over the whorehouse dining room tables. My and Willie's hair had already grown out, but this was the first time I felt like I had normal hair. Conductive jelly worked as well as baldness to get the messages in and out of my subdural net. Barring emergencies, Willie wasn't ever going to do drode work again.

Somewhere in the Mississippi below Tennessee, while Joe and Miriam went to get Loba and Dorcas, Willie was able to have sex with me, carefully, with lots of sweat.

Kearney grabbed me as soon as I began to dream. He jammed a baby nuke between my legs, but Willie shot him before the bomb stuffed up my snatch could explode. I woke paralyzed, terrified that I'd never escape, that I'd die blown to bits. Willie cuddled me, saying, "Allison, Kearney's dead. Remember?"

"You were in the dream. You shot him." I didn't tell Willie his dream self hadn't quite been fast enough, that I had a bomb up my snatch.

Loba bought Willie a retina job. We watched a puppet opera performing *Carmen* at an old opera house in Natchez while the job was done. Willie came out with better vision than he'd had since becoming a drode head. The doctor also closed his electrode holes, but the net and transformer were still in Willie's skull.

For the next three nights, I turned into a little girl. One night, I turned my parents in to the police, remembering the car's license plate. The second night, I joined the child gang and ran on half-dead legs from Kearneys who kept popping up everywhere. Willie, not Jergen, opened the door that saved me. The third night, I stood to let them kill me and they circled me, baffled. Willie said, "Allison, you okay? Not like last night?"

I said, "I don't need to be so afraid. They're only dreams."

Willie said, "Dorcas made a play for me."

Now I felt paralyzed. I managed to say, "I'd rather we be faithful, but thanks for telling me."

"I wouldn't have her," Willie said. "She hasn't really been hurt by this world."

"She kept expecting some university would reward her for being a good girl. Or for being a rich girl."

"The more fool she, then," Willie said.

I rolled over and kissed Willie, gently. "I like being with someone who's had it rough, too." Had Jergen and I kissed so gently?

Willie said, "Did she check the news nets when you were in Natchez?"

"She did disappear during the opera intermission."

Willie said, "We'll fix your retinas in New Orleans."

"Will Loba get Dorcas's retinas rebuilt, too?"

Willie said, "The reward for her is enormous. She is advertised all over the world. Loba is afraid even her connections would sell out Dorcas."

I said, "I'm learning a lot from Dorcas. She seems a little uneasy about it, but then the Movement taught me a lot about biology earlier."

Finally, after weeks traveling up the Mississippi, down the Mississippi, or parked at various marinas, we arrived at New Orleans. The river had stopped the wildfires started by my bomb from getting the city. *Full circle. Will the circle be unbroken?* The ground seemed strange underfoot after the weeks on the river. We giggled at each other as we lurched on the unwavy, unwaked ground, then took a taxi to Loba's retina doctor.

Dorcas's head swung slightly when she located a public news node. I wondered if she'd mapped Willie's new retinas, how many of us she'd betray before the Feds arranged an accident for her.

"Stay until my retinas are done," I asked her.

"Oh, fierce Allison, are you afraid?"

"Nanotech can screw up," I said.

"Loba knows best," Dorcas said.

We got out of the taxi in a pretty condo district built to look like the French Quarter, only without the wrought iron, then walked back a couple blocks to the clinic. The doctor was a woman. I said, "A woman from São Paulo said you could help."

Dorcas said, "How long will it take?"

"An hour."

I wondered if Dorcas planned to come back. She kissed me on the cheek and said, "I'll be back in an hour."

The doctor said in a Latin accent, "I have known your Brazilian friend for many years. You can always trust her."

I said, "She's been like a mother to me." I felt like crying. Everyone dies in the end, but the mothers try to keep their children going as long as possible. And Loba made such a good mother substitute for me, stern but concerned.

"Can we trust that American redhair?"

I shrugged. "You might consider moving."

"We always do," the woman doctor said. "I understand you hate being drugged, but the visual distortions as the machines work might be unpleasant."

"It's okay."

"You've been rebuilt before?"

"Yes."

She led me inside and sat me down in a chair. Then she pulled on gloves and opened two foil-sealed packets, pulled out two silver-stained pads. "Close the eyes," she said. I obeyed, felt the chill of nanomachines so tiny they were liquid against my eyelids. They ran between my eyelashes and around my eyeballs.

"One, *dos, tres, quatro, cinco,* you may open your eyes now."

My vision wobbled and wavered as the nanomachines rebuilt my retinas to fit a fake identity, perhaps a dead woman's, or a woman who'd disappeared, or perhaps a completely invented woman.

When the hour was up, Dorcas came back, smiling. I knew she'd arranged to meet her parents, hoped they'd be supportive, hoped the Feds weren't riding a trace down to us.

I looked back at the doctor who burned the recalled nanomachines. *"Vayo con mercia,"* I said, not sure I'd spoken anything in real Spanish. *Go with mercy.*

Dorcas said, "Let's get back. I've got a taxi waiting outside."

I felt like now would be a good time to walk, but the woman doctor looked out the window at the cab and said, "He's trustworthy."

Good momma Loba, keep an eye on Dorcas. I asked, "Do we owe you anything?"

"It's paid. Don't get caught," the woman said.

We got in the cab. Dorcas said, "I figured we're headed out of the country from here. Loba's renting a jet or something. I've got to go to the airport to check it out."

I said, hazarding a guess, "So your parents are going to meet you there."

"We had an unbreakable code, not a cipher. Don't tell Loba. My dad doesn't like the Feds any better than the rest of us."

"Shit, Dorcas, why?" Then realized Dorcas had to have her own way, with insects, with men, with universities, all on her own terms. Was I that bad?

"I want to tell them I'm okay. Don't tell Loba, please."

"Loba's already told. This is her cab driver."

The driver said, "Excuse me, miss. Let me arrange the one to drive you to the airport." He picked up his radio mike and said, *"Uno secundo, por favor."* More Spanish that was street names and numbers. He wrote out a number for Dorcas and said, "Very good man. He'll pick you up here."

Dorcas got out of the taxi. I looked back at her as we left her on the pavement. She looked lost to me.

The taxi driver walked me back to the barges. Joe was watching the gangways. I said, "She's meeting her parents at the airport."

"We can't hold her captive," Joe said.

I asked, "Why the fuck not?"

"We know what Dorcas can do with insects," Joe said.

I hugged Willie when I got on board, then asked, "Loba, will we take her back after she meet her parents?"

"Perhaps it will be okay," Loba said. "Her parents don't seem to have alerted the Federales."

Joe said, "She's a spoiled brat."

Loba said, "But a gifted spoiled brat. I believe her latest product will be pupating in a couple of days. We'll be gone then."

"Out of the country?" I asked.

Loba said, "It depends on what happens at the airport. She may try to betray us, but I don't think the Feds would let her live long if they can't catch us."

Willie said, "Allison and I learned a lot from her."

SIXTEEN

ADULT CHILD AND IMAGO

Now Dorcas had space to work but the rest of her group avoided her, made excuses. All except Allison, who reminded Dorcas unpleasantly of an ambitious graduate student.

The day Allison had her eyes rebuilt was the day Dorcas planned to meet her parents. After the morning session, Allison smiled and washed the electrolyte jelly out of her hair. She said, "After today, I won't be Allison anymore."

"You'll still have the electric works in your brain," Dorcas said. Perhaps, she thought, I can come back to them. She suspected that she hadn't made the right decision, but she was tired of Loba telling her what to do, tired of being the unattached single woman—Loba and Sue didn't count as they had a certain singularity no man could penetrate.

So Dorcas made her arrangements and got out of the cab. She waited on the steaming pavement until another cab pulled up beside her. "Do you have the number?" the man asked. Dorcas handed him the slip of paper the first driver gave her, then got in the cab. "To the airport."

"Perhaps your parents will be understanding," the driver said. "If not, we need to know."

"What's wrong with you that you're with them?"

The driver pulled off into a parking space. He twisted his body so he could lift a leg over the front seat. The shoe wasn't fitted for an ordinary human foot.

Dorcas said, "You could get it fixed."

The man pulled his leg back and stared at Dorcas without speaking. He started the car and pulled back into traffic. They drove on to the airport.

Dorcas went to the information counter and asked, "Are Mr. and Mrs. Hudson in yet?"

The man at the counter looked through a stack of paper messages and said, "They're at the Holiday Inn. Room ten-fourteen."

"Will I need a car to take me there?"

"I would recommend it," the man said.

The driver waited for Dorcas. She said, "I need to go to the Holiday Inn."

"What room?"

Dorcas wondered why she would tell him that, but the group had given her everything she needed for her insects. "Can I really go back if you keep an eye on me?"

"If we understand what happened," the man said. He started the car, pulled away from the curb and drove about a third of a mile to the hotel, another building like any international airport hotel, still being built or remodelled.

Dorcas said, "Room ten-fourteen, then."

"You shouldn't do this."

"I need to check on them. They're my parents." She closed her eyes and visualized refineries, oil pumps rocking like metal dinosaurs.

The driver didn't open the door for her, couldn't move quickly with his crippled feet. Dorcas got out and walked into the hotel as though she belonged. She did. Her parents were there.

Room 1014. A man who looked like early photographs of her father opened the door. He appeared to be in his late twenties. Dorcas never remembered him looking so young. "Dad?"

"Well, you haven't changed," her father said.

Her mother came out, younger than Dorcas. Dorcas asked, "Do you think you were followed?"

"No," her father said. "Would you like tea, coffee?"

"A soda?"

"Emily, make Dorcas a soda," her father said. Dorcas was almost shocked to hear her mother's name applied to this young woman.

Her mother poured a canned drink into a glass, added an ice cube from the refrigerator. She looked at Dorcas in the mirror, her real back to Dorcas, then shrugged.

"I've got this secret job. The Feds are just pretending to be looking for me."

Emily turned and handed Dorcas her drink. Paul said, "Dorcas, we know better. You've been gene-hacking for eco-terrorists."

"There's money in it. You were always one for market opportunities." Dorcas drank the soda her mother had given her.

Her mother said, "Dorcas, you've been a disappointment to us since you were in high school."

"Not that we didn't spoil you," her father said. "But our doctor thought you were our best genetic combination."

"Yes, Daddy, I'm your gourmet child." The ice cube had melted unnaturally quickly.

Her mother said, "Sit down, Dorcas. We feel we owe you an explanation for what we've done."

Dorcas felt her body shift. "It was in the drink? Nanotech? You're changing me. Please change my retinas. Loba couldn't risk it because I'm wanted everywhere."

"Yes," her mother said. "We know how we'd raise you this time."

Paul said, "It's not like we're killing you. We're just going to reduce you to babyhood."

Emily said, "You need to lie down, dear. Paul, go get the plastic sheet and the cryogenic unit, in case she stops before term."

Dorcas said, "I'll drown in my own tissue."

"Don't worry, dear, we've got all the necessary life support. We're just using your uterus."

Dorcas felt her womb filling. "No, mother, please." Her toes turned to jelly.

After the nanomachines scavenged what they needed, her father vacuumed away the rest of her feet. Dorcas said, "But it won't be me. I'm my memories."

Her mother said, "Would you like sedation, dear?"

"Mom, how long will this take?"

Her father said, "We put in a massive set of machines so they could be quicker reassembling you."

"How quick?"

"A few hours."

Dorcas tried to get up, but she seemed disconnected from her dissolving body. "But will it keep my memories?"

Her mother said, "It would be more humane to sedate her," and reached for a needle. Dorcas felt the needle go in.

Her father said, just as she faded away, "Your memories aren't our baby."

Dorcas's clone stirred in her womb as she completely died. The nanomachines stopped while Emily and Paul removed their new daughter, then disassembled the rest of the bio-matrix.

Emily said to Paul, "Are you sure the machines redid her retinas?"

Dorcas's father nodded. "We wouldn't want the Feds to embarrass the family."

They wrapped the newborn baby in a blanket. A man appeared to be watching them, but he was a Chicano cripple, no one of consequence.

Loba heard that Dorcas entered a room with two other adults. Two adults and a baby left. The toilet and septic system were full of undifferentiated proteins.

She said to Willie, "In another thirty years, perhaps she'll work for us again."

SEVENTEEN

THE END OF THE BEGINNING OF THE INSECT ERA

After Dorcas, we flew out of New Orleans and over the burnt husks of oil tanks and refineries. The land, though, was mostly green again behind the island beaches with their radioactive sands. Degradation and partial recovery, at least for the natural world. Life evolved in a high-radiation environment, but not in a high-sulfur-dioxide one.

We crossed Mexico and the Pacific with the eggs, pupae, and instars of Dorcas's insects.

I said, "Willie and I learned a lot working with her. More than enough to duplicate her prior designs."

I loved the group, tiny and cohesive. Dorcas would have fractured us. We were a human Klein bottle, interpenetrating. We finally made it out of the prisons of our various pasts.

We flew into Peking with a hundred thousand insect eggs mailed ahead of us in plastic airhose segments concealed in thick but ordinary letters, an old trick fish collectors used to send eggs into embargoed countries.

Dust ground from rock by ancient glaciers flew over head, filled with lunged wasps that hated the scent of blood.

Someday, we'd conquer ourselves.

TOR
BOOKS The Best in Science Fiction

MOTHER OF STORMS • John Barnes
From one of the hottest new nanes in SF: a shattering epic of global catastrophe, virtual reality, and human courage, in the manner of *Lucifer's Hammer, Neuromancer,* and *The Forge of God.*

BEYOND THE GATE • Dave Wolverton
The insectoid dronons threaten to enslave the human race in the sequel to *The Golden Queen.*

TROUBLE AND HER FRIENDS • Melissa Scott
Lambda Award-winning cyberpunk SF adventure that the *Philadelphia Inquirer* called "provocative, well-written and thoroughly entertaining."

THE GATHERING FLAME • Debra Doyle and James D. Macdonald
The Domina of Entibor obeys no law save her own.

WILDLIFE • James Patrick Kelly
"A brilliant evocation of future possibilities that establishes Kelly as a leading shaper of the genre."—*Booklist*

THE VOICES OF HEAVEN • Frederik Pohl
"A solid and engaging read from one of the genre's surest hands."—*Kirkus Reviews*

MOVING MARS • Greg Bear
The Nebula Award-winning novel of war between Earth and its colonists on Mars.

NEPTUNE CROSSING • Jeffrey A. Carver
"A roaring, cross-the-solar-system adventure of the first water."—Jack McDevitt

TOR
BOOKS The Best in Science Fiction

MOTHER OF STORMS • John Barnes
From one of the hottest new names in SF: a shattering epic of global catastrophe, virtual reality, and human courage, in the manner of *Lucifer's Hammer*, *Neuromancer*, and *The Forge of God*.

THE GOLDEN QUEEN • Dave Wolverton
A heroic band of humans sets out to save the galaxy from alien invaders by the bestselling author of *Star Wars: The Courtship of Princess Leia*.

TROUBLE AND HER FRIENDS • Melissa Scott
Lambda Award-winning cyberpunk SF adventure that the *Philadelphia Inquirer* called "provocative, well-written and thoroughly entertaining."

THE GATHERING FLAME • Debra Doyle and
James D. Macdonald
The Domina of Entibor obeys no law save her own.

WILDLIFE • James Patrick Kelly
"A brilliant evocation of future possibilities that establishes Kelly as a leading shaper of the genre."—*Booklist*

THE VOICES OF HEAVEN • Frederik Pohl
"A solid and engaging read from one of the genre's surest hands."—*Kirkus Reviews*

MOVING MARS • Greg Bear
The Nebula Award-winning novel of war between Earth and its colonists on Mars.

NEPTUNE CROSSING • Jeffrey A. Carver
"A roaring, cross-the-solar-system adventure of the first water."—Jack McDevitt

---

Call toll-free 1-800-288-2131 to use your major credit card or clip and mail this form below to order by mail

- ✂

Send to: Publishers Book and Audio Mailing Service
PO Box 120159, Staten Island, NY 10312-0004

❏ 533453	**Mother Of Storms**..................$5.99/$6.99	❏ 534158	**Wildlife**....................................$4.99/$5.99
❏ 552555	**The Golden Queen** ....$5.99/$6.99	❏ 524802	**Moving Mars** ....$5.99/$6.99
❏ 522133	**Trouble and Her Friends**..........$4.99/$5.99	❏ 535189	**The Voices of Heaven** ....$5.99/$6.99
❏ 534956	**Gathering Flame** ....$5.99/$6.99	❏ 535154	**Neptune Crossing**..................$5.99/$6.99

Please send me the following books checked above. I am enclosing $_____. (Please add $1.50 for the first book, and 50¢ for each additional book to cover postage and handling. Send check or money order only—no CODs).

Name _____

Address _____ City _____ State _____ Zip_____